The Fall

CRIMSON WORLDS IX

Jay Allan

Crimson Worlds Series

Marines (Crimson Worlds I)
The Cost of Victory (Crimson Worlds II)
A Little Rebellion (Crimson Worlds III)
The First Imperium (Crimson Worlds IV)
The Line Must Hold (Crimson Worlds V)
To Hell's Heart (Crimson Worlds VI)
The Shadow Legions(Crimson Worlds VII)
Even Legends Die (Crimson Worlds VIII)
The Fall (Crimson Worlds IX)

War Stories (Crimson World Prequels)

Also By Jay Allan

The Dragon's Banner

Gehenna Dawn (Portal Worlds I)
The Ten Thousand (Portal Worlds II)

www.crimsonworlds.com

The Fall

The Fall is a work of fiction. All names, characters, incidents, and locations are fictitious. Any resemblance to actual persons, living or dead, events or places is entirely coincidental.

Copyright © 2014 Jay Allan Books

All rights reserved.

ISBN: 978-0692313084

Hell is empty and all the devils are here.
- William Shakespeare, The Tempest

Chapter 1

Modified Cargo Hold
MCS Sand Devil
Beta Carolis System

"Where is Gavin Stark?" Cain spoke slowly, clearly. He didn't raise his voice, didn't speak a threatening word, but his tone was menace itself. His cold eyes bored into those of the terrified figure lying prone before him, and those eyes held death in their gaze. Cain was the image of the perfect warrior, a veteran who'd seen combat everywhere man's hand had touched, but now he had shed the badges of the Corps, the insignia of the honorable Marine. He was a killer now, merciless in his relentless pursuit of revenge.

He held a pistol in his right hand, its grip worn smooth from long use. His face was impassive, a chiseled visage as cold as marble. His gray fatigues were rumpled and worn, and they were spattered with blood, though none of it was his.

The cargo hold was empty, cold. Cain's frozen words echoed off the ceiling 10 meters above. There was a man on the bare metal floor, lying prostrate before him. He was the sole survivor of Cain's last encounter with Gavin Stark's henchmen, and his torn suit was covered with the blood of his companions.

The captive was a seasoned agent, one of Stark's cold-blooded killers, well-trained and accustomed to withstanding interrogation and danger. But there was something about Cain's stare, his voice. It aroused a primal fear, an almost supernatural terror, and the prisoner began to shake uncontrollably. "I don't know anything," he rasped piteously.

Cain extended his arm, aiming the pistol at the prisoner's knee, staring right into the terrified man's eyes as he pulled the trigger, without threat, without hesitation. The shot was loud, and it echoed through the empty hold. The miserable captive screamed in agony and helpless fear as his knee exploded in a spray of blood and shattered bone. He fell onto his side, his arms reaching out for his stricken leg.

"Where is Gavin Stark?" Cain didn't move. His tone hadn't changed.

The agent rolled onto his back, his hands still clutching at the remains of his knee as he screamed again. He'd been a remorseless killer, one of Stark's brutal agents, but now he was broken, lying on the ground, tears streaming down his face. The pain from his knee was almost unbearable, but there was something else too, a feeling he struggled to understand, a frigid dread that consumed him utterly. He'd worked with some of the most brutal killers mankind had ever produced, but he'd never encountered anything like the frozen hatred of Erik Cain. The grim Marine didn't yell; he didn't threaten. He didn't even appear to be angry. But there was a darkness there that even this assassin from Alliance Intelligence couldn't comprehend.

He'd heard of Erik Cain, of course. Few were unaware of the Marines' great hero, the stone cold general who had commanded the legendary defense of Sandoval before leading his crack troops to the Rim for the final battles against the First Imperium. But the man in the room now was something different. This wasn't the military hero known to so many, the grim but honorable commander who'd led his Marines wherever the bugle called. There was an eerie coldness to this man, a complete lack of humanity, of emotion. Whatever Cain had been before, there was no doubt he had been changed. He was an avatar of vengeance now, a man utterly without pity, an unstoppable force that would allow nothing to interfere with the mission. Not mercy, not fatigue, not even the call to battle he had followed for so long. Nothing.

Cain looked down at the crumpled wreck of a man lying

before him. He didn't feel anger or hatred, at least not as he'd known those emotions before. He felt nothing. There was only one focus for the terrible rage that had taken hold of his soul, a single enemy that consumed Erik Cain's every thought. Cain would kill as many of Stark's people as he had to, he would die himself if necessary, but Elias Holm's murderer would not escape him. He had made that vow the day of Holm's funeral, and for six months he'd pursued his prey, through countless systems and across lightyears of empty space.

Cain knew Holm would be the first to try to reach him, to stop him from pursuing his dangerous and deadly vendetta. To warn him his pursuit of revenge could lead to his own destruction. He could hear the dead general's voice in his mind, telling him vengeance would serve no purpose, that his place was in the field, where the Marines were fighting a series of desperate battles against Stark's clone armies. He knew all of that, but it didn't matter. There was nothing left, nothing but the all-consuming need for vengeance.

He told himself he'd never have left the Corps, abandoned his Marines in the middle of a fight, if he hadn't had someone as capable as Cate Gilson to lead them. He didn't know if he believed that or not, but he tried to convince himself. But the truth was darker, less certain. He wasn't sure anything could have stopped him from going after Stark, not duty, not responsibility, not even love. He'd left them all behind, his Marines, the war, Sarah. Erik Cain, the man, loved Sarah Linden with every fiber of his being. But the man was gone now, and only the creature remained, like some legendary beast living only to fulfill its deadly purpose. He was like an animal now, a ceaseless predator, and he'd never stop, never slow in the chase. Not until his prey was dead.

He didn't know if Stark's death would make Holm rest any easier, but he knew he didn't have a choice. He would do whatever he had to, stop at nothing to find his enemy. Perhaps when the deed was done, when Holm and the countless others who had died as a result of Stark's quest for power were avenged, Cain the man could return and move forward, to live a life, as normal men did. He supposed it was possible, but he just didn't know. And right now, he didn't care.

Cain knew on some level he hadn't truly abandoned his comrades. He still fought the same enemy they did. Gavin Stark was more than Elias Holm's murderer, more than a man responsible for millions of deaths. He was the sole commander of the Shadow Legions, the prime mover behind every battle the Marines were fighting. Killing Stark would not only avenge Holm's death; it might very well end the entire war. Stark was a paranoid of epic proportions, and Cain doubted the megalomaniac would have allowed anyone else enough power or knowledge to effectively succeed him. If Stark died, his scheme to dominate all mankind would also die.

He slid his arm to the side, calmly aiming at his victim's other knee. "Where is Gavin Stark?" His cold eyes bored into those of the pathetic weeping creature at his feet.

"No…please, no." The prisoner was lying on his side, his blood-covered hands still clutching at the stricken knee. "I don't know…I really don't know. Stark doesn't tell…"

Another shot rang out, and the prisoner howled again in shock and pain. He fell back to the floor, screaming in agony, his voice low and raw. He lay on his back, his legs covered in blood. "No," he howled, saliva dripping down his chin as he did. "Please…please…" His voice was thick, throaty. He looked up at Cain, his eyes wide with terror.

His cries for mercy were lost on the pitiless Marine. Cain's focus was total, his blood like ice in his veins. He barely even heard his victim's cries, and there wasn't the faintest trace of pity in him. He walked over and stood above the prisoner, staring down as he gripped the pistol tightly in his hand. He looked at his victim for a while, perhaps half a minute. The agent was completely broken, he decided. If he'd known anything, he would have told Cain already. It was another dead end. Another lead turned to useless ash.

Cain's arm moved slowly, bringing the pistol to bear on the whimpering man's head.

The prisoner howled and cried for mercy, sobbing piteously.

"Please…no," he begged. "Please…"

Cain felt nothing as he stared down at the miserable wreck of a man lying before him, covered in his own blood. There was no sympathy, no mercy. Nothing but frustration at another dead end. This man was a cold-blooded assassin. He'd chosen his path, made the decision to become one of Stark's murderers. Perhaps his victims would rest easier when he had joined them in death.

Cain stared down his arm into the prisoner's tear-filled eyes. "Where is Gavin Stark," he repeated coldly. But he knew the prisoner didn't know, and his finger tightened slowly around the trigger.

"Get anything?" James Teller walked down the short corridor, clad in his own rumpled gray Marine fatigues. His boots clanged loudly on the metal deck.

"Nothing." Cain wore the same uniform, but his was stained with blood. "Just another dead end." There were patches of loose threads on the collars of both men's clothing, where their rank insignia had been torn off. Teller and Cain were on a mission, but it was a personal vendetta, and neither felt they could wear their Corps symbols of rank until it was done. They had no intention of behaving like Marines on this operation, of being constrained by the honor of the Corps…or by any code of conduct. To destroy Gavin Stark they would become like him, think as he did, adopt the same tactics. Sometimes, they had decided, it takes a monster to destroy a monster.

Teller nodded. "We got another report from Vance's people, Erik." His voice was somber. "The fighting on Earth is continuing to escalate. There have been repeated nuclear exchanges in all the battlezones. It's all tactical so far…no one's started obliterating cities yet, but Vance thinks it's only a matter of time unless he can figure some way to intervene."

"What does he expect us to do about it?" Cain's voice was raw. "Earth can go to hell all by itself, without our help. We've got a job to do." He started walking down the corridor toward the Torch's small bridge. Roderick Vance had given Cain the ship to hunt down Gavin Stark. The sleek Martian vessels were the fastest things in space and, with the new scramblers Vance's people had installed, the Sand Devil was difficult to detect at anything but close range.

Teller fell in beside Cain. "I don't suppose there's anything we can do." He paused. "Still, so many people are dying. It's hard to believe it's come to this." Teller had his own grudge against the Alliance's government and the entrenched politicians who ruled with an iron fist, but he wasn't as absolute in his hatred of all things Earth as Cain. His childhood had been a difficult one, but not as horrific as the nightmare his friend had survived.

Erik Cain had seen his family expelled from their home and cast into a violent urban wasteland. His father, mother, and sisters had been brutally murdered, and he'd been left to survive alone on the streets when he was eleven. The Corps had found him in his death chamber, convicted by an unjust court and facing imminent execution.

The woman he loved had survived a similar ordeal, brutalized and forced to flee with a price on her head, compelled to survive in the crumbing belts of ancient, almost-abandoned suburbs surrounding the Alliance's cities. She had suffered things she still found it difficult to speak of, even with him.

For all the empathy and loyalty he could show those close to him, there was a side of Cain capable of incredible coldness. He had turned his back on his homeworld, and that was the last word as far as he was concerned. The judgment had been made, the die cast. He blamed Earth and its people for the horrors he and Sarah – and millions of others – had endured, and didn't care if they were careening toward their doom.

The hatch to the bridge slid open as he stepped forward, and he entered the tiny control center. The captain sat in the center of the room, overseeing three other officers manning their posts. Ben Jennings was a decorated officer of the Martian Confederation's navy, a combat veteran with years of experience. Cain knew Jennings should be skippering a Martian battleship, not ferrying a handful of once, and hopefully future, Marines around, hunting one man.

But that man was Gavin Stark, the former head of Alliance intelligence and the commander of the Shadow Legions, a brilliant psychopath determined to seize power over all mankind. Vance understood Cain's need for vengeance. Elias Holm had been a man respected by all those he'd worked with. Holm had been one of the great Alliance heroes of the Third Frontier War, and he'd gone on to lead the ground forces facing the robotic legions of the First Imperium, saving all humanity in the process.

But Vance knew Holm had been more than a hero to Cain. Their relationship had been like that between father and son, and he realized the enraged and grief-stricken Marine would go after his mentor's murderer with an unstoppable fury. He knew it would be futile to try to stop Cain, so he decided to help him. If Cain could find Stark and kill him, he might accomplish more than a division of fully-armored Marines. There was far more at stake than Cain's own personal vendetta. Stark was a mastermind, a psychotic paranoid who kept every aspect of his program running directly through himself. He didn't trust subordinates with too much knowledge and power, and he deliberately kept his top operatives in the dark about the whole picture. So if Cain could take him out, his entire operation might collapse in on itself.

"Any new communications, Captain?" Teller looked over at Jennings. He'd expected an update from Cate Gilson by now. They'd been out of range of the Commnet system for over a week, at least the uncompromised sections. The Shadow Legions had cut off a large part of the overall network, making communications spotty and difficult for the Alliance forces and their allies.

"Nothing, General." Teller wasn't technically a general at the moment. Neither was Cain. But Jennings was scrupulous in calling them by their Marine ranks regardless. Some things you earned for life, and these two men would be always generals to him, even if they spent the rest of their lives playing checkers on some Rim world. "There's been very little incoming traffic from the area around Columbia. I suspect Shadow Legion forces have cut the net as some point rimward from here."

Cain frowned. Stark's Shadow Legion soldiers were everywhere, dug in on 40 colony worlds and far outnumbering the Marines and their allies. But their fleet had remained hidden. Stark was a psychopath, but he was also a genius and a master strategist. And he had been keeping his ships out of combat, using them only to escort invasion forces before pulling them back to whatever hiding place he'd established. He wasn't afraid of many things, but one of the few things that did scare him was Augustus Garret.

The Alliance's exceptional admiral had become the scourge of space, striking terror in the hearts of those standing against him. Garret's strategies were brilliant – well planned and unorthodox, and his crews worshipped him, ready to follow him to the center of a fiery nova if that's where he led them. His reputation had been unparalleled even before the First Imperium War, but now he was regarded, by friend and foe alike, as the greatest naval commander in history, an invincible, unstoppable force. His complete destruction of most of the CAC navy nine months before had only increased his fearsome reputation.

Teller looked at Cain, and he saw his friend had the same concerned look. Gilson's last communication had been two weeks before. The Marines and their Janissary allies had liberated a few small colony worlds, mostly in systems that were strategically located to serve as forward bases of operation, but now Gilson was planning a move against Columbia.

Cain knew the planet well, and his mind drifted back across the years. He'd first served under Holm on Columbia, in the dark days after the Slaughter Pen, when the Alliance forces were on the run. Cain had been a sergeant then, and a newly promoted one at that.

They'd managed to defend the planet, barely, but the cost had been high…including Erik Cain coming as close to a nuclear explosion as a man could without actually dying. He'd spent months in the hospital, and then another year and a half at the Academy, before he returned to the fight. When he next led an assault, it would be as a captain…and the Alliance would be on the road to recovery from its earlier defeats.

"You think the Columbia operation is underway?" Teller tried to hide his concern, but he was only marginally successful. Columbia was a crucial target, one of the Alliance's biggest and most important colonies. But Stark knew that too, and he'd sent a massive invasion force to take the planet. There had been a few early reports from the defenders, but nothing since, and it was generally assumed they'd been overwhelmed and destroyed – and the Shadow Legions had been digging in for months. There was little doubt in Teller's mind – or Cain's – that the liberation of the planet would be a bloodbath.

"I don't know, Jim." Cain's voice was grim, somber. They both had friends in that invasion force, Marines of course, but also some of the Janissaries. The two forces, allies now after years as enemies, had fought together initially against the First Imperium and then again on Armstrong, where the Janissaries had saved Cain's forces from destruction. He felt a twinge in his stomach. It seemed wrong for his friends to be going into a brutal fight without him. But he knew he had no choice. He had to follow through on what he was doing. He had to kill Gavin Stark.

He turned and stared at Teller. "I just don't know," he repeated. He took a deep breath and exhaled. "But they've got their job to do, and we've got ours." He turned to face Teller. "And that job is finding the man behind all of this."

He looked down at the floor for a few seconds, thinking, analyzing everything they knew. "Things are coming to a head on Earth," he said suddenly. "If I know Gavin Stark, he's going to do everything he can to push the Superpowers over the brink so he can come in and pick up the pieces."

"But Roderick Vance's expedition destroyed his base." Teller's voice was grim. The Martian nuclear attack had obliterated Stark's secret facility destroying almost a million of his Shadow Legion clones. It had killed at least another million Alliance citizens as well, victims of radiation and fallout from the bombardment.

"That was a help, but I seriously doubt Gavin Stark had all his Earth-based resources in one place." Cain had sworn he would never again underestimate Stark, and he was determined to make good on that pledge. "Vance's attack hurt him, no doubt, but it's a certainty he's got more clones stashed somewhere." He paused. "And when he's pushed the Superpowers to the final confrontation, he'll release them against the last remnants of their armies." Another pause. "And then he'll rule Earth. All of it."

Cain had a hunch, nothing but a guess really, but the more he thought about it, the more it made sense. Stark was stalemated in the colonies, too afraid of Garret to do anything but dig in on the worlds he occupied and hope the Corps dashed itself to pieces assaulting his defenses. But Earth was a different story.

He turned back toward Jennings. "Captain..." Cain stared straight ahead, but his thoughts were elsewhere, imagining the plans going through Stark's twisted mind. "...please plot a course to the Sol system." Yes, he thought with any icy hatred, that's where we'll find him. There to finish the job at home while Garret's fleet is busy escorting the Columbia invasion force. "Fastest possible time, if you please, Captain. No matter how much time we need to spend buttoned up in the tanks."

Cain stared straight ahead, his eyes glazed over, his fists clenched. I know you'll be there, he thought darkly. I've finally got you, you son of a bitch.

Chapter 2

Admiral's Workroom
AS Pershing
Orbiting Columbia, Eta Cassiopeiae II

Augustus Garret sat at his desk, staring across at General Catherine Gilson, acting Commandant of the Alliance Marine Corps. It had been more than half a year, but it was still a shock to look at that chair and not see Elias Holm sitting there. Garret and Holm had forged a highly effective partnership over their years in command of the respective services, and a close friendship as well. Now Holm was gone, another friend and comrade lost to the endless wars that seemed to plague man wherever he went.

Garret had seen so many killed in his years of battle there was nothing left inside but an aching numbness. He'd witnessed more death and suffering than any man was intended to endure, but duty owned his soul, and it commanded him ever onward, wherever the call of battle echoed out to him.

The struggle against Gavin Stark's Shadow Legions was his fourth war. He'd been blooded in the Second Frontier War, and he'd gotten his first taste of true sacrifice in that conflict. He'd survived that struggle, and the pain and loss it had caused him, to become a hero leading the massively expanded fleets of the Third Frontier War. But it wasn't until the First Imperium War that he became a true legend, the most feared and celebrated warrior in human space, and perhaps in all history itself.

His list of victories had grown, one great battle after another won, but no triumph, no matter how swift or complete, ever seemed to achieve peace. Now he was at war again, not facing the robotic legions of long-dead aliens, but against a human monster, a psychopathic genius bent on total domination of mankind. It never ended, he thought grimly, the constant sacrifice, the endless bloodshed. Now he would lead his people into the fight again, but would victory this time bring a lasting peace or just more suffering and death?

Gilson was fidgeting nervously, clearly uncomfortable to be sitting on the fleet flagship while her Marines were preparing to hit the ground. Indeed, she had fully intended to go down with the first wave, ignoring all objections from her officers. Finally, Garret had prevailed on her that her duty was to coordinate the entire attack, not to get herself killed in some pointless gesture. She owed it to her Marines, he had said. She owed it to them to stay alive and give them the leadership they needed to win and survive this new battle.

Gilson had been ready to argue, but she, like the rest of her fellow officers, considered Garret to be the overall Alliance commander, though officially he only led the navy. Unable to ignore Garret's wishes, she reluctantly agreed to manage the invasion from the flagship. Augustus Garret was famous throughout occupied space, the man who had stopped the First Imperium and saved mankind from total destruction. Elias Holm, Erik Cain – and Gilson herself – had all won their own share of fame and glory in that terrible conflict, but Fleet Admiral Garret had received the largest share of acclaim, even from his own peers, though he wanted none of it.

Garret hated the hero worship, the senseless acclaim he received wherever he went. His own people were the worst offenders, and he'd come to dread that starry eyed look they gave him, the awestruck silence in the ranks as he passed by. He'd long ago lost his taste for glory, far too familiar with its often heartrending price. The victory against the First Imperium had saved humanity, but it had cost Garret his soul. In his own mind he wasn't a hero; he was a butcher, leading thousands to their deaths and worse. The fact that those sacrifices were necessary, that they had saved millions, was enough reason to do what he had done, but not to forgive himself for the cost. He'd sacrificed friendship, even love, to achieve his victories, and the taste was bitter in his mouth.

He'd never forgive himself for what he had done in that final battle on the frontier, how he'd left his best friend and 40,000 Marines and naval personnel behind, trapped at the mercy of a massive fleet of First Imperium vessels. His friends and comrades had told him again and again he'd had no choice, and Garret himself knew that was true. But no one else seemed to understand it just didn't matter. Some acts were so horrifying, so soul-killing, no amount of justification could make a difference. Some things you did killed the part of you that made you human.

"The first waves will be launching in three minutes." Ali Khaled sat next to Gilson. The former Caliphate commander, now a fugitive from his nation along with all his men, sat next to Gilson, staring at a bank of monitors along the wall. Some showed live shots of the activities in the assault bays, while others displayed lists of stats and projected launch times.

"Yes." Gilson nodded, her own eyes fixed on the monitors. "General Heath is in command of the lead elements." Then-Colonel Heath had served well on Arcadia, when Gilson's forces returned from the frontier and reinforced the battered Marines James Teller and Elias Holm had led to the aid of the locals. She'd given him his star for it, and now he was commanding the advance elements of the invasion force, proof she thought grimly, that no good deed goes unpunished. Heath's people would be landing in the teeth of the enemy defenses, and they'd be outnumbered and under constant fire as they clawed to carve a foothold for the rest of the forces to land.

James Teller would have been her first choice to command the vanguard, but he was off with Erik Cain, chasing Gavin Stark. Teller was Cain's protégé, much as Cain had been Holm's. When Erik decided to hunt down Stark, Teller had followed him without a second thought. She had both men's stars in her desk, waiting for them to return and claim them. She'd wished more than once that they were with her, helping to lead the Corps into this new fight, but she understood why they had made the choices they had. And, if they were successful in finding and killing Stark, perhaps they would do more to end this war than the entire strike force about to invade Columbia. Maybe they could wear those stars again in peacetime, helping her rebuild the shattered Corps.

Nevertheless, Gilson had tried to convince Cain to stay, and Garret had thrown his own efforts behind hers. But Erik Cain was as stubborn as any human being who'd ever lived, and he grimly declined both their entreaties. Killing Stark was not only vengeance for General Holm, he'd declared, but the best way to defeat the Shadow Legions. Stark had been their enemy for years, secretly plotting against them before he declared openly and launched his Shadow Legions to conquer occupied space. He'd been a cancer consuming the body of the navy and the Corps, even as they struggled against the robot legions of the First Imperium. Stark had worked against them as far back as the Third Frontier War and the rebellions, engineering Rafael Samuels' treachery that had almost destroyed the Corps.

Lop the head off, Cain had said simply, and the body will die. There could be no peace while Stark lived. He was too capable, too intelligent – too evil. He would never stop, and no victory could be final while he still lived.

Garret and Gilson had argued with him, but they both knew Cain was right. If he and Teller succeeded, if they found and killed Gavin Stark, maybe this war could be stopped before the last veterans of the Corps and their Janissary allies were gone. Thousands were already dead, lost in the endless, brutal battles. Perhaps Cain's pursuit of vengeance could save the few who remained, and the Corps itself with them.

The three officers stared at the monitors, waiting for the launches to begin. There was an eerie quiet in the room, an absence that each of them felt keenly. They all knew Elias Holm was dead, of course, yet it seemed every time one of them turned around, they expected to see him standing there, calmly directing the invasion force. It had been six months, but the loss was still fresh, a wound that wouldn't heal.

Gilson's emotions were volatile. Despite her understanding of his motives and the potential rewards of his success, she was angry at Cain for leaving her to fill Holm's shoes by herself. Worse, she envied him. She wanted to hunt Stark down herself, to kill the psychopathic bastard with her own hands. Her feelings had been confusing at first, threatening to tear her apart, but she'd made peace with the whole thing. Cain was the right one to pursue Stark. She had been close to Holm, a loyal officer and a comrade through decades of brutal fighting, but Erik Cain had been like a son to the fallen Commandant. It was his right to go after Stark, even more than hers, and she'd come to realize and accept that.

Besides, Cain was the right man for the job. The grim Marine had a dark side, a coldness and a relentless determination Gilson knew she couldn't match. Cain would follow every lead, and he would do whatever had to be done to track his prey. Whatever had to be done - those were dangerous words, ones she wasn't sure she could back up with the brutal ferocity she knew Cain would.

"Admiral Garret, General Heath requests permission to commence his launch, sir." Tara Rourke's voice was clear and confident on the comlink. She'd been Garret's flag tactical officer for several years now, and he'd declared more than once that she was the best junior officer who'd ever served under him.

Garret glanced across the desk at Gilson. "It's your order, General." He flipped a button. "Your link is live."

Gilson nodded softly. "Attention all Marines, this is General Catherine Gilson." The Marines had liberated a number of smaller worlds over the past six months, but this was the first major planetary assault since Arcadia and Armstrong, and she could feel the tension in her gut. "You are about to liberate one of the oldest and most populated colony worlds in human-occupied space, a planet that has seen more than its share of war and destruction in its century of human habitation." She hoped it was still one of the most populated. The enemy had been there for 18 months, and the Columbians were well-known for their willingness to resist, whatever the cost. She was deathly afraid they had paid that price in blood.

"As always, you have my utmost confidence. You are battered and tired. We have all suffered terrible losses and grief. You have fought without rest, struggled from one end of human space to the other and even into the First Imperium itself. No men and women could be expected to do what you have done, let alone more. But you are Marines first, and men and women second. In the final accounting, that is all that matters. Marines are always ready to do the job, to fight whatever battles must be fought." She paused, taking a deep breath. "And there are struggles yet to be won."

She hesitated, pushing back the tears she could feel welling up in her eyes. "I know that General Holm would be proud to see you all today, ready to fight another battle for freedom. Know as you go forward into the fight once again that he is with you, as he will be forever. You are the Marines he helped to make you, and I know you will live up to that standard."

She glanced over at Khaled. "In this fight, as in our last one, we have allies, men who once fought against us, but now stand at our sides as friends. They are honorable warriors who march to the fire alongside us, and they have earned our trust and our respect. We are grateful for their aid and proud to fight at their sides."

She swallowed hard and sucked in another breath. "Go now, and fight with the valor all have come to expect from you. Go and free our people on Columbia and destroy the Shadow Legion invaders. Show the enemy just what Marines can do. Forward, to victory." She cut the line and turned toward Garret and nodded. "Commence the landing."

All around Columbia, men and women sprang into action at Gilson's order. Transports fired their thrusters, moving into low orbits, positioning themselves to launch their Marine and Janissary contingents into Columbia's upper atmosphere. Escort ships maneuvered to cover their movements, providing protection and close support. Farther out, the battlefleets and logistical trains were moved into position.

Columbia was surrounded by almost all the military might

Garret and Gilson could muster. The combined fleet was divided into three task forces plus the former Caliphate ships under Admiral Abbas. It was an awesome display of naval power, and Garret was practically daring Stark to come out of hiding with his fleet and offer battle.

Taskforce One was commanded by Elizabeth Arlington, and it was in close orbit, protecting the transport armada. The troopships themselves were in a long line, ready to begin launching dropships into the upper atmosphere. The Marines and Janissaries onboard were suited up and loaded onto their landing craft, waiting for the final order. Arlington's warships were in high orbit, covering the transports from any enemy that might slip past the heavier fleet units on station farther out.

Taskforce Two, under Admiral Michael Jacobs, had been the first units to approach the planet. They'd conducted a pre-invasion bombardment, blasting any enemy positions they could identify and target without undue danger to civilian populations. Jacob's ships were on the move now, half pulling away from the planet to rearm, the rest taking position to provide support to the Marines on the ground.

Taskforce Three, under Camille Harmon, was the largest, with most of the heavy capital ships. Harmon's force was organized for one mission, and one mission only, to blast the hell out of any enemy ships that tried to interfere with the invasion force. Her units were posted about three light minutes from the planet, along with Abbas' Caliphate ships. They hadn't detected any enemy naval presence, but they were on full alert anyway. Garret and Harmon were aware of Stark's unpredictability, and they weren't taking any chances. Harmon had scoutships patrolling the entire system, and her combat elements were ready to destroy any naval force that approached Columbia without authorization.

Garret stared at his screen, though he'd committed every detail of the fleet and operation to memory. He knew every ship under his command, and its position and its orders. His people were ready for whatever had to be done, and Gilson's as well. That wasn't what worried him. It was supply that most concerned him. They had managed to scrounge up enough to launch the Columbia invasion, but now the logistical situation was becoming dire. He was watching numbers scroll slowly across the screen, and his frown deepened as he thought about how low his stores had become.

Provisioning Gilson's Marines for the invasion had almost depleted the fleet's stores, and many of his own ships carried half-loads of missiles and other ordnance. He'd tried to contact the high command on Earth a dozen times, but he'd been unable to get through. There were no shipments of supplies coming through, no orders, no news. He'd tried to keep his focus on the crises at hand, but now he was really worried. What was happening on Earth?

"Good luck, Marines!" Captain Harlow's voice echoed loudly in the helmets of the Marines of A and B companies of the 3rd Battalion. They were the leading edge of the first wave, the first 350 men and women scheduled to hit the ground on Columbia.

The tradition of the ship's captain wishing the strike force luck had come down from the earliest days of the spaceborne Corps, and it had endured through three Frontier Wars, the struggle against the First Imperium, and now the battle to defeat Gavin Stark's Shadow Legions.

Lieutenant Callahan gritted his teeth. He knew the captain's address was the final thing he'd hear before the catapults fired and launched the heavy Liggett 10-man landers out into the edge of space above Columbia. Callahan was a veteran who'd fought in the rebellions as a private and the First Imperium War as a non-com. He'd received a battlefield promotion during the fighting on Armstrong, a reward bestowed on him by none other than the legendary Erik Cain himself.

He exhaled hard as the magnetic cannon accelerated his lander down the rails and through the open outer doors. His armor absorbed some of the g-forces, but he was still slammed back hard inside his suit, losing his breath for a few seconds before he adjusted. It was the same with every assault landing, but it was something you never got completely used to, no matter how many drops you made.

Callahan had no illusions about what he and his people faced down on Columbia's surface. They were all veterans, and they would do what had to be done. But the honor of leading the advance guard carried a heavy price. He knew casualties would be high, very high. And if the first Marines down failed to secure a perimeter, they could all be overwhelmed before the fleet could send down enough units to strengthen the landing zone. If the invasion of Columbia failed, if the enemy put up too strong a defense and General Gilson called off the rest of the landings, Callahan knew his people would all be KIA. He knew that because he was damned sure none of them would surrender.

Callahan glanced at his display, watching the five landers carrying his platoon descend into Columbia's atmosphere. The formation looked good, and they seemed to be right on schedule. If everything went according to plan, they'd be on the ground and in action in less than ten minutes.

He felt the lander bounce hard to one side as it tore through the thickening air. The Liggett landing craft was an improvement on the old Gordon, carrying ten armored Marines and a large cargo of ammunition and equipment. With four heavy duty laser turrets and enough ordnance to keep a squad supplied for hours, the Liggett was designed to land right in the teeth of an enemy position, blasting away in close support as its squad jumped right into battle.

"Projected landing in six minutes." The voice was female, calm and pleasant, typical for a fleet AI. Callahan knew everyone in the first wave had gotten the same announcement. He took a deep breath, preparing himself once again for battle. He knew his people were ready, that all the Corps was prepared to do what had to be done. His heart had swelled with pride when General Gilson addressed them, when she had invoked the name of Elias Holm. The Commandant had been beloved by every Marine in the Corps, and Callahan and his people were ready to lash out at the enemy that had taken their leader from them. The Corps would fight on Columbia with its usual tenacity and professionalism, but there would be something else here too, a ferocity driven by their pain of loss. The Marines was here to do battle for Elias Holm, and God help any who stood in their way.

"Four minutes until projected landing. All Marines, complete final diagnostic check on weapons systems."

Callahan's visor plate opened, and he could see the bright blue sky above Columbia. He was held rigidly in place, but he managed to glance down toward the ground as he checked his weapons. There was water below, nothing but a seemingly endless sea stretching as far as he could see. He knew his people were still thousands of kilometers from the inhabited areas of the planet, tearing through the atmosphere at 40,000 kph heading for the LZ just outside the capital city of Weston.

He could feel the lander's maneuvering thrusters kick in, and the small craft began to zigzag wildly. They were entering the inner defensive perimeter, and the Liggett's AI was conducting evasive maneuvers, trying to avoid the incoming AA fire. He could see the laser turrets whipping around, and he caught the barely perceptible flash of one of them firing. He knew that had probably been a surface-to-air missile heading for his lander and, in the back of his mind, he suspected that laser blast had saved his life. His and those of the other nine Marines bolted in next to him.

There was land below the Liggett now, and he could see they were much closer to the ground. He could make out terrain features ahead, and he tried to match them with the maps he'd studied in the pre-mission briefing.

"Two minutes to landing."

His own com unit activated, allowing him to contact the men and women of his platoon. He was about to speak when he saw a bright flash off to the extreme right. His eyes snapped back to his display, and he felt his stomach in his throat. There were only four Liggett's displayed. Lander 4 was gone. Just gone.

The shock of loss hit him hard. He'd understood they were going back into the fight, but it never seemed real until somebody got hit. Now it was official. They were back in the shit.

"Alright, Marines. Stay focused. We've got a job to do." But all he could think about was the crew of ship four. Hiller, Haggerty, Ash – Ash had saved his life on Armstrong. Now they were all gone.

"Thirty seconds to landing."

The AI snapped him back to the present. He had a job to do, and that came first, before everything. Ten of his people were dead, but the rest were counting on him. It was time to make these sons of bitches pay. And now the men and women of A Company had one more reason to waste these motherfuckers.

He felt the Liggett's braking rockets fire and then the slow, sickening drop as the lander floated down the last 30 meters, settling hard on the rocky ground. There was fire ripping all around them, the enemy already moving on the LZ determined to pinch it out before a second wave could get down.

"Let's go!" he shouted into the com, leaping from the lander and whipping around his assault rifle. "Company A...attack!"

The Marines were back on Columbia.

Chapter 3

Front Lines
120 Kilometers East of Paris
French Zone, Europa Federalis

Hans Werner peered out over the trench at the blackened and shattered ground in front of his position. The stretch of rolling hills had once been covered with rich vineyards, but now it was a blasted hell where nothing lived. The civilians who'd survived the initial battles had long since fled, and the ruin of war was everywhere.

Werner couldn't see the Europan positions from where he stood, but he knew they were there, a mere 3 kilometers ahead, a network of trenches as formidable as his, hidden by the low ridgeline. He'd assaulted that defensive position three times. Each of his meticulously planned attacks drove through the enemy defenses, only to bog down and falter for lack of supplies and reinforcements. The enemy had thrown themselves at his line as well, and each time his carefully positioned batteries and autocannons shredded the advancing formations, sending them back in disarray.

The casualties along the stalemated line had been almost too many to count. Werner had lost two million men in just the last six months, and he was certain the Europans had suffered even greater casualties. The CEL forces had seemed unstoppable on their initial drive toward Paris, but then the RIC allied with Europa Federalis and invaded the CEL's eastern provinces, draining away the resources that sustained Werner's offensive.

The Europan diplomatic victory was as effective as any

battlefield success, and Werner lost almost a million men without a battle, legions of his veterans sent to the eastern front to meet the new threat. His supplies and reinforcements trickled to almost nothing as well, and he'd been compelled to halt his advance and reorganize. The CEL's chance at a quick victory was lost, the victim of enemy diplomacy and the need to fight a 2-front war.

Werner had gained his fourth star during the early fighting along the Reims-Troyes Line, and he now commanded the four armies of 1st Army Group. He was the greatest hero of the war, at least in Europe, and the only CEL commander who had distinguished himself in the disastrous early battles. His steadfast defense along the southern edge of the front had likely saved the League from an ignominious defeat in the early months of the fighting, when the Europan forces surged forward shouting their battle cry, "Venger le sang de Marseille."

The still-unnamed world war had begun in Europe, between Europa Federalis and the Central European League, ignited by the nuclear destruction of Marseilles, an act of terrorism in which the CEL still denied any involvement. Repeated statements to that effect from Neu-Brandenberg had fallen on deaf ears, and the Paris government repudiated the century-long prohibition against terrestrial warfare and launched a massive invasion of their hated neighbors. That war had been raging for more than a year now, and both Powers, already prostrate from the worldwide economic depression, were on the verge of total collapse.

The conflict may have started along the banks of the Rhine, but once open war broke out between Superpowers, the conflagration spread, and now there was fighting in every corner of the globe. The Tokyo-based Pacific Rim Coalition joined their longtime Western Alliance allies in the conflict with the Chinese-dominated Central Asian Combine. The Caliphate honored its treaty obligations to their CAC partners, and the Alliance and PRC were soon fighting their two greatest rivals. That struggle had raged across the seas, where the Alliance and PRC had been largely victorious, and in southern Asia and Africa, where the

CAC-Caliphate armies had crushed most of their enemies.

The CAC and the Caliphate had won the diplomatic war as well, winning over both the RIC and the South American Empire as well as Europa Federalis. Hong Kong and New Medina had assembled their great power bloc with a combination of threats and promises, edging out the diplomats from Washbalt with the help of an extraordinary effort by Li An and her C1 operatives.

The Russian-Indian offensive against the CEL had been the price of bringing Europa Federalis into their league, and now five of Earth's Superpowers were aligned against the other three. Werner's attentions had been focused primarily on the theater where he commanded, but he knew the effects of the wider war would trickle down and affect his own armies. Already, his forces had been stripped of manpower and resources to support the tenuous defensive lines on the eastern front. He knew that would only get worse, as the Russians continued to mobilize and pour more troops into the combat zone. Eventually, he realized, if his forces became any weaker, even the battered Europans would reorganize and launch their own offensive.

He stared down at the orders he held in his hand. He'd read them three times already, but he found his eyes panning across the small 'pad again. He understood the reality behind the directive, but he still couldn't bring himself to believe what he was reading. He was to launch an immediate offensive to take the Europan capital of Paris, and he was authorized to use unlimited tactical and intermediate ranged nuclear weapons against any military targets, without consideration to civilian casualties.

Both sides had used nukes in the war, but they had been targeted and sporadic. Werner's orders called for a massive pre-attack bombardment, one that shattered the Europan defensive positions and their logistical centers behind the front. There would be millions of civilian casualties, no matter how carefully he targeted the strikes. He could only guess at the probable response, and how it would affect his advancing armies...and the rest of the world.

He felt a flush of anger toward the high command in Neu-Brandenburg, but he realized they had no choice. The CEL couldn't fight the Europans and the RIC at the same time, and the Alliance wasn't in a position to offer anything beyond minimal support. Taking out Europa Federalis was the only way the CEL could survive. If they knocked out their western enemy, they could consolidate their forces on the eastern front and hold out against the growing RIC pressure. It was a desperate plan, one he wanted to oppose. But he couldn't think of an alternative.

"Come here, Major." He shouted to his longtime aide.

Potsdorf had been with him since his days as a battalion commander. Then a lieutenant, he had followed Werner through his meteoric rise in rank, continuing to serve as his aide at each level of command.

"Yes, General." Potsdorf was running over, moving as quickly as he could in the deep muck of the trench. The aide was a tall man, with close-cropped blonde hair and a grim face. He stopped in front of the theater commander and stood at attention.

"Read this, Potsdorf." He handed the 'pad to his surprised aide.

"My God, sir." Potsdorf was still reading, but he'd gotten the gist of the order in the first few seconds. "This is a massive escalation."

"Indeed it is, Major." There was a sadness in Werner's voice. He was a soldier, and he would carry out his orders, but he couldn't help but think he was committing suicide as well. For him and for his soldiers, and possibly for the civilians back home too. The Europans would almost certainly respond in kind, and a battlefield that was already a nightmare would become a blasted, radioactive hell. What happened next rested with the politicians, but that was cold comfort to Werner. "But those are our orders, so we'd better do everything we can to make sure the troops are ready." He took a deep breath. "Because we're about to unleash hell."

Ryan Warren's head was pounding. He reached around and massaged the back of his neck, feeling the hard tightness of the

knotted muscles under his fingers. He glanced at the chronometer. He'd been at his desk for almost 15 hours, but he wasn't
even close to done. There was a half-eaten sandwich sitting off
to the side of workstation, the only food he'd touched all day. It
had been there for hours, and the edges were dried out and stale.
A stone cold cup of coffee, missing only a few sips, sat next to
the plate, equally forgotten.

Warren had lost 10 kilos since he had taken over Gavin
Stark's job, and he wondered how that master spy had seemed to
handle his myriad responsibilities with such effortless grace. He
suspected now that had been at least somewhat of a façade, that
Stark's brilliant leadership had come at its own cost. Still, it had
been weeks since he'd managed to sleep all night, and he wondered how any man could do this job for as long as Stark had.

For years Warren had dreamed about being Number One,
a goal that had seemed unattainable from his mid-level position in the massive spy agency. Now that circumstance had
made his wild ambition a reality, he longed only to flee from the
crushing responsibility, to go back to his small office and his old
manageable portfolio of work. He'd once ached for the power
he imagined Stark wielded, but now, with war raging across the
globe and revolution and disorder at home, he saw nothing but
endless obligation. No matter what he managed to accomplish,
another ten problems were waiting for his attention.

Things were going downhill. Fast. He'd been Number One
for ten months now, but he was still trying to rebuild an Alliance
Intelligence ravaged by the nuclear destruction of its headquarters. The personnel losses had been severe, and key agents were
missing, even those who shouldn't have been in Washbalt when
HQ was destroyed. There was something wrong, something
he couldn't explain fully. He was sure of that. But he couldn't
figure out what it was.

The devastated and massively shrunken Alliance Intelligence
had only a fraction of its earlier resources, and more problems
than ever to address. There was war raging across the globe, and
the Alliance had suffered some key defeats, making its position
ever more precarious. Warren wouldn't characterize the war to

date as a disaster, but he couldn't say things were going well either.

The navy had gained control of the seas, largely as a result of Admiral Young's extraordinary leadership, but the naval victories had been costly, and losses had been high. The remaining fleets were strong enough to control the oceans themselves, but too weak to project force close to land, where the enemy's ground batteries and missiles could come into play.

The Cog pacification program had begun to achieve some sporadic successes. The initial implementation had been nothing short of a disaster, the Cog enlisted men disobeying their officers and refusing to execute their kill orders. Warren had overestimated the discipline of the armed forces, assuming the Cog soldiers would do as they were told, out of sheer self-preservation if nothing else. They'd all known the price of disobedience, but many of them had mutinied anyway, and the initial attacks against the rioting Cogs had been a stunning failure.

Warren's people had since reestablished control over the kill units, transferring in more crew from the middle classes and the lowest ranks of the political class. His people had taken charge of the captured mutineers from the military authorities, executing them with extreme brutality in front of their fellow soldiers. He knew there was a limit to what such harsh measures could accomplish, that if he pushed too hard, he would only feed rebellion. But time wasn't on his side, and if he couldn't scare the soldiers into submission, all would be lost. He'd actually had contingency plans to nuke several cities where the Cog rebellions were the most severe, but President Oliver had put those on hold.

Oliver had a reputation for strength and intelligence, one Warren now realized was entirely undeserved. The Alliance's longtime president was a bully with some instinctive political skill, but nothing more. He had maintained power for so many years through momentum and threats, and he'd been lucky not to encounter a capable adversary in that time. The current crisis had entirely overwhelmed him, and he'd lost his nerve more than once when risky actions were called for. Warren had thought about making a move to unseat Oliver, but he hadn't pulled the trigger. He had no doubt it was the move Gavin Stark would have made, but the last thing Alliance Intelligence's new chief wanted was more responsibility.

He had more pressing matters than planning a coup. He'd managed to pacify most of the cities, but there were several problem spots remaining. Manhattan was the worst of all, and the Cogs had rampaged through the Protected Zone in an orgy of rape and murder. The enraged lower classes had fallen on everyone they'd encountered, members of the middle class as well as the Political families and Corporate Magnates. The entire city had been shut down, and the bodies of the unburied dead filled the streets. Even the secure areas occupied by the highest levels of the political classes had been ransacked, their pampered inhabitants brutalized and tortured to death in the streets.

He'd repeatedly sent in kill flights, but the rebellious Cogs had taken refuge underground in the vast network of old rail tunnels that crisscrossed the city. The problem had festered for months now, but he simply didn't have enough ground troops available to clean out the entrenched Cogs, not with the demands for manpower coming in from the combat zones. Starvation would do his job for him eventually, at least once the surviving Cogs exhausted the dwindling food supplies.

Diplomacy had been a black mark on his record as well, and he could find little accomplishment there to celebrate. His decimated agency had failed to provide the covert support the Alliance diplomats needed. He knew Li An had gotten the better of him in the race for allies, and her manipulations had helped the CAC assemble a bloc of five Powers lined up against the Alliance and its allies. He'd been an operative all his life, but it still amazed him how far a little sex and blackmail could go toward directing international affairs.

Warren had known the ancient CAC spy was a master manipulator, and he realized she had taken him to school in the frantic espionage that surrounded the various negotiations. The prelude to global war had seen the Powers scrambling for allies, and Li's CAC had decisively won that struggle.

The ancient Li An had been a match even for Stark himself, or at least nearly so. No other adversary had challenged Alliance Intelligence's brilliant master so effectively. Indeed, Warren thought, she may have even gotten the best of him in the end. The perpetrator of the attack that destroyed Alliance Intelligence headquarters and killed Gavin Stark had never been identified, but C1 and its brilliant leader were at the top of everyone's suspect list. Even without proof, the incident had been a major factor in provoking the war now raging across the Earth.

"Number One, we have a priority one communication for you from Chancellor Schmidt."

His head whipped toward the com unit on his desk. Otto Schmidt was the Chancellor of the Central European League, President Oliver's counterpart in the CEL.

"Put him through immediately." Warren felt a knot in his empty stomach. He could speculate on a number of reasons the CEL Chancellor would contact him, but none of them were good news.

"Mr. Warren?" He could hear the exhaustion in the voice on the com, and he could tell immediately there was no AI translating. The Chancellor spoke flawless English with only the slightest accent, a major improvement over Warren's poor mastery of German.

"Yes, Mr. Chancellor. This is a rare honor. How may I help you?" His voice was tentative, confused. Schmidt should rightfully have contacted Oliver, not him.

"I have been unable to reach President Oliver despite several attempts, and it is vital that I speak to someone at the top levels of your government immediately." They both knew the head of Alliance Intelligence was one of the most powerful members of the government, despite being ranked fairly far down on official lists of seniority.

Warren held back a sigh. He knew Oliver was nearing a total breakdown, but he couldn't imagine the fool being unavailable to an allied head of state during wartime. "I am sure I can help you, Chancellor."

"Conditions on our eastern front have been deteriorating rapidly as the RIC continues to mobilize and reinforce its armies."

"We are aware of the pressure your forces are experiencing on both fronts. As you know, we are increasing our shipments of…"

"Pardon my interruption, Mr. Warren, but I am aware that your government is doing everything possible to aid our war effort. Unfortunately, the sum total of this is insufficient to alter the tactical situation." He paused. "Unless we take immediate drastic measures to defeat Europa Federalis, we will be crushed between two enemies."

Warren felt his stomach roll at the word drastic. He knew immediately what the Chancellor was going to say, and his mind raced at the likely consequences.

"As per our treaty obligations, I am advising you that at 11PM Washbalt time, General Werner's First Army Group will launch an offensive to break through the Europan lines and capture Paris. The attack will be preceded by a hurricane bombardment, including unlimited tactical and intermediate-range nuclear and chemical ordnance." Schmidt paused for an instant, the gravity of what he was saying laying heavily on him as he spoke. "I have authorized and instructed General Werner to restrict the bombardment to targets of military significance, however, I have also advised him that potential collateral damage resulting from his attack is not a consideration."

Warren took a breath. In less than two hours, the CEL's army was going to unleash a massive bombardment that would kill hundreds of thousands, and probably millions, of Europan civilians. His mind was running wild with the potential consequences. He knew there was no way to stop the CEL from following through. It was their only chance. If they didn't knock the Europans out of the war, they were finished. If they won a complete victory on the western front, they could rush General Werner and his veterans to the east. Werner was their star commander, and his troops the best they had. Maybe they could at least stalemate the invading RIC armies.

"Thank you for the notice, Chancellor." He swallowed hard.

"My best wishes to General Werner and his men." He paused. "And to all of us."

"Thank you, Mr. Warren. You will of course pass this on to President Oliver and the other members of your Cabinet?" It was more a statement than a question.

"Of course, Chancellor." Schmidt cut the line. Warren sat still for a few seconds, trying to organize his thoughts. He had to get Alliance Intelligence locked down, in case this thing escalated wildly. He punched at his workstation, pulling up the emergency protocols for potential worldwide nuclear exchanges. All the years he'd longed for Stark's job, and now that he was here, he might find himself presiding over the biggest catastrophe in human history.

He put his face in his hands. There was one thing he had to do first. He hit the com unit. "I need to see President Oliver. Now." The fool couldn't have gotten too far. They were all locked down deep under the Virginia countryside, with Stonewall protocols in full effect. "All personnel are to stop whatever they are doing and locate the president immediately."

Warren sighed. The fool was probably drunk or strung out somewhere. Perhaps he had to revisit that coup idea. Oliver was losing his shit, and the Alliance couldn't afford a leader right now who was caving under the pressure. Warren didn't want Oliver's job, but he was beginning to realize he might have to take it anyway.

Chapter 4

Base Omega
Asteroid Belt
Altair System

Gavin Stark sat at his desk, a half-finished Scotch sitting neglected alongside his workstation. His mind was in a dozen places at once, reviewing reports, examining force deployments, updating supply manifests. His paranoid mind was virtually incapable of trusting anyone, and he micromanaged every aspect of the massive campaign now underway.

Stark was a true genius, his brilliant mind an accident of genetics, an unlikely mutation that gave him analytical ability far in excess of most humans. He was different in other ways as well, a man with few true emotions. He could feel rage, certainly, but even that was only a manifestation of his singular focus, a direction of frustration toward those who interfered with his plans. But emotions like love, loyalty, friendship – they were mostly beyond his ability to feel and understand. He'd only ever had one friend. Jack Dutton had been his mentor and confidante, and the old man's death had severed the only connection Stark had to his humanity.

For all his evil, for the millions of deaths he'd caused and the countless more who would die as his plans progressed, Stark wasn't really a sadist. He would torture a captive without hesitation or pity, but only to gain information he needed or to instill useful fear in those who witnessed such brutality. He rarely tormented enemies simply to gain satisfaction from their suffering, and he rapidly lost interest in those who had opposed him once they were no longer a threat. He was cold, determined, almost robotic in his actions, and he rarely allowed himself to pursue pointless vendettas that did nothing to further his plans.

Only a few adversaries, those who had truly and repeatedly interfered with his efforts, those who had thwarted him and stood in his way again and again, earned his lasting enmity. At the top of this list, two men stood above all others, and they were both the target of Stark's eternal wrath. He hated Augustus Garret and Erik Cain with a passion utterly inconsistent with his normal cold-blooded demeanor, and his temper flared when he even thought of his greatest enemies.

He'd taken an unacceptable personal risk to attempt an assassination of Cain on Armstrong. He had missed his nemesis but ended up killing Elias Holm instead. He'd been frustrated that Cain escaped him, but Holm was another enemy, and Stark knew the Marine Commandant's death would shatter Erik Cain. He reveled in the hurt he had caused, even as he scolded himself for taking such a terrible risk. It was unlike him, and he was beginning to realize that his enmity for the Marines and their allies was affecting his normal calm and rational demeanor. He struggled against the hatred he felt and forced himself to remember his priorities. Power was what Stark truly craved, the total domination of all those around him. He knew he had been born to rule mankind, and now his plans were in their final stages. He was resolved to remain focused, to execute his plan meticulously, to follow through until humanity was his forever. Men would bow to him and beg his favor, and he would be their overlord.

He was using every facet of his malevolent intelligence, carefully analyzing his plans, reviewing the reports coming in from all across occupied space, trying to decide what to do next. Many of his schemes were progressing nicely, but he'd suffered setbacks as well, mostly at the hands of his old nemeses, the cursed Marines and Augustus Garret and his navy.

He leaned back in his chair and allowed himself a smile. Garret and his Marine allies were about to invade Columbia. Indeed, he thought, they are probably beginning their attack even now. It would be a brutal fight, he knew, one that might very well end in the defeat of his occupation forces. He'd managed to get significant reinforcements to his Shadow Legions there, and they controlled most of the planet's inhabited areas. The population had fled to the swamps and wilderness areas, continuing the fight with a futile, but annoying, partisan struggle.

Still, despite the strength of his defenders, he'd seen the Marines in action too many times to discount their chance of success. They were worked up into a frenzy by the death of their leader, and Stark knew they would hit the ground on Columbia like avenging angels, slaughtering all who stood in their way. But none of that mattered. However the battle turned out, it would be a win for Stark, at least in the long run.

Garret and the Marines were cut off from Earth, completely unaware of the disaster unfolding there. The Alliance navy and Marines were the best fighting forces in space, but they needed supplies to maintain their effectiveness, and soon they'd be down to throwing rocks. Stark's plans were long term by nature, and he knew he could eliminate even a victorious Marine Corps and navy by forcing them to expend their supplies and cutting them off from any replenishment.

The great Alliance shipyards at Wolf 359 had already been reduced to floating wreckage, and on every world the Shadow Legions had occupied, they had destroyed any facility capable of producing weapons or supplies for the armed forces. Garret's teams had already sabotaged the space-based shipyards and orbital factories of the other Superpowers, enlisting an unlikely team of traitors and deep cover operatives to achieve the goal. When the struggle on Earth reached its inevitable final phase, the terrestrial factories that had long supplied the space-based forces of the doomed Superpowers would also be gone, reduced to piles of radioactive slag. Then Garret would see what his vaunted fleet could accomplish with no weapons, no spare parts…and no hope of resupply. The Marines who survived the impending battle on Columbia could fight their next struggle with sticks and stones.

Stark sat silently, considering his plans. His own fleet was hidden in Altair's massive asteroid belt, ships powered down and running silent. He knew they didn't have a chance against Garret and his forces, at least not until the great admiral was out of ordnance. Then he could send his fleet to engage Garret, using unanswered missile volleys to blast the Alliance admiral's helpless ships to bits at long range...and destroy the "invincible" Augustus Garret once and for all. But before that day, he had one mission for Admiral Liang and his hidden fleet, a single obstacle remaining in the way of his total domination.

He was worried about Roderick Vance and the Martian Confederation. He'd planned to deal with them once he'd finished off Garret and the Marines, but now he decided to move up the timetable. Vance was enormously capable and, unlike the military leaders, he possessed the same sort of subtlety Stark himself did. The Martian spy was dangerous, and Stark had become worried about what he might be doing in the shadows, how he was feeding information to Garret and the rest of the Alliance leaders. Martian industry was still intact, and Vance could even supply Garret's fleet if Stark didn't do something about it. No, the Martian problem couldn't wait any longer. Vance and the Confederation were the last variable, and it was time to eliminate that uncertainty from the equation.

He reached out and activated his com. "Admiral Liang, please report to my office immediately." He took a deep breath. "I have a mission for the fleet."

Vance was walking along the esplanade, staring down into the water as it flowed beneath him. One day, the Red River would meander unhindered across the plains of a terraformed Mars, but now it was little more than a decorative water feature running around the domed periphery of the Ares Metroplex. A century of tireless effort had made significant changes to the Martian environment. The nuclear engines at the poles ran night and day, melting the massive ice caps and releasing oxygen and water vapor into the slowly-thickening atmosphere.

A man still couldn't breathe unassisted on the surface of the red planet, but the pressure had improved considerably, and the average temperature had increased by 40 degrees Kelvin. It was now possible to survive outside for limited periods with proper cold weather gear and an oxygen tank. Vance had done it himself, feeling a rush of pride in what the Confederation had managed to achieve in its 130 years of existence. He knew he wouldn't live to see running rivers and cloudy skies, but he hoped to take a walk outside one day before he died, unaided by breathing equipment and feeling the cool air on his bare face.

He looked up through the dome. Phobos was almost full, casting a faint glow across the sandy dunes, but Deimos had already set, and its light was gone from the night sky. Mars' two moons were small, but they were beautiful, he thought, somehow at home in the velvety night sky. The fact that he knew both of them housed extensive military and intelligence bases marred that serene image somewhat, and he momentarily longed for an age when Mars was safe, when her security no longer required people like him to stand on the line and hold off those who would see the Confederation destroyed, its people reduced to abject slaves.

He didn't know if that day would ever come. He knew what Erik Cain would say, but he found himself grasping at faint hopes for the best. Vance had lived most of his life certain he'd never meet his match in cynicism, but that was before his path had crossed that of the grim Alliance Marine. Cain didn't believe in much, nothing really, beyond the men and women who served at his side. He tended to expect the worst from everyone else and, more often than not, he had been right.

Vance was a cold man in many ways, and he was often seen as aloof and humorless. It wasn't entirely a fair assessment, but he'd accepted it as part of the life he'd chosen to lead. He could have enjoyed a luxurious existence running his family's massive business empire, but he knew his beloved Confederation existed in a dangerous universe, and he'd sworn to do whatever was necessary to ensure its survival. That often meant taking dark actions, and sometimes people died because of what he did. Often, in fact. It was part of the job, something he'd learned to live with, however uncomfortably.

His father had also been a loner, and he'd died when Vance was still a child. It wasn't until years later he learned his father had perished in the service of Mars, leading her intelligence agencies as he himself would one day. His family was one of the wealthiest on Mars. Indeed, they were one of the richest anywhere, but he learned it also had a long tradition of service to the Confederation, a history he chose to continue.

"Mr. Vance?" The voice came from behind a row of small trees, evergreens imported from the Pacific Northwest on Earth. The trees were almost extinct on their homeworld, but the Confederation's domes harbored samples of many plants no longer found on Earth.

"Yes, Jaquin, it's me." Vance held back a sigh. He'd arranged the meeting himself, but now he was resenting the intrusion into his quiet time. It wasn't rational, but he'd begun to think about how little of Roderick Vance truly remained beyond the servant to duty. Quiet, introspective moments had become precious to him, and he'd come to guard them jealously. He knew he wasn't likely to have much time to himself in the near future, not with the disasters unfolding all around him.

He quickly put aside such thoughts and forced his mind back to the present. If the Mars he dreamed about was ever to exist, Vance knew it had to survive first. He had to stay focused, do what duty called on him to do. His toils would buy the Confederation the future its people deserved, and generations of Martians would have a chance at life and freedom.

He turned to face his agent. Jaquin Diervos was one of his most reliable men, just back from a long and dangerous mission. "What do you have for me?"

"Well, sir..." The agent spoke softly, his voice tentative, uncertain. "...you were correct. The Caliphate orbital factories at Persis have been destroyed in series of nuclear explosions. The official position is that Admiral Abbas and his fleet are responsible, that they are heretics and traitors who have defected from the Caliphate." Of course that was the official position only for communications with those already aware Abbas had declared his fleet unaligned with the home government. The masses living in the Caliphate, and the millions serving in its armies on Earth had no idea anything at all was amiss in the colonies.

"Abbas, my ass." Vance took a deep breath. "Abbas wouldn't have taken action against a Caliphate colony. He only went rogue because the Caliph proscribed him, along with dozens of other officers guilty of no offense beyond serving bravely alongside the Alliance navy in the war with the First Imperium."

"That is what they are saying, Mr. Vance." The spy's tone suggested he didn't believe it any more than Vance.

"Garret wouldn't have done it either. Not when he was allied with the Caliphate fleet." Vance looked out over the river, the lights of the city rippling off the slowly moving water. "It had to be Stark." He paused, thinking quietly for a few seconds. "But why would he bother with a target like that? With the Caliphate fleet gone rogue and Persis still loyal to the home government, what purpose was served by blasting a bunch of unused factories to slag?"

"There have been similar incidents, sir." The agent stepped out of the shadows and moved closer to Vance, lowering his voice as he did. "Facilities have also been destroyed on San Rafael, Constantia, and several other worlds." He paused. "It appears that all of the interstellar production assets and shipyards of the Superpowers have been targeted and destroyed in incidents that resemble terrorist activity."

Vance stood quietly, imagining the brilliance it had taken to mastermind such a widespread series of operations. He reminded himself again to be cautious, to never underestimate Gavin Stark. "He is systematically destroying every facility capable of supplying an interstellar fleet." Vance stared down into the water, the lights of the city dancing on its gently rippling surface. Why, he thought, why would Stark waste resources and take the risk to destroy those facilities? Most war production was still Earth-based, so...

Of course! It all made sense. Stark was betting on the destruction of the Earth-based facilities as well. All of them. That was how he planned to defeat Garret. He was going to starve him of supplies and ordnance and wait until his fleet was helpless. Vance felt a cold chill in his stomach. Stark was really planning to take his insane scheme all the way. He was going to manipulate the Powers into full-scale nuclear exchanges, a final battle that would destroy all the cities and factories on Earth. Once the Superpowers had obliterated each other and Garret's helpless fleet was destroyed, Stark would have all the time in the world to establish control. There would be no one left to oppose him. No one but Mars.

Vance's head snapped around, staring back at his surprised agent. "We need to get back to headquarters. Now." He turned without explanation, waving for the agent to follow. He'd assumed Stark was holding his fleet back to preserve its strength for an eventual showdown with Garret. But if he was going to starve Garret out, that meant he could use his fleet someplace else. And if the Superpowers on Earth slipped into their final death struggle, there would only be one place left in occupied space where Garret's ships could rearm and resupply. Mars.

Chapter 5

LZ Holm
30 Kilometers East of Weston
Columbia, Eta Cassiopeiae II

Rod Heath crouched down behind piles of shattered masonry that had once been a small building, peering carefully out toward the enemy lines. The commander of the first wave was far forward, too far, he knew General Gilson would have said, but there wasn't much in the way of a rear area anyway. The LZ was small, and the enemy had been hitting it relentlessly, trying to pinch out the beachhead before the rest of the Marines could land. His people had been struggling to widen the tiny scrap of Columbia they controlled, but the enemy had reacted rapidly to the landing, and the Marines had fought hard for every meter of ground, paying the price in blood.

His people hadn't died passively though. The ground in front of his position was covered with the bodies of armored enemy soldiers. They had hit this location and hit it hard, but the defenders had held firm, driving them back with heavy losses. He could see from the numbers of dead lying along his side of the line that the defense had been a costly one.

Heath had lost count of his casualties since the landing. His AI could have given him a figure in an instant, accurate at least to the extent that fighting suits were still reporting and communication nets were active, but he'd told it not to. He knew well enough they were bad, and he wasn't ready to hear the numbers yet.

Things had been hard from the start. The enemy AA fire had

been thicker than expected, and his people suffered badly on the way in. The first wave had 500 casualties in the landing, almost all of them KIA when their Liggetts were shot down. That was over 10% of the total force, before a boot even touched the ground. Those losses had been far heavier than projected, and they had left weak spots in the OB all across the battlefield. He'd spent the first hour on the ground shifting troop concentrations, trying to plug holes to meet the enemy attacks. Now he had to get his people moving. Just hanging on wasn't going to get it done.

He looked around at the pockmarked and blackened ground. His forces had repelled multiple enemy assaults here, and by all accounts, they'd barely managed to hang on.

"Lieutenant, who's in command here?" He crouched low and walked toward an officer kneeling alone in shell hole. He glanced up at the display inside his helmet, IDing him as he approached. Callahan, Lt., commander of 1st Platoon, Company A, 2nd Battalion.

"I don't know, sir." Callahan's voice was hoarse, his tone vacant, stunned. He was clearly in some sort of shock, but he was still at his post. "My platoon was wiped out, General. I'm all that's left."

The words hit Heath like a hammer. He slid down into the muck of the water-filled hole and put his armored hand on Callahan's back. "I'm sorry son," he said softly, wishing he could talk to the officer without armor and com units between their words. "Things have been hard all across the line." His eyes drifted up, staring out over the temporarily still field. "Tell me what happened."

"I lost two of my boats coming in, sir." Callahan stared at the ground as he spoke. "The first was blown apart at high altitude. None of them even had a chance." He took a ragged breath. "The other was hit just before we landed. It tumbled over and crashed." He paused, and when he continued his voice was halting, cracking. "We got to them as soon as we could but…" He hesitated again, and Heath could hear the pain in his shallow breaths. "…but it was too late."

Heath had been in the Corps a long time, long enough to know there was really nothing to say. Men kept getting themselves into wars, and as long as they did, soldiers would fight those wars. The Marines considered themselves an elite fighting force, but they died just like any other men. And when they did, their comrades were expected to keep going, to fight the battle until it was won. Or until they were all dead.

"There was nothing you could have done, Lieutenant." He knew his words would be cold comfort, but they were all he had. "Any of us can get hit on the way down. We all know that when we bolt ourselves into those landers." His eyes darted up to his display. His AI was streaming Callahan's service record. Heath nodded as he read. The kid was hardcore, promoted from the ranks by none other than Erik Cain.

"I pulled everybody together the best I could, sir, but then they hit us almost immediately. There must have been 200 of them, just on our frontage. The first wave came in before we even got the autocannons out of the locker and deployed on the line. We did our best, sir, but they kept coming. And every time they did, I lost more of my people."

Heath looked out over the field in front of Callahan's position. He did a quick estimate and decided there were at least 150 bodies in front of the line the kid's platoon had defended. "It looks like your people gave 'em hell, son." He shook his head. He'd always considered dead enemy soldiers a poor trade for the loss of his own comrades, but he couldn't think of anything else to say, any way he could convince Callahan that his Marines had died for something worthwhile. Talk of causes and justifications was for aboard ship, when the fight was in prospect or the combat was over. There were reasons to fight, some even to die, but Heath knew well enough that down here, in the mud and blood, amid the stench of death and battle, men and women fought for one thing above all else – for the friends and comrades in the line next to them.

He knew warriors who survived their wars often mustered out and dispersed, resettling on various planets and going on to live out their lives, often never seeing their old comrades again. But on the battlefield, these men and women were closer than brothers and sisters. They shared a bond that couldn't be fully understood by anyone who hadn't felt it themselves. Heath couldn't imagine a harder thing than watching your entire platoon being slaughtered. He knew Callahan was wondering why he had survived, and on some level wishing he hadn't. But Heath was glad the young officer had made it. He knew he was going to need men like him in the hours and days ahead.

He was glancing at the AI's report on 2nd Battalion, and he barely caught a gasp before it escaped his lips. The battalion had launched with 604 Marines, and now it was down to 199 effectives. Major Bellas was dead, killed on the way down when his transport was blown out of the sky. Every company commander was dead or wounded, and half the platoon officers were down. He kept reading. The 1st Battalion wasn't much better off.

"Son, I know you're dealing with the loss of your people, but the job's just getting started here, and I need you." Heath's voice was sympathetic but also firm. "You've got to pull it together for me. I'm giving you a battlefield promotion to major, and I'm putting you in command of the remnants of 1st and 2nd Battalions."

It took a few seconds for Heath's words to sink in, and when they did Callahan's mind screamed, "No!" He wanted to run, to escape and hide somewhere. The thought of more responsibility, of another four or five hundred Marines under his command – dying under his command - was more than he could bear, and he could feel himself unraveling.

"Sir..." He paused. "I don't thin..."

"Listen to me, son." Heath's voice was soothing, but there was toughness there too. "You did it right here today. You were there for your Marines, and you held your position." He reached out with both hands, grabbing Callahan's armored shoulders. "Now we've got hundreds of other Marines, and they need someone to get them through this. They're stuck here, just like you." He could see Callahan shaking his head, but he continued anyway. "I need you to shake it off, son. If you have to torture yourself, do it later, when we're back aboard ship. Right now there are Marines who need you." Another pause. "I need you."

Callahan turned his head slowly, staring back at Heath. He wished he was anywhere else, even that an enemy bullet had found him and taken him down, but he knew he'd obey the general. Jack Callahan the man felt numb, dead - but there was still life in the Marine. He straightened himself up and looked back at the general.

"I'll do my best, sir." His voice was weak, his tone uncertain, but Heath knew at once he'd gotten through to him.

"I know you will, son." He turned and started to climb out of the shell hole. "Good luck, Major," he said as he crouched low and scrambled back toward the command post. There was an art to rallying fighting men, and Heath had learned from some of the best. The only thing they hadn't taught him was how not to hate himself after he did it.

"General, we have reports of fighting east of Weston." Hal Richmond came running into the tent, the excitement obvious in his high-pitched voice. He caught himself and straightened up. "I'm sorry, General. Request permission to make a report."

Jarrod Tyler was sitting on a small folding chair, wearing a pair of gray fatigue pants and a t-shirt that had once been white but was now some indeterminate shade of brownish-gray. His face was twisted into a frustrated scowl, the same expression he'd worn for months now. He'd failed to defeat the invaders who had come to ravage his world, and then he'd led his people into the swamps and badlands, seeking any fate for them save surrender. It was a choice that appeared noble, a soldier's last stand, but it had also thrown them all into a hellish nightmare, one it seemed few of them would survive.

The Columbians, most of them at least, had avoided capitulation, and they were still maintaining the fight. The war had become a guerilla battle now, Tyler's remaining warriors primarily engaged in raids targeting enemy supplies and patrols. But the cost had been staggering. They were short of everything – food, drugs, basic survival gear. Civilians began dying almost immediately, and the daily toll still continued. Diseases that could be healed with an injection killed for lack of proper medicine. Civilians weakened by malnutrition and unused to living outside in the cold and damp were easy targets for a variety of pathogens, and the overworked doctors and med techs did what they could as their supplies dwindled to nothing. Yet the people remained steadfast behind their leader, most of them at least.

There had been a few stillborn rebellions against his authority as dictator, but most of the Columbians were still with him. They lived their miserable lives in cold, leaky tents, watching their families slowly starve to death, but still they gave him their loyalty. He was grateful for the support, but it tore at him as well. Part of him wanted the people to hate him, to rise up and cast him aside. In many ways, their loyalty was his greatest source of pain, and it prevented him from shifting any responsibility for the holocaust on Columbia away from himself. With total power came total responsibility.

He bore the guilt, all of it. For failing to defeat the enemy in the field, for leading his people into the nightmare of continued resistance in the wildest areas of their world. He'd led them here, and they had followed, placing their trust in him to get them through this greatest trial.

Richmond's excited words pulled him from his deep retrospection. "Oh...Hal. Come in." Hal Richmond was his aide, or a makeshift assistant, at least. Tyler wouldn't have enlisted a 15 year old kid, but he took the boy in after his parents and sister died of infectious diseases that hadn't killed anyone in civilized societies for centuries.

"General, we have multiple reports of fighting east of Weston."

"Multiple reports?" Tyler's eyes widened. He'd thought he'd seen a few strange flashes in the sky the day before, but he'd discounted them. His people had been waiting for relief for a long time, and he'd just about given up. He knew the Marines would have come if they could have, so he assumed this enemy, whoever they were, had attacked other worlds as well. He'd assumed the Marines were committed elsewhere. Or worse, defeated.

"Yes, sir." Richmond was nervous and excited, but he held his composure well. "Two different hunter teams have reported in." His voice became darker. "And three more deployed to that area failed to check in and are missing." He paused. "Sir, could it be the invasion?"

That's what they'd been calling it. The invasion. Not Tyler, but his soldiers and the civilians of Columbia. Through all the death and hardship, they'd continued to believe the Marines would come and liberate them once again. Tyler had less faith. His didn't doubt the dedication of the Corps, but he also knew the Marines were only men and women. They'd gone right from the Third Frontier War into the Rebellions, and the survivors had poured their blood into the sands of a dozen worlds fighting off the robot legions of the First Imperium. The few who'd made it through that holocaust had returned to this new struggle. Tyler didn't doubt the Marines would come if they could; he doubted there were any Marines left.

Tyler looked back at his young aide. "It could be a lot of things, Hal. Maybe a separate group of refugees launching an attack."

"Or the Marines!" Richmond's eyes were bright with excitement. "It could be the Marines too, couldn't it?"

"I suppose it could, Hal." Tyler didn't want to let himself believe. He'd waited each day for help to come, watching his people die in these miserable swamps. But it was possible. He tried to force back his own excitement at the prospect.

"Hal, go get Lieutenants Paine and White." He waved toward the flap of the tent. "Tell them I've got a mission for them."

If the Marines had really landed, it was time to launch his own attack to support the landing. It would cost him all his remaining supplies and leave him nothing to defend the civilians. It was a last roll of the dice for Tyler and the remnants of Columbia's army. He had to be sure the Marines were actually here before he issued the order.

Paine and White were his two best men. If anybody could get to the bottom of what was going on, it was them. If they came back and told him there were Marines on Columbia, that would be enough for him to risk everything.

"But the LZ is surrounded, General." Arch Mantooth had been with Gilson since the beginning of the First Imperium War. She'd given him his eagles at the beginning of that conflict and his star after Arcadia. "You think we suffered heavy losses to the landers in the first wave, fresh after the bombardment and with whatever level of surprise we had?" His voice was raw. He hated counseling caution when fellow Marines were in trouble, but it wasn't going to help the men and women on the ground if they got another wave blown out of the sky.

"So what do we do, Arch? Send down a load of bodybags and say, 'so sorry! We can't get any help down to you?'" Her voice had been harsher than she'd intended. She knew Mantooth would be the last to abandon fellow Marines. And he was right. Getting a whole new batch of men and women shot to pieces wasn't going to do Heath's people any good.

Mantooth took a deep breath. "So what do we do, General?" There was a brittleness to his tone, a sensitivity that told Gilson her outburst had found its mark.

"We go in." The gravelly voice came from the far end of the table. Sam Thomas stared right at Gilson as he spoke. "It's what we do. We don't count the cost, we don't worry about shit we can't change. Liberating Columbia is important enough, but by God, there are Marines down there under fire." His volume had risen steadily, and now his roar practically shook the table. "That's all we need to know. That's all that's ever mattered." His eyes remained locked on Gilson's. "That's all Elias would have needed to know." Thomas knew he wasn't being fair using Holm's memory to manipulate Gilson, but he didn't care. He was too old for bullshit games, and he'd be damned if they were going to leave those Marines down there to be overwhelmed and destroyed.

"Sam, you know I would never abandon our people down there." Gilson knew he was working her, but that didn't stop his words from having exactly the effect he'd intended. "But how can we drop more troops into a pinpoint zone like that with the enemy on all sides?" She was staring at the map projected onto the table. "We'll have to set up a new LZ."

"For that to do any good, we'd have to set up the new zone at least 200 klicks from the first. Otherwise, we'll still be coming down right on top of the heavy enemy concentration." Mantooth was staring at the map as he spoke. "We'll just end up with two groups surrounded."

"There's no choice." Sam Thomas flashed his eyes toward Mantooth then back to Gilson. He slapped his hand down hard on the table. "We have to reinforce the original LZ." Thomas was well into his 80s, but years of rejuv treatments had taken at least 20 of those off his effective age. Still, he had every one of those years' worth of ornery stubbornness. "This is like Persis all over again."

Everyone present knew the history of the battle that ended the Second Frontier War, but Sam Thomas had actually been there. "It was Elias Holm and his battalion trapped down on the planet then, and by God, Viper Worthington wasn't about to leave any of his Marines behind, and damned the cost." He didn't add that Worthington had been killed in the final stages of his rescue mission, but everyone knew that already. Worthington's story was woven deeply into Corps legend, and first year boots knew the story of Persis.

Gilson sat quietly for a few seconds. "If only we had some atmospheric fighters," she said quietly. "A few squadrons could lay down a bombardment to provide close cover to the transports." She shook her head. It was pointless to wish for something she knew they didn't have. All their fighter wings were gone, destroyed in the endless series of battles they had fought.

"I can give you close support." Elizabeth Arlington had been sitting quietly in the corner while the Marines debated their next move, but now she spoke up.

Gilson turned to face her longtime friend. "How, Lizzie? There's not an atmospheric fighter in the fleet."

"No, but we've got plenty of fast attack ships, especially the Lightning-class birds."

Gilson looked confused. "Those ships aren't streamlined

for atmospheric flight, Lizzie."

Arlington just stared back at her friend. "Not officially, no. But they're pretty sleek craft, and they have a tougher frame than most ships their size. With a good enough pilot..."

"You can't be serious. The risk would be..."

"No more than your Marines are taking, Cate." Arlington looked around the table. "I came up through the suicide boats, and my piloting stats were the best in the wing."

"You want to go yourself?" Gilson's tone was one of shock. "You've got a whole task force to command, and you're talking about taking a suicidal run in a fast attack ship?"

"I'm the least essential officer in the fleet. I've got Admiral Garret on my flagship. That makes me as extraneous as an appendix." She took a deep breath. "And I'd wager I could find 3 or 4 other volunteers to pilot some additional ships."

"Lizzie..." Gilson's voice was hoarse, her throat dry. Arlington was one of her closest friends, and she was talking about throwing her life away on a desperate strafing run. But the men and women on the ground were her Marines, and they needed help.

"I'm OK, Cate." Arlington knew her friend was worried about her, as she had been since Terrence Compton and his people were trapped behind the barrier, stuck in First Imperium space facing almost certain death. Her halting and fitful romance with Compton had been one of the worst kept secrets in the fleet, but only Gilson and a few others knew just how much she had loved him, and how badly his loss had hurt her. "I can do this." She locked her eyes on Gilson's. "And I will come back. I'm not trying to commit suicide."

Gilson closed her eyes and nodded. There wasn't any other choice. Without some close air support, her second wave would be decimated before it even hit the ground. And if she did nothing, Heath and his people would be wiped out.

"OK, Lizzie." She fought to get the words out. "When can you be ready?"

Chapter 6

Flag Bridge
MCS John Carter
Near the Saturn Relay Station
Sol System

Duncan Campbell stood on the flag bridge of John Carter, staring at the incoming vessels on the plotting screen. Carter had been his ship, and he'd captained her for two years before Roderick Vance sent him to Earth to destroy Gavin Stark's main clone production facility. He'd completed that mission without a hitch...unless you considered hundreds of thousands of innocent civilians dead from radiation poisoning to be a hitch.

Vance had known the consequences of his orders, and Campbell had as well. John Carter's ex-skipper had done what had to be done, and the nightmares that had invaded his sleep since were his problem, one he kept to himself. The scar on his soul was no less a battle wound than a bullet would have delivered, and he knew he would carry it the rest of his life.

Campbell had completed another mission for Vance, a wild, all caution to the wind race to the planet Armstrong to deliver a warning to Erik Cain. He'd burnt out his ship in that one, barely managing to get through to the planet and crash land. He was badly injured, but he delivered his message as ordered. Sarah Linden had tended to his wounds, saving his life and putting him back together with remarkable efficiency. Now he was back, and his reward was waiting for him when he arrived. Admiral's stars and command of the main fleet.

Campbell wondered if the massive promotion was based

on his skill as a naval officer or the fact that Roderick Vance could count on him to follow his orders no matter what, even to slaughter millions if his command required it. He didn't know, but he suspected it was a combination of the two, with a bit of his father's influence thrown in as well.

He leaned back in his chair, shifting, trying to find an angle where his back didn't hurt. Dr. Linden had done remarkable work just saving his life, and she'd wanted him to stay in the hospital for at least another month. But duty called, and Campbell insisted on leaving as soon as he was able. The ride back to Mars, trapped in the tanks while another one of Vance's Torch speeders tore through space at almost 50g, hadn't helped his partially healed spine any, and now he often found himself in considerable pain.

"Scanner report?" He glanced at the communications console. He'd taken Lieutenant Christensen with him when he moved to the flag bridge, bumping her up to Lieutenant Commander in the process.

"The unidentified ships are still on an intercept course, Admiral." She paused, looking down at her workstation. "Estimated time to extreme combat range, 23 minutes."

Unidentified my ass, Campbell thought. Those are Gavin Stark's ships. Vance had warned him they might be coming, a sudden and urgent communique that was short on details. He'd managed to concentrate the fleet just in time.

He'd been surprised at first, but the more he thought about it, the more sense it made. Admiral Garret was at Columbia with his combined fleet, supporting the Marine invasion of the planet. It was a perfect time for Stark to make a move against Mars, and there he was, right on schedule.

"Bring the fleet to red alert, Commander." Campbell took a deep breath. Stark's fleet outnumbered his by a considerable margin, but Campbell had faith in his people. They were free Martians, defending their planet against a tyrant who would make them into slaves. They would do whatever had to be done.

"Yes, Admiral." She paused a few seconds before continuing. "All ships report red alert status."

He stared at the screen watching the enemy ships approach. The formation was standard, unimaginative, but it was also solid, right out of the textbook. John Carter and its twin, Sword of Ares, were bigger and stronger than anything the enemy fleet had, but Campbell only had another 4 battleships. The incoming armada had 12, and enough punch to take out every ship in Campbell's fleet.

"I want every weapons crew on the fleet to conduct full diagnostics on their targeting systems."

"Yes, sir." Christensen relayed the command.

Campbell could practically hear the groans on the other ships. Naval crews hated routine tasks, especially right before entering battle. But Campbell didn't give a shit. A minor recalibration of a targeting system could be the difference between a miss and a critical hit, and if the Martian Fleet was going to survive the next few hours, it was going to need every pinpoint shot it could manage. Besides, he'd rather have them scrambling to run superfluous tests than sitting in their seats for 20 minutes staring at the massive enemy fleet bearing down on them.

He looked down at his workstation, punching the keys to bring up a tactical map. He knew he was facing a hell of an introduction to fleet command, and if he was going to win, he had to think outside the box. His two massive battlewagons had the heaviest laser armaments of any ships in space. If he could get them close enough, their x-ray lasers would cut Stark's older capital ships into scrap. But the enemy knew that too. The Carter and the Sword of Ares would attract missile fire from every ship in the enemy fleet. They'd be gutted before they entered laser range.

His eyes moved to the large circle on the edge of the battle map. Saturn. Maybe, he thought…just maybe. He punched in some calculations, programming a simulation. It was close, but if he timed it just right, and if the enemy didn't alter their trajectory, it just might work.

"Commander Linken, plot a course for John Carter and Sword of Ares directly toward Saturn."

Linken was another refugee from Campbell's old bridge crew

who'd followed his commander to his new post. He turned and glanced back at the admiral with a quizzical look on his face. "Yes, sir," he stammered.

"Transmit your course calculation to the helm and to Sword of Ares when you are ready." He turned his head and looked over toward Christensen. "Commander, get me Captain Oswald on Sword of Ares."

Maybe, he thought. Just maybe this will work.

Liang Chang stared at the main display. The enemy fleet was dividing into two sections. Its two biggest battleships were detaching from the main force, heading for the protection of Saturn. Their battleline was already outnumbered; without the superbattleships they didn't have a chance.

"All ships, increase thrust to 4g." Chang wanted to close and finish off the Martian fleet before their heavy units could reverse course. Once the rest of the fleet was destroyed, he could hunt down the giant battlewagons at will. He knew the two ships were awesomely powerful, but they wouldn't stand a chance against his whole fleet. Whatever the Martian commander was thinking, Liang was sure he had made a mistake, one that would cost him his fleet.

He was tempted to zip everybody up and blast away at full thrust, closing the distance that much faster, but he didn't want to fight the battle from the tanks. The Martians were outnumbered, but they had a reputation for professionalism, and he wasn't about to underestimate them. He knew his crews were no match for the Martians man for man, and he wanted them at their best for the battle. Naval commanders told themselves various things, but Liang knew that no crew ever made was as effective operating from the acceleration tanks, drugged up and half-crushed to death.

"Admiral Liang, we are approaching launch range." Vladimir Lugarin's voice was deep, his Russian accent thick. Stark had mandated English as the language to be used on his fleet, but there were many crew members, Liang himself, who were native to other tongues. Those who couldn't speak English used portable AIs to translate, but Lugarin thought he spoke English better than he did, and his AI was rarely activated.

"All ships prepare to launch externally-mounted ordnance." Liang spoke excellent English, like most of the elite classes in the CAC. It was an idiosyncrasy of CAC culture. The English-speaking Alliance had been the enemy for more than a century, and the United States and its allies before that. Yet, despite the almost xenophobic ethos the CAC had developed, and the mandated respect for ethnically pure culture imposed on the masses, it remained the custom for the upper classes to learn other languages, particularly English.

Lugarin worked his controls, sending the pre-fire orders to the ships of the fleet. Weapons crews were entering final missile plots and preparing to launch their deadly ordnance. In a few seconds, hundreds of gigatons of nuclear death would blast forth toward the Martian ships, and those vessels would respond with their own deadly volleys.

"All vessels report ready to launch, Admiral."

Liang sat quietly for a few seconds, inhaling deeply. He'd spent most of the past two years dreading his ultimate confrontation with Augustus Garret. Liang had been the CAC's senior admiral, the battle commander of its entire navy, but his inability to defeat the Alliance's brilliant combat leader had cost him his rank and position…and almost his life. Li An had promised him an unpleasant death as the price of his final failure, and Liang's only escape had been to throw himself on the mercy of her nemesis, Gavin Stark. He'd spent the years after in comfortable but total seclusion in Alliance Intelligence headquarters.

At first he'd thought Stark kept him alive just to annoy Li An, but one day the master spy came to visit, and he offered Liang an opportunity to return to fleet command. Liang jumped at the chance, but the realization that sooner or later he would have to face his old nemesis had weighed on him since. Liang was an experienced commander, but he knew he couldn't beat Garret, not without a massive superiority he was unlikely to have. When he got the order to ready the fleet, he felt a flush of panic ripple through his body, but then he realized they were moving against the Martians and not Garret.

Relieved of the burden of facing the brilliant Alliance admiral, he welcomed the chance at a battle to redeem his reputation. Now he was back in the Sol system, facing the last major spacefleet other than his and Garret's. When it was destroyed, the Shadow Legions would be one step closer to total victory. Liang wasn't comfortable relying on Stark's gratitude, but he was sure it was preferable to enduring his wrath.

He stared over at Lugarin. "All ships are to launch at once."

Stark sat quietly on Spectre's cramped bridge, as the ship zipped past the asteroid belt bound for Mars. The two other vessels of her class flanked her in a tight formation, moving at the same velocity on matching trajectories. Wraith and Ghost were on their maiden voyages, the two newest additions to Stark's fleet.

The Martian Confederation controlled most of the outer solar system, and they had outposts and scanning stations on every planet and moon. But Spectre and her sisters were very special vessels, virtually undetectable to any known scanning technology. They had slipped past the Confederation's detection net, and now they were heading straight for the Red Planet itself.

He twisted in his chair, trying to get comfortable. Stark hated space travel. In fact, he hated being off Earth. He wanted to rule mankind's colony worlds, but he didn't want to spend any more time there than necessary. The colonists were an unruly lot, prone to ask a lot of questions and argue when they were told what to do. That was something he would deal with decisively when he took control. The colonials would learn to obey their master, those who survived the transition, at least.

The one part of his plan he regretted was the complete destruction of Earth's cities. He'd initially hoped to preserve some level of civilization, but Roderick Vance had wrecked that plan with his nuclear attack on the Dakota facility. In an instant, Stark lost more than two-thirds of the manpower he had to move against the Superpowers. His original idea had been to seize control when the Powers' armies were on the verge of collapse, but before they started nuking each other's cities. He'd had close to 1.5 million fully-armored clone soldiers ready to go, but Vance had cost him a million of those. The Dakota facility had been completely obliterated, and everyone there had perished.

He could still succeed with the 350,000 he had left, but he needed the Powers to destroy each other first. His remaining troops would simply sweep down over the post-apocalyptic hell and impose his rule on the scattered and stunned survivors. A few government installations would survive the holocaust, but 350,000 powered infantry was enough to deal with those. He would dig the surviving politicians out of their ratholes one by one, and when he was done, all mankind would serve him and his clone descendants forever.

He glanced down at the scanners. It appeared his little flotilla had remained undetected. They were on a carefully charted course straight for Mars. His ships engines were shut down, and he intended them to stay that way until they were about to enter orbit. He had no intention of giving the Martians any chance to spot him, not until it was too late. Once the deed was done his ships could run for it, and they were faster than anything in space, except perhaps one of the Martian Torches. But even Vance's superfast craft would have a hard time catching one of his Spectre-class ships before they slipped back into stealth mode and disappeared from the Martian's scopes.

Stark allowed himself a smile. Even as his little flotilla approached Mars, he knew his fleet was engaging the Martians somewhere in the outer system. Admiral Liang was probably on his flag bridge, Stark thought, even now working himself up into his own lackluster version of a battle frenzy. Liang was a mediocre commander at best, one whose former master had been trying for ten years to carry out a death sentence she'd placed on his head.

Thwarting Li An all those years had been its own special pleasure, but Liang had become useful in his own right. He wasn't an Augustus Garret, nothing close, but he was the best

Stark had available. Admirals with fleet command experience were hard to find, especially ones willing to see their old comrades sacrificed along with everyone else. Stark prized moral ambiguity in his subordinates. Men who were motivated solely by personal gain were easier to control. It tended to make things far less complicated.

Liang had enough strength to take out the Confederation's fleet, but Stark was far from confident. The admiral could easily snatch defeat from the jaws of victory, and the Confederation had a reputation for placing talented commanders in charge of its fleets. But Stark didn't care, not really. All he wanted was for Liang to cripple the Martian fleet, take them out of any future fight. If he suffered even greater losses himself, even if he lost the battle and retreated in disarray, it was of no account. Liang thought he was leading the attack to cripple the Confederation, and Stark had encouraged that belief. But the former CAC admiral and his fleet were a diversion, nothing more.

Gavin Stark was going to deal with the Martian Confederation himself.

"Admiral Ross is reporting heavy damage to all battleline ships, Admiral." There was concern in Christensen's voice, and sadness. The Martian Fleet wasn't as large as those of the other Superpowers, and it was manned almost totally by career officers and enlisted personnel. Almost everyone on John Carter had friends and relatives on the other ships, and it was hard to think about what they were going through fighting against an overwhelming enemy. Especially when John Carter and Sword of Ares appeared to be running away, escaping while the rest of the fleet held off the enemy.

"Very well, Commander." Campbell felt the worry and guilt as much as any of his crew, but he kept his voice calm and even. He knew if he didn't set the example for his people, no one else would. Besides, they weren't abandoning their comrades. Once Carter and Sword of Mars completed their slingshot move around Saturn, they would emerge behind Stark's fleet, at close range with laser batteries firing full. Then it would be a fight to the death.

His ships had left a trail of buoys behind as they arced around the solar system's second largest planet, so they'd been able to maintain communications and follow reports of the battle. The Martian ships had been hit hard by the enemy's massive missile barrage, but they'd managed to score nearly as many hits with their own smaller volleys, and they'd destroyed one of Stark's battleships with targeted attacks. The Martian capital ships were all damaged, but none of them had been taken out of the fight.

Campbell allowed himself a smile. David Ross was a brilliant officer, one Campbell had been confident to leave in charge of the main fleet while he led the flanking move. Whoever was commanding Stark's ships, it was clear he was no match for Ross in an even fight. Campbell's smile faded. Too bad it's not an even fight, he thought grimly.

"We're about to lose contact with the fleet, Admiral."

The buoys had extended the time Campbell's two ships could stay in contact with the rest of the fleet, but now they were entering the inner zone of Saturn's magnetic field. They would lose contact for 18 minutes, and then they would emerge behind Stark's fleet.

"C'mon, David," Campbell whispered to himself. "Hold it together for another 20 minutes, and we'll be there." He closed his eyes, imagining the hell his people were going through. Twenty minutes, he thought. Just hang on for another twenty minutes. But he knew that was a long time.

Chapter 7

Front Lines
120 kilometers east of Paris
French Zone, Europa Federalis

Werner stared out from inside the heavy command vehicle. There were mushroom clouds in a long line stretching across the Europan lines, and more rising up in the distance behind. He'd hesitated as long as he could before launching the deadly barrage, but his orders were explicit, and they left him no latitude at all.

He'd been reluctant to escalate the conflict so significantly, but once he moved to execute his orders, he found the entire episode began to feed on itself, compelling him to increase the intensity of the attack even beyond the minimum requirements imposed by the high command. He knew his attack would almost certainly prompt a response in kind. Facing certain escalation, he realized he had to make his first strike count, and he actually added to the target list and increased the number of warheads used, hoping to gain as much advantage as he could from hitting first.

His forces were advancing now, moving almost without resistance through the shattered remnants of the Europan lines. He knew that wouldn't last. He'd hit the enemy as hard as he could, but he knew they would still have enough surviving batteries and rocket launchers for a retaliatory strike. He was surprised it hadn't happened yet, but he knew that only meant he'd taken the enemy by surprise. That would buy him a few hours, nothing more. Then his own troops would be bracketed by nuclear explosions and bombarded with nerve gas. His command centers and supply depots would be targeted and destroyed, and his surviving units would be scattered and disorganized.

His hospitals and rear areas would be flooded with wounded, soldiers with severe burns and radiation poisoning. Thousands would die waiting for care or for lack of medical supplies or adequate facilities. The roads that weren't destroyed in the blasts would be clogged with stunned and wounded survivors, separated from their decimated units and straggling aimlessly through the countryside. He knew it was coming, he could see it in his mind, but there was nothing he could do to stop it.

His people were as ready as they could be, though there were limited options to prepare for a massive nuclear bombardment. He'd dispersed his command and control and logistics as much as possible. He was riding around the wilderness in a glorified truck, not a very impressive headquarters for an army group commander. But he'd chosen mobility and anonymity over trying to dig deep enough to survive the inevitable strike that would obliterate his headquarters.

His hospitals were fully staffed and stocked with all the supplies and medicines he could obtain, and he'd moved them as far away as possible from any likely military targets. He had disbursed extra food and ammunition to his units, in anticipation of them receiving nothing else for a considerable time after the assault.

The Europan armies were already struggling with that hell, he knew, and they'd been far less prepared than his forces. With any luck, his people would endure the nuclear hell better than their enemies. But, however prepared he was, he knew it would be bad nevertheless. Within a few days, the men on the front lines might be fighting with rocks and using their empty rifles as clubs. The few that were still alive, at least.

"Sir, General Hoffman reports his forces have reached the outskirts of Fontainebleau. He has encountered only light resistance, and his troops have taken 200,000 prisoners." Potsdorf sounded excited. The aide was an experienced soldier, but he'd come so far, so fast, he couldn't fully grasp the implications of what was happening. Hoffman's army was halfway to Paris in just a few hours, and it looked like enemy resistance was falling away.

Werner nodded. "Thank you, Major." His voice was terse, clipped. Maybe Hoffman's people will get closer to Paris, thought. The Europans would have to be a bit more careful right dropping nukes right around their capital, he thought. The front line might actually be the safest place to be right now. "Give General Hoffman my regards, and advise him to press on to Paris will all possible speed."

Werner knew he should congratulate his army commander himself, but he just didn't have it in him. He knew the angel of death would be calling on his forces soon, and he was waiting. Waiting to see who survived.

"Attention all units, attention all units." All the com speakers crackled to life, a Highest Priority message coming through and overriding all other communications. "This is CEL detection station Gamma. We are tracking approximately 400 intermediate range missiles inbound for troop positions along the Europan front."

Werner took a deep breath. At least the waiting would be over soon. The Europan launch sites were not that far away. He figured his people had 2 minutes, maybe 3 before the incoming missiles started dropping nukes on them. And less time before the atomic-armed artillery began dropping nuclear shells on his lines.

"Let's find the closest thing to cover we can, boys." The command vehicle was the safest place to be. Its shielding wouldn't do much if a nuke landed too close, but it would offer some protection against radiation and minor blast damage. But most importantly, it was kilometers away from any headquarters or other priority target. "Over there, between those two rock outcrop…"

Werner saw the first flash and he turned away, putting his hands over his face. Fuck, he thought. The blast shield wasn't down. "We've got to…"

Another wave of blinding light poured into the cabin, and a

few second later, the blast wave shattered the heavy supposedly unbreakable glass of the forward viewport, sending razor sharp shards flying around the interior of the heavy vehicle.

Werner fell forward, trying to reach around to his back, groaning at the stabbing pain. He struggled to get up and check on the rest of the staff just as a third nuke detonated, this one even closer. He closed his eyes and took a deep breath. Then the shockwave came, and it lifted the 40 ton vehicle, slamming it into the heavy rock outcropping like a child's toy.

Axe stood on top of a mound of collapsed masonry, staring out over the rubble-strewn streets of the Manhattan Protected Zone. They're going to have to change the name, he thought with a vicious scowl. It's not very protected anymore. The elites who'd called this enclave home were mostly dead now, those who hadn't managed to escape, at least.

Most of them hadn't died easily. The Cogs of New York had been passive for a long time, generation after generation meekly accepting their position on society's lowest rung. Caught between the oppressive government and the vicious gangs, they'd lived lives of fear and poverty for over a century. But now that had changed, and the anger and hatred, so long buried and kept in place by fear, erupted, and the Cogs went mad with rage and violence.

The mob turned into a wild animal, lashing out at all those who had oppressed them. The enraged Cogs stormed the government buildings, ignoring the losses as they threw themselves against the heavily-armed police. They dragged out the security forces who had gunned so many of them down, tearing them to shreds in the street. They chased the terrified middle classes and politicians alike, massacring them all in an orgy of bloodletting. Gang members were tortured to death by those they had victimized for so long, and the mangled corpses of the victims were everywhere.

It was vengeance for a century of suffering and oppression, and it was deadly and indiscriminant. The mob wanted blood. It wanted revenge, not justice, and it fell on anyone who reeked even faintly of privilege.

It had been a risk coming back to Manhattan, but Axe had to see for himself what was going on. He wore the rags of a Cog worker, and he carried a pistol he'd taken off a dead cop. He knew the mob would tear him to shreds if they realized he'd been one of the gang leaders, but he stumbled through the streets looking lost, like a Cog who had come into the Protected Zone with the mob and was just walking around.

He'd left the rest of his small group behind, in the mostly-abandoned areas that had once been called Queens. He'd told them to scavenge whatever food and equipment they could find and wait for him. He knew his few remaining men were loyal, but most of them were stupid too, and he couldn't take the risk of bringing them into the Zone. One hint that he and his people were former gangers, and the mob would be on them in an instant. He wasn't willing to risk one of them saying something foolish or giving way who they were. No, he thought, Tank and the others are good in a fight, but that was close to useless against 100,000 screaming Cogs worked up into a bloodlust.

He'd come to satisfy his curiosity in part, and also to scrounge up anything useful from the Protected Zone. The wastelands of Long Island had been abandoned for over a century, and there was very little useful to be found outside the city itself. The fall of the Protected Zone was an unmatched opportunity to plunder, though he realized he had arrived rather late to the party. The Cogs had lived in squalor and poverty for generations, but when they broke into the neighborhoods of their former masters, they proved to be skilled looters.

Axe was heading to Sector A, the elite enclave where the wealthiest and most powerful citizens of Manhattan had lived. He knew the rioting Cogs had worked the place over already, but he suspected there was still swag to be gained on the upper levels of the super-luxury buildings. The government had shut down the reactors, leaving most of the city without power, and it took a very determined looter to climb 300 flights of stairs to the top of a kilometer-high building. There was probably a lot of virgin territory up there, and those apartments up in the sky

would be the homes of the most powerful Politicians and Magnates, filled with valuables he could only imagine.

There were probably residents still hiding on those upper
floors too, locked up in their luxurious apartments, hoping
against hope the government would crush the rebelling Cogs
and save them. He gripped the pistol tightly in his hand and
readjusted the sack he'd slung over his shoulder. He had half a
dozen weapons in there, and some spare ammo too. He knew
he might have some fighting to do, and he wanted to be ready.

He took a few more steps before he heard it. The sound of
engines from above, approaching rapidly. Gunships. He swung
his head back and forth, looking for someplace to take cover.
He started toward a large building, rushing for the open hole
where the main doorway had been.

"Here, this way."

The voice came from behind, and he spun around. It was a
Cog, an old man, filthy and disheveled, but wearing a cashmere
overcoat that had cost its original owner more than its present
wearer had earned in his entire life.

"Come," he repeated. "To the tunnels. We'll be safe in the
tunnels."

Axe hesitated, but just for an instant. Then he followed his
instincts and ran toward the man. The Cog led him around the
corner and pointed. "There, he said."

There was a large hole in the pavement, and below Axe
could see tunnels stretching off in both directions. Of course,
he thought, the ancient train lines. There were subterranean
tunnels stretching all over New York City, artifacts of an age
when the city was vastly larger with a population 7 or 8 times
what it had now. His gang had used some of the ancient tunnels
in Brooklyn to store supplies and get from one place to another.
They were deep in places. A perfect place to take cover.

He heard the sound of autocannon fire. The gunships were
attacking, blasting down everyone in the streets. The old man
motioned again, and he crouched down, carefully extending his
leg into the hole. Axe moved over to the edge, looking down.
There was a ladder, stretching down to the ground 6 or 7 meters

below. It was a rickety looking affair, but the sound of gun-fire was getting closer, and Ace decided he didn't have a better choice. He waited for the old man to climb down a couple meters, and he lowered his foot carefully onto one of the rungs and climbed down into the semi-darkness.

Warren walked slowly into the dark room. His agents had located the president almost immediately. It hadn't been difficult. The entire government was operating under Stonewall protocols, and that meant everyone of significant importance was in the massive federal complex deep under the Virginia countryside. Oliver's people had tried to get to him, but they'd been too timid to demand entry to his private quarters, fleeing in a panic when he cursed them and threw things at the door.

Warren's agents were considerably less squeamish, and they had their orders. He suspected there would be repercussions from arresting the president's guards, but he'd deal with that when it became a problem. With the way things were going, it didn't even make his top ten list of concerns.

"President Oliver?" Warren let the door close behind him, and he turned on the lights.

"What is it?" The voice was slurred, angry. Oliver was lying on the floor, one leg propped up on the sofa. He was wearing a suit, but the jacket had been discarded and the rest of it was stained and wrinkled.

Warren took a few steps forward then he recoiled at the reek that suddenly hit him. It was alcohol and vomit and days-old sweat. "It's Ryan Warren, sir." Dammit, Warren thought. He's cracked completely.

"Warren?" Oliver growled. "I said I was…wasn't to b…be disturbed." He struggled to sit up, and he glared at Warren.

"Mr. President, the situation in Europe is dire. The CEL Chancellor was trying to reach you. They launched a massive tactical nuclear strike on the Europan positions several hours ago." Warren paused, trying to determine if anything he said was getting through to Oliver. "Sir, we just got word that the Europans retaliated with their own bombardment. Over 1,000 nuclear warheads and shells have been detonated across north-eastern France and Southwestern Germany."

"Why wasn't I informed immediately," Oliver roared. He tried to stand up, but he fell back down and stared up at Ryan.

"Mr. President, we have been trying to brief you for hours. We…" Ryan stopped abruptly. Oliver was clearly incapable of handling the current situation. The Alliance was entering the greatest crisis of its existence, and its president was drunk and strung out. There was no time to deal with him in his current state, no room for any mistakes right now. Not if the Alliance was going to have any chance at weathering this storm.

There had been no news from the Europan-CEL front beyond word of the shared nuclear exchanges. Warren had no idea which power would emerge from the cataclysm in the stronger position or if, indeed, either power still possessed any meaningful military strength in the affected areas.

Mutual destruction would be a win for the enemy. With no hope of reinforcing the makeshift forces the CEL had cobbled together to delay the RIC armies, its collapse was almost certain. A quick victory in the west was their only chance, but it seemed unlikely they would still possess the strength to deal with the growing Russian forces. A CEL capitulation would leave the Alliance and the PRC alone, fighting the rest of the world. Warren knew the Alliance could take any other single Power, but sooner or later, a five to two struggle had to end in defeat.

He took a deep breath and pulled a small gun from his pocket. There was a silencer attached to the short barrel. All his life he'd dreamed of acquiring power, of imposing his will on others. Now he was on the brink of assuming total control over the Alliance, or at least making his play for absolute power, and he wished for anything else. The Alliance was crumbling. Indeed, the entire world faced a crisis like none before in its long and troubled history.

Oliver looked up and saw the gun. "What the hell…"

Warren pulled the trigger. The president of the Alliance fell back, his body rolling off the couch and landing face down on the floor. Warren knew Oliver was dead, but he believed in being sure, and he put two more shots into the back of his head. "Consider yourself impeached, Mr. President."

He stared at Oliver's body, watching the pool of blood around his head slowly expanding on the polished wood floor. Shooting Oliver was the easy part, he knew. Next, he had to consolidate control, and he had to do it immediately. The Alliance was full of ambitious politicians and generals, and he had to have everything locked down before word got out that Oliver was dead.

He turned and walked back the way he had come, tapping the plate to open the door. He looked toward the cluster of agents standing around the in the hallway. They were his best operatives, his inner circle. "We've got a lot of work to do." He spoke softly, gravely. "No one gets into this room until I say so. I want a dozen guards posted. Intelligence security, and men of unquestioned reliability."

"Yes, Number One." The title was more traditional than specifically accurate. Warren hadn't had time to reconstitute the Directorate, and he was the only one in Alliance Intelligence who currently bore the traditional numerical title. Still, he thought it had a nice ring to it.

"We need to round up all Presidential Security. It won't be long before someone realizes the duty guards are missing. We need to find every one of them, on and off duty." He paused, and sighed. "And liquidate them all. They're too big a security risk." It was no time for carelessness or half-measures.

The senior agent nodded. "Understood, Number One."

"And we need to get control of the nuclear arsenals and bring the top military officers onboard. Let's review the files on all the key generals and admirals and come up with an action plan on how to control them." Warren was a big believer in using a well-crafted combination of bribery and threats to control people, something he'd learned working under Gavin Stark.

"Stay here until you can get this door properly guarded and then meet me in the command center. There is much to be done." Warren turned and headed toward the elevator bank. It was going to be a busy night. By morning he'd either be the unquestioned master of the Alliance...or he'd be dead.

Chapter 8

Flag Bridge
MCS Rhodes
Near Saturn
Sol System

David Ross stared straight ahead, through the haze and smoke hanging in the air of his flag bridge. Rhodes was badly damaged, and there were internal fires and multiple systems down. But one of the reactors was still online, and half her laser turrets were still operational and blazing away at the enemy. She had fight left in her yet.

Ross' subordinates had tried to convince him to transfer the flag, but he'd refused every time. If Rhodes still had a weapon to fire and a reactor left to power it, her admiral would stay with her, and if she succumbed then he would go down with her. Ross was a bit of a romantic, and he tended to personify his ships. Abandoning a vessel that was still giving its all to the fight just seemed wrong to him. His staff tended to think he would have been more at home on the deck of a wooden ship, cutlass in hand, fighting to the bitter end.

"Report from Celestia, Admiral. Captain Pharris is dead. Celestia's bridge is destroyed, and the 1st officer is running the ship from the emergency control center." Janet Randall had been Ross' tactical officer since his first ship command, and she'd come with him on every posting since.

"Very well, Commander." His voice was like iron. Neil Pharris had been his classmate at the Academy, and a good friend in his younger days, though they'd grown less close as duty and responsibility took more of their time. He felt for the men and women dying on his ships, and their comrades struggling to keep tortured machinery working, but they needed one thing from him now, above all else. Strength. They could have their own fears, cry for their own pain, but they needed to see their commander as a pillar of solid stone.

"Order the reserve squadrons to attack." He'd kept back 2 groups of fast attack ships, six boats in all. It wasn't much against the 10 remaining battleships of the enemy line, but the strategy was unorthodox, and he would have surprise on his side. The ships were small and fragile, and they would earn their "suicide boat" nickname making close in runs at battleships. But their plasma torpedoes were extremely powerful weapons at point blank range. A few well-placed hits could gut a capital ship, especially one already damaged in the protracted fight.

Ross sat in his chair, impassive, watching the battle continue to unfold. He brushed aside thoughts about Pharris' daughter and what he would tell her about her father. His living crews needed him now. There would be time to mourn the dead later. If anyone survived.

The fleets had approached each other at low velocities, and now they were in a protracted energy weapons duel. In normal circumstances, he'd have had his smaller fleet come in at high speed, trying to overcome his numerical disadvantage with superior maneuver. But that wasn't an option here. The Martian fleet had one overriding mission. At all costs, they had to keep Stark's fleet away from Mars itself. Even a few warships could wreak havoc if they got through. The Martian cities were covered with hyper-polycarbonate domes, protecting their citizens from the planet's extreme conditions. They were incredibly strong under normal circumstances, but an attack from space would destroy one completely, exposing the city below to the harsh realities of the Martian surface.

He sat and watched the data streaming in from the fleet. He'd lost two cruisers already, and half a dozen smaller ships, and most of the other vessels in the fleet had suffered varying degrees of damage ranging from serious to catastrophic.

He watched the scanners, his eyes focused on six small blips. He knew he was sending those crews, most of them at least, to their deaths, but there was no choice. He needed to break up the enemy attack to buy some time…and the attack ships could do just that.

He saw them streak toward their targets, accelerating at 30g right for the enemy battleline. Their crews were zipped up in their tanks, and Ross couldn't imagine a worse way to die if they were hit.

"The enemy line is diverting fire toward the attack ships." Randall's tone told him that she too realized just how little chance those crews had of making it back. "Our battleline units are reporting reduced fire."

Ross winced as he saw one of the attack ships disappear on the scanner. Then another. A third of the force was gone just like that, but the others closed to attack range. He watched as they concentrated on a single enemy battleship. It was a big vessel, an Alliance Yorktown class, and it was already heavily damaged and trailing atmosphere and fluids.

The attack ships came on in two waves of two, blasting their thrusters at full power in a zigzag pattern, trying to dodge the battlewagon's heavy point defense. Ross' eyes were glued to the scanner, watching as they approached firing range. One of the attack ships disappeared just before it fired, but the other three launched their torpedoes and blasted away at full thrust, altering their vectors to clear the close-range defensive fire of the target. One of the blips flashed brightly, but it didn't disappear. The ship had been hit but not destroyed. Whether it was still capable of escaping – or indeed, if anyone onboard was still alive – was still unclear.

Ross' eyes darted to the big red oval representing the enemy battleship. He watched three tiny dots move into it one after another, and the AI began displaying damage reports to the side of the map. A few seconds later, the oval vanished, and the AI reported the complete destruction of the ship. The Alliance Yorktowns were the biggest warships in space besides the Confederation's two monster superbattleships, and now the enemy only had one left. The flagship.

The flag bridge erupted in cheers as the report came in, and another when all three attack ships blasted through the enemy's intercept zone and into the clear. A 50% survival rate was far higher than Ross had expected, and he sighed quietly in gratitude.

He glanced up at the chronometer. Less than five minutes left, he thought, thinking about Campbell and the two massive dreadnoughts now working their way around Saturn. He took a deep breath and stared at the tactical screen. He knew five minutes could stretch out like an eternity.

"All batteries, prepare to fire." Campbell was sitting on the front edge of his seat, leaning forward, his hands gripping the sides of his chair like vices. The posture was bad, and his back hurt like hell, but he didn't care. It was almost time.

The last 17 minutes had stretched on like an eternity, one long second slowly yielding to the next. His mind had been running wild with scenarios of hell unleashed on the rest of his fleet. He could see the nuclear explosions in his head, gargantuan warheads detonating in space all around his ships. The blasts wouldn't look like much in space, just a brief flash of intense light. But any ship within a few kilometers would be hit with a massive burst of radiation. Hulls would melt, armor would buckle. Men and women would die.

The missile exchange would be over by now, he realized. Whatever damage it had wrought was done, and whatever was left of the Confederation's navy would be fighting a laser duel with Stark's fleet. The Martian ships had strong energy weapon complements, and he knew that would help. But numbers would tell the tale in the end. Each of his ships would be facing two or three enemy vessels, and that kind of mathematics usually asserted itself before a battle was over.

With any luck, Campbell hoped, the enemy commander assumed the two biggest Martian battleships had fled, the Confederation unwilling to risk their most powerful and modern vessels in a losing fight. If the fool bought it, Campbell would have a precious few moments of total surprise. He hoped it would be enough.

John Carter and Sword of Ares had picked up a lot of speed whipping around Saturn's gravity well, and in a few seconds, a targeted blast of thrust would send them heading right toward the rear of Stark's fleet.

"All personnel prepare for thrust." He watched as Christensen relayed his command. They were going to fire the thrusters at 8g for 30 seconds. That was a lot to handle outside of the tanks, and he knew there would be injuries. But his people could take it for half a minute, and it would send the two massive ships on a direct line to the rear of the enemy fleet, already in energy weapons range.

"Thrust in 3, 2, 1…now." He held on to his chair, feeling the crushing pressure as Carter's massive engines blasted the vessel ahead at 8g. He struggled to breathe, sweat trickling down the side of his face as he forced air into his tortured lungs. His spine felt as if it would sever in his chair, torn into two pieces by the massive force of the acceleration.

His eyes moved toward the chronometer, and he realized that only ten seconds had passed. He gritted his teeth and endured the pain and discomfort, counting down to himself. Ten, eight. "He turned toward Christensen's workstation, ready to give the command as soon as the engines disengaged.

Four, he thought, desperately sucking in another breath. Three, two, one. He felt the relief almost immediately as John Carter went briefly into free fall and then fired her positioning engines, restoring a reasonable facsimile of gravity to the occupied areas of the ship.

"Commander Christensen…" Campbell's voice was cold, and in his eyes he held death itself. "All batteries, fire."

"It looks like a battle going on, Erik." Teller sat next to Cain in the Torch's wardroom, looking at the display on the wall. "Near Saturn."

Cain sat stone still, his eyes staring across the room at nothing in particular. "Of course. It all makes sense." He turned to face Teller. "Garret's at Columbia supporting the invasion there." His voice was like granite, and there wasn't a hint of doubt in his tone. "Stark could bring his fleet out of hiding without fear of Garret finding and destroying it. So he made his move on Mars."

"Mars?" Teller looked confused. "Why would he pick a fight with the Confederation when he's already dealing with the situation on Earth and the war in the colonies?"

Cain took a deep breath and exhaled loudly. "Because he's already won in the colonies." Cain's words were grim, with a brutal edge to them. "Cate Gilson will probably manage to retake Columbia, but what will be left of the Corps? The casualties there will be enormous, and the supplies expended impossible to replace." He stared at Teller for a few seconds before continuing. "The truth is, we're done, James. The Corps is finished. The men and women Cate is leading down to the surface of Columbia are the tattered remnants, and half of them will never leave that planet. How many have we lost? How many are left from the survivors of the Third Frontier War? Ten percent? Is it even that many?"

Cain's words hit Teller like an avalanche. Erik Cain had a dark side. That was nothing surprising to anyone who knew the man. But Teller had never seen him so utterly convinced the Marines couldn't prevail. Cain was one of the pillars of the Corps, a man who might be Commandant right now if he hadn't chosen to chase after Gavin Stark instead. He'd never lost hope before, not even during the lowest nadir of the First Imperium War.

"But even if the casualties on Columbia are heavy, we can always rebuild. The Corps has suffered losses before, but as long as a cadre remains, we can go on and regain our strength." Teller was struggling to convince himself as much as Cain, but he couldn't keep the uncertainty out of his voice.

"Rebuild? How? Where?" Cain's tone was relentlessly grim. "The Academy is basically a ruin, and all the arms production industry that had sprouted up on Armstrong was destroyed in the fighting." He turned back, looking off aimlessly across the room. "Stark is systematically destroying every facility capable of supporting the Corps or the fleet. When the Superpowers begin their last dance and start nuking each other into the dark ages, there will only be one place with high tech military production facilities left."

"Mars." Teller stared at Cain. "Vance would supply the Corps and Garret's fleet too if he is able. Stark has to destroy the Confederation's industry, or his plans can't succeed."

Cain nodded slowly. "We always forget two things when we're dealing with Gavin Stark…how smart he really is and just how far he is willing to go." There was icy hatred in Cain's voice, but a strange note of perverse respect as well. The grim Marine would sacrifice his own life to destroy Stark, but he couldn't help feeling a bit of amazement at a human being so capable. Cain wondered what Gavin Stark could have accomplished if he'd put his genius toward something more useful than the single-minded pursuit of power.

He sighed softly. Cain knew humanity shared the blame for that, and man had sown the seeds of his own destruction. Stark was a creature of the perverse world into which he was born. The endless political games, the oppression, the jealously-guarded class-structure. Erik Cain was a Marine through and through, and the Corps had his complete and eternal loyalty, but in his heart he believed that humanity had created the nightmare that was destroying it. If they'd stood up and fought for their freedom somewhere along the line, if they'd taken the time to see and understand what was happening to them instead of listening to platitudes and blindly following leaders, perhaps the world would have been different. Perhaps his world would have been different…or Sarah's.

Cain was only 50 years old. Even without rejuv therapy, his mother and father should still be alive, and his sisters as well. But they weren't. For him, his parents would always be 40, and his sisters just nine years old, the ages they were when the stark violence that haunted the lives of the Cogs struck his family.

He hadn't thought about them for years, not really. It was all part of a past he'd blocked, tried to forget. There was nothing there but pain. But now that humanity was facing its final struggle against an eternity of tyranny, his old memories flooded back. His last image of his sisters had been that of two little girls, lying in the ruins of their tattered mattress, shot a dozen times each. If that was the world Gavin Stark was going to destroy, if the monsters who'd allowed people to live the way the Cogs did were to be his victims, Cain thought perhaps he should stand aside and let it all happen. Did mankind even deserve to survive?

Cain struggled constantly with the dark side of his soul, fought hard to be a good man when all he saw around him was evil and brutality. He knew he would have stood aside if Stark were just fighting to subjugate Earth. He would allow the people there to fight their own battles, and to pay the price for their decades of craven compliance to those so unfit to lead them. But Stark was after the colonies too, and Cain had sworn to defend those with his life. He was far from confident that mankind in space would choose a different path than their forefathers had on Earth, but he knew they deserved the chance at least, either to forge a bold new path toward freedom, or to make the same mistakes again and descend into slavery.

But most of all, he was after Stark to avenge Elias Holm. The Commandant had been a role model to Cain, an example of something he'd long doubted could exist – a truly good man. The Corps had saved Cain from death and the squalor and misery of Earth, but it was Holm who had helped him become the man he had. Stark would pay for taking that life. He would pay if it was the last thing Erik Cain ever did.

Ross watched the display as another dreadnought disappeared from the enemy line. Admiral Campbell's surprise had been total. The two superbattleships had come around Saturn hard, x-ray lasers blasting. They'd taken out three of Stark's damaged battleships in the first few minutes, before the defenders managed to come about and return fire.

Now the enemy was maneuvering to concentrate on Campbell's ships. Ross was countering by closing with his own vessel. The battle was entering its final stage, a close-in knife fight to the death. "The battleline will accelerate toward the enemy at 3g."

"Yes, sir." Randall relayed the order. A few seconds later she turned back toward Ross. "Admiral, Celestia is Status 111."

Ross' head snapped around toward his display, and he focused on the reports streaming in from the stricken battleship. Status 111 was the Confederation's version of the Alliance Code Omega. It meant a ship was past saving and that its total destruction was imminent.

"All personnel on Celestia are to abandon…" He stopped abruptly as the small blue oval disappeared from his screen. He hadn't really expected to get through the battle without losses, but it still hurt to see a battleship with a crew of almost 1,000 blown to bits.

"All other capital ships are to continue toward the enemy, firing laser batteries full." He grabbed the armrests of his chair as Rhodes shook hard. He could hear distant sounds of explosions, and the lights dimmed for a few seconds. That was too close to the reactor, he thought. Another one of those, and we're out of this fight.

He felt suddenly lighter, no longer struggling under the 3g of pressure from the engines' thrust. He flipped on the intraship com direct to Rhodes' bridge. "What's happening, Tom?" Thomas Jacoby had been Ross' flag captain since he'd gotten his admiral's stars, first on the cruiser Dionysus and then on Rhodes.

"We've got trouble in the conduit from the reactor to the engines. I'm afraid 1.5g is all I can give you now." He paused, and Ross could hear shouting in the background. "Sir, I strongly suggest you transfer your flag."

"C'mon, Tom, we're not starting all that…"

"Admiral, I'm serious. We've got fires out of control all through the engineering spaces. It will be a miracle if we can keep the power on, even if we manage to maintain reactor containment." His voice was raw, harried. Ross could tell he was serious.

"Run your ship, Captain." Ross knew Jacoby didn't have

time to waste talking to him. "Do the best you can, Tom. And I'll run my flag bridge. Right here on Rhodes."

Ross figured he'd hear from Jacoby again in a few minutes, badgering him to take a shuttle over to one of the other battleships, but he didn't. The two never spoke again. The damage control parties fighting to save Rhodes' reactor from the fires failed in their frantic efforts, and one minute, forty-two seconds later the battleship lost containment in its fusion core. For a few seconds, she shone like a miniature sun. Then she was gone.

Chapter 9

LZ Holm
30 Kilometers East of Weston
Columbia, Eta Cassiopeiae II

"Keep that ammunition moving." Callahan had set up his command post about 100 meters from the front line. It had taken over an hour to sort out and reorganize the shattered remnants of his two battalions, but he'd managed to get a strong defense in place before the enemy finished reforming and launched a fresh attack.

He had pulled half his Marines back from the line, holding them in reserve to plug any gaps, but he'd detached all the auto-cannons, doubling them up along the perimeter. The concentrated fire had shattered the last attack, and a thousand enemy dead were scattered in front of his position. It had been a great victory, but a fleeting one that he couldn't repeat without more ammunition.

He'd wanted to give up when his platoon was wiped out, but General Heath had reminded him he was a Marine. And something else too. The general made him think about whether he wanted his men to have died in a futile battle that ended in the slaughter of the rest of the forces on Columbia, or if he wanted their sacrifice to mean something. He couldn't bring his Marines back, but he could give their deaths meaning by helping to hold out, and then pressing on until Columbia was once again free.

"This is all we could get, sir." The corporal was leading a squad of men, each pair of them carrying a heavy crate full of autocannon rounds. It looked like a lot of ammo, but Callahan knew it wasn't, at least not at the rate his people were expending it. "The supply depot is almost empty."

Callahan nodded. "Just get all that distributed along the line." He turned and walked back toward his reserve formations. He suspected he was going to need them when the heavy weapons ran out of ammunition, and he wanted them ready to go.

"Major, they're coming again." Lieutenant Mellas was Callahan's new aide, a platoon leader who ended up out of a job when the new major combined three of his shattered units into one formation. Mellas was up on the line, and Callahan could tell from the tension in his voice the new attack was a big one.

"On my way," he snapped back to Mellas. He flipped the com channel back to the sergeant in charge of the ammo detail. "Get those rounds distributed. Now." He turned and raced back toward the front line. He knew the entire force was running out of ammunition, and when they did, it would be over. The LZ would be overrun and the survivors gunned down.

He felt a rush of anger that no new waves had come to the aid of the Marines on the surface, but he knew the realities. The advance guard had been tasked to expand the LZ, but they'd been hemmed in and pushed back instead. Trying to bring down new forces into a pinpoint zone surrounded on all sides by the enemy was suicide. Half the landers would get blasted before they even touched down.

General Gilson was one of the oldest sweats in the Corps. He knew she would do anything to save the men and women on the ground. Anything but losing twice as many Marines in a failed attempt to relieve them. He doubted there were more than 2,000 of the original 5,000 still alive, and any relief attempt would lose more than that just trying to land.

He trotted up to the front, sliding into a deep foxhole. There were half a dozen Marines there, including two crouched down toward the front, manning one of the heavy autocannons and firing on full auto.

The troops were focused on the advancing enemy, and they

didn't notice his rank at first. His armor looked just like theirs, and it bore no special insignia. An officer's best chance to avoid becoming sniper bait was to look just like everyone else. A major was a juicy target, and one who strutted around looking like an important officer was just asking to be picked off.

"Major, sir!" The corporal in command turned abruptly, having just noticed Callahan's data on his display.

"As you were, corporal." Callahan pushed forward through the ankle-deep mud toward the front edge of the hole. "I'm just here to get a look." He peered out at the approaching enemy and gasped.

There were hundreds of troops advancing, no, more than a thousand, and it looked like there were fresh columns moving up behind them. The second he peaked over the edge of the foxhole he knew his people were done. The enemy was coming in massive force, far more than his Marines could defeat. They would sweep through the LZ and overrun the entire position, and that would be the end of the first wave, and the invasion of Columbia.

He pulled his assault rifle from his back. His people might be doomed, but there was one thing he was damned sure about. They would sell their lives dearly. The enemy might overwhelm the LZ and repulse the Marine invasion, but they were going to pay a heavy price to do it.

He watched the attackers approaching. They looked just like Marines, the same as the troops on Armstrong. They were leap-frogging forward across the ravaged battlefield, taking cover in shellholes and shattered buildings. Half of them were firing at any time, providing cover for their advancing units. Callahan wished his people were facing a less disciplined force, one that would just charge across the field. But they were fighting a mirror image of themselves.

He flipped on his com. "All reserve formations advance now. Reinforce the forward line." There was no point keeping anyone back now. His people would do most of their damage while the enemy was coming in, and he wanted every gun on the line.

He leaned forward, steadying himself and bringing his own weapon to bear. His command didn't have a rifle to spare. He was about to fire when he heard the sound of approaching aircraft. He stared at his display, but he couldn't believe what it told him. He leaned back and looked up in stunned silence at the massive craft swooping down from the sky.

Elizabeth Arlington stared down at the ground below. My God, she thought, the LZ is being overrun. "Alright squadron, we need to make this count, and we need to do it now. It's the last chance those Marines on the ground have."

She pushed hard on the throttle, driving Typhoon down to 2000 meters and zipping along the rocky ground south of the battlefield. The fast attack ship was a small vessel in a space battle, where it used its speed and maneuverability to zip around the heavier fleet units. But it was massive and cumbersome compared to an atmospheric fighter, or even a heavy bomber.

She'd sold the attack ships as almost streamlined for atmospheric flight, but that had been an exaggeration if not an outright lie. It had been enough at least to get her Marine allies to accept the plan. She'd snuck the whole thing past Garret, who would have known immediately how full of shit she was. Technically, she didn't need his direct permission, and that would be her story. The ships were from her task force, and she was in command. Still, she suspected she would get quite a talking to…if she made it back that is.

There had been at least a shred of truth to her story. The fast attack ships were easier to handle in an atmosphere than something like a battleship or a cruiser. It was at least possible to fly the things in air, but it took everything a top pilot had and then some. None of that mattered, though. She knew the Marines didn't have a chance without air support, and she couldn't stand to watch them abandoned and left behind.

She'd watched comrades abandoned once before, and she knew she'd never forget it. She hadn't even had the chance to say goodbye to Compton. She'd just sat on her flagship and watched the massive First Imperium explosive seal off the warp gate, trapping half the fleet, including the man she loved, with hundreds of enemy ships. She knew, even through the hurt and heartbreak, that there had been no choice then. If Garret hadn't blown the warp gate, the last of the fleet would have been obliterated, and all mankind would have been destroyed. But there was a choice this time, or at least a chance. And she was going to make sure those men and women on the ground got it.

She felt the ship shake hard, buffeted by air currents it was never intended to navigate, and she compensated as much as she could. She glanced at the hull temperature readout. It was 1100 degrees and rising. Damn, she thought, I'm going to have to throttle back on the speed.

Her eyes were locked on her screen, and her moist palms gripped the controls. She had her long brown hair pulled back in a ponytail and tied tightly in a knot behind her head. Her neck was hot and moist with sweat, and she could feel her heart pounding in her ears. Her ego had told her she could do this, and now she had to make good on that.

The Lightning-class attack ships carried a normal complement of 68 officers and crew, but she'd cut that down to a barely manageable eight per vessel. She had no engineering crew, no backups of any kind. The mission was stunningly dangerous, and she didn't want to risk anyone needlessly. But the lack of support staff meant any damage, even a routine malfunction could be fatal. And the Lightnings weren't built to withstand the rigors of atmospheric flight, so an overtaxed system could fail at any time.

She felt a twinge of guilt. Her people were volunteers, 39 other men and women in the five ships now streaking toward the LZ. But she didn't fool herself. When an admiral asked for volunteers, especially when she too was going, she knew there was tremendous pressure to step forward. She truly wanted to be at the controls. She was scared, certainly, but the thought of leaving more comrades behind was unthinkable to her. She wondered if the others were as committed as she, or if they were just following their admiral out of loyalty and duty.

"Attention, attack wing Flaming Death." She had come up

with the name, something she thought the leathernecks on the ground would appreciate. "Spread out into attack positions." She hadn't had time to make too many mods to the ships, but her engineers had managed to attach ground attack pods to the birds. It made them even harder to fly in an atmosphere, but the cluster bombs were deadly against ground targets.

"We're each going to hit them with one plasma torpedo." The attack ships' primary weapon system was deadly in space, but she had no idea how it would perform in an atmosphere. "Drop those in the enemy rear. We're not here to fry our own guys." She'd personally shoot the careless son of a bitch who hit the Marine positions out of carelessness.

She took a deep breath. "Then we'll turn once and come back low over the close in enemy concentrations and hit them with the cluster bombs." She nudged the throttle, bringing her ship into the lead position for the attack. "That's it…then we're out of here, so make those shots count."

She swung her ship around, angling for a group of columns marching up from the enemy rear. "OK, gunner, let's nail those bastards!" She struggled to hold the ship steady, bringing it around to cross over the heaviest troop concentrations. She held her breath, waiting for Specialist Samars to let loose the plasma torpedo. It was a dangerous plan. If the atmosphere proved to be too hard on the fragile containment system, the thing could blow the second it left the tube. If that happened, Typhoon would be gone, vaporized by its own malfunctioning weapon, with nothing but a few surviving chunks left to hit the ground.

The ship shook hard as it released its deadly ordnance, and her eyes flashed to the display, watching the weapon descend toward the ground. She let out a breath, and watched the blip move directly to the target area.

"Alright!" The cheering along the line was deafening, and Callahan instructed his AI to reduce the volume on the unitwide com. There was a second sun on the horizon for a few seconds, a billowing white cloud of energy and death that engulfed the enemy rear areas.

Callahan hadn't known what to make of the massive craft that had passed overhead, but he was pretty sure now they were friendlies. Ground pounders didn't see the outsides of space-craft very often, so none of his people recognized their own fast attack ships. But they'd just vaporized hundreds, no thousands of the enemy, he thought, and that was good enough for him.

"Alright you grunts, stop watching the show and keep fir-ing." The big aircraft had slammed the enemy rear areas, but there were still plenty of troops closer to his lines, enough to overrun the whole LZ, especially if his people let up their inten-sity, even for a few seconds.

He set the example himself, leaning toward the front of the hole and whipping his rifle around. He had been picking targets before, but the enemy's lead elements were getting closer now, and he switched to full auto. He focused on a group of enemy troopers and fired, hitting at least two and sending the others scrambling for cover.

His elation at the air bombardment began to fade as he real-ized there were still too many enemy troops moving toward his troops. They'd been firing as they advanced and bombarding Callahan's positions with mortar fire. Three of the six Marines sharing his foxhole had been hit. One was dead and two wounded. One of the injured Marines was still on the line, firing along with her comrades. The other was barely conscious, and his medical AI and trauma control system were the only things keeping him alive.

"Marines, this is Admiral Arlington." The voice came through on his com. He could hear stress in her voice but ela-tion as well. "Keep your heads down, guys. We're going to do another run closer in."

Admiral Arlington, he thought with a shock. What the hell is the task force commander doing down here? "You heard the admiral. Everybody down." He slipped back and leaned down, covering his head with his arms as he did. He could hear the sounds of the ships approaching again, and he could only imag-ine what they were about to unleash on the hordes of troops out on that plain.

He waited, listening to his own breath and waiting for the attack to begin. Each second dragged out for an eternity, and it seemed like he'd been waiting forever when he heard the ships roar by. It sounded and felt like they were directly overhead, and in their wake came the explosions. It started with a few, out in the field, less than 500 meters from his position. Then the intensity increased, hundreds of bombs landing all along the enemy lines. He imagined the cluster bombs tearing apart the enemy formations, cutting the attackers down by the hundreds.

He knew he should stay low, but he couldn't resist taking a look for himself. He stared out at a vision of hell itself, a roiling smoke filled nightmare of death and destruction. There were a few hundred of the enemy still standing, mostly those closest to his position, but the rest of the field was gone, engulfed by the flames.

"Up, now. All of you." He opened fire on the closest group of enemy survivors. They were stunned, trapped between his line and the fires. But he'd be damned if any of them were going to get away. "Fire. Kill the sons of bitches before they get a chance to run."

It only took a minute for his people to wipe out the trapped enemy troopers, and another two or three for the hellfire on the field to begin to dissipate. Callahan stood and looked out over the blackened and blasted plain. The enemy forces were shattered, at least two thirds of their numbers down, the rest reeling in retreat.

He felt a rush of elation, but it cooled quickly when he saw the columns of smoke rising in the distance to the south. Two of the attack ships had been unable to pull out of their low altitude attack runs, and they crashed a few kilometers to the south. Those crews had saved his people; they had salvaged the entire invasion, but they had paid for it too. He was still staring when his com unit crackled back to life.

"Attention Marines, this is General Gilson, inbound with the second wave. We estimate landing in one-eight minutes."

The cheering was even louder this time, and Marines were

holding their rifles in the air and waving their arms. Callahan smiled and took a deep breath, but his eyes were still staring back off to the south, toward those towers of thick, black smoke. The next Marine he heard talking shit about the navy was going to get a hell of a beating.

"All units, you heard General Gilson." It was General Heath, and his voice was edged with steel. "All units are to advance and clear the enemy from the field." He paused for an instant. "It's time to expand the LZ."

Chapter 10

Front Lines
120 kilometers east of Paris
French Zone, Europa Federalis

The light was hazy, cutting in and out. Werner tried to focus, but he couldn't shake himself out of the heavy daze. He was confused, his mind fuzzy, disconnected. He was lying on his side, and he became aware of pain in his legs, his back. He tried to sit up, but he couldn't manage it. Then he realized a heavy support had fallen on him, pinning him to the side of his over- turned vehicle.

He could hear sounds. They were coming from different directions, but he couldn't place them. He could feel pulling, sense someone tugging at him. His body moved, and a wave of pain took him. He cried out and the pressure stopped. He looked up again. He could see everything around him a little better, and his mind began to clear. It was his men, his escort. They were leaning over him, trying to get him out of his stricken vehicle.

Yes, he remembered slowly. The command vehicle. The explosions. The last shockwave had slammed into the big truck, smashing it into one of the rock outcroppings. He turned his head slowly, looking around, his vision coming back, gradually at first then more quickly.

He could see the truck had been badly damaged, and there was debris everywhere. The driver was still sitting in his seat, and Werner could tell the man was dead, even with his still-fuzzy vision. His head was turned at a grotesque angle, and there was blood covering his entire upper body.

"General…" He heard the voices. They seemed soft at first, far away. "…General Werner…" He tried to concentrate, and he could hear the sounds, closer, louder. "…sir, can you answer?"

"Status?" His voice was raw, and the word scraped its way coarsely from his parched throat. His memory was coming back, and he wanted to know what had happened to his army.

He felt something on his lips, something cool, wet. "Here, sir. Drink. At least a little." He felt the water on his mouth, pouring down the side of his face, his neck. He tried swallowing, hard, painfully. The water slid down his throat. The coolness felt good, driving back the pain a little.

"Status," he repeated, his voice clearer and louder this time.

"Unknown, General." It was a different voice. Werner looked up and saw an officer looking down at him, a familiar one. "They hit us hard, sir." Potsdorf stared at 1st Army Group's commander in chief, his faced caked in filth and his shoulder covered with a rough bandage, half soaked through with blood. The aide took a deep, painful breath. "We've got to get you to the field hospital, sir."

Werner felt some strength returning, and he pulled himself up. "No. I need to get an idea of the overall situation first." He looked down at the chunk of metal lying across his legs. "Get this off me." He could tell his legs weren't severely injured. His back hurt like fire though, and he could feel the slickness of blood everywhere. He reached around and ran his hand over his back. When he pulled it back it was wet, red. "Just get my doctor in here. I need these cuts on my back fused or stitched up." He still felt weak, lightheaded. He could see from the slick redness all around that he'd lost a lot of blood.

"I'm sorry, sir. Doctor Hoffen is dead. He was crushed by the command vehicle." Potsdorf was waving as he spoke, directing several soldiers to move the structural support off Werner's legs.

Werner closed his eyes for a second. Just like that, he thought. I'm in one place, Hoffen is a few meters away. I end up with cuts and bruises and he is crushed by 40 tons of armored vehicle. He knew wars were won by men and tactics, and materiel too, but sometimes he was still stunned by the random nature of it all. One man stands on a line and survives a battle, the solider next to him is torn to pieces by enemy fire. It doesn't matter that both are veterans, equally skilled at combat. Fortune still smiles on one and smites the other.

"Mmmmmpph." Werner felt a sudden wave of pain as three soldiers struggled to pull the heavy chunk of steel from his legs. The three men picked it up and moved it to the side, letting it fall again with a loud crash.

"Are you OK, sir?" Potsdorf was alarmed at the outburst, but he looked down and was immediately relieved when he saw Werner moving his legs. "You really need some rest, sir."

"Rest, Potsdorf?" Werner was almost amused at the suggestion, proof that a touch of levity, however brief, could make its way into any situation. "Do you really think I have the time to rest right now? That any of us do?" The battered general pulled himself up, sitting on a chunk of metal that had once been a workstation. "Now, I need somebody to stitch up my back before I bleed to death, and I don't care who does it." His eyes settled on his aide. "You, Potsdorf. You do it."

Potsdorf looked like he might panic for an instant, but he nodded and reached to his side, pulling a small first aid kit from his belt. The doctor would have used the fuser, which was a quicker and better solution, but all his instruments were under the command truck, crushed as flat as their owner.

Potsdorf moved around behind Werner, slowly pulling off the general's jacket. His shirt was soaked through with blood, plastered to his skin. Potsdorf took a small pair of scissors and gently cut the back of the garment. He barely held back a gasp when he saw Werner's back. There was a single deep gash right between the shoulder blades, where a big shard had hit him. It was surrounded by at least a dozen other cuts, less deep but still gushing blood.

"Sir, I don't have any anesthetic or painkillers…" His voice was tentative, uncertain.

"Potsdorf, we just got nuked. There are almost certainly hundreds of thousands dead out there. We don't even know if we still have an army." He started to turn to look back toward the aide, but a wave of pain changed his mind. "Do you really think some stitches are going to be more than I can handle?"

"OK, sir." The aide still didn't sound very confident, but he picked up a pair of forceps and started pulling shards of glass from his commander's back. Werner twitched once or twice, but he didn't say a word about the pain.

"I need some coms," he said, his voice tight as Potsdorf sewed up his wounds. "Who is still in action out there?"

"Steiner is trying to set up the portable comlink, sir." The aide spoke slowly, his mind focused on Werner's back. "It was damaged, but he thinks he might be able to manage a temporary fix."

Werner stared at the ground while Potsdorf finished his attempt at first aid. He needed coms more than anything. He had to find out what was going on with his armies. He was out of the net, and he figured they'd be looking for him, if there was anyone left to look, that is. For all he knew, no one was on the net. He tried to imagine the nightmare out there, the apocalyptic hell covering the entire battlefield. How many of his people were dead? How many were straggling around, wounded, sick from radiation, trying to find their way to an aid station? How many of the survivors would still be alive in a day? A week?

He clenched his fists. He had to get on the com and find out what had happened to his armies.

"More reports from the Europan-CEL front, Number... excuse me, Mr. President." The agent nodded respectfully to Warren.

"Yes, go on." Warren didn't really care what they called him. Besides, whatever else he was, he was still Number One. He had no intention of trusting anyone else with control of Alliance Intelligence, whether he was president or not. He knew just how deadly a tool the agency was, even in its shrunken, post-Gavin Stark incarnation.

He'd taken the office of the presidency simply because if offered some semblance of continuity for public consumption. The official story was simple. Warren had assumed the interim presidency after Oliver's untimely and tragic death following surgery for a long time genetic illness. It was at least moderately believable, and it had only required a few additional liquidations, Oliver's doctor among them, of course.

Convincing the generals and admirals, and a few other key personnel, to go along with his assumption of power had been easier than he'd expected. Most of them were more concerned with whether they'd be alive in a week than worrying about their own ambitions. Warren was amused at the dousing effect fear had on the lust for power. He felt it himself. He'd tried to give Oliver every chance, but the man had lost control, and it wasn't a time to be tolerant of weak leadership. After a lifetime of craving power for its own sake, he'd ended up taking it out of fear. Fear of what would happen if the mentally broken Oliver continued to lead the Alliance.

He stared down at the 'pad, reading the latest dispatches. The Europans had responded in kind to the CEL's nuclear attack. By all accounts, the entire battlefield was a nuclear and chemical hell, and there was little hard data on what formations were still in the field, if any.

"This is where we're going to lose the war," he whispered softly, mostly to himself. The Alliance and the PRC might be able to defeat the Caliphate and the CAC, and hold the South Americans at bay while doing it, but if the CEL was destroyed, Warren knew he'd have Europa Federalis and the Russian-Indian Confederacy on his ass too.

He sighed. He didn't know what, if anything, had survived from Werner's victorious armies. But even if the brilliant general managed to push forward through the maelstrom and seize Paris, it was very unlikely he'd have enough strength left turn around and salvage the situation on the CEL's eastern front. Taking out Europa Federalis would be helpful, but the CEL was exhausted after its death struggle with its longtime enemy, too prostrate to mount a prolonged defense against the growing

Russian-Indian armies. Worse, he'd been hearing unconfirmed rumors that a Caliphate army was forming up for an invasion of the CEL from the south.

The world was on the brink of an unmitigated disaster already, but Werner couldn't think of anything to do but escalate further. The CEL was going to have to go nuclear on its eastern front as well, and the Alliance was going to have to help. The list of potential repercussions was sobering, but he couldn't come up with another plan that didn't ultimately lead to total defeat.

He looked up at the agent standing next to him. "Send a Priority One flash communication to Admiral Vellinghausen. He is to prepare for a tactical nuclear bombardment of targets along the CEL-RIC front."

"Yes, Mr. President." The agent showed no emotion, not even the slightest break in his stone cold expression at an order that meant, at the very least, millions would die.

My God, Warren thought. Gavin Stark really did recruit and train an army of sociopaths. He wondered if he was any different – or just another of Stark's prototype human monsters, a man incapable of caring about the misery and death he unleashed on others. He'd done his share of terrible things in the service of Alliance Intelligence, and he'd never been unduly troubled by guilt or remorse. But things were different now. The fate of the entire world was at stake, and Warren was feeling uncertainties he'd never before experienced. Is this guilt, he wondered?

"Advise him he will have a target list within four hours." Guilt or no, he was too far in now. The Alliance was in too deep to pull back. There could only be victory in this war, or total and utter defeat, and Warren would rather die in the ashes than be dragged before the Caliph or Li An in shackles. "And get me Chancellor Schmidt immediately."

"Yes, Mr. President." The agent nodded and turned around, hurrying out of the office to carry out his orders.

Warren took a deep breath, looking around the room. Oliver's tastes were much flashier than his own, and hated just about everything the former president had selected, from his enormous desk to the various bits and pieces that lay on the shelves and tables around the room. He wondered what it would be like to assume the presidency during a different time, one when redecorating an office was a priority.

The com buzzed. "Mr. President, we have Chancellor Schmidt on the line." Warren's finger paused over the flashing button. It was time to convince the head of the CEL to launch most of the rest of his nuclear arsenal at the invading Russian armies. The bombs in the west had blasted and poisoned lands in Europa Federalis, but in the east the fighting was all on CEL territory. The civilians who would become collateral damage were citizens of the CEL. The industry and infrastructure destroyed would be the CEL's.

Warren knew Schmidt was under enormous stress, the chancellor's situation even more desperate than the one he was facing. But it was the only way, the only chance to avoid a road that led to almost certain defeat. Even if it left the CEL prostrate, its own armies virtually destroyed.

"Mr. Chancellor, I have a proposal to discuss with you."

Axe moved through the tunnels slowly, carefully. He had a portable light – he'd killed to get it – but he had no idea how much power it had left, and he was being cautious. He was fairly certain the tunnel led into the heart of Sector A. His people had used it before, to make special deliveries to the elite zone. There were a number of substances the elites craved, items that were illegal and unobtainable through legitimate channels.

For a price, the gangs had offered whatever the privileged and powerful desired. Axe's people had delivered various narcotics through these tunnels, as well as attractive Cog women, sold as sex slaves and written off as random victims of street violence. They'd even brought in a steady stream of young Cog men for a specific client, a Senator who'd fancied himself a gifted martial artist and who treated himself from time to time to the spectacle of beating drugged opponents to death in his own private arena.

Axe had willingly participated in sordid business of this sort for the gang, first as a junior member, willing to do anything to escape the miserable existence of a Cog factory worker, and later as he climbed through the ranks, eventually becoming the leader.

As he rose to the top, he became increasingly aware of the perverse relationship between the gangs and the government. At first, he'd view Alliance Gov as the enemy, and he hated and despised the police who occasionally launched reprisals against the gangs. But later he learned that the gangs were actually allied with the government. The violence in the ghettoes, and the atmosphere of constant fear it propagated, kept the Cogs beaten down, too focused on their daily struggle to survive to even think about rebelling against the government.

The gangs served other purposes as well, keeping the privileged Political Classes well supplied with luxuries and perversions the government thought were best kept in the shadows.

The gang leaders themselves made a devil's bargain, promising enough random violence to keep the Cogs down while also sacrificing a tithe of their own low level members to police action. The young Axe, a junior gang member making risky runs into the Protected Zone, had viewed the police as the hated enemy, but when he advanced up the chain of command, he came to realize they were all part of an elaborate charade, one that existed solely to support Alliance Gov's control of every aspect of life and society.

Axe had moved up through the gang a step at a time, and at each level he had done what was expected of him, killing without question, dragging helpless captives to their fates as the playthings of the wealthy Politicians. He'd done what he had to do, to escape the factories and to stay alive. But now he felt remorse, and he questioned the foulness of the system he had served.

He was a violent creature, he knew, dangerous and feral. He'd just killed a man for his flashlight. But he didn't think he could go back to the old system, coolly sacrificing his own people to the hated police while serving his masters at Alliance Gov. Whatever he did going forward, he swore to himself it would be genuine. Never again would he serve Alliance Gov, nor would he ever again betray those he led, men and women who swore loyalty to him.

He would kill again, he was sure, but only to serve his own purposes, to survive and to bring his people through the destruction and chaos that were spreading everywhere. Even killing for a flashlight made more sense to him than playing the twisted game with Alliance Government. His act had been a brutal one, unforgivable perhaps, but there was at least a base honesty to it. He had needed the light to survive in the tunnels, and he had done what he had to do to get it. He knew the Cogs would turn on each other when they began to run low on plundered supplies. Men would do what he had done and worse. They would do what they had to do to survive. And he intended to be long gone from the city before things reached that stage.

Chapter 11

Flag Bridge
MCS John Carter
Near Saturn
Sol System

Duncan Campbell stared at the display, watching the report of Rhodes' destruction in stunned silence. It all felt strangely detached, a small icon disappearing from a computer screen, along with a stream of data confirming that the Martian battleship had lost power to its fusion core containment. The reality – that one of his oldest friends, and over 900 veteran spacers had just been vaporized – seemed an amorphous concept.

The Martian admiral felt the emotion welling up inside of him, and he clamped down hard, driving it into a deep place in his mind until he had time for it. He had ships in the fight that needed his attention, and live crews fighting an enemy that still outnumbered them. He would mourn the dead later.

His eyes scanned the tactical display. The battle was going fairly well overall, better at least than he could have dared hope. But well was a relative term when you were badly outnumbered, and he knew his fleet was on its last legs. Celestia and Rhodes were gone, and every other ship in the battleline, including John Carter and Sword of Ares, were heavily damaged.

He panned across the icons representing enemy ships. Stark's vessels had all been stolen from various other powers, and most of them were in the Martian naval database, making them easy to pick out. His eyes stopped on one battleship, a Yorktown class behemoth. It was positioned behind the battleline, and it was the last of the big Alliance ships in the fleet. Liang's flagship.

"Get me Captain Oswald now." It was time to up the ante, time to see what Liang Chang was truly made of.

"I've got Captain Oswald, sir."

"Captain, do you see that Yorktown sitting behind the enemy battleline?"

"Yes, sir. She's tucked in there nice and neat." Oswald had a deep booming voice, and it lost nothing in the transmission across 20,000 kilometers of empty space.

"Would you say that's Liang's flagship?"

"I'd bet money on it, sir."

Campbell took a deep breath. "Let's find out. I want you to head straight for that ship, Brian. Ignore everything else. I'll do the same." His eyes darted back to the display for an instant. "It's time to give Admiral Liang something to think about."

"Yes, sir." Oswald emphasized both words with a tone of deep approval. He was all for taking the battle to Stark's admiral and damned the consequences.

Campbell knew those consequences could be severe. As soon as Liang realized they were coming after him, all hell would break loose. He'd probably order every ship in his fleet to attack the two huge battlewagons. Carter and Sword of Mars were tough vessels, the largest and most powerful tools of war ever built by man, but they weren't indestructible. If they took enough damage they could be obliterated, just like Celestia and Rhodes.

"Good luck, Brian."

"And to you, sir."

Campbell took a deep breath and dialed up John Carter's bridge. "Will, set a course directly toward contact Sierra-2. I want all batteries targeted at that ship."

Will Cartwright had taken over command of John Carter when the newly minted Admiral Campbell moved to the flag bridge. Cartwright had been Campbell's first officer, and there was no one he trusted more. In fact, he'd asked Roderick Vance point blank to promote Cartwright and make him his flag cap-

tain. There had been a number of senior officer on the list waiting for a battleship command, but Vance acceded to the wishes
of his new Admiral. If Campbell was going to take control of
the whole fleet, Vance had reasoned, he had the right to the flag
captain of his choosing.

"Yes, sir. Target Sierra-2." There was a brief pause. "Initiating 3g thrust in twenty seconds."

An instant later, the message repeated on the shipwide com.
"All personnel prepare for immediate 3g maneuvers."

Campbell could hear Cartwright shouting commands
through the open com. A few seconds later: "All batteries are
targeting contact Sierra-2, Admiral."

Campbell closed the com line and stared straight ahead, imagining Liang's reaction. The former-CAC admiral wasn't a fool,
but he wasn't known for his personal courage either. Campbell wondered whether the fear of Gavin Stark was enough to
stiffen his spine.

"Sword of Ares is on a parallel course, 20,700 kilometers
to our port, Admiral. Both ships on a direct vector for enemy
contact Sierra-2."

Campbell's expression morphed slowly into a hard, feral
gaze. I'm coming for you, Liang Chang, he thought. And the
shades of David Ross and the crews of Celestia and Rhodes are
with me.

"Time to see what we are all made of," he whispered to
himself.

Cain was thinking, wracking his brain trying to figure out
how Stark was planning to come at Mars. The fleet battle now
raging was a diversion, he was sure of that. Stark was too sub-
tle, too clever to wager such a crucial part of his plan on the
vagaries of success in battle. Stark was a lot of things, but he
wasn't a soldier, a warrior. He didn't have the capacity to trust
in the men serving under him to do what was necessary. No,
Cain thought, he would have planned something else, something
sleeker, more direct.

"We're getting close to Mars." Teller walked up behind Cain.

"I had the captain do a full scan. Nothing. The scope is clear."

"Of course, it's clear. Stark knows he could never have gotten a ship through the Confederation's net without being detected." He paused for a few seconds, looking up with a strange expression on his face. "A normal ship, at least."

"Normal ship?" Teller was confused.

"How did he get away on Armstrong?"

Teller walked around Cain's chair, staring down at his friend. "He slipped past the fleet, I guess."

"Slipped past Augustus Garret?" Cain's voice was becoming firmer, his conviction growing. "Not likely." His eyes darted up toward Teller's. "No, James, not just any ship. Stark must have some kind of stealth ship, something that can evade normal detection."

"A stealth ship?" Teller sounded unconvinced. "That's a bit of a stretch, wouldn't you say?"

"Not really." Cain was nodding as he spoke. "What else could it be? After Stark killed Elias, Admiral Garret clamped down the tightest blockade occupied space has ever seen, but the son of a bitch got through it somehow anyway." Cain knew he was working a hunch, but the more he thought about it, the more he was sure he was right. "We know the navy's been working on stealth technology for a long time, and Stark would have had access to everything through Alliance Intelligence." The pieces were beginning to slide into place in Cain's mind. No one in the Alliance would have been better positioned to steal promising new technologies – and eliminate anyone who knew anything about them. "Think about it. Who would have had an easier time diverting any new research to his own purposes?"

Teller was listening, but his expression remained skeptical. It just seemed too out there for him to embrace.

"Think about it, James. We're always underestimating Stark, always one step behind him. I've fallen into that trap before, but never again." He paused and stared at Teller with icy eyes. "Never."

Cain stood up. "That's why his fleet is invading the system. Stark wanted to draw the Confederation's warships away from

Mars." He paused again. "That means he must be planning something…now." He moved quickly toward the door. "Come on, James. We've got to get to the bridge."

He slipped through the open hatch and into the corridor, heading for the ship's small control center.

Teller chased behind. "Erik, wait. Don't you think we're moving a little too quickly here? This is only a guess after all."

"It's the best thing we've got." Cain didn't break a stride. "And my gut tells me I'm right, James." Cain waved his hand over the plate next to the bridge entrance, and the hatch slid open. He walked inside and looked over toward the command chair. "Captain Jennings, I need to speak with Roderick Vance. Now."

Jennings turned toward the unexpected visitor. "Immediately, General Cain." Vance had sent Jennings to aid Cain, with the specific instructions to do anything the Marine general asked. The head of Martian Intelligence respected Cain and trusted his judgment, perhaps even more in some ways than his own Marine colleagues. Cain and Vance were similar creatures, the 'cold fish' of their respective services. Vance knew Cain was deadly serious in his pursuit of Gavin Stark, and he wanted to help any way he could. And he knew if anyone could track stark down and rid the universe of Stark's loathsome presence, it was Erik Cain, by sheer determination if nothing else.

"This is Sand Devil to Confederation Control. I have a clearance level one communique for Roderick Vance." Sand Devil's captain handled the communication himself. A clearance level one message could only be made by a ship's captain or higher. It was the Confederation's top priority communications protocol, used only for serious emergencies. Vance had been clear that Jennings was to use the channel for any messages from Cain.

"Vance here." The communications desk rerouted the message almost instantaneously.

Jennings handed Cain a headset. He reached out and grabbed it, strapping it on. "Cain here, Roderick." He paused, but only for an instant. He was about to hurl the Confederation into frenzy of activity, like a child kicking an anthill. He wondered for a second if Teller was right, if he was overreacting. But he shoved that aside. He knew he was right. He just knew it.

"I believe Stark's attack is a diversion, Roderick, an attempt to draw your fleet away from Mars."

"Why would he want to…" Vance's voice stopped suddenly, and Cain could hear alarms in the background. Erik turned and looked at Teller then his eyes shot over to Jennings. "Captain, run a scan of…"

"Already doing it, General. We're picking up multiple missile launches from high orbit." He snapped his head around toward Cain. "We can't detect any launch platforms, sir, but we're tracking 36 inbound delivery vehicles entering the Martian atmosphere. "It's like they came out of nowhere." The captain's voice was loud, brittle. "Preliminary analysis suggests multiple surface targets, including the Ares Metroplex, Argos, Tharsis City, and Olympia."

Cain felt his stomach tighten as Jennings rattled off the names of the four largest cities on Mars. My God, he thought. We're too late.

"I said a planetwide level one alert." Vance was shouting into the com unit. He almost never lost his composure, but now he was facing the most dangerous crisis of his life, and he'd let it happen. He'd sent the entire fleet to face Stark's invading ships, secure in the knowledge that nothing could come through either of Sol's warp gates without being tracked every kilometer by his detection grid. He'd played into Stark's hands again, and this time hundreds of thousands of innocent Martians would pay the price.

"I want all personnel into the shelters immediately." There were klaxons sounding off all around, and he could hear the scrambling of boots in the corridor outside. His hands worked the com controls. "All planetary defense units, we are tracking 36 incoming enemy missiles. Interception is absolutely essential at all costs. Fire at will." He knew the anti-assault batteries would get some of them, probably most of them. But he also knew some would get through, especially since they were probably MIRVs, with at least half a dozen warheads each.

"All atmospheric fighter squadrons are to scramble at once." He knew the aircraft would be too late, but there was a small chance they might pick off one or two of the enemy missiles, and anything would help right now. Besides, they'd be safer in the air than on the ground anyway.

The door slid open and a squad of armed and armored Martian Marines poured into the room. "We're here to get you to a secure location, Mr. Vance." The sergeant waved his arm, and four of his men surrounded Vance, gently leading him toward the door.

"Wait," Vance yelled. "I have…"

"I'm sorry, Mr. Vance, but there is no time." The sergeant stepped out of the way, motioning for the Marines to move the head of Martian Intelligence out into the hall.

Vance was going to argue, but he knew the standard procedures even better than the sergeant did. All council members were to be taken to the underground shelter in the event of a level one alert. Vance knew the Marines would do whatever they had to do, but they would get him to safety whether he wanted to go or not.

He followed along, flipping on the portable comlink on his wrist. "I want full updates," he yelled as the Marines hustled him down the corridor toward the emergency lift.

No, he thought to himself. This can't be happening. He'd helped to design the Martian early warning systems himself, and there was no way a ship should have been able to get so close to Mars without being detected. He leaned over the wrist com and yelled, "Get General Cain on this line immediately."

"Roderick, I'm here. They're missiles, and they're tracking for your four biggest cities." Vance already knew what Cain was telling him, but the words hit him like a sledgehammer anyway.

"Who?" he stammered as the Marines shoved him into the lift. "Who launched the attack?"

"We don't know." Cain's voice was busy, distracted. "We can't detect any ships in orbit. I think Stark has…" The high speed lift descended rapidly toward the secure underground bunker of the Martian Council, and Vance's portable com lost the connection. He stared aimlessly toward the small control panel thinking one thing again and again. How?

Stark sat in his chair on the bridge and watched the missile tracking data on the main display. He tended to remain impassive and unreadable in front of the crew, but he couldn't keep a small smile off his face. His stealth ships had managed to sneak into Mars orbit and launch their ordnance. He knew the Martians would fire everything they had at his missiles, but they'd never get them all. And his barrage didn't have to destroy every square kilometer of inhabited Mars or kill all the Martians. All they had to do was crack the domes of four cities, and single near miss was enough to do the job. There wasn't any appreciable military support infrastructure anywhere else on Mars, and if the bombardment took out its targets, Garret and the Marines would lose their last hope of refit and resupply. And Stark would be one step closer to mastery over mankind.

He watched the plotting screen. Soon, his 36 delivery vehicles would separate into 216 individual warheads. The stealth ships weren't large, and they couldn't carry a lot of ordnance. The bombs were small, 100 kilotons each, hardly comparable to the 100 megaton city killers the Superpowers would soon be hurling at each other, or the 500 megaton monsters the battlefleets were launching out by Saturn. But 100 kilotons was more than enough to shatter a city's dome, even one built from reinforced hyper-polycarbonate.

He could see the Martian response in action. Anti-missile rockets were streaking up through the sky, locking onto his launch vehicles with considerable accuracy. He knew the ground-based lasers were active too, tracking the inbound missiles and waiting for them to come into their shorter range. The defense was spot on, the reactions times extraordinary. The Confederation lived in the shadow of Earth, ever fearful of the navies of the Superpowers, and the Martian defensive systems were leading edge. But Stark knew all that, and he'd planned around it.

"Separate MIRVs." He spoke softly, matter-of-factly.

"Sir, the entry vehicles are still…"

"Separate MIRVs," Stark repeated, every aspect of his tone a blood-chilling threat. "Now."

"Yes, Number One." The captain gestured to the tactical officer who turned and worked the controls.

"Vehicle separation complete." The officer's voice was cracking, tense.

Stark smiled. Now Vance's people had 216 targets to chase and less than six minutes to go. It was as good as done.

He leaned back, and closed his eyes for a moment, savoring his impending triumph. Then his ship shook wildly, and the lights went dark for a few seconds. He bolted upright and looked around the small bridge, his eyes settling on the captain. "What the hell was that?"

"We're detecting something, sir. It's very faint. It could be a small amount of debris or some frozen liquids, but we don't have enough data to be sure." Cain had ordered the Torch to target the area where the missiles first entered its scanning plot. The stealth ship had to be there, at least it must have been when the ordnance was fired. Cain knew Stark wasn't the type to trust anyone else with a job this important. He'd be there himself. Cain was sure of it. And he was betting the psychopathic bastard would have stayed in orbit to make sure the job was done.

"Fire again!" Cain's voice was frightening, like something out a legend, the cold wailing of the undead, come to claim the living. "Blanket the entire area."

Cain knew the Torch was a lightly-armed ship, and he longed for something with more power, even a suicide boat. But he had what he had, and there was no use wasting time on idle wishes. "Maintain fire, full dispersion pattern." Hopefully, Stark's stealth vessels were similarly fragile.

"Yes, sir." The Torch's lights dimmed briefly every time its lasers fired. "More debris, General. We definitely hit something."

"Concentrate fire on the area around the debris field." Cain was standing in the middle of the bridge, fists clenched. He knew Stark was out there somewhere and, by God, he was going to kill the son of a bitch.

"General, we've got something on the scope. It looks like a ship of some kind, but the AI is drawing a blank on ID."

Cain turned toward the captain and stared at him with death in his eyes. "Fire."

Stark was fuming, wondering how some tiny ship in Martian orbit had picked off his location. He'd detected the ship when it arrived, but he wasn't about to give his position away by attacking it. It looked like a courier ship or a small scout, nothing to worry about. At least that's what he'd thought.

"Get us out of here now." Ghost had been hit worse than Spectre, and its stealth system had been knocked out. He'd ordered it to fight the enemy vessel while Wraith and Spectre escaped, and to proceed to the warp gate and head back to Base Omega. Stark had another destination in mind for the other two ships, but he couldn't risk anyone following the damaged Ghost there.

"Spectre control, this is Gavin Stark." He looked down at his board.

"Spectre control." The AI's voice was cold, impersonal. "Voice pattern identified, Stark, Gavin. Awaiting orders."

"Download destination delta-gamma-one-one into navigational computer."

"Selected course information is password protected. Access code is required."

"Access code alpha-zeta-gamma-delta-delta-three-six-one-eight."

"Access code accepted. Course delta-gamma-one-one now active in navigation system."

"Engage navigation. Maximum acceleration." A smile crept back on Stark's lips. He had one more surprise up his sleeve.

"Engaged."

Stark leaned back, breathing as deeply as he could, as 4 gees pushed down on him. In a few seconds, he would be away from Mars, and on his way to his last base, a refuge so secret, no one but the Shadow Legion personnel stationed there knew it existed. Most of those who built it were still posted there, and the others were gone, sacrificed to the needs of security. It was his refuge for the final phase, and from there he would direct the end game of his plan to impose his rule on Earth.

Cain pulled himself up and shuffled over to an empty chair. He'd been so intent on finding the ship he knew had to be there, he hadn't considered they might decide to fight back. The Torch had taken a hit. It was just a glancing blow, but Vance's amazing speedsters weren't warships, not by any measure, and the blast had knocked Cain off his feet. Another hit or two and that would be the end of Sand Devil.

"Maintain fire, captain. We've got the thing on scanners now, and we need to blast the fucker dead on." The enemy vessel didn't appear to be any stronger than the Torch, and Cain figured one more solid hit would disable it at least.

"Erik…"

Cain turned his head toward Teller. The Marine was sitting at another workstation, monitoring the enemy missiles. As soon as he saw his friend's face, he knew. "The Ares Metroplex?"

Teller nodded grimly. "Three detonations around the city. The second one cracked the dome. The last one shattered it."

Cain felt a tightness in his stomach, and he hoped there had been enough time for Vance's people to evacuate the population, though he doubted everyone got out. He stared at the display for a second, hoping Vance at least had gotten to safety. Then he took a breath and turned back to the captain, who was looking at Teller, his face a mask of shock and pain.

"Captain!" Cain's shout was primal, and it shook the officer from his funk. "We need to take out that ship, and we need to do it now! Those are the bastards who just blasted the Metroplex." Cain knew how to reach the baser instincts of men, to shake them from sadness and fear and channel their anger and longing for vengeance into an irresistible force.

"Full power to the lasers. Fire!" Cain shouted, his roar seeming to shake the ship's structural supports. His eyes were focused on the plotting screen, and an instant later, the ship went dark, every scrap of power from its straining reactor pumped into the weapons systems. A few seconds later, the power came back, and Cain focused on the screen. It was blank. Nothing but floating debris and chunks of ice and frozen gasses. The enemy ship was gone.

Cain felt a rush of satisfaction, but something didn't feel right. He looked down at the screen, reviewing the scanning data from the enemy ship. His eyes stopped on the tonnage figure, 3,500. There was no way a ship that size could fire 36 MIRVs. He felt his chest tighten, and rage flowed through his body. There had to be more than one ship. They hadn't killed Stark. They'd destroyed the ship the bastard had left behind to cover his escape. Cain clenched his fists and screamed.

Liang stared at small screen on his display, watching the ships converge from two directions. The Martian battleline had been savaged, two of its four battleships destroyed outright and the other two badly damaged. But the surviving ships, along with their attached cruisers and destroyers were heading directly for his flagship, firing with all their remaining weaponry.

The two Martian superbattleships were coming in from the other side, their deadly x-ray lasers ignoring every other target, blasting away at him as well. He felt a chill go down his spine. This was no normal battle formation. The Martian admiral was coming for him! And every vessel remaining in the Martian fleet was bearing down.

"Pull us back," he shouted to his tactical officer. "Get us behind the battle line." Liang could feel the cold, clammy sweat on his neck, and he took a deep breath. "All other ships are to engage the enemy fleet while we draw them in."

"Yes, Admiral." The officer relayed the order to engineering, and he turned back toward Liang. "We'll be engaging the engines in 30 second, sir. Prepare for 3g thrust." He sent the orders to the rest of the fleet, ordering them to hold position and engage the incoming enemy ships. He doubted they'd view Liang's flight as 'drawing the enemy in,' but they knew they were close to victory, and none of them wanted to risk Gavin Stark's wrath. They didn't have much respect for Liang, but they were scared to death of Stark. They served the most conscienceless killer in all of occupied space, and they knew how he felt about anything less than total success.

"The battleline is covering our retreat, Admiral."

"Very well," Liang said softly, trying to hide his fear. There was something about this Martian admiral that reminded him of Augustus Garret. Not in raw military talent, perhaps, but in terms of cold-blooded persistence. And the thought terrified him.

Campbell was slammed back hard into his command chair as John Carter took another hit. The ship was surrounded, enemy cruisers and destroyers coming in from all sides to make deadly attack runs. But that was a problem for the damage control parties. Carter's captain, and her gunners, were focused on one target and nothing else.

Liang's flagship was trying to withdraw under the cover of its screening vessels, but Captain Cartwright had managed to keep John Carter right behind its prey. The Martian behemoth had massive damage, and she was streaming frozen gas and fluids behind her, but she was still in the fight. Sword of Ares was trying to keep up, but she'd lost two of her engines, and she was down to a single reactor running at 50%. Campbell knew the vessel and its crew couldn't be in better hands than Brian Oswald's, but he still gave the superbattleship no more than even odds of survival.

Campbell was silent, his discipline keeping the pain and loss all around him at bay. The battle wasn't over yet, and it was still to be decided if those who'd died had done so in vain or in a noble victory. Win or lose, the Martian admiral knew his fleet was all but destroyed, and he was determined to inflict as much loss as possible on Stark's forces in return. His people had given worse than they'd gotten, but it remained to be seen if they would overcome their numerical inferiority in the end.

John Carter shook again as she took a direct hit from one

of the enemy battleships. The lights flickered, but all her systems remained functional. Campbell had his headset on, the line to Captain Cartwright's bridge open. "Keep us on target, Will. And keep those batteries firing full." The x-ray lasers were tearing Liang's ship apart, each blast ripping through multiple decks, destroying everything in its path. Campbell knew Liang's ship couldn't take much more, but he knew his own savaged behemoth was also nearing the end of its incredible endurance. And John Carter had half the enemy fleet trying to take her down.

Campbell snapped his head toward the com station. "All vessels, cease pursuit of the enemy flagship, and direct all fire on vessels attacking John Carter." The Martian flagship would deal with Liang's vessel herself, as long as the rest of the fleet could get some of the attackers off her ass and buy her some time.

Christensen relayed the command, and all along the battleline, the battered Martian ships came around and fell on the vessels chasing John Carter. They struck like starving wolves, spewing death and destruction from every remaining gun, and all across the confused, intermixed lines, ships were blown apart and men and women died.

"Search harder, Captain." Cain was leaning over the captain's shoulder, staring at the data streaming across the screen. He didn't understand most of it; he'd spent his life fighting on the ground, not piloting spaceships around. But he knew there had to be something there, and he was going to find it if it was the last thing he ever did. "There has to be some way to track that ship."

"I'm running scanner sweeps in all directions, General. There is nothing. No energy trail, no radiation. Nothing to track."

Cain's face was like iron. "We hit another ship, Captain. You know we did. We must have done some kind damage, even if it was minimal. There has to be something we can trace, even bits of debris."

"Yes," the Captain said softly. "That's an idea. Maybe debris. They wouldn't have had time to patch anything before they took off." His hands raced over the workstation, eyes glued to the screen. "I think I have something." He leaned over the scope, staring intently. "It's a faint trail, bits of plasti-steel and other materials, probably from the hull." He flipped a few controls and put his face back to the scope. "We just might be able to follow it, General." His face snapped up. "But we need to go now."

Cain nodded and slapped his hand down on the console. "Then let's go. Just don't lose that trail, whatever you do." Cain tried not to sound too threatening with the last bit, but then again, he thought, a little extra motivation wouldn't hurt the captain's concentration.

Chapter 12

Dead Man's Ridge
Halfway Between LZ Holm and Weston
Columbia, Eta Cassiopeiae II

"Keep up that fire. Don't give those bastards a chance to reform." Callahan was crouched down, just behind his line on the reverse slope of the ridge. It had been named after one of the first families to settle on Columbia, but one of his non-coms had rechristened it Dead Man's Ridge. Callahan didn't know, but considering Columbia's violent history, he suspected the new name might just stick.

His people had advanced 15 klicks, moving straight toward Columbia's capital...its ruins, at least. The scanning runs had confirmed that most of Weston had been leveled by a number of tactical nuclear warheads. By all indications, the detonations had taken place months before, probably during the final days of the planetary army's defensive efforts. Callahan couldn't imagine what those last days of fighting had been like. The Columbians had a reputation for never giving up, and he wondered how much of the civilian population had died in the fighting – and in the reprisals he suspected their resistance had provoked.

He crouched down and walked along the line, checking on each platoon in turn. He'd been continually reorganizing, combining shattered formations to keep his units on the line closer to full strength. Moving troops around on an OB didn't create any more of them though, and he'd had trouble manning his section of the line, at least until General Mantooth led a bunch of fresh units from the second wave forward and cut the area he had to cover in half.

The bizarre air attack, followed by the almost-immediate landing of the second wave had stabilized the Marines' position on Columbia. The enemy's forward units had been almost obliterated, and the first ten klicks of the advance had required little more than walking straight ahead.

Now the Shadow Legion defense was stiffening, and the Marines had been forced to fight against a series of enemy delaying actions over the last five klicks. Callahan's people were just mopping up the last of these, a strongpoint that had put up a hell of a fight.

"Major, it looks like the enemy is setting up a strong defensive line just east of Weston." It was General Heath on the com. "Finish reducing the enemy position and halt your forces." Callahan could hear Heath's exhaustion, despite the general's best efforts to hide it. "We've got the third wave coming down now, and we'll wait until they are deployed before we continue forward and assault the new line."

"Yes, sir. Understood." He didn't like the idea of giving the enemy time to reorder themselves, but it was worth the wait to add the reinforcements to the line. The third wave consisted mostly of Janissaries, and the Marines deeply respected their new allies, if for no other reason than the fact that they'd had to fight them for so many years, and they knew how tough they were. Besides, his people could use a rest, however brief. He was about to move up and check on the reduction of the enemy strongpoint when his com crackled back to life.

"Major Callahan, I've got two…ah…visitors here. I think you should come over immediately, sir." It was Lieutenant Bevin, the commander of the platoon on Callahan's extreme left.

"Visitors? What the hell are you talking about, Matt?" There was a touch of annoyance in Callahan's voice. Things were in better shape than they'd been a few hours before, but he still didn't have time for bullshit.

"Sir, I'm serious. They say they're from the planetary army."

Callahan's head snapped instinctively toward the south, in

the direction of Bevin's position. "They're what?" He'd heard the lieutenant perfectly, but he still couldn't reconcile with what he'd been told. He hadn't dared to hope that any of the locals had managed to hold out so long against a force as deadly as the Shadow Legions.

"They say they're officers from the planetary army, sir. They claim there are over 1,500 men still in arms. Apparently, they withdrew to the swamps with most of the civilian population, and they've been fighting a guerilla war for the past eight months."

"I'll be right there, Bevin." He turned and started jogging south, crouching low to keep behind the cover of the low ridge. This, I've got to report, he thought. He flipped his com to the emergency circuit. "This is Major Callahan...I need to speak with General Gilson immediately."

"What am I going to do with you, Elizabeth?" Garret had intended to give Arlington the scolding of her life, but as soon as he saw her, his mind filled with memories. Garret had known for a long time how Terrance Compton felt about Arlington, and he'd encouraged his friend to ignore notions of propriety and act on his feelings. Compton hadn't listened, of course. No more than Garret had expected him to. His oldest friend was as unorthodox as he was when leading a fleet into battle, but he was an old stick in the mud in other ways.

Garret could see immediately that Arlington was still devastated by Compton's loss, and his anger immediately drained away. He knew he'd never get over losing his lifelong friend. Why should he expect Arlington to endure the loss of the man she loved any better? But he still had to deal with her somehow. He couldn't let her become a wild daredevil, risking her life recklessly until her luck finally ran out. He owed that much to Compton if not to her.

"I am sorry, sir. However, I would like to add that technically, I did not exceed my authority as task force commander." She looked back at him sheepishly.

"Technically, Elizabeth?" Garret glared back at her, but

there was no real anger in his eyes. "Is it my understanding that you feel you should get off on a technicality?" He paused. "Is it possible you could have imagined that I would not have wanted to know about this operation before it was launched? You've been too smart an officer for too long to start playing dumb now."

"No, sir." Her voice was soft, but she held her own and didn't flinch. Augustus Garret was like a demigod in the Alliance navy, and there were few officers who could stand firm and endure his disapproval. Arlington was one of them.

"Then why didn't you advise me before you went ahead? We were, after all, on the same ship. Were we not?"

"Yes, sir, we were on the same ship." She stood rigidly and held his gaze. "I didn't tell you because I was afraid if I did you would order me not to go."

"You were afraid I would cancel the operation?"

She nodded, almost imperceptibly. "In part, sir." She paused.

"What else?"

She took a breath. "I was afraid you wouldn't let me go personally, even if you allowed the operation to proceed. And I…" She stopped and took a deep breath.

"Please continue, Admiral." Garret's voice was stern but compassionate as well.

"I couldn't order anyone to go on that mission unless I went along." She hesitated for a few seconds before continuing, her voice becoming more strained as she did. "And I couldn't abandon those Marines down there, Admiral. I couldn't bear for us to leave our own behind. Again." She gasped out the last word, barely holding back her tears.

"Elizabeth…" Garret felt her words like a punch in the gut. He walked over and put his hand on her shoulder. "I miss him too. And I'll never forgive myself for what I did."

Arlington stared into Garret's eyes, hearing the pain in his voice, and realizing for the first time that it was always there. She couldn't imagine the guilt and burden Augustus Garret carried, the cumulative pain that was the inevitable byproduct of his long and storied career.

Arlington was still devastated by Compton's loss, but hearing Garret blame himself so profoundly stirred another response in her. "It wasn't your fault, sir. There wasn't a choice. I know that. I always have." Her voice was cracking, but she kept her eyes locked on Garret's and continued. "He...he knows it too, sir." She paused, drawing in a ragged breath. "You know he does."

Garret nodded. "Yes, I know." He noted the present tense in her comment. He hoped she managed to cling to belief that Compton was still alive out there somewhere, but he tended to doubt it. Arlington was as cold a realist as he was, and they both knew how many First Imperium ships were in that system. Compton was an extremely talented officer and a veteran of almost 50 years of interstellar warfare. If anyone could have gotten his people out of that system, it was him, but the odds were very long indeed. "In fact, I never told you this, Elizabeth, but the last message we received from him told me to pull the rest of the fleet out and blow the warp gate. He knew there wasn't another alternative." Garret understood everything he was telling her, but he also knew that realization did nothing to ease his own guilt and pain. He doubted it would for Arlington either.

She stared back at him with a sad, thoughtful expression on her face, but she didn't say anything. There was nothing to say. Compton was gone, and nothing either of them could do would change that. Now, she had done what she felt she had to do, and she knew she would do it again in the same situation. She would accept whatever punishment Garret chose to level at her, but she wasn't sorry for what she'd done, and she wouldn't lie and say she was.

Garret looked at her silently for a few seconds. "Well, Elizabeth, as much as I want to scold you, I can't argue that you saved thousands of Marines on the ground, far more than the 24 crew that were lost on your expedition." Garret had never intended to punish her seriously. In the end, he'd asked himself what he would have done in her situation. He tried to lie to himself, but he couldn't. He knew he'd have gone in as well, and if he'd had a commander who might have overruled him, he'd probably have pulled the same thing she had.

"So, let's just say congratulations on pulling it off. I spoke with General Gilson, and I believe the Corps is going to award you a medal – assuming any of us survive this campaign, that is." He smiled at her, trying to ease her concerns. Elizabeth Arlington had enough pain without him adding his disapproval to the mix. "As far as any reprimand, let's just say you will come to me next time…and trust me to support you. And we'll leave it at that."

"Thank you, sir. I will…trust you next time."

He forced a tiny smile onto his lips, and he was glad to see she managed one too.

Elaine Samitch worked feverishly under the harsh portable lights. She was awash in blood, desperately trying to save a young Marine. The kid had been shot to pieces, and she wasn't sure how he'd even made it to the aid station alive. His suit's trauma control system had proven its worth and then some.

He couldn't have been more than 21 or 22, one of the last wave of new recruits to make it through camp before the fighting on Armstrong had put a stop to Marine training and recruitment. The Corps had been under enormous pressure to replace losses after the brutal battles of the First Imperium War, and the vaunted Marine regimen had been drastically shortened, its vast program of physical and academic training cut to the bone.

The casualties had always been higher among the newest Marines, a blood tax war exacted from those newest to its horrors. Samitch had seen that since the days of the Third Frontier War. But these latest young Marines had been rushed through training and sent half-ready to the battlefields. Their losses had been nothing short of catastrophic, and there weren't many left from those last few classes.

Samitch was in charge of the entire medical team on Columbia. She'd come down with the second wave and set up the main field hospital and two aid stations. She had more people landing with the third wave, and she intended to set up a forward hospital closer to the action, handing off the unit in the LZ to her second-in-command.

It felt strange to be in charge. She'd spent years as Sarah Linden's executive officer, but now she was tasked with running the show without her friend and mentor. Sarah was on the hospital ship Boyer, and if fleet rumors had any substance, she was close to breaking the conditioning of the man who was still the only Shadow Legion prisoner taken in the war.

Anderson-45 had been a senior officer, captured on Armstrong in a freak circumstance, when his suit malfunctioned and failed to execute its kill function. The idea of an army killing its own soldiers rather than risking their capture was just another of the many horrors to spring forth from Gavin Stark's twisted mind.

The Marines, who'd been fighting a brutal deathmatch against Anderson-45's comrades, were shocked to find that their new prisoner seemed to harbor no hatred or bad feelings toward them. Indeed, he'd shown a remarkably unemotional point of view toward the fighting.

Sarah had been working feverishly since they'd taken the captive, trying to find a way to undo the mental and emotional conditioning that compelled the Shadow Legions to blindly follow their orders. It had been a long and frustrating process, but Sarah had finally made some substantial progress.

She'd planned to put her work on hold to go down to Columbia and head up the medical operation, but Generals Gilson, Merrick, Heath - all the Marine top brass – tried to convince her to stay at her work. Sarah Linden had led the medical team for every major invasion for 15 years, and she argued vehemently against staying behind. But when Admiral Garret threw his lot in with the Marines, she'd grudgingly given in and turned command over to Samitch.

She knew they were right in their arguments. If she could finally break through Anderson-45's conditioning, she might be able to develop a way to make the Shadow Legions stand down en masse. If she was successful, she could end the war almost immediately, without spilling another drop of Marine blood.

Samitch was sure Sarah would find the answer. Sarah Linden wasn't just the senior medical officer in the Corps, she was one of the most brilliant doctors of her generation, one who had saved thousands of lives through her tireless efforts. If there was anyone in the Corps who could do the job, it was her. Every Marine officer from Gilson to Samitch agreed on that.

Samitch knew her own job was to fill Sarah's enormous shoes, to do whatever it took to save the men and women who were fighting the battles, to patch their broken bodies together and to keep the operation running tirelessly, no matter how long it took or how many wounded Marines came in. She had admired Sarah for years, served under her, learned from her. The two had been friends as long as either could remember, and there was no way Samitch was going to fail – either Sarah Linden or the Marines who needed her.

She stared down at her bloodsoaked hands, clenched into fists of frustration and anger, and she wanted to scream. The kid on the table was dead.

"I don't even know how this is possible, Isaac." General Catherine Gilson was walking quickly across the muddy, pock-marked ground. "It's been almost a year and a half since the initial invasion, and you can see how much force the enemy pumped into here." She was fully armored, but like Merrick, she had her helmet retracted. "How could the native army still be in the field?"

"It would be a mistake to under-estimate a partisan force, Cate." Isaac Merrick walked alongside Gilson. Especially one that is well led.

Merrick had come to the Corps by the strangest of routes. He'd begun as their enemy. Merrick was a member of one of Earth's top Political families, and he'd been a general in the Alliance army, sent to Arcadia during the rebellions to put down the local forces. He'd gotten a taste of just what good men and women fighting for their homes could accomplish, and he never forgot it.

He'd also come to realize he'd been fighting on the wrong side and, after the rebellions ended, he emigrated to Armstrong where he served as a consultant to the Marines for a while before the Corps recognized his general's commission and inducted him formally. It was the first and only time someone from a different fighting force had been taken into the ranks.

"I know, Isaac, but they must have been outnumbered 5-1." She paused. "No, probably even worse than that. And the difference in equipment and armaments had to be enormous."

"Well, I guess we will see." He gestured ahead to the cluster of armored Marines gathered around two men wearing older, bulkier fighting suits with helmets retracted.

The two senior officers moved toward the group. Gilson looked at General Heath. "Well, Rod, what have we got here?"

Heath gestured toward Callahan. "Major Callahan's people made contact, General." He took a step back and looked at the two strangers. "General Catherine Gilson, may I present Lieutenants Reginald White and Tony Paine of the Columbia Defense Force."

"Gentlemen." Gilson nodded toward the two Columbians. "I must say, I am surprised to find you still in arms after all this time."

Paine spoke first. "General Gilson, I can't tell you how happy we are to see you. You and all your Marines. It has been a difficult fight, and we sorely need your help."

"I suspect you vastly understate what your people have been through, Lieutenant. It is a testament to your endurance and élan that you are still in the fight."

White allowed himself a grim smile. "That is General Tyler's doing. We would have fallen long ago without his leadership." White's voice was somber, but his respect for Tyler was clear.

"Did you retreat to the swamps after the enemy nuked Weston, Lieutenant?" Gilson's voice was gentle, sympathetic. She suspected most of the surviving Columbians had lost friends and relatives when the capital was destroyed.

White glanced over at Paine then back to Gilson, a confused expression on his face. "No, General. We fought on for quite some time in our lines south of the city before we retreated into the swamps." He paused for a few seconds. "And the enemy didn't nuke Weston." He glanced at the assembled generals. "We did."

"You did?" Merrick spoke first, the shock in his voice relaying what they all felt.

"Yes, sir. General Tyler ordered the city evacuated when we couldn't hold it any longer, and we staged a fighting withdrawal while the civilians escaped to the south." He panned his eyes over the assembled Marines. "When the enemy was moving through the city en masse, General Tyler launched the bombardment. We think we killed as many as 5,000 in that attack."

Gilson looked over at Merrick, unable to keep the surprise out of her expression. She turned toward the two guests. "Well, Lieutenants, I can see everything I've heard about Columbians was correct." She turned toward Merrick. "Isaac, take our guests back to headquarters, and have them show you exactly where their people are. I can only imagine if they've got the whole population hunkered down in those swamps they must need food and meds. Badly."

"Thank you, General." Paine's voice betrayed the stress and tension his people had been under. "That would be most helpful." He glanced at White and nodded. "And weapons too, if it's not too much trouble, General." His face hardened. "Because our stocks are almost exhausted, and it's time to clear these vermin off of Columbia once and for all."

"Of course, Lieutenant. Go with General Merrick, and we'll get you everything we can." She took a look at Paine and then turned her head toward White. They were both thin and gaunt, their eyes sunken deeply in heavily-lined faces. She could see they had the hearts of lions, but she wondered when they'd had their last decent meal. She looked over at Merrick. "And make sure our guests get something to eat, Isaac."

"Yes, General." Merrick gestured with his arm. "If you gentlemen will accompany me."

Gilson watched them walk back toward HQ, but there was only one thought in her mind. She'd heard the stories about

Columbia before, about how the people were crazy, how even the children in the street would fight against an invader. She'd never especially believed any of it. Until now. The legends fell far short. The Columbians were 100% certifiably insane. And she loved them for it.

Chapter 13

Sector A
Midtown Protected Zone
New York City, US Zone, Western Alliance

Axe smashed the entry plate with a chunk of broken masonry, exposing the mechanism beneath. He'd stopped to rest half a dozen times on the way up, but he was still breathing hard, his neck and back soaked with sweat. He'd stopped counting the flights of stairs less than halfway up, but he knew it had been over 300 to the top.

He stared at the wiring of the door lock, looking for the override switch. Breaking into apartments was a useful skill for a gang member, one he'd learned years before. It wasn't terribly difficult, especially since this unit was in a high security building in a section of Manhattan that was normally protected like a fortress. In normal times, he'd have never gotten into Sector A, and certainly not into the building itself. The apartment lock itself wasn't terribly formidable since no one was supposed to get in the building uninvited.

He slipped his finger under the catch and pulled. He heard a loud click as the door popped out of the locking mechanism. He stepped in front of the now-unlocked hatch and pressed his hands hard against it, pulling it slowly open.

He stopped when the door was halfway open, and he slid through the opening, holding his pistol in front of him, ready for any trouble. He was at the top of one of the best buildings in Sector A. He figured he might as well go right for the top. He didn't want to stay too long. He just wanted to get the best plunder he could in a few hours and get out. Besides, the wealthier and more influential the occupant, the likelier it was they'd been able to get out before the Cogs broke through and began their rampage, and that meant the apartment would probably be deserted. Axe wasn't looking for trouble. He'd fight if he had to, but he was just as happy to ransack an empty apartment or two.

He stepped out of the entryway into an expansive room, at least 20 meters long. There were floor-to-ceiling windows along two walls, and they looked out above the Protected Zone and across the Hudson River. The furnishings were the finest Axe had ever seen, massive sofas and chairs covered in silk and other expensive materials.

One look at the opulent luxury was enough to remind him why the Cogs had burst into the Protected Zone with blood and hatred in their hearts. Axe knew the owners of this apartment hadn't created anything of value or earned their money through hard work. They'd had the good fortune to be born into a family with strong political influence, and they owed their plush lifestyle to that fact alone.

Axe felt a surge of anger, a revulsion that this system had gone on for so long. He wondered what had gone through the heads of the Politicos who hadn't been able to escape, their last thoughts before the despised mobs tore them to pieces in the streets. They'd never had a reason to fear the Cogs, and they'd come to view them as less than human, some sub-species beneath themselves and the others in the Political Class.

Axe knew he was a deeply flawed man, a killer and a manipulator, but at least he had done the things he'd done to survive, and to drag himself from the hopeless squalor. He hadn't viewed his victims as being beneath him. His outlook was more feral, a contest for survival that pitted men against each other. He'd lived fairly well as a gang leader, but the luxury he was now witnessing was as alien to him as it would have been to any factory worker from Brooklyn or the Bronx.

He moved from room to room, gathering everything small that looked valuable. He'd found a duffle bag, and he was filling it. He'd stared in wonder at the sack, slowly realizing it was real leather, and that it must have cost more than a Cog worker made in a year.

He worked his way down a long hall, to what looked like a study or an office. There was a large desk, and he moved over to it, setting the bag down as he tried to force open the locked drawers.

He looked around the top of the desk, searching for something he could use to pry it open when he heard a sound coming from across the room. His eyes snapped up and he held the pistol in front of him, ready to fire. He stood still, listening.

He heard the sound again, and he moved toward it. It was coming from behind a small, locked door. He picked up a heavy marble bust and smashed the access plate. He reached his fingers inside and poked around. The override control was the same as the one in the main entrance. He pulled the release, and he heard the latch click, disengaging the lock.

He gripped the door hard and shoved it to the side, sticking his head through the opening and looking around the room. He caught movement, and his arm snapped up, bringing the pistol to bear. He was ready to shoot, but his eyes focused on the room's occupant, and he stopped. There was a girl huddled against the wall, cringing, trying to conceal her face and her tears. She couldn't have been more than 14, maybe 15, and she was covered in bruises and small burns.

The girl was terrified, curled up in a fetal position in the corner. She was wearing a thin white slip, shivering both from fear and cold. She was thin, almost emaciated, but he could see immediately she was very pretty. His stomach clenched as he realized why she was there, and he felt his body tense with anger.

"I'm not going to hurt you." He spoke slowly, his tone soft, soothing.

The girl shied away, pressing herself against the wall and burying her face in her hands. Axe stood in the doorway for a few seconds, trying to decide what to do. He was in a hurry. He wanted to be out of Manhattan by dark, and he didn't have time for this.

He turned to walk back into the study, but he stopped after a few steps. He could hear the girl sobbing softly. He looked back and got a better glimpse of her. She was thin as a rail, and he suddenly realized she'd been locked in the room with no food and very little water. There was a heavy stench, sweat and piss and shit. She'd obviously been trapped there for days without access to a bathroom.

"I want you to listen to me." Axe was cursing himself in his head for getting involved, but he just couldn't bring himself to leave her without one attempt to reach her. "I have nothing to do with the people who lived here, with whoever did this to you." He took a single step forward, and she flinched. "I am just here to steal anything I can use, and then I am leaving Manhattan." He thought honesty might convince her better than anything else.

She was sitting in the corner with her legs bent at the knees and her arms wrapped around. Her head moved slowly, looking tentatively in his direction.

"I do not want to hurt you. I will leave you alone if you want, but I am going somewhere safe, and you can come with me if you'd like." He paused, standing still, making no moves toward her. "My name is Axe."

She was silent for a moment, sitting and rocking her body back and forth nervously. "Ellie," she finally said. "My name is Ellie." Her voice was barely a whisper.

"Ellie, there is no power or water on, but I'm sure we can find you something to eat and drink." He stood stone still, not wanting to scare her now that she was responding. "Can you walk? We can go to the kitchen and see what is there."

She stood up slowly, wobbling a bit as she did. Axe could see how weak she was. She turned and looked at him. "You will let me go?"

Axe nodded. "Yes." He gestured toward the hallway. "Let's get you something to eat, and when you're done, you can come with me or you go anywhere else you want. Your choice."

Axe knew he wasn't a good man, not by any reasonable definition, but he was suddenly overcome with disgust at the monsters who ruled the Alliance. Generations of unquestioned power and unchecked privilege had turned the entrenched Political classes into a hideous grotesque, a remorseless group of creatures focused only on their own power and personal pleasure.

He tried to keep a pleasant expression on his face. The last thing he wanted to do was scare Ellie away. He knew the girl wouldn't last an hour on the streets alone. He wasn't sure why he cared, but he did.

"Come on." He motioned toward the door. "Let's go see what we can find to eat. I'm hungry too."

She moved slowly, cautiously toward the door, hunger and thirst momentarily pushing her fear aside. She limped as she moved across the room, and Axe could see she bruises at various stages of healing. It looked like she'd been beaten at least several different times recently. He stood still as she passed by him and walked into the study, and then he followed her toward the kitchen.

For all his external show of calm, inside his mind his rage was boiling and hatred was seething. He knew one thing for sure. The next Alliance Gov hack he ran into was going to die, and probably not pleasantly.

"Preliminary reports suggest that the CEL nuclear attack on the eastern front has halted the Russian-Indian advance. It is too early for meaningful casualty reports, but it is clear they are substantial. It is unlikely the RIC forces will be able to regroup and resume the offensive, at least for some time." Anne Jackson was one of Warren's key people at Alliance Intelligence. He had grudgingly named her Number Two, and tasked her with acting as his effective chief of staff.

He'd initially planned a relatively bloodless transition as president but, in the end, consolidating his position with a minimum of risk had required a significant amount of killing. He'd had most of Oliver's staff terminated, replacing anyone of suspect loyalty with his own agents. He might have been less draconian if the situation hadn't been so dire, but he couldn't take any chances of internal disruption, not now.

He looked up at Jackson. "Please continue, Number Two."

"The Russian counter-barrage appears to have been extremely effective. The CEL positions were hit with three successive bombardments." She paused. "I am making suppositions, but I would say it is very unlikely that any CEL formations have survived on the eastern front, or at least none that are likely to return to combat effectiveness. If the RIC is able to reassemble and resupply a significant force, they will have an open road into the CEL."

Warren sighed. "Well, I suppose a temporary stalemate is the best we could have hoped for on the CEL-RIC front. We'll just have to hope the RIC's history for poor organization and logistics continues uninterrupted." He leaned back and stared at the large map on the display. "It appears, at least, that General Werner has survived on the western front and has managed to reorganize at least a portion of his army group."

"Yes, Mr. President." Jackson swiped a finger across the small 'pad in her hands, and the display zoomed in to show the area around Paris. "It appears that he has two corps-sized formations advancing on the Europan capital even now. It is unclear what resistance the Europans are able to mount, but it is likely that Werner will soon take the city." She hesitated and looked at Warren. "We must consider the likely Europan response if their capital falls."

Warren nodded. "Indeed we do." The loss of a capital meant different things to the various Powers. The fall of Washbalt would be a costly loss, but the Alliance had numerous other major urban and industrial centers. But Paris was in every way the heart of Europa Federalis, and the French politicians who ran the Superpower would probably react rashly to its loss.

"Perhaps you should contact the Chancellor, sir, and encourage him to order General Werner to delay his advance."

Werner exhaled loudly. "That would probably be the best idea right now, Anne, but consider the CEL position. They have been on a total war footing for over a year. They have had over 5,000,000 casualties since the fighting began, and that doesn't include what they lost in the nuclear exchanges over the past three days. They are exhausted, unable to mount even a token defense in the east. General Werner and his armies are the only positive they have, and their only hope is to win the war in the west so they can send their great commander and his survivors to the east."

"But sir, the fall of Paris is more likely to instigate a major escalation than to end the war in the west."

"I'm inclined to agree with you, Number Two, though I'm not sure I would if I was in Chancellor Schmidt's shoes." He stared at his new chief of staff. "And there is the rub. The CEL is more desperate than we are at present, and wild gambles are more likely to appeal to them." He paused. "I will speak with the Chancellor, but I doubt he will order his top general to stop on the threshold of seizing the enemy capital. Would we exercise that kind of restraint if we'd suffered 5,000,000 casualties?"

Warren didn't wait for an answer. "Let's move on to other matters. Any status updates on the other fronts?"

Jackson shook her head. "I'm afraid not, sir." She tapped her 'pad, and the map of Europe disappeared, replaced by one of Africa and western Asia. "General Lauria is all but defeated in Africa. We have effectively lost the resource zone there, and the Caliphate is in almost total control of the continent." She glanced up at the map, gesturing toward a cluster of small blue squares representing the last Alliance forces. "It is time to consider a plan to evacuate General Lauria and his army before they are completely destroyed."

Warren stared at the map. "How many effectives is he down to?"

"He claims 275,000, but reports from our agents on the scene suggest a considerably lower figure, perhaps 120,000."

"Fuck Lauria." Warren's voice was thick with disgust. "He barely put up a fight, and he's spent most of the campaign retreating across the continent. We'd be lucky to get 75,000 of his troops out of there even with a full effort, and it's not worth the resources to try it. Not to save the shattered and demoralized remnants of a broken army." His face was twisted into a determined frown. "Maybe when they realize there is no escape they'll at least put up a decent fight."

"Yes, sir." Jackson's voice was businesslike, non-committal. She had no stake in whether the troops in Africa escaped, but she was surprised at Warren's decision. She'd known him for a long time, and she'd thought he lacked the brutal decisiveness his job required. Now she was reevaluating, trying to figure out how Warren was adapting to his myriad new responsibilities.

"So we have been driven out of Asia, driven out of Africa." He stared at the map, but he wasn't seeing anything. He was deep in thought. "It appears we are at a stalemate of sorts, and not one that is not to our advantage. The Caliphate and the CAC have no easier time reaching the rest of our possessions than we do of striking theirs, but they now possess superior resources than we do."

"That is true, sir. Though, at least we have time for further mobilization and reorganization."

"And what will happen while we are calling up reservists and training new recruits, Number Two?" Warren stared right across the table. "The RIC and Caliphate will get organized and crush the CEL." He took a quick breath. "And the CAC will focus on the PRC. With enough support from the Caliphate, they may even successfully invade. Admiral Young has performed admirably, but I doubt he can defeat the combined CAC and Caliphate navies, and if the enemy is able to establish local dominance, the PRC could be in trouble."

"So what do you propose, sir?" Jackson returned Warren's stare, a nervous look on her face.

"Well, it's a sideshow, but we have to knock the South Americans down. They'll never successfully invade up Central America, but bogging them down in the jungles isn't enough. We've got to weaken CAC-Caliphate power bloc any way we can, and right now the empire is the most vulnerable to our forces. Advise General Dougherty I want a detailed plan for the destruction of the empire. And I want it by the end of the day tomorrow."

"Yes sir." She hesitated, waiting to see if he would add anything. "And what else, Mr. President?" she finally said.

He looked back at her, and for an instant his mask of confidence failed him. "I have no idea, Anne."

She was about to respond when the com unit buzzed. "Mr. President, I have an incoming communication for you, sir."

Not now, Warren thought. I don't have time for this. "Who is it?" he barked.

"It is Minister Li from the CAC, sir. And she says it is urgent."

Chapter 14

Flag Bridge
MCS John Carter
Near Saturn
Sol System

Duncan Campbell coughed hard, choking on the smoke and toxic fumes hanging thick in the air of his savaged flag bridge. John Carter was a wreck floating through space, a broken vessel trailing great plumes of frozen gas and liquid behind its twisted and battered hull. She had given her all to the fight, struggled with every scrap of might and resolve she and her crew could muster.

Campbell picked up a portable mask and strapped it on his head, breathing deeply. It was hard to position the breather with one arm, but that's all he had. His left arm was useless, broken in several places, and bleeding heavily where a piece of shattered bone had punctured the skin. The stricken appendage throbbed, and any movement at all sent a red hot pain racing up to his shoulder. The lower half of the arm was twisted out at a grotesque angle, a visual manifestation of how badly mangled it was. The medics had rushed to his station when they first arrived, but he'd ordered them to tend to the others first. Many of his people more seriously injured than he was.

The pure air cleared his head almost immediately, and he looked around at the battered wreckage of his command center. The bridge was dimly lit, and only the emergency lights and the most vital workstations were functioning. John Carter was gutted, and there were still fires raging throughout the vastness of her hull. Her exhausted damage control teams worked tire-lessly to save what was left of the ship, and gunners, navigators, stewards - everyone else onboard - had been drafted into the effort. Campbell had ordered Carter's last functioning reactor shut down, for fear the damaged unit might lose containment. The lack of power wasn't helping the repair effort, but Campbell couldn't take the risk. Even a microsecond's failure of the containment field would turn John Carter into a small, short-lived sun.

The admiral had taken tactical control of the ship when Captain Cartwright and most of the bridge crew were killed by a well-placed enemy laser pulse. The shot had blown out a huge section of the hull, and Cartwright and most of his people had been killed instantly, their bodies blasted out into space.

Cartwright almost made it through, Campbell thought sadly. The shot that had killed him was almost the last one fired by Liang's beleaguered flagship. John Carter had followed its prey mercilessly, pounding it again and again. An instant after the blast that had killed Cartwright, Liang's ship was bracketed by four x-ray lasers from John Carter, and the big vessel disap-peared in a maelstrom of nuclear fury.

Campbell's strategy had paid off, despite the horrendous cost. With its commander reduced to his component atoms, the battered enemy fleet broke up and fled, making a run for the warp gate. Conventional strategy would have called for a vigor-ous pursuit, but Campbell knew his fleet had nothing left. They had completed their mission, driven the invaders back, paying a terrible price for the outcome he was sure many would call a victory. He'd ordered all ships to hold their positions and con-centrate on damage control. He'd lost enough people and ships, and now it was time to save what he had left.

Campbell didn't have a complete picture of just how badly his forces had been hurt, but he knew nearly half his ships had been destroyed outright. He was still waiting for casualty figures and final damage reports from most of the others, but he knew the news wouldn't be good. He'd lost a lot of friends in the bat-tle. Some he knew about already, and he was sure there would be others as the reports came in. Thousands of loyal naval crew had been slaughtered, manning their stations to the end. He had his emotional wall up now, and he didn't feel much, but he knew it would hit him hard later, when he finally took off his stars and faced what had happened as a man and not an admiral sworn to duty above all things.

Many of his ships had full or partial losses of power and damage to their com systems. He suspected it would be days before he had a reliable idea of just how badly the fleet had been damaged. He feared for the worst, and he knew it would be a long time before Mars would once again put a credible battle-fleet into space.

He looked around the flag bridge, now serving as John Carter's control center as well. There were broken structural members lying around, including one that had killed two of his staff. There were torn conduits laying twisted on the deck. They were inert now, but before he'd shut down the reactor, they'd been live, dancing around the floor carrying enough voltage to fry a man in an instant. He tried to imagine scenes from around the ship, in areas less protected than the flag bridge. He suspected whole sections had been blown out, vast sections of the ship exposed to space. He knew there were fires raging out of control, damaging intact systems and sucking precious oxygen from inhabited areas of the stricken vessel.

He took a deep breath. His crews had done their duty, they had earned the gratitude of the people of the Confederation with their courage and their fortitude. Whatever the cost, Stark's fleet had been driven back to the warp gate and out of the Sol system.

"Admiral…"

It was Christensen, and the instant he heard her tone he knew something was very wrong. His head snapped around, and he saw her face, and the tears streaming down her cheeks. "What is it, Lia?" His stomach tightened into a knot. Christensen was a hardnosed officer, a veteran not easily upset. Anything that brought tears to her eyes at her post had to be catastrophic.

"We just got a communique from Mars, sir." Her voice was

soft, her words choked with emotion. "The enemy got ships past us somehow. They attacked Mars while we were fighting." She hesitated, sniffling, trying to get the words out. "The Metroplex, Argos, Olympia…they're all gone sir."

Campbell felt as if a frozen hand had clenched his spine. Gone? How was it possible? The battle, the victory his men and women had paid for with their sweat and blood. It had all been pointless. They had failed…they had failed to defend their people.

He imagined the great cities of Mars, their massive domes shattered, their deserted streets as frozen as the lifeless surface of the Red Planet. How many were dead? Had the populations made it to the underground shelters? Or had they died with the cities?

He sat stone still, feeling as if he would vomit at any second. His thoughts were racing, a frantic uncontrollable maelstrom raging in his head. He struggled to focus, to remain in control. He knew what he had to do. He wasn't sure it would help, but it was the only option.

"Lieutenant…" His voice was as firm as he could keep it. He was trying to set the example for Christensen and the rest of his people. They were shocked, devastated, wounded. But Mars still needed them, possibly more than ever. "…I want the reactor restarted immediately. All ships capable of maneuver are to be ready in 30 minutes." He looked around the ruins of the flag bridge, at the stunned faces staring back at him. "We're going home."

"The trail is faint, General. It's extremely difficult to follow." The stress in Jenning's voice was obvious. He was trying not to lose a trail he wasn't even sure existed. He was half convinced they were following nothing at all. The tiny bits of debris, a gram or less in some cases, were far from conclusive evidence that a ship had come this way. Especially a ship whose existence was barely more than a theory to begin with. They'd destroyed one vessel in Mars orbit, but it was pure conjecture that there had been more than one there.

"Stay on it, Captain. This course leads into the asteroid belt." Cain's voice was solid, definitive. There wasn't a doubt in his mind they were following a vessel, and he was equally certain Gavin Stark was aboard.

"It's a perfect place for a secret base. It could be an asteroid in a thinly explored region or even one disguised as a mining base."

Cain's obsession with Stark was driving him to push Jennings hard, but there was another reason too. Cain was no stranger to pain and loss, but he couldn't imagine what Jennings was feeling, having witnessed the devastating attack on his homeworld. In his experience, there was no better way to handle personal pain than diving in and surrendering to duty. Cain was a normal man in many ways, but when he stepped onto a battlefield, he shoved his humanity away, into a deep part of his mind. The warrior had little use for the man and his weaknesses.

"Yes, General."

Jennings had his orders, and those were to do whatever Erik Cain requested. His mind kept drifting back to Mars, wondering how bad the damage had truly been, but he was a warrior, and he would do his duty. He didn't have Cain's ability to bury his pain, but he was a veteran, and it showed. "If they are heading for an asteroid base, we will know soon."

Cain sat down at one of the workstations. He was edgy, jumpy. He'd been up and down 20 times during the short trip from Mars to the asteroid belt. He'd been pursuing Gavin Stark for six grueling months, from one end of occupied space to the other, and for two decades before that, he and his Marines had struggled against the bastard's schemes. He could feel the excitement of bringing the long battle to an end. His hands were shaking with anticipation, and deep inside him, the monster that gave Erik Cain his strength was ready to taste blood.

"General, it appears the enemy vessel is decelerating." The trail of debris was thicker, denser, and Sand Devil's scanners were picking up something that might be a tiny leakage of energy from the stealth vessel.

"Cut all power. Now." Cain's voice was soft, an instinctive reaction to his desire to hide from the enemy's scanners. The Torch wasn't a stealth ship, but on minimal energy output it would be hard to detect at this range. "Scanners on full passive mode."

Cain's nervous energy almost drove him out of his seat again, but he forced himself to stay still. He was watching the scanning report, waiting. The seconds seemed to stretch into an eternity as he sat there staring at the screen. Had he finally found Gavin Stark?

"Stand back, Captain." Vance roared, almost shaking the very foundations of the bunker. "I am going to suit up, and I am going to the surface, and no one is going to stop me." He glared at the Marine officer with eyes that could melt solid plasti-steel. "Do you understand me?"

The officer stood firm. Anyone else would have cringed and obsequiously surrendered to Vance's demands, but the Marine was made of sterner stuff, and he returned the stare with equal resolve. "If you are going out there, sir, I must insist that you take an appropriate escort. I will assemble a reinforced company to go with you."

"A company?" Vance respected the captain, and he realized the officer was only doing his duty to protect him. But he also knew there weren't any Marines to spare right now. The whole planet was in crisis, and he couldn't even guess at how many emergencies were waiting to be addressed. "How about a squad?" He stared at the officer for a few seconds. "Come on, Captain. We both know no one landed on the surface. The enemy did what they intended to do, but this isn't an invasion. A squad is more than enough escort."

The captain nodded grudgingly. "Very well, sir. But you need to wear armor."

Vance was going to argue, but he knew there was no point. The captain was right. He had to wear an enviro-suit anyway, and some kind of radiation shielding as well. He might as well get it all in one with a Marine fighting suit.

"Very well, Captain. If it doesn't take too much time to find me one."

The officer spun around. "Sergeant Givens," he snapped.

"Yes, sir." The Marine stood at attention.

"You are to escort Mr. Vance to the armor bay and assist him in getting into one of the all-purpose suits." The captain's voice was like steel amid the crisis. "You will then assemble a squad and escort him to the surface. You are to stay with him anywhere he chooses to go." His eyes narrowed. "I hold you responsible for his safety. Understood?"

"Yes, Captain. Understood."

The captain turned toward Vance. "If you will go with the Sergeant, sir, he will see to your needs."

"Thank you, Captain." Vance looked over to the waiting non-com. "Lead on, Sergeant."

"Sir!" The Marine nodded and turned around, leading Vance out into the hall toward the armor bay. The corridors were busy, filled with Marine personnel and emergency service workers rushing from one disaster to the next.

Vance still felt sick, and he was struggling to come to terms with the enormity of the catastrophe he had just witnessed. He blamed himself for it all, for letting Gavin Stark get the better of him. If he'd been more careful, considered the situation more deeply, maybe things would have been different. He knew better intellectually. War was war, and if it went on long enough, destruction spread everywhere. But he still couldn't shake the feeling that he'd missed something, been duped by Stark once again. Perhaps he should have suspected Stark's stealth ships, or at least realized the invasion force at Saturn was just a diversion.

Things could be worse, he thought grimly. For all the devastation that had been wrought on the surface, most of the people had been evacuated in time. The original settlers had built underground cities and only years later constructed the great domes on the surface. There were kilometers of semi-abandoned corridors and old dwellings that had sat empty for half a century.

Vance and his predecessors had been extremely cautious, ever fearful of a war with one or more of the Earth Superpowers, and the tunnels were well-stocked with emergency supplies and equipment. The population was far larger than it had been when the subterranean dwellings were last inhabited, but Vance knew they would manage somehow. Most of the people would survive, though standards of living would plummet. Mars' economy was in ruins, and its people would live in overcrowded apartments and depend almost entirely on government aid to survive. Freedom would be lost, at least for a generation or more. He and the council would have to rule like dictators, control every resource the planet still possessed. If they didn't, Martian civilization would never survive.

The domed megafarms had not been damaged, at least. That was something to be thankful for. Stark had clearly been out to destroy Martian industry, not to depopulate the planet. Mars was already dependent on imported food. If the farm domes had been cracked, the situation would have been impossible.

"We're here, sir." The sergeant's voice pulled Vance from his thoughts. "The general-purpose suits are against that wall. The armorer will help you with the adjustments." He gestured across the room. "With your permission, I will go assemble the escort squad."

"Yes, Sergeant. Thank you." Vance walked across the room toward the row of hulking suits lined up in racks against the wall. The fighting suits were an imposing sight, the ultimate weapons of war. The Martian armor was the most advanced of any of the Superpowers, better even than the suits of the Alliance Marine Corps. A trained Marine wore his armor like a second skin, but Vance knew his would be cumbersome and uncomfortable. The Marine suits were customized to be a perfect fit for their wearers, men and women who'd been trained in their use for years. Vance would wear a generic suit, designed for emergency use. Still, he'd be far better protected than he would in an enviro-suit.

"Sir, it is an honor." The Marine armorer stood at attention.

"Relax, Corporal. We've no need for ceremony now." Vance took another look at the hulking suit, it's osmium-iridium armor plating covered with a deep black coating, the material of the programmable camouflage system. "Let's see if we can squeeze me into one of these monsters." He sighed softly. "I need to get to the surface and see what is going on up there."

"Let's get the boys suited up, James." There was grim anticipation in Cain's voice, and an ominous tone that chilled the room around him.

The ship they'd been pursuing had finally landed, and Cain's guess had been right. They touched down on an old asteroid base. A quick scan of the asteroid and its history only increased Cain's confidence. This was Gavin Stark's base, and he was there to oversee the final phase of his plans on Earth. He was sure of it.

"I'm on it, Erik." Teller slipped through the open hatch and headed toward the assembly area. The Torch was a tiny vessel, and he and Cain had only been able to bring a squad with them. It was a very special formation, all veterans, most with service dating back to the Third Frontier War. Every one of them was a volunteer, and they'd left their rank insignia, from sergeant's stripes to colonel's eagles behind. They weren't Marines now. They were hunters. And they were about to begin the final battle with their prey.

Cain stared at the data screen. The asteroid had been one of the first to be mined, back in the days of the old United States and its fledgling space force. It had been worked for more than 50 years before it was finally abandoned, all its easily extractable resources mined out. It had passed from the investment consortium that had developed it to the Alliance Government when all private businesses were nationalized. It had been ignored for decades, a forgotten piece of interplanetary real estate, long ago replaced by richer finds.

Forgotten until Stark found it, Cain thought. The asteroid was perfect for his needs. There would be kilometers of mining tunnels already excavated, making it much easier to build a secure underground base. And it was in a remote section of the asteroid belt, far from the heavily trafficked shipping lanes. A perfect choice, he thought. Just what he expected from Gavin

Stark.

"I'm here, you son of a bitch." Cain was whispering to himself, his voice a barely audible growl. "It's almost time for our last dance." His face was like a marble statue, twisted into a menacing frown. He took a deep breath, staring one last time at the viewscreen displaying the irregularly-shaped asteroid. Then he turned and walked toward the cargo hold.

It was time for the final showdown.

Chapter 15

Dead Man's Ridge
Halfway Between LZ Holm and Weston
Columbia, Eta Cassiopeiae II

"General Tyler, it is a pleasure to meet you. Major Craig Mandrake, Alliance Marines Corps at your service."

Tyler stood in front of the armored Marine, and he allowed himself a rare smile. "It is my pleasure, Major. I can't tell you how relieved I am to see Alliance Marines back on Columbia." He exhaled loudly. "And just in time too. I don't know how much longer we could have held out." Tyler appeared to be an unstoppable force to those around him, a man without weakness, without emotion. But that was a show for the benefit of his people. Inside, he was exhausted to his core, and he doubted he could have held things together much longer.

"Well, we are here, General. Almost the entire Corps." That was technically true, though the Corps was a shadow of its former size and strength. "And we're landing supplies for your people even now. Food, meds, weapons." He stared at Tyler, and he could see through the façade, to the man below. He had an idea of the burden Tyler had been carrying for more than a year, and he had nothing but respect for Columbia's military commander.

"Again, Major, I don't know how to thank you. We have a lot of hungry mouths to feed down here." Tyler was still having trouble convincing himself that after all the time that had passed, help had finally come. He'd been rock solid in front of his soldiers and the civilians, but inside he'd all but given up hope.

"We're just doing our jobs, General. I'm sorry it took so long, but there's been trouble all across occupied space." Mandrake was one of the few Marine officers who hadn't been surprised when he heard there were Columbian forces still holding out. He'd been the liaison to Kara Sander's army on Arcadia, and he'd gotten a good taste of what desperate partisans fighting for their homes could accomplish.

"I've got a reinforced battalion coming down at this LZ to support your forces, General." Mandrake gestured south, toward the landing area. The stubby Liggett landers were still coming in toward the center of the field, with heavier transport sleds setting down on the perimeter. "My people are putting together a com center with an orbital uplink. You're too far south for conventional ground communications with the primary LZ, but fleetcom will patch you through to General Gilson."

Tyler nodded. "I am very anxious to speak with the General." Tyler had recognized a number of names among the Marines landing on Columbia, but there was one famous leatherneck no one had mentioned, a man Tyler had long respected and was anxious to meet. "Is General Cain with the invasion force, Major?"

"I'm afraid not. General Cain is...ah...on another mission." Mandrake paused for a moment, wondering himself where Cain's desperate quest had taken him. He knew why the General had gone, and he suspected he would have done the same thing in Cain's shoes. But many of the Marines landing on Columbia were Cain's people, and they missed their legendary commander. They would do their duty, no one doubted that, but there was a spark missing, part of what had sustained them through their great battles.

"I'm sorry I won't have the chance to meet General Cain. He is quite famous on Columbia. He fought here under General Holm during the Third Frontier War, as a sergeant if you can believe that." Tyler's eyes flashed behind Mandrake, watching as a lander his the ground, and the ten Marines onboard leapt out and formed up in an instant. All the stories he'd heard about the

Marines seemed to be true.

"Yes, General Cain's exploits on Columbia have found their way into Marine lore, along with many of his other battles."

"Is General Holm with the fleet? He is regarded as nothing less than a savior on Columbia. His birthday is a planetwide holiday."

Mandrake felt his stomach clench. He hadn't thought about it before, but of course no one on Columbia could have known. "I'm afraid General Holm is dead." His voice was gentle, touched with his own lingering sadness. "He was killed near the end of the fighting on Armstrong." Murdered, Mandrake thought, by a psychopath after the battle was over.

Tyler stared back for a moment, silent, his face blank with shock. "That is terrible news, Major." His voice was a sliver of what it had been, and he stared down at the ground. "Columbia will always be deeply in the General's debt. He will be sincerely mourned, and he will be remembered on this world as long as men live here."

Mandrake felt a wave of grief coming on, but he pushed it back. There was work to do, and no time to dwell on what couldn't be changed. "General Holm would want us to focus on duty and not on him." He extended an armored hand, gently touching Tyler's shoulder. "Let's see to getting these supplies distributed." He gestured toward the LZ, where large piles of crates were already stacked up, waiting to be moved to wherever they were needed.

"I will organize civilian details at once, so no combat strength is diverted." Tyler was still in shock, but he was forcing himself back to the present situation.

"It would also be helpful if you can share any intel you have on enemy strength and dispositions." Mandrake's voice returned to normal. "I suspect you have considerably more data than we do, and I'm certain General Gilson would find it extremely valuable."

The prospect of hitting the enemy energized Tyler. "Let's go to my command post, Major. We have considerable information, and I'm sure it will be very useful to General Gilson."

The open field was engulfed with great billowing clouds of green steam, spreading out, obscuring the entire plain. The bilious gas was radioactive, and it interfered with most scanning devices. The Shadow Legion soldiers were dug in across the line, but they had never seen a bombardment like this before, and they were uncertain what to expect.

The gas was called Smoke, and only one force used it in combat. Behind its creeping cover, serried ranks of Janissaries formed up for battle, their lines rigid and perfect. They were warriors with as proud and storied a history as the Marines they had fought for so long.

Farooq stood just behind the first wave, wearing the same brown armor as his soldiers. They had been the Caliphate's elite warriors for a century, and they'd faced the Marines in countless battles throughout occupied space. The two forces had hated each other and fought with unparalleled savagery, with no quarter asked or given. But there had been respect as well, and a grudging acceptance by each that the other was the only military formation that could fight them on anything like equal terms.

Things had changed now, and the Janissaries were outcast, proscribed by the Caliph after they had rebelled, angered by an attempted purge of their senior officers. They had fought alongside their old enemies against the legions of the First Imperium, and by the time that war was won, old foes had become new friends. Now they were ready to fight alongside the Marines again, to help them sweep the Shadow Legions from Columbia.

"First Orta, advance." Farooq's voice blared through the com units, and over 1,000 Janissaries advanced as one. They moved swiftly behind the rolling barrage of Smoke, closing the distance to the enemy as quickly as possible.

Farooq stood and watched his vanguard advance into the swirling green mist. "Second Orta, advance." He snapped out the orders, and the next rank of soldiers marched forward in lockstep, following their brethren onto the Smoke-covered battlefield.

"Third Orta, advance." Farooq turned and joined the third

wave, following the marching soldiers into the heavy clouds.

His people were heading for the enemy's most important position, a 2 kilometer section of the line covering the main approach to Weston. If the attack succeeded, the Shadow Legion forces would be split in two, and the Janissaries would control high ground that dominated both flanks.

Farooq stepped into the opaque clouds, moving carefully forward. He knew his lines were slowed by their own camouflage system, but that couldn't be helped. You couldn't even see your feet in a Smoke could, and it wasn't going to do anyone any good taking a nasty fall in armor.

He could hear the enemy fire up ahead. He knew his display was next to useless – the Smoke obscured the Janissaries' scanners as effectively as the enemy's. He wouldn't know how effective the enemy fire had been until his people emerged from the billowing clouds, right on top of the enemy line.

His people were holding their fire as they advanced. It was a standard Janissary tactic. Their method of war tended toward the theatrical and, coupled with their fearsome reputation, it undermined the morale of their enemies. Unless, of course, they were facing Marines, who tended to ignore the scary show and hold firm despite the Janissaries' best mind games. Or worse, when they were fighting a group of clones designed to be copies of the Marines, but conditioned to remove all fear and human weakness.

Still, Farooq had ordered the usual tactics. Firing while they advanced would only give away their positions within the rolling clouds, and that would increase their own casualties far more than any damage they could hope to inflict on the entrenched enemy. The best chance was to close as quickly as possible, and to break the line by sheer force.

The Janissaries had their orders, and Farooq couldn't change them now, even if he wanted to. The Smoke obscured communications as well as scanners. His people would move forward and break the enemy line. Or they would falter and rout. And he knew if his men broke, that would mean that at least half of them were dead already.

He pushed steadily forward. He guessed he was about half-way across the field, which meant his front line was already engaging. His external speakers were picking up heavy fire from farther forward, confirmation that the fight was underway.

He checked his directional display, making sure he wasn't straying too far inside the thick green clouds. Nothing worked in the Smoke except a basic compass, but that was enough for him to keep his bearings. In another minute or so, he guessed, he'd be up on the line, three full ortas of his troops pushed forward into the fight. Then it would be a brutal struggle to see who broke first.

"OK, Marines. It looks like the Janissaries are breaking through." Callahan was crouched behind the edge of the make-shift trench. He'd been following the attack of the Caliphate troops on his display, and he could see they were pushing forward. He could feel them breaking through.

"Prepare to advance." He turned back toward Paine and White, who were both prone beneath the lip of the trench. "I want you guys to stay back when we go in." His eyes panned up and down their battered suits of nearly-ancient powered armor.

"With all due respect, sir, we'd prefer to advance with your forces." There was an edge to White's voice, not resentment exactly, but it was clear he had no intention of cowering in a trench while the Marines went in.

"I mean no disrespect to your fighting abilities, but you are emissaries from General Tyler, and…"

"Don't worry about it, Major. General Tyler knows us, and he'd expect us to be in the front line of any attack." It was Paine this time, and he had the same slightly crazy tone to his voice. Callahan suspected Paine and White were two of Tyler's best soldiers, and probably his worst discipline problems too.

"As you wish, gentlemen." They weren't in Callahan's line of command anyway, so there was no point in arguing when it was clear he wasn't going to get anywhere. "But keep your heads down. I don't want to explain to General Gilson how I got you both killed."

"Fair enough, sir." White nodded. "We'll be careful."

Callahan returned the nod, but he didn't feel much better. He had the distinct impression that caution was something in neither man's skillset.

He glanced back to his display just as his comlink crackled to life. It was Farooq's voice coming through loud and clear. "Major Callahan, Colonel Venti, the enemy is withdrawing from the central position. You may advance when ready." The Caliphate commander sounded exhausted. Callahan wasn't surprised. Farooq had thrown his people at the strongest part of the enemy line, the linchpin of the entire position. It was an unorthodox move, a daring effort to compromise the entire enemy position. It looked like they'd won, but Callahan didn't even want to guess at their losses.

"All right, Marines. These people may be cheap copies of us, but now it's time to show them how the real thing fights. All units forward." He roared the command through the com, doing all he could to rally his Marines and work them into a frenzy. This was the big fight, the most crucial few hours of the entire campaign. If the enemy was driven back, they'd have nowhere to go. The radioactive ruins of Weston lay to the south and the ocean to the north. The enemy could only fall back to the west, but that led into the mountains, a deathtrap for a retreating army.

"Let's go, boys." He shouted back to Paine and White, and then he slammed his helmet shut and moved forward. He ran about 20 meters and dove down behind a tiny fold in the ground, dropping low and firing a few times as he scouted out his next piece of cover. His units were zigzagging forward, half of each platoon covering the rest as it advanced. The long-range fire probably wouldn't cause many casualties, but it would keep the enemy's heads down while the forward group advanced.

The enemy fire was heavy, but Callahan knew their position was already compromised, with the Janissaries directing fire down on their flanks. His people just had to keep up the pressure, driving forward and taking the ground. Then the enemy would be forced back into the rugged foothills behind their lines.

He could see Paine and White advancing off to his right, moving quickly, completely ignoring his instructions to be cautious. He'd already decided the two had to be a major headache for General Tyler, but now he was realizing they were tremendous warriors as well. He could see they knew their way around a battlefield as well as he did. He just hoped their luck didn't run out on his watch.

He surged forward to the next cover, a pile of shattered masonry that had once been a small building. It was about 20 meters ahead, and he took a deep breath and ran for it. The fire was getting heavier as his forces closed on the enemy line, and he could see Marines down now. He dove for the cover of the debris and did a combat roll, finishing in a prone position with his rifle at the ready. He could see the enemy trench line now, just visible though the haze and smoke of the battlefield.

He looked up to the right, to the hills in the background. Farooq's men were there, and as soon as they got set up, they would dominate the ground behind the trenches. If Callahan's Marines could drive the enemy out of their fortifications, Farooq's gunners would massacre them on the retreat.

"Keep moving, Marines!" he yelled into the com. "Take those trenches." He took another breath, hopping over the broken pile of concrete and running forward.

"You have waited for this day, my soldiers. You have bled for it." Tyler stood on a small rise, looking out at the 1,500 troops he still commanded, the last remnants of Columbia's once powerful army. "You have seen our people driven from their homes, forced to live like animals in the wilderness. You have seen the dead in the streets, civilians…children."

He raised his arms in the air. "Well, that ends now!"

The crowd roared, men and women raising their battered rifles into the air and shouting his name. "Tyler!"

"Today we take back our world. Today we begin the final campaign, fighting alongside the Alliance Marines, who have once again come to Columbia to battle an invader." He looked over toward Mandrake and a small cluster of his officers. "It is an honor and a privilege to serve alongside these men and women, to go into battle with such illustrious veterans and heroes."

The shouts of the soldiers were becoming louder, and they cheered wildly every time Tyler mentioned the Marines. It was an angry, excited, screaming mob, ready to march into hell itself to drive the Shadow Legions from their world.

"Now, we will take our vengeance, my soldiers. Now, we will make the invaders pay for every centimeter of our world and every drop of Columbian blood that has been spilled." He waved his arms wildly, working the soldiers into a frenzy. "The orders are attack. Attack, attack, attack. Keep fighting until no enemy lives to breath Columbian air!" He held his own rifle above his head. "Now, to your units, and forward to meet the enemy."

The soldiers shouted his name again and again. "Tyler, Tyler, Tyler…"

"To your units, and may even God forsake our wretched enemy." He stood and watched as the ragged soldiers streamed toward their rally points. He'd reorganized his shrunken army into four battalions, and now he watched his troops forming into those newly-designated groups. They were ready for the fight ahead, as ready as any warriors who had ever lived. He knew they would sustain Columbia's reputation as a world that would not tolerate invaders. Today, the Shadow Legions would curse the day they set foot on Columbian soil.

Tyler stepped down from the hill, walking over toward Mandrake and his command group. "Good luck to all of you." He extended his hand toward the major.

"And to you, General Tyler, and all of your people." He grasped the Columbian dictator's hand. "And may our victory be swift and easy." He knew it would be neither, but it helped him on some level to imagine it was possible.

Mandrake turned back to his officers. "To your posts. We move out in five minutes." The cluster of Marines nodded crisply and trotted off to their units.

The Marine battalion would be spearheading the attack. Less

than half of Tyler's troops were armored, and Mandrake had insisted the exhausted Columbian warriors form up behind his fresh Marines. It had taken some convincing, but Tyler finally agreed.

Mandrake had been impressed by Tyler's strength and tenacity. The Columbian general reminded him of Kara Sanders on Arcadia. The two partisan leaders had the same incredible tenacity, an utter refusal to give up no matter what the odds. Kara had lived through some dark days to see her world liberated, and Mandrake was determined to see Tyler did as well.

His thoughts drifted back to Arcadia. Kara had made quite an impression on him, and he found himself thinking of her often. He scolded himself when she slipped into his mind, pushing the thoughts back. He didn't have time for such nonsense now. She was lightyears away, and he had a job to do. Mandrake was a realist. If the Corps was going to defeat the Shadow Legions, not only on Columbia but everywhere, he knew not many of them would survive. His future was more likely death in battle on some colony world than hearth and home with Kara Sanders. But despite his efforts and all his discipline, she kept creeping back into his thoughts.

"All companies report ready to advance, sir." Lieutenant Grove was his aide, a young officer who'd come up during the struggle with the First Imperium. "And General Tyler reports his forces are also ready."

Mandrake took a deep breath and looked out toward the assembled formations. He turned slowly and stared back at Grove, uttering a single word.

"Attack."

Callahan spun around and fired, his shot taking down an enemy trooper about to fire on one of his people. The battle was a confused mess, both sides swirling in and around the bloodsoaked trenches, the attackers pressing their assault with unwavering fortitude, and the defenders refusing to yield a centimeter.

The fighting was down to blades in places, the hyper-thin

edges of the deadly knives slicing right through armor and the flesh below. The enemy resistance was toughest right around Callahan, which was why he was there. He'd led three assaults up the narrow trench line, trying to break through, but the enemy troopers held on, throwing them back each time. Losses on both sides were enormous, and the forces remained locked in a bloody fight to the death.

The enemy had tried to reinforce the trench line, but Farooq's Janissaries had opened fire on the advancing troops, shattering their formations and sending the survivors retreating in a disordered mess.

Strategy and tactics no longer mattered. The battle was down to guts and determination, and the side who hung on longest, who outlasted the fortitude of their opponents, would have the victory.

Callahan had been in the thick of the fighting since his forces had streamed into the trenches. He knew his people had to see him, and he did everything he could to set the example and strengthen the will of his beleaguered Marines. He had his assault rifle in one arm, and his molecular blade extended on the other. His back was against the wall of the trench, and he had gunned down at least a dozen of the enemy and killed two with his blade.

He could see Paine and White, standing back to back, fighting enemy troops coming at them from two sides. The ancient armor the Columbians wore didn't carry the super-sharp molecular blades, but the two fought on, firing with such deadly accuracy no enemy was able to close to hand to hand range.

Callahan had lost count of his casualties, but he was sure his people had killed more of the enemy than they'd lost. The Shadow Legions troopers weren't easy to distinguish from his own people at first sight. They wore the same armor, carried the same weapons. The suit AIs tracked friend or foe transponders, and they warned a Marine if he was about to fire at a friendly target, but looking at the piles of bodies in the trench, it was hard to see whose they were.

He swung around, firing at a fresh group of enemy soldiers

rushing toward him. He'd taken down two when the third managed to bring his rifle around and fire. Callahan felt the impact on his leg. It wasn't pain, at least not at first. Just a strange realization he'd been hit. The pain came a second later, but it was gone in an instant, as his suit's trauma control system flooded his bloodstream with painkillers and other meds.

"Give me some poppers, Ian." He'd named his AI after his father, who'd also been a Marine. Ian Callahan had died on Tau Ceti III, during the disastrous operation known to history as the Slaughter Pen, and his namesake had accompanied his son into a dozen campaigns.

Callahan felt the amphetamines flowing through his body, counteracting his exhaustion and the effects of the painkillers. He couldn't afford to be groggy now. He leaned back into the trench wall, taking the weight off his stricken leg. The soldier who'd shot him was dead already, killed by his own return fire.

There were enemies coming at him from every direction. He chanced a quick look at his display, glancing up as he fired desperately into the approaching soldiers. He could see it immediately. His people were losing the fight. They had fought with great courage and tenacity, but there were just too many of the enemy. At least half his people were down, and the rest were split up into groups, desperately trying to hold out against the enemy troopers swarming them.

He knew he was almost done too. It wouldn't be long before one of his attackers took him down. He gritted his teeth and kept firing, spraying the area around him with hypervelocity projectiles. If he was going to die here, he was resolved to do it well. To die like a Marine.

He felt another shot, this one on his arm. He sank down to his knees, still firing as yet another round hit him. He could feel the blood pooling inside his armor, and the pain as the medical system tried to force expanding foam into the wounds to stop the blood loss.

This was it. After all his battles, this was where it ended. He tried to clear his head, groaned as he raised his rifle with his good arm. There were at least a dozen enemy soldiers moving toward him, bringing their rifles to bear.

Suddenly, one of his attackers fell. Then another. The rest of them turned quickly, but it did them no good. They went down one after the other, until they were all dead. Callahan wasn't sure what was happening, and he drifted on the edge of consciousness.

"Are you OK, sir?" It was Paine, and he was crouching above him, looking down.

He coughed, trying to clear his throat. He was wounded, but the med system was stabilizing everything and replacing his lost blood with synthetic. He felt another wave of uppers flooding his bloodstream, and his lucidity started returning.

"I'm alright." It was a bit of an overstatement, he thought, but he wasn't dead, and he'd damned sure expected to be by now. "Thanks for the assist."

"Any time, sir." There was a strange sound in Paine's voice, a ferociousness he hadn't heard before. "Any chance to kill these Shadow motherfuckers is worth it. Saving a comrade is just a bonus."

Callahan felt a little chill at Paine's tone. The two Columbian officers had been nothing but friendly with him, but now he started to understand what watching your world occupied, its people brutalized and killed, did to a man. There was a hatred in Paine's voice toward the Shadow Legions more intense than anything he'd ever encountered.

He pulled himself up, propping his back against the edge of the trench. Paine and White may have saved him, but his people were still losing the fight. He was about to order a retreat when he saw shadows looming over the edge of the trench. Dark forms moved up to the lip and leapt in, molecular blades protruding from both arms.

It was the Janissaries. Farooq's men had come around, and they were pouring into the trench from the enemy rear. Callahan let out a wild battlecry, recoiling at the pain of the exertion. The Janissaries had come.

He looked up at Paine, who was hovering over him. "Go," he screamed. "I'll be fine. It's time to finish these bastards!"

Chapter 16

WAS Boyer
High Orbit
Columbia, Eta Cassiopeiae II

Sarah Linden was staring at her workstation trying to focus. She was close to solving the problem, and she knew it. There was something missing, some last piece of the puzzle that had eluded her. She was determined to figure it out, but she was having trouble concentrating. Her thoughts kept drifting down to the surface, to the overloaded field hospitals she knew she should be commanding. It felt wrong to be sitting in her nice, sterile lab while Marines were fighting and dying in the mud and filth of the battlefield. For 20 years she had been there, just behind the lines, waiting to do whatever was necessary to save those men and women. Her field hospitals had been in abandoned buildings, tents, even caves, but everywhere she had gone, Marines who would have died survived their wounds. She understood all the logic and the rationale for why she'd stayed behind, but that didn't make it any easier to accept.

It was one more distraction, adding to the anguish and pain already tearing at her insides as she tried to unravel the mysteries of Anderson-45's conditioning. She knew success might render battles like the one going on now obsolete. The Shadow Legions followed their orders because they were conditioned to do so, not out of any real loyalty to Gavin Stark. If she could break that hold, give the thousands of clones access to the free will she knew existed somewhere within each of them, she could end the war and destroy Stark's bid for power in one stroke.

Her hand slipped into her pocket, her fingers closing gently around something small and cold. Erik Cain had left his Marine ring behind on her table when he left Armstrong in search of Gavin Stark. Some might suggest he hadn't taken it with him for the same reason he'd left his general's stars behind, but Sarah knew him better than anyone, and she understood perfectly. For the first time in all his wars and his desperate battles, Erik didn't expect to come back. He'd left the ring so she would have something of him if he died on his quest.

A military life filled with almost ceaseless combat had left Cain with few personal possessions, and he'd left her the thing he'd had that was most precious to him. She'd known as soon as she came in and saw it laying there. She'd burst into tears then, but now she'd resolved to keep the thing with her at all times, not as a remembrance of a lover she would never see again, but as a sign of her belief he would return to her, as he always had before. She refused to give up, even to consider the possibility that Erik would lose his battle with Stark, that he would die far away from her, on some distant planet or ship. No, she'd sworn to herself. Not after all they'd been through together. It just couldn't end that way.

"Colonel Linden?" It was Alicia Wing, her lab assistant. She was at the doorway, peering cautiously inside. She'd become accustomed to Sarah's frequent moments of introspection, and she tried to respect her privacy. Wing had only met Cain twice, but the general was famous…and besides, everyone in the Corps knew the story of Erik Cain and Sarah Linden.

"Yes, Alicia?" Sarah's voice was strained at first, but she quickly got control of herself. "What is it?"

Wing cleared her throat. She realized from Sarah's expression she'd come at a bad time, but the news she had just couldn't wait. "Colonel, we have the new brainscan results back from Anderson-45."

Linden had been testing a variety of cures on Anderson-45, but she'd been unable to break the conditioning that compelled the clone-soldier to follow orders from his commanders without question. She'd broken the code to issue commands, and she could activate the programming and give him her own orders.

But nothing she tried would make him ignore properly-issued commands. Despite all her efforts, she was still stuck.

She'd ruled out any form of surgery or other physical changes made to Anderson-45's brain, but she kept coming back to that. She'd exhausted every purely behavioral option. There had to be something physical. There was no other answer.

"Did we find anything?" The last scan had been by far the most comprehensive, and it had taken Boyer's AI almost two days to crunch the data.

"Yes!" The excitement in Wing's voice was unmistakable. "I think we may be on the road to solving this."

Sarah stood up abruptly. She pushed aside the worries and sadness and guilt, focusing entirely what Wing had told her. "Let's get it up on the screen." She walked over to the main AI control panel. "Display Anderson-45 brainscan A-11."

"Displaying primary results on main screen, Doctor Linden." Medical AIs all seemed to speak with variations of the same female voice. It was designed to be pleasant and calm, but it also got annoying after hearing too many subtly different versions.

Sarah stared at the screen as a graphic of Anderson-45's DNA moved slowly across. She watched as section after section went by. "What is that?" She paused the display, zooming in on a small area. "This genomic sequence doesn't match the original Anderson DNA." She punched at the keyboard, bringing up a similar graphic on the screen. She zoomed in, staring hard at the two side by side.

She turned toward Wing. "They modified the original Anderson's DNA." It had taken a monumental effort, but Sarah's people had found the records of the original Anderson, a retired Marine Stark's people had kidnapped so they could use his DNA for his series of officer clones. "We need to identify this sequence immediately."

"The AI is already working on it, Colonel. It looks related to brain function." It was clear Wing was sure they'd found what they'd been looking for.

"That would explain why we've been unsuccessful so far."

She was intrigued, but not entirely convinced yet. "If they managed to create some kind of genetic susceptibility to the conditioning, it might defeat any purely psychological effort to deprogram."

Wing nodded. "The AI agrees." The excitement drained from her voice. "But it hasn't developed any proposed method for dealing with the situation."

Sarah stared at the two segments of DNA. "That's the problem. It's one thing to identify the alleles that give some-one brown eyes instead of blue ones and quite another to do anything about the fact that a subject has brown eyes." She felt the frustration building inside her, and she cursed Gavin Stark's thoroughness. "They're hardwired to accept their condition-ing." She was talking to herself as much as to Wing. "So how do we get around that?"

Augustus Garret sat quietly in his quarters, reviewing reports from the surface. He was following the action on the ground, but more out of curiosity than anything else. The land battle was Gilson's turf, and she was more than capable of directing her Marines. If she wanted support from the fleet, she would let him know. And even if she did, he'd still have nothing to do. He'd already ordered his task force commanders to honor any request from General Gilson or one of her deputies.

In truth, Garret was bored. He'd escorted Gilson's trans-ports to Columbia and remained in orbit to protect the Marines on the ground, but he knew they didn't need anything from him. They faced a brutal fight, but it was one Garret could do little to aid.

Garret was sure Stark wasn't going to risk his fleet at Colum-bia, but he also knew he couldn't take the chance. If he pulled out now and Stark's ships did show up, the Marines on the ground would be in deep shit. They'd lose all support and satel-lite com, and they'd be under the guns of the enemy fleet. And Garret knew Stark would be a hell of a lot less cautious about bombarding an Alliance planet than he had been.

No, he was stuck where he was, with nothing to do but won-

der what was going on elsewhere…and listen to the ghosts that
tormented his lonely hours. He knew people wondered at his
stamina and the relentlessness with which he fought his battles,
but the truth would have shocked them all. His hours of tireless effort and the grating tension of command were his most
contented ones. At least his thoughts were occupied, diverted
from the sorrow and remembrance that plagued his idle time.

Garret wondered what he would do if his people managed
to defeat Stark and win the war. Would there really be a lasting
peace? And if there was, could he survive it?

Augustus Garret was the perfect warrior, a legend throughout occupied space, but all that success in battle had come at a
horrendous cost. He knew he had survived too long, given too
many eulogies for lost friends, and the shadows of those who
had died around him loomed large during his hours of solitude.

The AI interrupted his brooding with its gentle chime.
"Admiral Mondragon is here."

"Open the door." Garret straightened himself up, brushing
his wrinkled uniform into some semblance of neatness. "Francisco, thank you for coming so quickly."

"Of course, sir." The heavyset officer walked into the room,
snapping to attention and saluting.

"Have a seat, Francisco." Garret gestured to one of the
other chairs around the small table. "Let's keep this an informal
chat, shall we?"

"Yes, Admiral." Mondragon pulled the chair out and slowly
sat down. "What can I do for you, sir?" Mondragon hadn't
started his career in the Alliance navy. He'd emigrated from
the Europan fleet near the end of the First Imperium War. His
service as part of Garret's combined fleet had opened his eyes
to the Alliance navy's professionalism and skill, in stark contrast
to the Europan fleet, clogged with rampant cronyism and insti-
tutionalized corruption. His Basque heritage gave him no particular love for Europa Federalis, which was more an occupier
of his homeland than a government representative of its people
and their wishes. With Garret's approval, he'd resigned his commission and joined the Alliance navy.

"As you know, Francisco, we are out of communication with the Sol system, most likely because Stark's forces have interdicted the Commnet network somewhere between here and there."

Mondragon nodded. "Yes, sir. I'm inclined to agree with that assessment."

"I doubt Stark will make a naval move against Columbia, not with the whole fleet here. However, I cannot take the risk of leaving the Marine foothold unprotected just in case. Stark could have a ship powered down in the outer system, waiting to warn him in the event the fleet departs." He paused for an instant and added, "Indeed, he almost certainly has pickets out beyond our detection range." He looked across the table at Mondragon.

"Yes, sir. I understand." A short pause. "And agree."

I considered splitting the fleet, leaving part here to cover Columbia and sending the rest to Sol, but I decided against that as well. Without better intelligence on the extent of Stark's fleet, we might be inviting disaster by allowing him to attack a portion of our total force and defeating it in detail." Like the rest of his comrades, Garret had become somewhat paranoid about Stark and what he might do. None of them had ever faced an adversary so brilliant and capable, and it had them all second-guessing every move.

Mondragon nodded, though he thought Garret was being overly conservative. He didn't think Stark could defeat the Alliance's great admiral even if he had only half his ships. And a commander like Camille Harmon or Mike Jacobs could give any attacking force a hell of a fight too.

"But we need to know what is going on back on Earth and in the rest of the Sol system." He paused, his eyes finding Mondragon's. "I'd like to put together a small task group, all fast ships culled from the rest of the fleet units. I want to send it to Sol to see what is going on there, and to take whatever action may be necessary." He took a deep breath. "I want you to command that task group, Francisco, and I'd like you to leave as soon as possible."

Mondragon stared back, a stunned look on his face. "I'd be honored, Admiral."

Garret sighed softly. "Don't be so honored, Francisco. This isn't running an errand. I'm talking about a very dangerous mission. Stark's fleet is out there, but so are the remnants of the other Powers' navies. And we have no idea what they are doing, or even whose orders they are under." His tone was grim. It was clear he didn't like sending any of his people out in a small, vulnerable group. "Anyone you encounter may be an enemy... and probably will be. If you're attacked, you won't have any battleline, just a few light cruisers and fast attack ships."

"I understand, sir." Mondragon knew everything Garret said was true, but he couldn't help but feel a rush of pride that the great admiral was trusting him with a mission of this sort. "Have you designated a roster of ships for the mission?"

Garret nodded. He picked up a small 'pad from the table and ran his finger across. "Here. Twelve light cruisers and 24 attack ships. They're all newer vessels, completely undamaged. They're the fastest ships we've got."

Mondragon nodded. "Thank you again, Admiral Garret. I cannot properly express how much your confidence means to me."

Garret nodded and forced a smile. "Then you best go get ready. I'd like you to leave in 12 hours."

Mondragon stood up abruptly. "Yes, sir!"

Garret rose as well and extended his hand. "Good luck, Francisco. I will have orders out to the ships within the hour, and they will be assembled for you by 2200 fleet time."

"Thank you, sir." He shook Garret's hand and walked quickly through the door.

Garret watched him leave, the false smile fading from his lips. He knew Mondragon would face all kinds of dangers on the way to Sol, if he made it at all. But Garret had to try to make contact with someone - the high command on Earth, Roderick Vance, anyone. He had to know what was going on.

Garret wondered if Mondragon would have been so excited if he knew his beloved admiral didn't think he had more than a 50% chance of reaching Sol and coming back alive. For the thousandth time, Augustus Garret sighed, wondering if any of his ambitious officers realized that the top command was nothing but a curse. The glory was false, a glittering prize that turned to dust in one's hands, and the burden of supreme leadership sapped the soul of anyone who wielded it, leaving nothing but the dried out husk of a man and a uniform covered in pointless medals.

Chapter 17

Cargo Hold
MCS Sand Devil
Just Off Asteroid 175405
Sol System

"I want everyone to be extremely careful. No mistakes."
Cain stood on the edge of Sand Devil's depressurized cargo
hold, gripping a handhold and looking though the open hatch
into space. "This is dangerous, and none of us have been
trained for it."

He was about to lead his small force out of the Martian vessel, through 500 meters of open space to the asteroid's surface.
It was a bold plan. Some would call it crazy, but Cain's companions were the cream of the elite, and they would have jumped
into the sun if he'd ordered it.

Cain had fought once before on an asteroid, though it had
been substantially larger than the one looming beneath him now,
and he'd gotten there through far more conventional means.
He'd been a private then, and he'd only had to follow orders.
Now, he was in charge.

"When you push off, you've got to pay attention. If your
direction is bad, you're screwed. There's no way we can get to
you if you're off-target. You'll end up in deep space." Cain
stared out at the looming bulk of the asteroid. "And don't push
off too hard. This thing's got minimal gravity to worry about,
but you can give yourself a hell of a velocity off the ship with
the macros in your legs." He pointed out the hatch toward the
asteroid. "And that thing's almost solid iron."

The ten Marines with him were the best of the Corps, veterans of dozens of landings and battles. But it was still carelessness that got Marines killed, even experienced ones. Cain didn't really expect any of them to come back from this mission, but if they were going to expend their lives, he wanted it to be chasing down Gavin Stark, not smashing into an asteroid or launching themselves on a slow tour of the solar system.

"All this takes is true aim and a gentle push off." Cain had never operated in space himself, though he'd commanded a Seal team once, and he'd watched them maneuver around the outside of a space station. But Seals had specialized training and suits designed for work in space. The Marine armor could sustain life in the frigid vacuum, but it lacked the positioning jets of the Seal equipment.

Captain Jennings had brought Sand Devil around the opposite side of the asteroid from Stark's base. The small transport ship didn't have the armament to blast the better-base, and Cain had directed him to approach without coming near the facility. He suspected Stark had enough scanners deployed to pick them up, but he was betting the base itself was lightly armed, with no weapons deployed on the opposite end of the asteroid. It wouldn't take much to destroy the fragile Torch, and Cain wasn't about to chance a direct move on the base itself.

"I'll go first." Cain's voice was clear, emotionless. "I want one of you to follow every 30 seconds." He looked around at the cluster of armored Marines standing in the bay, holding on to whatever they could. "I mean 30 full seconds. One of you at a time. Stay calm, and think through everything before you make a move. Understood?"

He got a series of acknowledgements over the com. He nodded once and turned away from his people, looking back out into space. He leaned forward, positioning his feet on the edge of the cargo bay hatch and took a last look ahead, toward the looming bulk of asteroid 175405. He could feel his heart pounding in his ears and the sweat pouring down his neck and covering his hands.

Cain had a reputation for fearlessness, but that was all nonsense. He knew fear very well, and that was just what he was feeling. There was something about space, the endless emptiness waiting to swallow something as small and insignificant as a man. He tried to focus, but images filled his mind, him floating helplessly in the endless blackness, without hope of rescue, arguing with Hector, trying to convince the AI to administer a suicide dose of tranquilizers. He gritted his teeth and forced everything out of his mind. Everything but the task at hand.

He took a deep breath and pushed off gently. He moved slowly, weightlessly through the blackness. He could see the rocky surface ahead, becoming larger as he drew closer. His direction was true; he was going to hit the asteroid. If he hadn't pushed off too hard he would be OK.

It felt like he'd been floating forever, drifting steadily closer but never reaching his destination. He could see the surface closely now, the fine dust covering its iron bulk, the small pebbles strewn across the surface. Then it was upon him. He reached out to cushion the impact. He felt a jarring up his arm, and be bounced off the surface, rising about five meters before coming down again slowly and landing on the gray, dust-covered rock.

He stood up slowly, carefully, looking back up to the ship, no more than a small dot to him now. He knew he was OK, but he checked all his readouts anyway. "I'm down without incident."

"Got you, Erik." It was Teller's voice, and Cain could hear the relief. "Breyer's coming down now." They had agreed that Cain would lead the group down, and Teller would bring up the rear.

Cain looked up, trying to spot Breyer, but he didn't see anything. A man in a charcoal gray suit of armor was hard to spot against the blackness of space. "Hector, activate display."

The AI responded immediately, and the familiar shimmering blue image was projected against the inside of Cain's visor. His eyes went to a small icon, halfway from the ship to the surface. It looked like Breyer was on target to land about half a klick from Cain's position.

He watched as the graphic moved slowly toward the asteroid. Finally, his com unit crackled to life.

"Breyer here. Down without incident."

Cain felt himself exhale loudly. His people could do this. He was starting to believe they could all make it down.

"What the hell is going on here?" Stark was raging, losing control of the fierce temper that was one of his only true emotions.

"Sir, we had a brief contact when your ship approached, but it vanished before we could get any solid data. Now, it appears that an unidentified vessel is positioned on the far side of the asteroid." The officer's voice was shaky. Delivering bad news to Stark was never pleasant, but it was downright dangerous when it smacked of any level of incompetence.

"Destroy the ship." Stark was nearly apoplectic with anger. "Now!"

"Sir, it is outside of the firing arc of our defensive laser batteries."

Stark's fists were clenched tightly. He'd rushed the completion of this base. It had been one of the final projects, and he'd been nearing the end of his stolen resources. The base's primary defense was supposed to be secrecy not weapons, yet here he was with some kind of vessel less than a kilometer away.

"Get me the data from the remote scanners." Stark sat down hard, punching at the keys of his workstation like he was trying to put his fingers through the keyboard. He took one look at the image, and he felt a new wave of anger and frustration. "That is a Martian Torch." His words were dripping with rage. "It is a Martian Intelligence spy vessel." He looked around the small control center. "What is it doing right outside my base?" His voice was menace itself.

There was no answer. The terrified staff just sat quietly, trying not to make eye contact. "I want a platoon with heavy rocket launchers on the surface immediately. That ship is close enough to hit from the ground, and I want it destroyed!"

"Yes, sir." The tactical officer punched a series of keys, sending an alert to the Shadow Legion barracks. He turned back toward Stark and said nervously, "The duty platoon is scrambling now, sir."

"What is that ship doing?" Stark whispered to himself. "How the hell did they follow me here?"

"I'm glad to see you down here in one piece." Cain walked up to Teller and slapped his armored hand on his friend's shoulder. "Everybody made it." It had taken about half an hour to get them all landed and gathered together. The Marines had come down over a 2 kilometer area, but now they were organized and ready to move out. No one had been injured, and all their equipment was undamaged. It was the best Cain could have hoped for.

"That's a ride I hope I never have to take again." Teller turned and looked back at the rest of the Marines. "So, let's go do this. What do you say?"

Cain nodded, a greatly exaggerated gesture in a fighting suit. "All of you remember, your leg servos have enough power to launch you at escape velocity off this rock. And even if you jump a little off the ground, it will take forever for you to come back down. So stay low and shuffle along."

There was a chorus of yessirs on the com. Cain nodded again and started walking cautiously over the hard, dusty surface. It was time to go kill Gavin Stark.

They walked along in single file, following their pre-programmed displays toward the end of the asteroid that housed Stark's base. They moved slowly, carefully, but they still had a few minor issues. Breyer tripped over a small rock and inadvertently leapt into the air. It took half a minute for the asteroid's miniscule gravity to bring him back down to the surface. If he'd have been in a combat situation, he'd have been shot 50 times before he landed.

They'd gone about 4 kilometers when Cain stopped dead. "Bogies up ahead." He crouched down low, sliding over to take cover behind a large rock outcropping. "Spread out. Get some cover, all of you."

The unit sprang into action, the veterans moving swiftly into position to deal with the approaching threat. It was only a few seconds before they were ready, eleven Marines crouched behind good cover and ready for whatever was approaching.

Cain stared at the monitor. He wasn't sure if the enemy soldiers had spotted him yet, but he knew it was only a matter of time. They were carrying several large items, but he couldn't make out what they were.

"Rocket launchers." Hector's voice interrupted Cain's concentration. "H-104 heavy rocket launchers. Almost useless in ground combat in this environment. Most likely intended to target the Sand Devil."

Of course, Cain thought. Stark's people detected the ship, but they didn't have any weapons they could bring to bear on the opposite end of the asteroid. But the ship was close enough for ground troops to hit with rockets. That also explained why they didn't seem aware his people were there. They were focused on the ship, and they'd neglected to scan the surface carefully.

It was an advantage, but a fleeting one. The enemy could detect his people at any second. He didn't have proof they were hostiles, but it seemed inconceivable to him they weren't. "Fire," he yelled into the com, taking aim with his rifle and pulling the trigger.

"Sir, the surface team is reporting they have been engaged by unidentified soldiers."

Stark's head snapped around. Fuck, he thought. That ship somehow landed a ground force. "They are to eradicate the invaders. At once." He felt the frustration almost overcoming him. His final plan was about to unfold, and in 72 hours there would be nothing on Earth but radioactive ruins and stunned, defenseless refugees. And 300,000 of his Shadow Legion soldiers, ready to establish his control over every centimeter of the globe. He couldn't allow anything to interfere. Not now.

"Sound the alarm. All forces are to deploy to repel the invaders."

"Yes, sir." The officer pulled a lever, and the klaxons started sounding.

Stark's mind was racing, trying to analyze the situation. How did they find him? No, he thought, that's not important now. It didn't matter anymore. His base had been compromised. But had the Torch been able to get word back to anyone? Mars was in an uproar, too busy dealing with the consequences of his attack, and his based was surrounded by a jamming field. Still, he needed three more days, and that was a long time if his secrecy was at risk.

"Send another platoon to the surface. And I want those rocket launchers firing. That ship must be destroyed at once."

"Yes, sir."

"And get me video feed from the ground team. Immediately." Stark was trying to restrain his anger, but the rage was obvious in his voice.

"Done, sir."

Stark stared at his workstation's display, watching the scene on the surface. He glanced down at the notation below the picture. The relay was from the senior section leader. That meant the lieutenant and the platoon sergeant were already down. He could see his people were caught out in an open area, taking heavy fire from behind a line of large rock outcroppings. They were being cut down like a row of crops.

He stared at the image, trying to get a good look at the troopers firing at his men. They were well hidden, but finally he got a glimpse, recognizing the armor immediately. The attackers were Marines. What the hell were Alliance Marines doing on his asteroid?

Cain was firing his assault rifle, picking off the enemy soldiers in bunches of 2 or 3. His people had caught Stark's soldiers on a large open stretch of rock, and they were able to gun them down from the relative cover of a line of boulders and outcroppings. It looked like the enemy was platoon strength, but Cain's people had taken half of them down in the initial exchange, and they hadn't lost anyone yet.

He saw a few of the enemy troopers trying to get around the flank, to a rugged area where they would have some cover. "To the right," he said into the com, as he turned his rifle and picked off two of the enemy who had almost made it into cover. "Finish them off."

Up and down the line, his men fired on full auto, wiping out the last of the enemy platoon. "Cease fire." Cain stared out around the rock, looking cautiously over the field. "I think we got them all." He glanced up at his display, and he felt sick. There were eleven small icons displayed, and one of them was flashing red. "Hardy?" In his gut, he knew the lieutenant was dead, but part of him held out hope anyway. "Lieutenant Hardy, report."

Nothing. "James, go check out Hardy." Teller was closer to the stricken lieutenant.

Cain turned back, looking out over the battlefield, now strewn with enemy bodies. He'd never expected to maintain any level of surprise on the operation, but he hadn't been ready for a firefight on the surface either.

"Hardy's dead." It was Teller's voice. "He caught a shot in the head. Must have looked out too far trying to line up a shot."

Lieutenant Hardy had over ten years of combat experience, and his death was a reminder that even veterans could be careless. And one instant of poor judgment, one moment of weakened vigilance, was all it took to get a Marine killed.

"Alright, guys. Let's stay focused." Cain knew he didn't have to remind his veterans, but he did it anyway. The mission came first. It always did.

"Wraith is to launch at once and destroy the enemy vessel." His stealth ships were lightly armed and armored, not really designed for combat. But neither was the Martian Torch. And Stark was fairly certain the enemy vessel had been damaged in the exchange at Mars.

The Martian ship had begun to move away from the asteroid, leaving the Marines on the surface behind. It was a cold, calculated move, one more suited to him than his often overly sentimental enemies. It reminded him of Erik Cain, though he put that thought out of his mind. Cain would be on Columbia, fighting against the Shadow Legion army there, not prowling around the Sol system.

"And I want Spectre prepared to launch on short notice." He'd planned to direct the final phase of the Earth campaign from the base, but if his location was compromised he could easily be attacked before it was completed. He was still trying to analyze the entire sequence of events, to make the soundest choice possible. But if he decided to abandon the base, he wanted his ship ready to go.

"Yes, sir." The officer turned and relayed to order. "Sir, maintenance reports that Spectre is under repair. Her rear stabilizers were loose, sir, and her dampening field had a slight leak." He looked back at the readout. "Engineering says the repairs will be complete in less than an hour."

His head spun around. "Tell them minutes count."

We were trailing debris, he thought angrily. Of course! That's how they followed me here. If Wraith destroyed the enemy vessel before it could get a message back to Mars, perhaps the base location would stay secret. But he couldn't be sure, and it was too close to the endgame to start taking unnecessary chances.

He knew what he had to do. Wraith would destroy the enemy vessel before it could escape the base's jamming field and get a message back to Mars. And his people would wipe out the Marines on the surface. But he still wasn't going to take any needless risks. As soon as Spectre's repairs were finished, he'd take off in the stealth ship and direct the rest of the struggle for Earth from there. It wasn't ideal, but it was better than ending up stuck on the base if the enemy knew he was there.

"I want a report from the surface. Is 2nd Platoon engaged yet?"

Jennings sat on Sand Devil's bridge, staring at the contact on his scope. It was one of Stark's stealth ships. He was sure of that. And it was coming after him.

He turned and looked at his small bridge crew, two other officers besides himself. A Torch wasn't a very big ship and, aside from speed, its capabilities were seriously limited. But Stark's stealth ships were similar, and Jennings suspected the two vessels would be a close match in a straight up fight. Should he button the crew up in the tanks and try to outrun the enemy ship? Or should he stand and fight?

He knew the right answer. He had to get out of the enemy's jamming zone and get word back to Mars – whatever was left of it, at least – about Stark's base. Stark was a war criminal, one now responsible for thousands, if not millions, of deaths on Mars, another toll added to the list of bodies crushed under his heel in his grab for power.

But Jennings was a man, not a machine, and emotion played into his decision. Besides, there was no guarantee he could outrun Stark's ship before it could take Sand Devil out. Fleeing was as dangerous an option as standing and fighting. At least that's what he told himself. Because Ben Jennings wasn't going to run. Not after what Stark and his people had done to Mars.

"All hands to battlestations," he growled. "Prepare to engage enemy vessel."

The bridge crew snapped into action, working feverishly at their stations under the red light of the battlestations lamps.

"Laser batteries one and two report ready, Captain." Lieutenant Verason's voice was firm and thick with resolve. There was no doubt he agreed with the captain's decision. "The enemy is coming around the asteroid. They will be in our field of fire in 45 seconds, sir.

"All weapons, fire as soon you have a target." He knew the enemy captain would give the same orders. In a few more seconds, the two ships would be face to face in each other's firing arcs at point blank range. After that, it wouldn't take more than a few seconds to decide the issue.

Chapter 18

Federal Base Zeta
Western Virginia Region
US Zone, Western Alliance

"Minster Li, I could not agree more that any further deterioration of the international situation must be averted at all costs, but I find it difficult to imagine a scenario under which either of us can trust the other." Warren was sitting in his office – Francis Oliver's until two days before – speaking with the head of C1, the CAC's primary intelligence agency. Li An was a legend in the intelligence community, and her trail of achievements – and bodies – stretched back decades before his own birth.

"Yes, Mr. Warren. I'm afraid therein lies the crux of the matter." Li An spoke flawless English. According to the dossier Warren had hurriedly read, she was completely fluent in the primary language of every Superpower.

"We must decide now, Mr. Warren, you and I, if that is to be the cause of mankind's destruction." Her voice was weak, and Warren was shocked at how frail she sounded. He'd been taught to fear her and respect her abilities since his first day in training, and he had to remind himself he was talking to one of the deadliest and most intelligent spies who'd ever lived. She sounded like a sick old woman. Indeed, she was a sick old woman. But he suspected there was still venom left in the aged viper.

"So what is it, specifically, that you propose, Minister Li?" Warren was determined not to fall for whatever trap she was laying for him, but there was something about her voice that caught his interest. Was it honesty? Did he even remember what that sounded like?

There was a moment of silence on the line. "I propose that we end this disastrous conflict at all costs. We are now teetering on the edge of total destruction, a final confrontation that will obliterate us all. We must decide if anything is more important than avoiding this fate. Is there any territorial ambition worth more than survival?" She paused. "We are surrounded by fools, you and I, by imbeciles driven by greed, by pride. Fools too stupid to think for themselves and make decisions based on rationality."

"Again, Minister Li, I agree in principal with your words, but I do not know exactly what you would have me do." His voice was direct, to the point. In spite of a lifetime of hating and fearing C1's fearsome leader, Warren found himself liking the woman on the com. She sounded so clear, so straightforward. Was that all part of her game, he wondered? Was she trying to gain an edge on him, something that would allow the CAC to win the final victory?

"Mr. Warren, the original purpose of my call was to determine if I can place my trust in you." She took a deep, raspy breath. "Your predecessor, whose manipulations are largely responsible for the current war, was brilliant, but he was not a trustworthy man." She used the past tense, but she wasn't entirely convinced Stark was dead. She couldn't help but think he was out there somewhere, directing events like some master puppeteer. She'd tried to investigate, to pick up his trail, but every lead had been a dead end.

"Gavin Stark was a monster to the core, while I am simply a human being who wears a monster's mask upon occasion." She rasped again, struggling for air. "I believe you and I are made of similar stuff, Mr. Warren, and that you are not the creature your former master was." She paused. "For that reason, I will trust you." She cleared her throat again, throwing herself into a small coughing spasm. "You must excuse me, Mr. Warren. I am not as young and well as I once was."

"I understand, Minister Li. Please continue when you are able." There was an odd tone to Warren's voice. In spite of his suspicions, he wanted to hear what Li had to say.

"My initial plan had been to propose to you that the two of us take actions to seize control of our respective governments, preparatory to a phased reduction in our war footings. This would be followed by a renewed peace and a reaffirmation of the Treaty of Paris." There was a short pause on the line. "I believe however, if my intelligence is correct, that you have already taken control of the Alliance." She paused briefly. "Congratulations on a flawlessly executed operation."

"That is correct, Minister Li. I have accepted the presidency on an interim basis upon the tragic death of President Oliver, pending implementation of a more final succession plan."

"Well said, Mr. Warren." There was something to her tone, a weariness perhaps. Li An had played the game for a long time, and now, near the end of her long life, she craved nothing more than directness. She knew how power worked and how rarely men gave it up voluntarily. Ryan Warren might call himself interim president, but she suspected the only thing that would remove him from office was a well-placed bullet, like the one that had likely ended Oliver's tenure.

"Since you have already completed the first phase of my proposed plan, I suggest the following. Give me 72 hours to complete my own coup here and seize control of the CAC. It is unlikely to surprise you that I have many assets in position, ready to move as soon as I give the order." There was a brief silence. "I have never desired the top position, greatly preferring to remain in my lower profile post at C1. However, there is no remaining option. The fools on the Committee will lead us to disaster unless something is done at once."

"What do you want from me, Minister Li?"

"Nothing. I simply ask that you exert all efforts to restrain further escalation of the conflict for 72 hours. If I am successful, in three days we will take matching steps to deescalate and to pressure our allies to do the same."

Warren was silent. After a few seconds, Li added, "I know it all sounds quite desperate, Mr. Warren, but I would submit to you we are past the point of anything less than desperation."

She gave him a few seconds to think about it then she added, "Consider this if you have lingering doubts." Another pause, and more coughing. "I have already placed my trust in you as a show of good faith. I have no doubt you record all communications on this line. I have willingly stated my proposal to you, and a simple recording of that would be sufficient cause for my immediate execution were you to forward it to anyone on the Committee."

Warren considered her words carefully. He knew she was one of the smartest, most capable women who'd ever lived, and one of the most deceitful when it served her purposes. But she had exposed herself willingly, far more than he had. He couldn't imagine why she would have done that unless she was genuine.

"Why, Minister? Why take such a risk?"

There was a small noise on the com, almost a chuckle. "Because, Mr. Warren, though no doubt most consider me a terrible old woman, and one rotten to the core as well, I am a patriot. I love my nation, and I have no desire to see it buried under radioactive ash. I am old. Very, very old. If I am to leave behind a legacy, let it be this. That I helped us to stop at the brink and not fall into the abyss."

Warren sat quietly for a few seconds. He'd put the headset on determined not to believe anything Li An told him, but now he realized he did. Everything she said made sense, and she was putting herself on the line more than she was asking him to. He didn't want to see the Alliance utterly destroyed any more than she did the CAC. And he had no doubt that was where they were heading.

"Very well, Minister Li. Unless my hand is forced, I will refrain from any escalations for 72 hours. Contact me when you have completed your operation, and we will discuss the scale down of hostilities."

"Thank you, Mr. Warren."

"Thank you, Minister Li." Warren's finger hovered over the disconnect button. "And good luck to you." He cut the line and sat back, realizing he meant it sincerely. He hoped she pulled it off. Maybe she had just saved the world with her call.

"General Emmerich's division is about to enter the Paris suburbs, sir." Potsdorf turned and looked over at Werner. "They are reporting extremely light resistance."

Werner was sitting on a long bench along the inside of a squad transport. His mobile command center had been destroyed, and the armored combat vehicle was the best thing he'd been able to find. "He is to advance into the city, exercising extreme caution. I repeat, extreme caution." Werner twisted uncomfortably, desperately wishing he could scratch himself. The heavy protective gear was almost unbelievably uncomfortable, but there was no choice. There were radiation hotspots and drifting clouds of nerve gas all over the battlefield.

Reports were still coming in, but Werner was sure his armies had suffered casualties in excess of 30% in the bombardments, and possibly as high 60%. Beyond the outright dead and wounded, his forces were hopelessly scattered, thousands of troops roaming the countryside, trying to find their units, or what was left of them.

He had even less idea of the condition of the Europan forces, but anecdotal evidence from the field suggested they were even worse off. Werner had managed to reorganize half a dozen divisions with at least some balance of men, armor, and artillery, though each of them was barley a third its regulation strength. They hadn't run into any formed Europan forces at all, nothing except scattered and disorganized groups. It had taken four days to reach the outskirts of Paris, and now they were on the verge of taking the Europan capital without a major fight.

Werner knew things were bad on the eastern front. The nuclear exchanges there had thrown both armies into disarray, but the RIC had more reserves to send up, and the CEL didn't. In the end it would be simple mathematics. Unless he could force Europa Federalis to surrender in time to move his armies to the east.

He wasn't even sure that would be enough. He still didn't have an accurate report on his remaining strength, and most of the troops still in the field were poorly supplied and exhausted. But he knew it was the only chance, so he pushed his shattered forces forward. To Paris.

The streets were clogged with terrified crowds trying to flee to the west and south. Ravennes didn't know how the word had spread so quickly, but everyone in Paris seemed to know the CEL forces were moving into the city. Gaston Ravennes was the commander of the city guard, what was left of it. The army had drafted replacements from his people three times over the last year, and after the nuclear duel to the east, half of the rest had deserted and run. He had less than 200 men to try and keep order over a city with 3,000,000 terrified, fleeing civilians.

He'd believed the propaganda, the reports the government offices kept issuing, promising that the Europan armies would stop the invaders before they reached the city. He'd believed them until two days before, when he saw the convoys leaving the government district, taking the politicos and their families to relative safety to the west and south.

Now he knew the city was about to fall, and he had no idea how the CEL would treat anyone who stayed behind. The two Powers had been bitter enemies for 150 years, and the fighting had been brutal even before the nuclear exchanges inflicted their devastating losses. He couldn't imagine the CEL troops were in the mood to be gentle with an occupied city.

He'd sent his own family to his relations in Brittany, getting them out just before the mass panic started, but he'd stayed behind, unwilling to abandon what remained of his gendarmes.

He'd heard there were problems in other areas as well. Europa Federalis was a political entity that controlled a dozen previously independent nations, and the consolidation that created the Superpower had not been a gentle one. Many regions had been pushed into the amalgamation by force, and resentment still simmered throughout the provinces. The brutality of the National Police had kept these complaints in the shadows, but now many areas were in open revolt, rising up as the oppressive national government fell deeper into its death throes.

Ravennes turned abruptly, the sound of a fight catching his attention. He ran over, pulling out his com unit and calling for a squad of his men. He reached down toward his pistol, but his hand stopped halfway there. No, he thought, I need to keep things calm, not start shooting people. It was a departure from normal procedure. According to the book, any civilians who became unruly threatened the public good, and they were to be stopped by whatever means necessary. But Ravennes knew in his gut the old ways were gone. The day of the Superpowers was passing and, without truly understanding, Gaston Ravennes had an idea that things would never be the same.

"Please, please, citizens." He ran forward, waving his arms. "Please keep order. You will be able to move more quickly if you simply stay in your place."

"It's one of them!" The cry came from somewhere in the crowd. It was repeated, again and again, coming from all around.

Ravennes suddenly felt a coldness move through his body, a realization that all authority had broken down. He was a symbol of the old regime, his uniform a beacon signaling to all, here is the focus for your rage.

He knew he was in trouble, that the uniform that had for so long almost assured him of obedience now marked him as a target. He thought about drawing the pistol, but there were thousands around him. He might shoot three or four before they took him down, but the violence would only enrage them further.

He moved slowly away, as if pulling back from a wild animal. But it was too late. The shouts grew louder and more violent. The mob was screaming for his blood. He turned and ran, trying to find a place to hide, just as two of his men jogged up to him.

"Run," he cried to them. "The mob is out of control."

The three of them tried to push down the clogged street, past a stream of people unaware of the mob's focus. "Let's get to the precinct building. It's not far." There was desperation in his voice as he pushed his way forward.

He could hear the mob behind him, chasing, shouting to

those closer to him. He felt a punch. Then another. The people in the streets right around them were turning angry, feral, becoming part of the bloodthirsty crowd.

There was a sharp pain in his ribs. Someone had hit him with something, a stick or a rod of some kind. He lost his breath, but he kept pushing forward, desperately trying to escape.

He felt hands grabbing at him, trying to hold him back, but he struggled free and kept going. He saw one of his men go down under the surging mass of people and, a few seconds later, the other. He still drove himself forward, through the pain and fear. He was an animal now, driven by pure instinct, trying to escape any way he could. He pulled out the pistol and started firing, shooting at anyone near him.

A roar rose from the crowd, a merciless sound of pure hatred, as they closed on him from all sides. He fired as quickly as he could. He'd hit five, six, maybe seven of the enraged citizens, but then he felt arms grabbing him from behind.

His body fell hard, slammed into the pavement, and he could feel the pain from dozens of blows. He was surrounded, and the crowd was kicking at him and throwing things, at least a dozen of them right around him, howling for blood.

He tried to roll over, to protect himself anyway he could, but he couldn't move. He coughed, and a huge glob of blood sprayed out of his mouth. The pain was unbearable, and he screamed in agony and rage. He tried to crawl free, but then he just stopped. Everything was quiet now, and the pain was gone. The light became dimmer, and he felt himself fading slowly, until the darkness took him.

Axe waded through the waist-high water, moving as quickly as he could through the ancient, crumbling tunnel. The stolen flashlight was down to the last of its power, shining a dim light that was only useful for about a meter in front of him. "I think we're almost to the Queens side. My people are waiting there."

The girl followed right behind him. She'd been skittish at first, afraid to get too close to him. But he'd taken her to the kitchen and helped her find some food that hadn't spoiled. She was a little waif of a girl, but she'd have given Tank a run for his money packing away the food. He had no idea how long she'd been locked up with nothing to eat, but he knew he wanted to kill whoever had left her there, whoever did what had been done to her.

She'd still shied away from him in the apartment, but when they got down into the streets she recoiled at the surging, violent masses and followed along. He told her she could come with him, but he didn't try to convince her. She didn't answer him, but she trailed behind, staying a few meters back. Now, in the darkness of the flooded, rat-infested tunnels, she was right on his heels.

Axe pushed forward, trying not to think about the century or more of filth in the reeking, black water. He could feel the grade of the tunnel rising, and the water level began to drop off. He'd taken a tunnel into the Protected Zone, and he already felt like he'd walked as far as he had before. He was beginning to get worried he'd taken a wrong turn when he finally saw a faint glow farther ahead. He hurried his pace, anxious to get out into the sunlight.

He walked slowly up toward the light, the water dropping away as the tunnel rose. The entrance was partially covered by a cave in, but there was enough of an opening to squeeze through. He looked around, realizing he had come out through a different tunnel than the one he'd taken in. He climbed up and onto a crumbling concrete platform, turning around and offering his hand to Ellie. She shied away for a second, but then she reached up and took hold, letting him pull her up and into the light.

He turned and looked across the river at the kilometer-high towers of the Protected Zone, getting his bearings. He knew immediately he was too far south. His men were waiting about half a kilometer from where he was standing.

"This way," he said, pointing north. "If you want to come with me and my people, we need to walk this way for a few minutes." He paused, trying to gauge her reaction. "If you want to go off on your own, I won't stop you, but you'll be safer with us." He knew the girl didn't stand a chance by herself, but he was worried if he pushed her too hard she'd run. He still couldn't understand why he cared so much, but he did. He felt rage about the way she'd been treated, and just thinking about it infuriated him. He'd seen plenty of people brutalized, indeed he'd done more than a few terrible things himself - but there was something about Ellie, something that made him want to protect her.

"I will go with you." Her voice was soft, high-pitched with a gentle sadness to it. It was the first time she'd spoken to him.

He smiled, adjusting the heavy bag slung over his shoulder. "Then let's go." He looked up to the north and then east, through the ancient ruins of Queens to the deserted lands beyond. "It's time to leave this place."

Chapter 19

Hill 68
Just West of the Ruins of Weston
Columbia, Eta Cassiopeiae II

"Attention all units. Attention all units. Code Orange." The warning was issued directly from the fleetcom circuit, and it blasted out of every com unit on Columbia, overriding all other messages. Marines, Janissaries, and Columbian soldiers all got the word at once. The enemy had gone nuclear.

General Gilson had expected the move and, after the Janissaries spearheaded the big breakthrough, she'd ordered all units into extended order, deployed to minimize their vulnerability to enhanced weapons. The enemy was losing the battle for Columbia, and she knew they wouldn't go down without causing as much damage as they could. They'd fought to the death everywhere else, and she didn't expect things to be different on Columbia.

She'd moved forward from her HQ, intent on getting a close look at what was going on. Now she was standing on the front lines, looking out from a hill Heath's Marines had just taken. The fight had been a vicious one, with heavy losses on both sides, but Major Callahan's battered 1st Battalion had won the victory. Neither Heath nor Callahan were there to savor the triumph. The major had been seriously wounded in the initial breakthrough. He'd been taken to an aid station, and later evac'd to the hospital ship Boyer.

General Heath had put himself at the head of his dwindling forces and charged through the breech, driving the enemy into the rugged terrain west of the capital. He'd been killed in the final stages of the advance, as his Marines were assaulting the last of the enemy strongpoints. He'd died a hero, on the vanguard of the advance, surrounded by his Marines.

Gilson felt the loss keenly. Heath had been her protégé, much as Cain had been to Holm. He'd served under her for years, and she'd seen his career advance with tremendous pride. She knew he'd only done what he had to do. Marines didn't lead from behind, and casualties were always high, even among senior officers. Heath's name would be added to the considerable roster of Marine generals killed in action. It was a list of heroes, and Rod Heath would join such illustrious company as Elias Holm and Darius Jax.

Gilson felt sick when she first got the word, but it quickly passed, becoming almost like a fact she hadn't considered yet. It was a coldness borne of necessity, of the need to stay strong in the face of any losses. It made her a good commander, she knew that much. But she wasn't all that crazy about herself as a human being. What does it say about someone, she thought, when you can give a friend half a minute of grief and then put him out of your mind, like he'd never existed?

She ducked down below the crest of the hill, heading for a ragged line of trenches Callahan's people had taken before assaulting the hill itself. She knew she'd poked her nose out farther than she should have, and she was lucky she hadn't joined that list of dead generals herself.

She crouched to keep herself low, and she ran, diving head-first into the trench. Code Orange alerts were serious, and they rarely gave much lead time. Her landing was less graceful than befitted her position, but at least she'd gotten into cover in time. Marine fighting suits were tough. With a little help from the terrain, they could protect their wearer even from nearby nuclear explosions. But no armor was going to save a slow Marine who was caught out on open ground too close to a detonation.

She pulled herself partially up, looking around the trench. The rest of Callahan's Marines were sitting prone, heads ducked and waiting for the nuclear blasts or the all clear. She was aware of the casualties suffered by the entire expeditionary force, but she was still shocked to see how few remained from two full battalions. Numbers on a screen were one thing; actually seeing the men and women – and the massive gaps in their ranks – was another. Callahan's people were part of Heath's vanguard, and they'd paid a high price for that honor.

"General Gilson?"

The voice was on her com, but the speaker was crawling up right beside her. She glanced up at her projection, but there was no ID displayed. One look at the man's antique armor told her why.

"Lieutenant Paine?" She'd almost forgotten that she'd allowed the two Columbian officers hook up with Callahan's bunch.

"Yes, sir."

"What are you still doing this far forward?" She was surprised to find the envoy from General Tyler in a trench along the very edge of the front line.

"This is where the fight is, General." It could have been a flippant remark, but it wasn't. Paine was deadly serious.

"Where is Lieutenant White?" She hadn't expected the two envoys to dive headfirst into the fighting when she'd allowed them to hook up with Callahan's people.

"He's down the trench a ways." Paine gestured vaguely off to her right. "Have you heard anything from our people to the south, General?"

She was just about to tell him that Tyler's army was advancing north, supporting Major Mandrake's Marine battalion, but she was interrupted by a bright flash. Her visor blacked out automatically, and an instant later the sound and shockwave hit.

The ground shook like an earthquake, and sections of trench caved in, piles of rock and dirt sliding down like small avalanches. Structural supports were shattered like twigs, and dugouts all along the line collapsed. A few Marines were buried, but they managed to climb out from under the mounds of debris. Men and women ducked away from collapsed sections of trench, seeking better protection from the flying debris and the blasts of radiation they couldn't see but knew were there.

Another flash, more distant this time. Then another. The nukes were coming in.

"Issue the order." Sarah Linden was sitting outside the isolation chamber, watching Anderson-45 through the clear hyperpolycarbonate. He was sitting quietly, wearing only a set of surgical scrubs. There was a Marine standing next to him, fully clad in powered armor. There was padding affixed to his fighting suit, heavy wadding fastened all across the chest and torso.

"Issuing order now, Colonel." Alicia pressed a button on her console. Inside the chamber, the AI spoke, issuing a command to the sitting Anderson-45. It had taken a number of failed attempts to get the procedure down, and after every failure, Sarah had tirelessly reworked the formula. But now she had it figured out. She couldn't stop Anderson-45 from following an order, but she could issue one herself.

They were both expecting what happened, but they were still surprised at the ferocity with which Anderson-45 leapt up from his seat and ran toward the Marine, grabbing a chair as he did and swinging it into the armored form as hard as he could. He ducked to the side, as if he was expecting a return blow. He worked around the back of the Marine, grabbing a piece of the shattered chair and jabbing it at his adversary.

Sarah watched for a second in stunned silence then she yelled, "Issue the stand down order."

Alicia pressed a button on the console, and the AI's voice filled the room again. "Cease combat. Stand down."

Anderson-45 dropped the chair leg and stood at attention, making no hostile move toward the Marine standing less than a meter away.

"Anderson, are you OK?" Sarah leaned over and spoke softly into the microphone.

"Yes, Dr. Linden. I am fine." The Shadow Legion soldier stood where he was, making no move to sit down or renew his attack on the Marine.

She flipped off the microphone. "You see, Alicia. Right

there." She was pointing to Anderson-45's total body scan. "I was right. It piggybacks on the immune system, triggering an automated response, much like the creation of antibodies. Except instead of fighting invading organisms, it suppresses the subject's ability to resist the command." She turned toward her assistant. "It's like turning off free will and replacing it with a compulsion to obey."

Her eyes moved up to the brainscan. "It's all done through involuntary systems. The subject never has any control, not even a conscious knowledge of the effect. He just obeys, without even knowing why."

"You were right, Colonel. We should be able to customize a drug to counteract it. Like an immunosuppressant, but targeted at this specific effect. It would block the compulsion, leaving the subject to decide how to respond. They could still obey, but they would have to choose to do so." She sighed and looked at Sarah. "Considering their level of discipline, it doesn't seem likely they'd simply begin disobeying orders, even if they had the ability to do so."

Sarah took a deep breath. Alicia was right. "They might ignore suicidal orders or something of an extremely brutal nature, much like a Marine would." She looked down at the table. The Marines were extremely disciplined. An order would have to be highly immoral for most of them to disobey. But the Corps had an esprit de corps the Shadow Legions couldn't match. Perhaps the clone soldiers would be more likely to rebel against authority if their conditioning was neutralized. It was worth a try, at least.

"Let's move forward along this line. If we can punch in our parameters, the medical AI should be able to come up with a formula in a few hours." She turned and looked back into the room. Anderson-45 was still standing in place. He'd made no effort to sit or make himself comfortable. Sarah shook her head. The clones had no experience at all exercising free will. If she suddenly gave it to them, the results might be unpredictable.

She turned toward Alicia. "Synthesizing the drug is the least of our worries."

Her assistant looked at her with a quizzical look.

"Even if it works, how do we administer it to thousands of clones buttoned up in armor all across a battlefield?" She sighed. She knew she could beat this problem and help Stark's clones claim their free will as sentient beings. But she was starting to realize it wasn't going to help win the war.

She could treat any prisoners who were captured, but she couldn't think of any way to "weaponize" a cure and use it to disable the enemy in the field. And since, the Shadow Legions didn't surrender, that could mean all her work was for nothing.

Tara Rourke sat at her workstation, staring at the strange memo on her screen. There was no sender listed, and the message was brief, just six words. The ides of March are come.

Her eyes were fixed on the message, and she was unable to turn away. It felt like a bomb had exploded in her head. She wanted to scream, but she sat there silently, under the control of some strange compulsion. She didn't understand, but she couldn't make herself cry for help. Her head pounded, and she felt like she was losing herself, her consciousness slipping away.

She felt her body stand up, but she wasn't controlling it. She tried to force herself to sit, but she couldn't. Her body turned and walked slowly toward the hatch. "I will be back in a few minutes. Greaves, you're in charge while I'm gone." She didn't know where the words had come from.

She could hear her own voice, but she wasn't controlling it. She could see the main hatch ahead of her, but she had no idea what was happening. She felt waves of emotion – anger, fear, frustration. She couldn't make her body stop moving. She couldn't do anything but watch helplessly as something she couldn't see or feel controlled her.

She walked into the corridor and down to the bank of lifts. She waved her hand over the panel, and one of the doors opened. She stepped inside and said, "Level 9."

What was going on, she wondered helplessly, what am I doing? Her quarters were on level 9. Why was she going to her quarters?

She walked slowly down the corridor, her head nodding greetings to crew members as they passed each other. She tried to shout out to them, to plea for their help, but she was locked away, unable to control anything. She watched helplessly as her body walked to her quarters. Her palm pressed against the ID pad, and the door slid open. She could feel the cool glass of the pad on her hand, but she couldn't control her movements.

Her body walked inside and over to a small bank of drawers. She opened the bottom one and reached to the back, pulling out a small box. She recognized it immediately. She'd brought it back from her last leave, almost four years before. She hadn't touched it since, hadn't even thought about it, and now she realized she couldn't remember how she'd gotten it. She thought about it, and as she did, she realized she had almost no memories of that leave. It was all a blur. She remembered arriving on Armstrong, but the next thing she could picture was reporting back for duty two weeks later.

Her hand reached inside the box, pulling out something cold and hard. A small pistol. Her consciousness struggled, trying desperately to regain control of her body, but to no avail. Her hand slipped into her uniform's utility pocket, dropping the gun gently inside.

She turned again and walked toward the door and out into the hallway. She was screaming inside, trying to break out of the strange prison in her mind, but whatever was controlling her was too strong, and all her efforts were in vain.

She saw the bank of lifts ahead, and she felt herself touch the plate again and slip inside one of the cars. "Level 3," she heard herself say.

What is going on? Her thoughts were racing, frantically trying to figure out what was happening to her. Questions swirled in her mind. Why can't I remember that leave? Where am I going? How did I get this pistol?

The lift stopped, and she stepped out onto the deck, walking slowly down the short corridor. There was a door ahead with a Marine guard standing in front of it. Admiral Garret's quarters. What the hell was happening? Why was she going to see Garret with a gun in her pocket? She let out a primal scream, but her mouth remained still, silent.

"I would like to see the admiral if he is available, Corporal." She heard her own words, and she struggled again to take control, to scream to the guard for help. But she was still trapped.

"Yes, Commander." The Marine turned and punched a button to the side of the door, activating the AI. "Commander Rourke is here, and she wishes to see the Admiral."

Rourke still didn't understand what was going on, but she was beginning to panic. She tried again to break out, to control her body, to shout out, but to no avail.

The door opened a few seconds later. "You may enter, Commander." The guard stepped aside.

She tried to hold her body back, but she moved forward anyway, stepping into Garret's quarters. Space was at a huge premium on ships, but a fleet admiral warranted a sizable suite. The main room was about 8 meters long, with a small food station to one side. The space was divided roughly in half, with a living area on one side and a large workspace on the other. Garret sat at the desk, staring at his computer screen with a distant look on his face.

The admiral looked up and smiled. "Hello, Tara. What's up? Is anything wrong?" He stood up slowly and started to walk around the desk.

"No, sir. Nothing is wrong."

She felt her hand slip into her pocket. No, she thought. Please, God, no! She struggled, her mind throwing itself at the strange mental barrier. She focused on her hand, trying to pull it out of her pocket away from the gun, but no amount of effort made a difference.

She tried to shout out a warning, but she couldn't control her mouth either. She could feel her lips pursed lightly together in a faint smile.

"Well what can I do for..." Garret saw the pistol in her hand. "What is this, Tara? What are you..."

The first shot rang out, and Garret fell back over his desk, rolling to the side and falling off. By the time he hit the ground, she'd shot him twice more.

Tara screamed, but not a sound escaped her lips. She was overcome with the horror of what was happening, and she looked distantly through her eyes as her body walked around the desk, extending her arm toward Garret's unmoving form. She struggled and focused on pulling back, but to no avail. She could feel her fingers tightening to fire again, shooting again and again. Then the door slipped open and the Marine guard came running in. His assault rifle was leveled at her, firing.

She felt the impact, more as a piece of information than pain, and her body pitched around, the gun falling from her outstretched hand. She felt another shot, and another, and then she was back to normal, unrestrained and in control of herself. Waves of pain swept through her stricken body.

She held her hands out in front of her, screaming, "No," but the Marine fired again. She felt the impact on her chest, like a sledgehammer, and she fell back, landing next to Garret, her hand falling back into the pool of blood spreading out from the admiral's savaged body.

She heard the shouts of the Marine, his frantic calls for help, but it was all far away, dim and distant as she slid into darkness.

Chapter 20

Bridge
MCS Sand Devil
Just Off Asteroid 175405
Sol System

"Twenty seconds." Lieutenant Verason was counting down in five second increments, staring at his scope, watching as the enemy vessel made its way closer, coming around from behind the asteroid.

"Gunners, check your firing solutions." Jennings sat in the command chair, calmly watching the enemy approaching. The two ships would be nose to nose in a few seconds, and within a minute after that, only one of them would be left. "We're only going to get one chance to win this."

"Fifteen seconds."

Jennings pulled his helmet down over his head, snapping it shut. The other officers on the bridge had already sealed theirs. The emergency suits they all wore would keep them alive if the hull lost its integrity. The slim pressure suits weren't good for extended use in the frigid vacuum of space, but they would give their wearers fifteen minutes or so to get to an escape pod.

"Ten seconds."

Jennings tightened his safety straps and opened the valve on his supplemental oxygen. If the hull was breached, his suit would automatically switch from outside air to the small tank.

"Five seconds."

He took a deep breath and locked his eyes on the screen, watching the small oval move slowly out from behind the gray image of the asteroid. Three, two, one…he counted down the last few seconds in his head.

The lights went out, leaving only the dim red hue of the battlestations lamps to light the bridge. Jennings knew his gunners had fired immediately as the enemy ship came onto their targeting screens, and every spare joule of output from the reactor had been diverted into the laser blasts.

An instant later, the ship shook hard, and damage alarms went off in every compartment. Jennings looked down at his screen, pulling up damage control reports. Sand Devil had been hit. It was bad, but Jennings could tell immediately it could have been worse. His ship was hurt, but she was still in the fight.

"Damage assessment," he snapped to Verason.

"Uncertain, Captain." He was frantically working the scope, but there were intermittent power failures in the system, and he was having trouble getting reliable data. "It looks like we scored at least one solid hit, sir, but the scanners are damaged, and I can't get a solid read.

"Engineering, more power to the guns." Jennings knew it would take about 30 seconds to recharge Sand Devil's lasers, and he was afraid the next shot would be the last.

"Negative, sir. We've already got all non-essential output routed to weapons."

"Cut all systems ten second prior to firing. Including life support." His people had their survival suits. Twenty seconds without vital systems was tolerable. And every joule pumped into to the lasers counted right now.

"Yes, Captain." The engineer's voice was tentative, but Jennings knew he'd obey the command.

"Firing in ten seconds." The chief gunner's voice echoed throughout the ship, just before the com shut down with every other system. Only the battery-powered lamps remained on. Even the workstations went dark.

Jennings counted off the seconds in his head. He knew his gunners were pros, veterans with years of service. But it was still hard sitting in near darkness, counting on someone else's skill to save your life. He was down to three on his countdown when the lights and computers came back on. The extra power had shaved a couple seconds off the recharge time.

"Yes!" It was the junior gunner, and his shout blared from every speaker on the ship. "Got him, sir."

Jennings looked down at his own screen, just as he heard a muffled explosion, and Sand Devil lurched hard and went into a fast roll. His straps held him in place, but it was a rough ride nevertheless. He turned toward Verason, who was frantically working his board. "Let's get that roll stabilized, Lieutenant."

"Working on it, sir."

Jennings could feel the thrust as Verason fired positioning engines along carefully calculated vectors, slowing the ship's vicious spin. He was staring at his screen, trying to focus. The enemy ship was gone. He worked his controls, rewinding the scanner data, trying to see if the vessel had engaged its stealth systems and slipped away.

"Enemy target destroyed, Captain." The chief gunner was on the com, sounding enormously pleased. "It was Fern, sir." The junior gunner had scored a direct hit, ripping through the guts of the stealth ship and starting a fatal chain reaction of secondary explosions. But the dying vessel had gotten off one last blast before its reactor blew, and that shot had sliced into Sand Devil like a power saw.

"All hands to damage control." Jennings and his people had destroyed the enemy vessel. Now they had to save their own ship from the same fate.

"I think I found a way in, Erik." It was Teller, and he was standing over what appeared to be a large metal hatch. It wasn't disguised or camouflaged in any way. "I don't think they expected anybody to come at them from the surface."

Cain walked over slowly. His mind was strangely calm, despite the fact that they'd just fought two platoons of enemy soldiers, and they were about to enter Stark's final stronghold.

He'd lost three more of his people in the last fight. Combat in a vacuum was unforgiving, and even a superficial wound could kill. Marine armor had a sophisticated repair system for patching holes, but it was still difficult to fix a serious breech in the airless void of space. The atmospheric control system increased internal pressure to compensate for the loss, buying time for the system to plug the hole, but if the breach was too big, there was nothing to be done.

Cleves had been killed by shot to the arm. In a normal fight, it wouldn't have even taken him out of the line, but it had come in at an angle, and it tore a large, jagged chunk from the elbow section of his armor. His comrades tried desperately to get a patch on, even after his automated system had failed, but they couldn't reseal his suit. He lasted a little over four minutes, but finally he succumbed.

Cain felt differently than he normally did in combat, seemingly less affected by the loss of his men. He was focused, all his thoughts directed to the final showdown with Gavin Stark, and nothing else mattered. He'd already written the entire expedition off as lost. This was a suicide mission, and he knew it. He'd already mourned his men and made peace with his own fate. All that mattered was killing Stark.

He found it oddly peaceful not to worry about an escape plan. All his thoughts were directed to one goal. His seething anger, the lust for vengeance that had taken control of him – all were aimed at one thing. Killing Gavin Stark.

"Let's blow this thing and go do what we came to do." Cain motioned to Breyer, who was carrying a large container.

The Marine walked up to the entrance and pulled a 25 centimeter sphere from the case. He punched at a tiny set of controls on the small pad attached to the explosive and set it down next to the metal hatch.

"Two minutes," he said as he began moving away, shuffling carefully but quickly toward a line of large rock outcroppings.

Cain and the others mirrored his movements, climbing methodically over the spine of 3-meter high rock wall and crouching down.

"Forty seconds." Hector was counting down every ten seconds.

Cain could feel a strange tingling throughout his body. He'd been chasing Stark for more than half a year, and before that he'd sparred at long distance with the spymaster, back as far as the Third Frontier War. Toward the end of that long conflict, Cain's animosity toward his newly-assigned political officer almost landed him in the brig – or in front of a firing squad. He hadn't realized it at the time, but the dispute with the political officer was one of his first conflicts with Stark. Or that Rafael Samuels, then the Commandant of the Corps, was Stark's creature, a traitor who still hadn't paid the price of his betrayal.

"Thirty seconds."

Now it was time. This would be the final reckoning. He knew the odds would be long, as they always seemed to be. Cain didn't hold out much hope of escaping, but he was determined to kill Stark before he died. Thoughts of his friends and comrades passed through his mind. Sarah, of course, but also Augustus Garret, Isaac Merrick, Cate Gilson. He'd been fortunate to encounter a number of good people in his life, and he was grateful to have known them all. He'd taped a last message to Sarah and left it behind. He hoped he'd managed to express what she meant to him. He knew his death would be hard for her, but she was strong, a Marine.

"Twenty seconds."

He felt another sadness, thinking of other friends lost. Elias Holm had died in his arms, but he hadn't been the first close friend Cain had lost. Most of his original squadmates died in the Third Frontier War, and his oldest friend in the Corps, Will Thompson, had been killed leading the rebellion on Arcadia. Terrence Compton had been trapped behind the Barrier, surrounded by a massive enemy fleet. How long, he wondered, had he and his people survived before they were overwhelmed?

"Ten seconds."

Then there was Jax. If Elias Holm had been like a father to Cain, Jax had been his brother. They met just before the Slaughter Pen, and they'd served together through Holm's famous campaigns at the end of the war. Cain still missed Jax, and his loss was a wound had that had never healed. Sometimes he still expected the massive Marine to walk around the corner and start arguing with him about something stupid. But he was gone, and his death had been Cain's fault. He'd been blinded by relentless rage and arrogance, and the robot warriors of the First Imperium defeated him in their first major battle. Jax had warned Cain, but he hadn't listened. In the end, Jax held the line while Cain brought up reserves to stabilize the position. But the last ditch defense cost Jax his life and, despite years of friends and comrades trying to convince him otherwise, Cain knew it had been his fault.

"Three seconds...two...one."

There was a loud boom, and the ground shook. A spray of shattered rock rained down everywhere, bouncing off the stones and fighting suits alike. Cain slowly looked out from behind his covered position. There was no sign of the hatch at all, just a large crater around the opening. He climbed up and over the rock wall, reminding himself to take it slow and not inadvertently launch himself into space. He shuffled through the rocky debris and looked down into the crater.

There was a passage below, now half covered with dust and debris. They were in.

The control center shook violently, and Stark had to hang on to the armrests to avoid being thrown to the ground. "What the hell was that?" he barked. But he knew already.

"It was an explosive on the surface, sir." The officer was staring into his scope, watching the data stream in. He froze for an instant then he turned toward Stark. "Sir, it appears enemy troops have blasted open one of the surface hatches." There was confusion in his voice, and most of all, fear.

Fucking Marines, he thought to himself, decades of hatred and frustration rising from the depths of his mind. He'd spent years developing the Shadow Legion clones, and he'd kidnapped real retired Marines to use as his models. He had equipped them the same and removed most of their ability to feel fear through conditioning and genetic manipulation. And they still couldn't defeat the Marines without a massive numerical superiority. What was it about those cursed warriors of the Corps? What was their secret?

"All personnel are to move against the intruders at once." He paused. "Anybody who kills one of those Marines stays alive." His voice was thick with frozen anger.

The officers around him stared back silently, intimidated by a threat they knew far too well could have been serious. "Yes, sir." The comm officer answered with as much firmness as he could muster, which was moderate at best.

"And call down to the landing bay. I want Spectre ready for takeoff in fifteen minutes, no excuses."

"Yes, sir."

Stark stared at his workstation, punching the keys to bring up a schematic of the base. For all the facility's recently revealed weaknesses, surveillance was not one of them. Stark liked to know what his people were doing at all times, and every corridor and room was covered by multiple cameras and spy devices.

He zoomed to the area of the breach. There were 7 small red dots moving down a corridor. Seven! He'd sent 80 men to the surface. Perhaps his people had taken out most of the enemy force before they'd gained access. That almost placated his rage until he realized the Martian Torch couldn't carry more than 10 or 20 Marines, not with their full armor and equipment. He hated the Marines with a raging passion, but he could help but admire their ability. He'd repeatedly tried to destroy them, yet here they were, invading his ultra-secret base. There weren't enough of them to prevail, but he was amazed they'd gotten so close.

He could see a series of small black icons moving down a hallway perpendicular to the Marines' corridor. They were his people, closing on the enemy, using the same tracking data he was.

Hopefully, his soldiers would perform better than the unfortunates on the surface. He couldn't imagine he didn't have enough manpower left to overcome 7 Marines. But he wasn't going to take any chances. He punched a long series of codes into his workstation, activating a secret directive known only to him. In 30 minutes, the station's reactor would go critical. And that would be the end of the Marines.

Stark stood up and walked silently from the command center and out into the hall. It was time to get off the station.

"I said I want 3g thrust now. Course 315,270,135." Jennings understood Verason's hesitation, but he'd never been in the habit of repeating his orders, and he wasn't about to start now.

"Yes, sir." The tactical officer acknowledged respectfully, but it was clear he still disagreed with the order.

Jennings didn't like leaving the Marines behind any more than Verason, but he had priorities, and Erik Cain would have been the first to agree. Besides, he wasn't abandoning the Marines. He was just going far enough to escape the station's jamming radius and get word back to Roderick Vance. Then Sand Devil would come back and support the Marines…if any of them were still alive.

"Three gee thrust commencing in five seconds. Three… two…one."

Jennings felt the force hit him, pushing him into his chair with the equivalent of 3 times his body weight. Thrust at 3g was uncomfortable, but it was tolerable, especially for short periods. He would have pushed the engines harder, to 5g or 6g, if he'd thought they'd take it. Sand Devil had won her duel with the enemy vessel, but she was severely wounded herself, and Jennings knew he had to treat her with care.

He knew Vance would want to know where Gavin Stark was, but he was less sure the Martian leader would be able to use that knowledge effectively. The fleet was still out at Saturn, and Jennings hadn't heard any reports on the status of the battle there. He didn't have any updated information on the situation on Mars itself, but he couldn't imagine it was good. The Martian emergency services were very well trained, and he was hopeful most of the population had been saved. But what about the cities they'd been building for over a century? Were they completely lost? Would the next generations of Martians live in holes in the ground, as the original colonists did? Was the civilization they'd created, a source of pride to every Martian, completely gone?

"I want 3g deceleration ready to go in 4 minutes, 30 seconds." In ten minutes they'd be outside Stark's jamming range, sitting at a dead stop. Then he could send his message and get back to the station. He didn't want to miss the final showdown.

Cain crouched down around the corner, his rifle poking just into the corridor. His people had been halfway down the hall when he heard the enemy troopers approaching. He snapped out a quick order, and they'd all gotten back under cover just in time. Getting caught in the open would have been the end of them all.

He'd been exchanging fire with the enemy down at the other end of the hall for a few minutes, ducking around to take well-timed shots just as his opponent was doing. He'd been faster and more accurate so far, and he'd managed to pick off two of the troopers facing him. He guessed one was only wounded, but he'd practically blown the other's head off. He counted that one as a pretty solid KIA.

"This isn't getting it done. We're stuck here, and they've got better intel. They can watch us, but we've got no idea what they've got coming our way." Cain was peering around the corner as he spoke. He took a quick shot and ducked back around, dodging a burst of return fire.

"We can't go down that hallway, Erik, and the other way is a dead end." Teller was standing right behind Cain. The only other way is back up to the surface." He didn't add that the way back was blocked by a pair of massive blast doors that had slammed down to restore pressurization to the inhabited areas of the station.

"No." Cain's voice was like iron. "We're not going back. Gavin Stark is in here somewhere, and we're going to find him." His voice dripped venom. "And we're going to kill him." He turned and looked past Teller. "Elliot, give me one of those charges."

Breyer reached into the container and pulled out another spherical explosive. "This is pretty close quarters for one of these, Erik." He had a doubtful expression on his face, but he handed the globe to Cain.

Cain poked around the corner, spraying the corridor on full auto. Then he reached back and took the explosive from Breyer. He punched five seconds on the timer and threw the sphere down the hallway, ducking back around and waving for his men to hit the ground.

The explosion was almost deafening, and a blast of fire came back down the corridor. An unarmored man would have been killed, or at least injured, but Cain's armored Marines were fine. He waited a few seconds, and he yelled, "Now, follow me."

Cain leapt to his feet and spun around the corner, racing down the blasted corridor, firing on full auto as he did. The walls were blackened and scorched and sections of the ceiling had collapsed. He leapt over the debris and whipped around the far corner, firing wildly as he turned on the enemy position.

He stopped shooting almost immediately. The corridor was shattered, and there were a dozen enemies down. Most of them were dead, but two of them were moving, trying to crawl away down the hall. Cain raised his rifle and riddled them both without hesitation.

"Erik…" Teller's voice expressed his disapproval.

"We don't have time for prisoners, James. We're here to kill Stark. Nothing else matters." Cain's voice was without emotion, nothing there but cold-blooded focus.

He turned and moved down the smoky corridor. "Let's go," he snapped. "It's time to find Stark."

"This is an urgent communique from Captain Jennings aboard Sand Devil to Roderick Vance." Jennings sat in his chair, speaking into the small microphone on his workstation. "I repeat, this is a top priority message for Roderick Vance."

Sand Devil had just cleared the jamming radius from Stark's base, and Jennings had directed all available power to the long range com unit. It would take about 12 minutes for the signal to reach Mars and another 12 for a response to travel all the way back. But Jennings had no intention of staying in place that long. He was going to send the message and get back to the asteroid base as quickly as possible.

"We have followed Gavin Stark to a previously unknown base in the asteroid belt. The Marines landed on the surface and are attempting to find Stark now, but they are heavily outnumbered. We broke away to send this message and will be returning as soon as transmission is complete. I am sending coordinates with this message, and I request any assistance that is available."

He took a deep breath. He doubted Vance had anything to spare, but the chance to destroy Stark was too important to pass by. He wondered if his communique would draw resources away from rescue operations. Would civilians die because of his message?

"Jennings, commanding Sand Devil, out." He turned toward the Verason. "Let's set a course back…"

"New contact, Captain. Bearing 135,180,090." The officer's face was pressed down to his scope. "Make that multiple contacts. Tracking 30+ ships now, sir."

Jennings felt his morale sink. Sand Devil was normally one of the fastest ships in space, but with her battle damage, she wasn't going to outrun anything. He took a deep breath. He knew his ship couldn't battle its way past a lifeboat right now, but he'd be damned if they were going down without a fight.

"Battlestations, Lieutenant."

Chapter 21

Ruins of the Ares Metroplex
Martian Confederation

Vance stared out over the battered buildings of the Ares Metroplex. The city wasn't destroyed, not completely. Many buildings were hardly damaged, and others were battered but clearly repairable. But the enormous dome, built of pure hyper-polycarbonate at an almost incalculable cost, was a total loss. The material was almost indestructible under normal use, but multiple nuclear explosions in close proximity had been too much, and it had collapsed in on itself.

It had fallen completely on one side, with massive shards raining down on the buildings below. Many of the structures in those areas had been flattened by the huge chunks of clear polymer, and most of the others were damaged. The center of the dome had fallen as well, but most of one side still stood, despite the loss of structural integrity, a testament to the strength of the material and the tremendous engineering that had gone into its construction. Mars' low gravity helped as well. Vance doubted any of the dome could have remained standing on Earth.

Vance had always been unemotional, able to focus on the facts of a situation, and push aside anything not pertinent to the matter at hand. He had a reputation for being cold and unfeeling and, while he understood why people had that opinion, it wasn't the truth. Vance was a true patriot, and he loved the Martian Confederation. His calm rationality, coldness to some, had always been used in service of his nation and his people. His rational mind approached things differently than most people, and his ability to remain calm and clear-minded was his most defining characteristic. Those who viewed him as cold were likely to substitute pointless emotion for rational action. They would tell themselves they cared more than a cold fish like Vance, but the Martian spymaster would do more good, and save more of his people, by remaining calm and rational.

Even Vance's legendary self-control was being put to the test now, as he looked out on the gray, broken remains of his city. He was silent now, grateful to be locked up in armor, his reactions hidden from everyone else. A century of work, over a hundred years of constant effort and toil, and it lay before him in ruins. The city was salvageable…possibly. But the dome was a total loss. The remnants still standing defiantly were a hindrance, not an aid. They would have to be taken down, slowly and carefully, and replaced. But replaced with what? Mars was prostrate now. Her industry was half destroyed and the rest lay abandoned under the shattered domes. He had no idea how they would manage the rebuilding. It would be many years before Martians returned to live on the surface and looked up to see the sun and the stars above them once again.

Gavin Stark had his revenge. Vance had destroyed Stark's Dakota base, and now Mars had paid the price. No, he thought to himself, that wasn't completely true. Part of Vance wanted to blame himself for provoking the attack by moving against the Shadow Legions facility on Earth, but he knew that wasn't the case. Stark would have attacked Mars no matter what.

His Shadow Legions would eventually win their war against the Marines, if only by overwhelming them with sheer numbers. But there was no way Stark could defeat Augustus Garret, not if the great admiral could supply and maintain his fleet. Sooner or later he would hunt Stark down, destroy the rest of his ships and strand all his people wherever they were. Stark couldn't win his war and establish his dominion across human space, not while Augustus Garret was still out there with his fleet.

No, he thought, cursing his own foolishness, Stark had to destroy any industry that could support Garret's ships. He realized now that Mars had always been part of Stark's agenda, and he cursed himself for his stupidity in not seeing it sooner. He had fallen for Stark's trap, sending his ships out to Saturn to intercept the enemy fleet and opening the approach to Mars for Stark's stealth vessels. It had been one big deception, and Stark had gotten the better of him. And his people had paid.

At least most of them were still alive. Looking at the wreckage around him, he knew that was more than he could have hoped for, though he didn't know how he and the rest of the council were going to keep them all alive. The covered farms still stood, and they would continue to produce food, but they had never provided more than half the planet's needs, even when the supporting services were functioning 100%. He knew they'd produce less now, possibly not even a third of what it would take to feed the masses of refuges jammed into the overcrowded underground cities.

If Earth slipped into the abyss and the Superpowers finally destroyed each other, he didn't know how the Martian government was going to feed everyone. Brief images of food riots and lotteries to determine who would live flashed through his mind, but he quickly pushed them back. He knew it was a likely future, but it wasn't one he was ready to face now.

At least the orbital fortresses were still manned and operational. Stark's ships had approached through stealth, and Mars' defenses were still strong, even without the fleet. If an enemy tried to launch an attack, they'd have a hell of a fight on their hands.

"Mr. Vance, we have received two high priority communiques addressed to you." The com unit in the armor was loud, reverberating in his helmet, and he recoiled at first.

"From whom?"

"One is from Admiral Campbell, sir."

Vance let out a long sigh. Campbell was alive. That meant some of the fleet, at least, had survived. "What does he report?"

"Admiral Campbell advises that the fleet has suffered crippling losses, with half his vessels destroyed and most of the rest seriously damaged." The communications officer paused. "He reports the enemy fleet suffered catastrophic damage as well, including the destruction of its flagship and the presumed death of Admiral Liang. The surviving ships fled from the battle area, bound for the Centauri warp gate. Admiral Campbell is on his way back to Mars with all his ships capable of making the trip. The most heavily damaged fleet units remained behind and are continuing damage control efforts."

Vance took a deep breath. A victory, although a Pyrrhic one. Still, it was good news. Campbell had done a fine job, though he'd been facing a diversionary force and not the real threat. But that had been Vance's mistake, an intel error, and it took nothing away from the honor due to Campbell and his crews.

At least some portion of the fleet survived, Vance thought. As badly damaged as he suspected most of the fleet units were, he was grateful now for any resources that remained available.

"Who sent the second communique?" Vance looked up to the sky as he spoke, still trying to imagine the shattered wreckage of the Confederation's once powerful navy.

"Captain Jennings, sir. He reports his ship was able to track an enemy contact to a base in the asteroid belt. He believes Gavin Stark is on that base."

Vance felt the adrenalin flow through his body like a wave. If Jennings had managed to find Stark…

"He engaged an enemy vessel and destroyed it, though his ship was badly damaged in the fight. He landed General Cain and his Marines on the asteroid, but he reports they are heavily outnumbered, and he fears they will be overwhelmed and destroyed."

"Did he provide coordinates for this base?"

"Yes, sir."

Vance turned abruptly and waved to his Marine escort, switching the com to the Marine channel. "Let's move, Sergeant, we're going back down to HQ." He started walking toward the bank of lifts. He had to get back to his office. He had to reach Admiral Campbell. Immediately.

"I think we've got the reactor stabilized, sir." Joseph Vandebaran was John Carter's chief engineer. Campbell could hear the exhaustion in his raw voice. They'd had to cut their thrust twice on the trip back to Mars, so Vandebaran could take the reactor offline and repair cracks in the containment system.

Campbell was impressed with the lieutenant commander's skill and tenacity. By all rights, John Carter should be in a scrap heap, or more likely blown to its component atoms. Vandebaran's efforts had kept the battered Martian flagship functioning and, despite the two short interruptions, on a steady course back to Mars.

Campbell sat in his command chair, trying to get a handle on things. He'd gone from the mortal danger of an apocalyptic battle to the restrained joy of a marginal victory - then to the shattering news that his home had been destroyed. Subsequent communiques had updated the initial reports, and Campbell and his people were relieved at the news that casualties had been fairly light, and most of the civilians had successfully withdrawn to the underground shelters. But the thought of Mars' great cities lying cold and deserted under shattered domes was too depressing to think about, at least while he was still responsible for the remnants of the fleet.

"Incoming communication, Admiral." Christensen had been at her station for 36 hours, and her voice was a raspy whisper. "It's from Mr. Vance, sir."

Campbell's head spun around toward the com station. "Patch it through to me here, Lieutenant."

"Yes, sir." She turned back toward her station. "Coming through now."

"Congratulations, Admiral Campbell. We only have patchy information, but it is clear that you performed with your typical skill and bravery and that your people distinguished themselves. Mars thanks you and your brave naval crews."

Campbell could hear the fatigue in Vance's tone too. He couldn't imagine what had been happening on Mars, the stress Vance was under trying to save the civilians in the wake of Stark's devastating attack. As hard a road as he had traveled the past few days, Campbell was grateful he wasn't in Vance's shoes.

He appreciated Vance's words of congratulations and support, but it was difficult to feel any joy after a battle so costly, and his victory, if that's what they were going to call it, was marred by its ultimate futility. They had destroyed enemy ships, possibly even killed Liang, but it had done nothing to protect Mars from attack.

"I cannot begin to understand the pain and fatigue your people are feeling right now or the enormous damage your vessels have suffered." Vance paused briefly. "But I must ask you to undertake another mission, one of the utmost importance. I am transmitting you the coordinates of a secret base located in the asteroid belt. We have excellent intelligence that Gavin Stark himself is present there. You are ordered to destroy the facility and to kill Stark." Vance's voice paused, and when he continued, his voice was thick with emotion. "This is the most important order I have ever issued, Duncan, and I am counting on you and your people to see it done, whatever the cost. The future of Mars, of all mankind may depend on destroying Stark now."

Campbell sat in his chair listening quietly as the message played. He felt the rage inside him beginning to boil, the anger and hatred for Stark taking control. The dead in his fleet, on Mars, even the thousands he himself had killed with his attack on the Dakota base – it was all because of Stark. He wondered if any single man in history had ever caused such massive death and devastation. His fleet was in no condition to undertake another mission, but that didn't matter, not at all. Gavin Stark had to die.

"I know your people are exhausted, and you have suffered terrible losses, but you must undertake this final effort. All of us on Mars are with you in spirit, and you carry the future of your nation with you into this last battle. Good luck to all of you, Duncan. Vance out."

Campbell stared straight ahead, all the doubts and pain gone, at least temporarily. "Lieutenant Christensen, advise Commander Vandebaran that I will need as much power as he can give me." He paused, his hands gripping the armrest of his chair. "And issue an order to all units of the fleet. We are changing course. We have one last battle to fight."

Chapter 22

Paris
French Zone
Europa Federalis

Werner walked down the Champs-Elysees, or what was left of it at least. His troops had not been gentle with Paris or its citizens, despite his orders to refrain from vandalism and looting. The war had been hard, and everyone still in the ranks had lost friends and comrades.

Europa Federalis had started the war, at least if you believed the CEL claims of innocence in the destruction of Marseilles, and as far as the CEL soldiers were concerned, it was time for them to pay the price. Much of the population had already fled by the time Werner's lead elements pushed into the city, and from the looks of things, the mob and the remnants of the gendarmerie had engaged in quite a battle of their own.

The Europan army itself was nowhere to be seen, and the few units still holding the line after the nuclear assault were easily pushed aside. Werner was cautious, still not sure if the enemy was truly prostrate or if they were pulling back to reorder themselves for a counter-attack. He knew that's what he would have done, using the capital to draw in his enemy and then hitting them with a massive assault around the flank.

He wanted to dig in, to fortify the city and consolidate his own meager supplies. But that wasn't an option. The RIC had suffered heavily in the nuclear exchanges on the eastern front, but they hadn't been as fully mobilized as the CEL. Before long they would be marching fresh formations through the shattered and radioactive terrain, and the CEL had nothing to meet them. General Heinsdorf had barely been able to put together two makeshift divisions from his scattered survivors. When fresh Russian-Indian forces arrived, they'd push right through to Neu-Brandenburg, and into the industrial heartland of the CEL. Unless Werner could finish off the Europans and rush his forces to the east.

"Potsdorf, I don't want any of these formations stopping." He knew the men would want to stay in Paris, at least until they'd gotten some rest and worked their way through the most promising loot. The government elites all had plush apartments in the city and expansive estates along the outskirts. But Werner intended to keep his sword in the enemy's back. The coast wasn't far, and pretty soon the enemy would run out of room to retreat. He hoped the high command would offer reasonable terms to entice the Europans to capitulate, but he suspected they would demand a humiliating surrender, even as they faced defeat in the east. And that meant he was going to have to crush every enemy formation remaining in the field, and do it quickly, before the RIC launched another offensive.

"Yes, sir."

The aide's voice broadcast his exhaustion. Werner knew all his men needed rest, but there was no time. He was planning to have two divisions on the road west by morning. He knew that wouldn't be popular with his soldiers, but there was no choice.

"General, we're getting a high priority communication for you." Potsdorf walked over, carrying a headset. "It's General Fritzen at GHQ."

Werner took the headset and put it on. "Werner here, sir."

"Werner, you are to stand firm in and around Paris. You are not to advance west of the city limits." Fritzen's voice was stilted, sour. It was clear he didn't agree with the orders.

"Sir, our best chance to defeat the enemy is now. Every day we give them is more time to round up stragglers and reform their scattered units."

"Save it, Werner. You're wasting your time trying to convince me. I already agree with you. But this is from the top.

Apparently, the Alliance is trying to work on some peace initiative to end all the fighting." Werner could tell his superior didn't think there was a chance in hell anything would come of that. "And we're to stand firm and not make any provocative moves for 72 hours."

"Sir…" Werner sighed softly. Three days was an eternity right now, but he knew there was no point arguing. "Yes, sir. Understood. Werner out."

He turned toward Potsdorf. The aide was waiting with an expectant look on his face. "Well, Major. It looks like we're holding up here for a while. Issue recall orders for the lead divisions. Have them take position in the western suburbs."

Potsdorf looked confused, but one glimpse at Werner's expression was all it took for him to keep it to himself. "Yes, sir," he said and turned to carry out the orders.

"Tank, Buck…" Axe increased his pace as soon as he saw his people standing around the tunnel entrance. The last day had been a difficult one, not only because of danger and hardship, but also because of the way he'd begun to think about things. He'd been an opportunist all his life, willing to do whatever it took to live a life above the squalor of the people around him.

Not the people…his people, he reminded himself. His parents had been Cogs, and he was a Cog too. He was still a survivor, willing to go to extreme measures to ensure the safety of his small band, but he was finding it harder to rationalize some of the violence and brutality. He kept seeing the face of the old man he'd killed, a human being who was now dead because Axe wanted his flashlight. He couldn't justify his action and, for the first time in a long time, he found that he deeply regretted what he had done. He saw the old man's face before his eyes, covered with blood and half submerged in the foul, black water. Just as Axe had left him.

He glanced back at Ellie, who had slowed to a stop at the sight of the other gang members. She eyed them fearfully, suspiciously. Axe had rescued her, taken her from a place where she'd been terribly mistreated. He'd been outraged about what had been done to her, but now he wondered if he was any different than the spoiled, deviant scum who had abused her.

He looked back at the girl. "Ellie, it's all right. These are friends."

She stayed where she was, an unconvinced expression on her face. She looked like she might bolt and run at any second. Axe knew she would die on her own, but he was afraid to be too insistent with her. She'd been through a lot, and she was very skittish. If he was too aggressive, she'd run for sure.

"Axe!" Buck turned and ran over. "We'd just about given up on you. Where'd you come from?" He glanced at the tunnel exit then back in the direction Axe had come from.

"Ended up in the wrong tunnel. Came out about half a kilometer south." He trudged forward a few more meters, extending his arms and embracing his friend. "I'm glad to be back. I got some decent stuff, but there's nothing left for us in New York. The politicos are all gone, escaped or killed by the mobs. And the food is running low. Pretty soon the Cogs will start fighting over what is left." He paused, his head turning slightly to stare across the river at the great towers of Manhattan. "Then they'll probably start eating each other." He couldn't imagine the nightmare developing in the Protected Zone, and he knew things were about to get much worse.

"What'd you find here, my friend?" Buck's voice was mocking, lecherous. He leered at the girl standing tentatively behind Axe. "You brought back something worthwhile, alright.

Axe's eyes darted back to Ellie, and he could see the girl was about to run. He turned to Buck. "That's enough of that." His tone was rugged, threatening. "She's under my protection. Anybody even looks at her funny, and I'll cut him into quivering chunks of meat." He gave Buck a frigid stare. "Understand me?"

Buck's faced flushed red with anger, but it passed as quickly as it had come. Axe had been his leader for years, and he was used to taking his orders. "Yeah, boss. I understand." There was a touch of bitterness in his voice, but he turned away from Ellie and stood next to the others.

"We're going to head back east. It's too dangerous in Manhattan, and everything is running out there anyway. Things are going to get a lot worse there and, eventually, some of the mob is going find its way out here." He glanced back across the river for a few seconds then turned away. "And we don't want to be anywhere near here when they do."

He turned back to Ellie. "We're going east, a long way from the city, from all that violence and insanity." His voice was soft, gentle. "Will you come with us?"

She stood silently, looking at the ground for a few seconds before she returned his gaze. "I'll come," she said meekly, her eyes darting nervously toward Buck and the others for an instant.

"Come," Axe said. "No one will hurt you. You have my word." He smiled and turned toward the shattered remnants of the road. "Now let's all get the hell out of here."

Li An sat in her office, reviewing her preparations with the thoroughness that had made her one of the most effective intelligence operatives on Earth. Long before she'd risen to command C1, she'd been a field agent with an unmatched record of success. She'd been willing to do anything to get the job done. Murder, bribery, blackmail, sex – with men or women – whatever it took. Now, she felt as if those days had returned, and she was once again prepared to do whatever was necessary. The stakes were higher than ever, perhaps even life or death, not just for her this time, but for the entire CAC. For the world itself.

She had her agents in place. Everything was prepared, waiting for her to give the word. She'd put the operation off for as long as she could, but now she realized there was no choice. She'd made her judgment on Ryan Warren. He seemed reasonable, far preferable to Gavin Stark. She didn't trust him, certainly. Li An didn't trust anyone. But Ryan seemed to understand as she did that there was no chance for victory in this war, only survival or death. She thought she could work with him, and if they controlled the CAC and the Alliance, they just may be able to pull mankind back from the brink.

She went over the status of her various teams in her head,

reviewing each aspect of the operation one last time. In her younger days, she hadn't been terribly bothered by how much blood got spilled as long as the objective was accomplished. The older Li An still put success first, but in recent years she had tried to keep the brutality down to the minimum required. She didn't know if she was just too tired for so much blood or if her own impending mortality had affected her in some way.

There was no room for restraint now. She had one chance, and only one, to eliminate all potential resistance. Anyone who might oppose her grab for power had to die in the initial onslaught, along with all of their guards and retainers. When she gave the final word to go, thousands of people would be killed, the entire head of the CAC lopped off in one clean stroke. There would be no one left to strike back. No one to challenge her total power.

She leaned back and closed her eyes for a few seconds. She was tired, more fatigued than she had ever been. Was it possible, she wondered, to live too long?

She'd dueled with Jack Dutton for decades. Stark's mentor had been one of her main adversaries for most of her life. She'd gotten the better of him sometimes, as he had of her. They'd even worked together a long time back, when the CAC and the Alliance had found themselves with common cause for a brief period. The two made a good, if short-lived team, and they'd taken the opportunity to have a torrid affair as well, one she still recalled with a degree of fondness, despite the fact that they'd been enemies for three-quarters of a century afterward. But Dutton was dead now. He'd had the good sense to let go of life before the world fell completely apart around him. She'd shed a rare tear when she'd been told of his death, and she drank to his memory – and wondered if he'd still had the scar from those bite marks she'd given him 75 years before.

"Were you the smart one, Jack?" She spoke silently to herself, as she sat in the dark, featureless office. "Are you better off dead, out of the game? Or am I, to still be here, with one chance to keep everything from falling apart?" She turned for the thousandth time, but the view still wasn't there. Her office in Wan Chai had a breathtaking vista of the Hong Kong sky-line, but now she was in the Combine's command bunker, deep beneath the South China Sea.

Well, she thought to herself. There is no point in sitting here and wishing for different times. Li An had always been a woman of action, not one prone to sitting and hoping for things to get better on their own. She punched a few keys, bringing up a login screen. She entered her password, 12 keystrokes followed by a second 8-digit code. She was about to give the command word when her screen went dark.

She reached over and tapped the edge of her monitor. Nothing. She leaned down and checked the connections. Everything looked fine. What the hell, she thought, as the door slid open, and her assistant stepped in.

"Daiyu, my workstation is malfunctioning."

"No, Minister Li, it is not." Daiyu stood just inside the door-way, wearing a form fitting silk dress. She was beautiful, even by the standards of Li's young protégés. There was a gun in her hand. "I have disconnected you from the net."

"You did what?" There was a rush of anger in Li's voice, and she pulled her head up from under the desk, freezing when she saw the gun.

"Please, Minister Li, put your hands on the desk. I believe I have removed most of your hidden weapons, but I do not wish to take the chance that there is one of which I am not aware." Her tone was silky smooth, just a touch of self-satisfaction slip-ping through her otherwise firm control.

"Why, Daiyu? Why betray me? And your country?" There was resignation in Li's voice. She'd escaped from 100 close calls in her long career, but she knew this time she was cornered. For the first time in her long life, she felt herself surrendering, giving in to failure.

"It is nothing personal, Minister Li. And as for my country, I came from the gutters of Shanghai. My mother was a maid for a mid-level government official. She cleaned his home, and when he wished, he used her like a whore. When he got tired of her, he cast her out, and we lived on the streets until she died. I joined C1 because it was a chance to improve my life, not out of any patriotic foolishness. I couldn't care less who wins this war. I am in this for my own gain.

"Who was it? Did Ryan Warren get to you?" Could she have been that wrong about Warren?

"No, Minister Li, not Ryan Warren."

Li's cloudy eyes brightened with realization. "Gavin Stark?"

"Very good, Minister. If one is going to make a bold move, it is best advised to choose the most capable ally, wouldn't you agree?"

So Stark was alive after all. He'd played them all for fools, and she didn't have a doubt that everything that had happened was his work. He had defeated her in the end, completely and utterly. Only now, as she faced her own death, did she truly recognize the genius of the man she had struggled against for so many years.

Her plans were in ruins. Indeed, she had even aided Stark. When Ryan Warren didn't hear from her, he would assume she had betrayed him somehow. Instead of pulling the Powers back from the brink, her actions would push them closer to the abyss. She felt despair and she looked back at the utter futility of her life. She wanted only death now, to join Dutton and leave the world to its destruction.

"He has promised me a position in his new empire." Daiyu stared at her former boss, gloating with satisfaction. "Preventing you and Ryan Warren from interfering with his plans will earn me great rewards, and a high place in the new order.

Li An stared back with pity in her eyes. "You poor stupid girl. You know nothing about Gavin Stark."

"That will be enough. I am sorry, Minister Li, but I have my instructions, and time is limited. She aimed the pistol at Li An's head and fired.

The ancient leader of C1 was slammed back hard, her chair tilting over and dropping her body to the ground with a soft thud. Daiyu stepped around the desk, looking down at the legendary head of C1. Li An was dead, that was obvious, but she emptied the pistol into her just to be sure.

She pulled a small data chip from her pocket, placing it on Li An's desk. It was evidence that would lead to Ryan Warren. When the Alliance was blamed for assassinating the head of C1 in the middle of the CAC's secure wartime facility, all restraint would be fall away. The stage would be set for Armageddon.

She turned and left the room, pausing to take hold of the doorframe. She was suddenly lightheaded. She took a breath and walked back toward her desk, making it about halfway before she fell to the ground, gasping for her last breath.

Gavin Stark did not leave loose ends.

Chapter 23

Control Center
MCS Sand Devil
120,000 kilometers from Asteroid 175405
Sol System

Jennings stared at the main display, watching the enemy fleet approaching, a cluster of 36 small icons moving directly toward his small ship. They had altered their vector to intercept Sand Devil, so there was no doubt his ship had been detected. Jennings knew he was staring at his death approaching. The damaged Torch couldn't fight off one vessel in its current condition, much less a whole fleet.

Verason had tried to get ship identification data on the fleet, or at least basic mass estimates, but the scanners were too damaged for anything like that. His barely functioning sensor suite told him 36 ships were approaching, but that was all. Not that it mattered. The Martian fleet was still out at Saturn, and he couldn't imagine Admiral Campbell could have made it back this far so quickly. Even if he could have, he had no reason to come this way. The Alliance forces under Admiral Garret were at Columbia supporting the Marine invasion there. The rest of the Superpowers' fleets were fighting each other out in the colonies, or they were in open revolt. He couldn't think of a scenario where these inbound ships were friendlies.

Jennings sighed softly. Eliminate all other possibilities, he thought, and you must be left with the truth. Those ships had to be Stark's, and that meant Sand Devil would be destroyed the instant they came into firing range. Then the armada would move to Stark's base, and Cain's people would die too. If they weren't already dead. And the chance to eliminate Stark before he achieved his final victory would be lost.

The Martian captain had faced death before and escaped, but he couldn't come up with a way to get his people out of this. Surrender was unthinkable, even if the enemy would accept it, and his ship was too battered to flee. He and his crew would fight, but he knew that was almost laughable. He doubted they would even damage an enemy vessel before they were blown to atoms.

"Resend the communication to Mars." They'd already transmitted, but Jennings wanted to be sure it got through. Roderick Vance had to know about Stark's base, especially if Sand Devil was destroyed and Cain's Marines overwhelmed. If they got the word to Mars, at least his people wouldn't die in vain. Perhaps Vance would find some way to strike at Stark.

"Resending, Captain." Verason sounded as resigned to his fate as Jennings. But there was no panic, no loss of focus. If he had to die, he was resolved to die well. "Message successfully transmitted, sir."

"Very well, Lieutenant." He was proud of his people, and he felt fortunate to command such dedicated warriors. He stared ahead as the wave of small ovals moving steadily across the display. "Now, please bring us to battlestations." Laughable or not, he was resolved his ship was not going down without a fight.

Cain spun around the corner, firing half a dozen bursts into the open air. The enemy had pulled back, leaving the corridor undefended. Two bodies were lying on the ground, victims of Cain's deadly shooting during the firefight, but no live enemy soldiers remained.

The Marines had fought three different enemy groups since entering the base, and they'd used one of their portable mines on the third, killing half a dozen enemy soldiers and blowing apart another section of Gavin Stark's base. The explosives had come in handy, but they only had one left, and Cain had it marked for the door of the control center.

Their navigation had been all guess work to this point, and Cain was following pure instinct now. If he was right, they were near the control center, and that seemed as likely a place to find Stark as any. He was anxious, and the closeness of his goal was like a weight around his neck. He reminded himself Stark had control of the base's surveillance systems. The Marines had destroyed every camera they found, but he doubted they'd gotten them all. Even if they had, the trail of destroyed surveillance systems pinpointed their location nearly as well as any camera. Stark wouldn't be waiting quietly to serve himself up to Cain's Marines; he would be ready. Cain wasn't sure what his adversary would do, but he was sure it would be something unexpected. Don't underestimate Stark, he reminded himself.

Breyer pulled up behind Cain, his rifle at the ready. There were hatches all along the corridor, and enemy soldiers could come out of any of them. "I'm running low on ammo, Erik. I've got this cartridge and two more."

"Me too." Halligan was right behind Breyer.

Cain knew they were all low on ammo. He was worse off than any of them, down to his last cartridge. But that meant nothing to him. When he was out of bullets, he'd use his blade. Or his armored fist. Or he'd jump out of his armor naked as the day he was born and rip the bastards apart with his bare hands. But Gavin Stark was not going to escape him.

"Let's make them count, boys." Cain ejected his empty magazine, slamming the final cartridge in place. "That looks like it might be the command center." He pointed down the corridor, to a set of double doors. He cranked up his magnification until he could read the small letters just above the access plate. Control Center. Well, Cain thought, that's an amusing breach of security for Stark, labeling the control room for us.

"OK, let's have that last mine." Cain reached behind him grabbing the heavy sphere as Breyer handed it up to him. He punched in a series of numbers, activating the explosive and setting it for ten seconds.

He turned and looked back at his five surviving companions. "You guys all ready?" They all nodded. "We've come a long way to get here, gentlemen. If this is to be our final fight, I say we make it a worthy one. Gavin Stark should have died years ago, and now we five will make certain he does. Killing the bastard is our only priority. Remember that. If Stark dies, we have won, and we will have saved our friends and comrades from death and slavery." He paused, his head panning slowly across the small group.

Cain extended his armored hand toward the Marines. "If we are marked to die here, I say for myself, I could not hope to fall in better company or alongside such brave and noble warriors." He took a deep breath. "The Corps forever."

"The Corps forever," they responded in unison, extending their own hands and laying them atop Cain's.

He turned and took another breath, pushing back the wave of emotions. He leaned around the corner, activating the explosive and sliding it down the hallway. He pulled back, waiting for the explosion. "I love you, Sarah," he whispered softly to himself.

The corridor erupted as the mine detonated, and Cain leapt to his feet. "Now, men. Follow me." And he ran around the corner, through the flames and billowing smoke.

"Attention unidentified vessel, this is Admiral Francisco Mondragon, Alliance navy, on the flagship Wellington. Do not make any hostile moves or attempt to flee, or you will be fired upon." His voice was heavy with suspicion.

Jennings heard the words blaring through the com, but it took a few seconds for realization to set in. He felt excitement flooding through his body as he stared at the phalanx of approaching vessels, now identified not as enemies, but as Alliance allies.

"Please identify yourself at once." Mondragon was impatient, demanding.

He looked over at Verason. "If you'd be so kind as to open a channel, Lieutenant." He couldn't hold back the smile forcing its way onto his lips. "Greetings, Admiral Mondragon. This is Captain Ben Jennings, commanding the Martian Confederation

Ship Sand Devil." He paused for an instant and added, "We are very glad to see you."

"Please accept my greetings, Captain." Mondragon's voice relaxed, shifting to a much friendlier tone. "We have just come from Columbia at Admiral Garret's orders to assemble a status report and to take any actions we deem prudent. Can you update us on recent events?"

Jennings exhaled hard. "Admiral, we have a lot of news to pass on, and I'm afraid almost none of it is good." He paused. "But you have come upon us in the middle of an urgent mission. We have discovered Gavin Stark's base in the asteroid belt, and we just landed General Cain and his people there, less than 100,000 kilometers from this position." Another pause, briefer than the last. "I'm afraid they are heavily outnumbered and probably in need of assistance, Admiral. We were about to return after transmitting a status report to Martian GHQ." The excitement slowly slipped away from his tone. "I'm afraid the general and his men are in a desperate situation. They may even be dead already."

"Lead us there, Captain." There was cold determination in Mondragon's voice. "We have a Marine contingent aboard, and I am certain they are ready to assist General Cain."

"My pleasure, Admiral Mondragon." He turned and motioned toward Verason. "We are transmitting coordinates to your fleet now." He hesitated, glancing over as his officer sent the data. "We have considerable battle damage, Admiral, and we are unable to accelerate at greater than 3g. I suggest that your lead vessels proceed immediately to the base as quickly as possible. Before it's too late."

"We're on the way, Captain." Mondragon's voice was like tempered steel. "Follow at your best speed." The Alliance admiral cut the line, and a few seconds later, the fleet began accelerating at 7g, heading directly for Stark's base.

"Let's make our best speed to follow, Lieutenant." Jennings leaned back and sighed. "We have an appointment with Gavin Stark."

Cain leapt through the shattered wreckage of the door, his eyes scanning the room, assessing any threats. There were half a dozen officers at their posts, but no armored troops. And no Gavin Stark.

"Ghomes, keep watch on the door."

"Yes, sir." Ghomes' response was as sharp as a razor.

Cain glanced quickly back, watching as the veteran sergeant moved to the entry, cautiously peering out into the corridor.

"All clear, General." Ghomes stood where he was, looking out into the hallway, his rifle at the ready.

Cain walked over toward one of the control room officers. He towered over the unarmored man, looking down like some monster from a children's nightmare. "Where is Gavin Stark?" she asked, his voice calm.

"You are mistaken. He is not…"

The officer's head exploded as Cain fired his assault rifle from 20 centimeters. "Wrong answer," he roared, his amplified voice almost shaking the structural supports. He walked down to the next station and aimed his gun at the terrified officer sitting there.

"Where is he? I know he was here, so where did he go?" Cain's gloved finger was poised on the trigger of his assault rifle.

Teller was standing behind Cain, watching uncomfortably. He understood his friend's motivations, but he couldn't understand how a man as loyal and honorable as Cain could become such a cold-blooded killer. When Cain said he would let nothing stand in his way, Teller understood he meant it. Literally. To Erik Cain, nothing was important enough to stand in the way of killing Gavin Stark, no covenant of civilized behavior, no hint of mercy.

The terrified officer glanced over at one of his comrades. He was shaking, and sweat was beading up along top of his head.

"Don't look at him." Cain spoke softly again, the raging anger of his outburst seemingly gone. "He's not the one who's going to blow your brains all over your workstation. That's me." He paused for a few seconds. "Now, I'm going to ask you one more time…and only one. Where is Gavin Stark?" Cain knew all of Stark's people were scared to death of their psychopathic master, and he'd be damned if he was going to allow them to be less terrified of him.

The miserable officer squirmed in his chair, his body shifting away from Cain's armored bulk. "He…"

"He what?" Cain moved the rifle up, holding it right in front of the officer's face. "Spit it out. You may make a live prisoner yet."

"He…he left." The prisoner glanced back to his comrade, who was shaking his head.

Cain whipped the rifle around and fired, his hypervelocity round tearing the target's head right off. "I told you not to look at him. Now tell me where Stark is." There was impatience in his tone now, and a deep coldness. A dark spirit of vengeance controlled Cain now, the man totally submerged, hidden beneath the elemental fury that was driving him.

"Down to the landing bay. The base was compromised, so he is leaving."

Cain spun around. "Let's go. We've got to stop him." He turned back, his eyes panning over the remaining officers sitting in their chairs. His arm began to move slowly.

Teller knew what Cain was going to do. "Erik, you take Elliott and Jack with you and chase after Stark. Douglas and I will handle the prisoners and see if we can shut down the launch sequence from here." He took a deep breath and held it. He wasn't going to have a dispute with Cain, but if he could save the prisoners' lives he would. He wasn't even sure why. He knew they were all cutthroats and murderers. Maybe he'd just seen enough senseless death.

Cain nodded. "Good. See what you can do. Anything to keep that ship from taking off." He turned his head. "Breyer, Halligan, with me." He moved to the door, pausing to take a quick look down the hallway before leaping through and breaking into a near run. He was close. Too close to let Stark slip away again.

Chapter 24

AS Boyer
Orbiting Columbia
Columbia, Eta Cassiopeiae II

"I think we've got it, Alicia." Sarah was staring through the clear polymer at Anderson-45. The prisoner was sitting quietly, staring at the armored Marine, but making no aggressive moves at all.

"He has made no effort to attack the subject, despite three separate orders to do so. There isn't even any discernible hostility. Not even a nasty look." She turned and looked at Sarah. "Do you realize what this means?" The excitement in her voice was obvious.

"Less than you think, Alicia." Sarah was pleased the drug was a success, but she understood the practical limitations of the breakthrough. "Apart from the problem of how to administer an injection to enemy powered infantry in the field, I remind you that this drug simply prevents the subject from acting on an artificial compulsion to violence." She looked through the window at Anderson-45.

"Anderson has been with us for over a year, Alicia. He has lived with us and had enough time to draw his own conclusions about us. He knows we mean him no harm, and he is now far more educated than any of the other clones on how he and his brethren came into being. He is an extraordinary subject, and I would be cautious about extrapolating too much from him on how the other clones will react."

She turned and looked back at Alicia. "The rest of the

Shadow Legions have been fighting us for more than two years, and they've seen thousands of their people killed. They have been told we are evil, the enemy…that their cause is the just one. They think we murder prisoners, not that their officers terminate their beaten and abandoned detachments before they are captured."

Her voice was showing her fatigue, and the frustration of trying to solve an insoluble problem. "Remember how we thought about the Janissaries? The hatred? Now they are our allies. Perspectives change, but they do not do so easily or quickly. It took a considerable amount of time for many Marines to adapt to the Janissaries' change of allegiance. I am sure some Marines still harbor resentments." She was frustrated, and her efforts to hide it had begun to fail utterly. "Do you think those soldiers in the field are just going to welcome us with open arms, even if we somehow find a way to administer the drug?" She turned and stepped away from the observation window.

Alicia looked at Anderson-45 for a few seconds then she turned back toward Sarah. "So, all this is pointless then, isn't it? Even if we manage to make everything work, we can't deliver it to the soldiers in the field. And even if we do that somehow, they will probably still fight us because they've known us as nothing but the enemy. So all the work we've done it pointless."

"That's true to an extent, Alicia. But Anderson-45 is proof there is always hope. He's learned we're not the enemy, and now we have the power to give him back his free will." She wiped her brow with her sleeve. "Perhaps we'll find a way to take more prisoners…or the war will end before all the Shadow Legion soldiers are killed."

Erik passed through her mind, his almost unfathomable stubbornness. She imagined trying to convince him he'd been wrong in his convictions for years, that everyone he thought was an enemy wasn't, that he'd simply been lied to by those he followed.

A wave of sadness passed over her as she thought about him. She was worried sick, of course, but she also knew how truly capable he was. She was afraid he might die in his quest to kill Stark, but she also knew he could succeed. His raw determination and his ability to focus on one thing were so powerful they still unnerved her at times.

"You mean we're doing all this work so we can help any enemies who survive after killing so many of our people?" There was a twinge of bitterness to Alicia's voice.

"Come on, Alicia, you know better than that." Sarah looked back at Anderson, still sitting quietly in the chamber. "Look at Anderson-45. He has no inherent hostility toward us. The clones are victims, created to be slave soldiers. But however they came to be, they are human beings, and if we capture them, we have to help them overcome their brainwashing."

Alicia stared back wordlessly. Finally, she said, "I know you're right, but it's hard not to be bitter." She sighed. "Besides, it doesn't feel like the war will ever end."

"I know, but…"

The com unit interrupted her. "Colonel Linden, we've received an emergency communication from Pershing." The bridge officer's voice was strained, almost distraught.

"What is it, Lieutenant?" Sarah felt her entire body tense. She knew from the tone it was something bad. Very bad.

"It's Admiral Garret, Colonel." The officer paused, trying to catch her breath, find her voice. It was clear she was crying. "There was an assassination attempt. He is in extremely critical condition."

No, Sarah thought, fighting back her own tears, not Augustus too. She clenched her fists and pushed back against the darkness that felt like it was closing in on her from all sides.

"Doctor Farnor requests your immediate assistance, Colonel."

Sarah took a deep, ragged breath, trying to hold on to her composure. "Tell Commander Farnor I'm on my way." She took one last look at Anderson-45 and, with a nod to Alicia, she was out the door.

"We suffered moderate losses, General Tyler." There was fatigue in Gilson's voice, but she was trying to hide it. "It's not the first time we've faced a nuclear attack. The enemy took their last shot, and it wasn't enough to stop us." She paused, and when she continued, her exhaustion was more obvious. "Now we just need to launch the final assault. It will be costly, but there is no other choice."

"Why don't you return the favor first, General?" Tyler's voice was grim. "Blow the hell out of them before you send your people in."

"We don't use nuclear weapons on Alliance worlds, General Tyler. Not unless there is no alternative."

"I think that policy has been overtaken by events, General." Tyler took a deep breath. "My people are beyond grateful to your Marines, General Gilson, and we know how much you have sacrificed, not only on Columbia, but against the First Imperium and fighting the Shadow Legions on other worlds. You can't afford any unnecessary losses, and the entire inhabited area of Columbia has already been ravaged, leaving little to preserve." Tyler's voice was firm, but there was a sadness there too, sorrow at what had become of his world.

"Once the fighting is over, we will have to rebuild far to the south anyway. It is plain to see the entire area around Weston is already devastated and poisoned with radiation. Another barrage will have virtually no incremental effect on that." He paused. "So, as the duly appointed dictator of Columbia, I officially authorize...no, I request that you utilize a nuclear bombardment to weaken the enemy as much as possible before launching your final offensive. The entire population has fled from the area now held by the enemy, so you can attack with no concern for civilian losses." He paused again then added, "We know your Marines can't afford to take any more casualties than necessary. I fear they will be needed elsewhere, not just on Columbia."

Gilson was silent for a few seconds, considering Tyler's extraordinary words. She knew life sometimes created bizarre situations, but she'd never imagined a friendly planet's head of state asking her to nuke his world.

"Since you put it that way, General Tyler, I will reconsider the policy on nuclear exchanges. Please issue orders to your people to cease their advance and adopt a defensive posture."

"Yes, General. My people will be ready in 30 minutes."

"Very well, General Tyler. In exactly 45 minutes, we will unleash hell."

"Another hundred microliters of Androthrindozine. Now!" The surgeon was bent over the medpod, working feverishly, his hands moving across Augustus Garret's chest. A dozen navy personnel stood around, watching in stunned silence.

"I want this room cleared," the surgeon roared, waving an arm at the onlookers as he did. "Right now." His eyes didn't move from Garret's still form. "And wipe this sweat off my forehead," he growled to one of the medtechs assisting him.

Garret had been shot 7 times, and he had major trauma to both the chest and head. He was in a deep coma and his prognosis was grim.

Sarah came rushing into the room. "Dr. Farnor, I came as soon as I got the message." She was shedding her clothes as she raced through the surgical theater to the decontamination chamber, grabbing a set of scrubs and slipping through the door.

She rushed out half a minute later, taking position on the opposite side of the medpod from Farnor. She looked up at the screen suspended above the Garret, reviewing the results of the admiral's medscans. "Full cardiac display," she snapped to the medical AI.

"Displaying full cardiac display, Doctor Linden." A hologram of Garret's heart appeared half a meter above his body. It was rotating slowly, and large shimmering white spots showed the damaged areas.

"We're not going to be able to save his heart, Vin. We've got to take it out now, and get him on life support."

Farnor glanced up for a second. "Are you sure, Sarah? So quickly?" His eyes dropped back to his work. "Don't you think we should at least try to save it?"

Vincent Farnor was a gifted surgeon, a navy commander, and the chief medical officer on Pershing, but Sarah Linden had seen more traumatic battlefield wounds than any medical professional in occupied space.

"It's a longshot, Vin. Maybe one chance in five." She reached up and pointed to a section of the hologram. "You see the damage to the epicardium? Even if we can handle the other problems, we're never going to be able to repair this. He needs a complete regeneration, and we don't have time to waste on procedures that aren't going to work in the end. We'll be lucky if we don't lose him in any event, but if we waste hours trying to repair his heart, we've got no chance to save him."

"Expand image to include lungs."

"Expanding hologram, Doctor Linden."   The image expanded, displaying Garret's entire chest cavity.

"See here?" Sarah was pointing to damaged areas of the left lung. "And here? If we remove the heart, we can access these areas, maybe save his lungs. If we try to repair the heart too we're not going to be able to repair the lung damage, and we'll end up losing them both...and him too. We have to move now. We don't have much time."

Farnor nodded. "You've got me convinced, Sarah. We'll have to put him in partial cryo-stasis."

"I agree." She wiped her forehead with her sleeve. "We're going to have a lot of work to do on that head wound too. Her eyes moved to the monitor about the medpod. "It looks like we caught a piece of luck there. The brain injury is tricky, but I don't think anything vital was damaged. If we can save him, he shouldn't have any neurological impairment."

She took a deep breath. "Induce partial cyro-stasis, 20%."

"Inducing cryo-stasis now, Doctor Linden. The patient will reach the 20% level in 40 seconds." The AI's voice was crisp and clear on the medpod's speakers.

"Alright, Vin, let's do this." She was focused like a laser, as she always was in the hospital. But her stomach was twisted into knots. Augustus Garret was one of the finest men she knew, and a leader everyone – in the navy and the Corps – respected and loved. How could this have happened? Why would Tara Rourke have tried to kill Garret? She'd been almost like a daughter to him.

Sarah was used to the pressure of battlefield hospitals, and she looked calm and cool as she sliced Garret's chest open with the laser scalpel. But inside she was a wreck. She knew she would do everything she could, put every bit of her skill and talent into treating Garret's wounds. But she also knew she had at best a 50% chance of saving his life. And she couldn't imagine losing Augustus Garret so soon after Holm.

I've got to save him, she thought. Somehow, I've got to save him.

Code Black. The word had gone out to every Alliance unit on Columbia. The counterpart to Code Orange, it meant that the Marines were about to launch a nuclear attack.

Tyler was suited up and on the front lines. Half a dozen people had tried to convince him that the ruler of the entire planet should be in a less exposed position, but one look at his eyes was enough to send them scurrying out of his way. Tyler wasn't going anywhere else. This is where his soldiers were, preparing for the final battle, and this was where he was going to stay.

It was almost time. In another 60 seconds, General Gilson's Marines would begin their nuclear bombardment, hitting the disordered and decimated Shadow Legions with a firestorm the likes of which they couldn't imagine, not even in their worst nightmares.

It hurt Tyler to see his world devastated, the hills and plains he'd hiked as a child turned into pitted wastelands, poisoned with radioactivity. But he had been the first one to tread that road, enticing the enemy into Weston and then destroying the capital with his own nuclear arsenal. It was a cold move, perhaps, one that had shocked most people. But Columbia wasn't a stretch of ground, nor a cluster of buildings. No, it was much more than that. Columbia was its people, and as long as any of them survived, it would go on.

Tyler doubted more than a million of his countrymen would be left when the losses were finally tallied. More than half the population had already died in the war. He didn't have confirmed numbers to support that, but he knew it was true. What did a city and the surrounding settlements mean next to that? Columbia was an entire planet, and when the war was over, he and Lucia would lead the people to the south, to build a new capital and start again, as the original settlers had. But first, the invaders had to be defeated, even if the cost was more destruction and a new cluster of radioactive hotspots.

"General Tyler, we have a message from Marine HQ, sir." It was Captain Ventnor on the com. "They are launching now, sir."

Tyler flipped on his display. The blue light was flickering, and it had a transparent look to it, making it hard to read. He wished for the thousandth time his people had been equipped with modern armor, like the Marines and the Shadow Legions, but that was beyond the means of any colony world. Columbia was one of the few colonies to have any of its defense forces equipped with fighting suits, and most of them were surplus from the Second Frontier War, 40 year old relics pitted against the most modern armor with four decades of research and development separating them.

He watched Gilson's barrage moving toward the enemy position. The targeting data was courtesy of Admiral Garret's fleet, which had positioned a string of recon satellites around the planet and tied Tyler's people into the overall communications net.

He followed the ground-launched missiles and the atomic shells moving toward the enemy positions, and he noticed a line of larger icons, fleet-launched ordnance moving down from orbit toward the same group of targets. He'd relieved Gilson of her obligation to refrain from atomic attacks on Alliance planets, and now she was going to make the strike count. The Marines had suffered horrendous losses, not only on Columbia, but in other battles as well. Now she was letting loose a devastating bombardment designed to virtually destroy the cornered enemy forces.

Tyler was with his people, ready to move forward as soon as the detonations were finished. He knew the Marines would be heading west, moving in on the heels of the bombardment to finish off the enemy. His people would be a part of that, advancing from the south with Major Mandrake's Marines. They would move right through the toxic wreckage of Weston and turn to the west, slipping in alongside the Marines to chase down and kill the last of the invaders. Then, Columbia would be free again.

It had seemed almost impossible during the long months of guerilla warfare, when Tyler had watched his people starve while he choked on the bitterness of defeat. Though he had never let on to anyone – not even Lucia – he'd given up hope, despairing that help would ever come. Now he felt ashamed that his faith had failed him, and he knew he had underestimated the Marines. They were sworn to defend worlds like Columbia, and nothing would keep them from fulfilling that duty. If Cate Gilson had been alone, the last surviving Marine, Tyler knew she would have come to Columbia, her assault rifle in hand, and the honor of the Corps in her heart.

We watched the small dots move to their target zones, expanding briefly on the screen and then vanishing as they detonated. He knew the flashes would be brighter than the sun, but his visor was down, protecting his eyes. The last thing he needed now was to be blinded by an atomic blast.

An instant later, the sound arrived, one great rolling boom after another, and the shockwaves hit, more annoyance at this range than serious danger, sending chunks of dirt and bits of wreckage flying.

The bombardment continued for almost ten minutes, and when it was done, over 200 warheads had exploded, ranging from 2 kiloton mortar rounds to 100 kiloton missiles fired from orbit.

He sat and listened to the com, waiting for the orders. His body was tense, and he struggled to keep himself still. He felt both exhaustion and exhilaration, and his mind was a blur. He had his rifle in his armored hands, and he could see his men to both sides of him, crouched down, ready to lunge forward, as soon as he ordered it.

It was time. It was finally time. When the word came, his soldiers would climb out of their trenches and advance. And the battle wouldn't stop until Columbia was clean of the foul stench of the invader. Tyler wasn't sure what Gilson's Marines would do, but he knew one thing for certain. None of his Columbian soldiers would take any prisoners. There was only one way to pay the enemy for what they had done to his world. They were an infection, and he intended to eradicate them, wherever they retreated, anyplace they tried to hide.

His com crackled to life. "All units, advance." It was General Gilson's voice. The final battle had begun.

Chapter 25

Federal Base Zeta
Western Virginia Region
US Zone, Western Alliance

Warren sat quietly at his desk. He was supposed to be reviewing troop dispositions, but he couldn't even see the screen in front of his eyes. His mind was elsewhere, deep in thought, wondering if he'd somehow been taken by An Li.

He'd been understandably suspicious of her motives when she first contacted him, but she hadn't asked anything too burdensome. All she'd wanted was for him to hold back on any escalation as long as the opposition did the same. He had leaned on the CEL to hold their advance from Paris for 72 hours, but that was about the only thing he'd done differently than he would have otherwise. Even before she called, he was trying to restrain the Alliance's escalation, working to keep things from sliding even further into chaos.

The delay by the CEL forces had been to their disadvantage, giving the shattered Europans an extra three days to try and reform, but it had hardly been decisive. He had a hard time convincing himself that's all Li An had been after. He'd reviewed her file, all the extensive data Alliance Intelligence had on her decades of C1 leadership. She didn't waste time on small matters. He couldn't imagine she had initiated the entire affair just to scam him into slowing the CEL advance on Paris for three miserable days.

Still, she was 18 hours overdue, and all his attempts to contact her had gone unanswered. She'd asked for 72 hours, and by all accounts, Li An was remarkably punctual. It was unlike her to miss a deadline, and even stranger that he couldn't get an answer from her. It had to be some kind of trick, some plan of hers to gain an edge.

He scolded himself for being naïve. He'd gone into the conversation with his guard up, but everything she said made sense, and she hadn't asked him to do anything he considered alarming. Gradually, she convinced him she was serious. Now, he was wondering…what did she really want? What was going on?

"It has to be something," he muttered to himself. "She's up to something I don't know about, and I need to figure out what." By all accounts, C1's chief did not waste her time.

In the days after his discussion with her, he'd found himself believing more and more of what she had said. Indeed, he'd been surprised when the deadline came and went, and still she hadn't contacted him.

He'd checked with his operatives in the CAC, but none had seen any signs of a power struggle or a coup. He knew Li An was stealthy in her operations, but seizing power in her situation required spilling a lot of blood…highly placed blood. There was no way his agents could have failed to pick something up, even if her bid for power had failed. Unless the coup never happened. And that meant he'd been scammed.

He looked at his screen, forcing himself to focus. He punched a few keys, scrolling between status reports. The Alliance and the CAC had no significant combat in progress. The Alliance armies had been chased out of every foothold in eastern Asia, and the remnant of the Combine's navy was going nowhere near Admiral Young and his fleet. There was a lull in the fighting.

What was it, he wondered, what could she be planning? Then it occurred to him. There was no tactical battle in prospect that would be aided by deceiving him in the short term. It had to be something strategic she was after.

Was she that crazy? Was the CAC Committee? Was this all some kind of game to get the jump on a strategic attack? Perhaps a decapitation strike…or even worse, an all-out assault?

He recoiled at the insanity of the idea, but the more he considered it, the more he realized that was all it could be. The Powers had managed to destroy each other's orbital detection grids early in the war, so maybe she thought she could goad the Alliance into lethargy and gain the 15 minutes the CAC needed to get off an unanswered strike. Perhaps she believed they could take out the Alliance's entire retaliatory capacity. Warren knew that was nearly impossible, but perhaps Li An and the Committee had convinced themselves otherwise.

It was insane, he thought. Absolutely crazy. But it was possible, even likely. He knew what he had to do.

He pressed his com unit. "Anne, can you come into my office?"

"On my way, Mr. President."

He turned and looked back at his workstation, pulling up nuclear strike scenarios. There were dozens of plans in the system, and they split into four basic categories. The first were targeted at the central government installations of each of the enemy Superpowers. These "decapitation" strikes were designed to eliminate all levels of the enemy leadership, creating a power vacuum that would leave a nation exposed and vulnerable to conventional conquest.

The second and third types targeted enemy military power only, either with or without a decapitation component. Level two plans were intended to completely destroy an enemy's strategic forces only, while level three schemes were broader, designed to wipe out the entire military establishment of a Superpower.

"All useless," Warren muttered. Any of the strikes would invite a retaliatory response, and none of the plans could guarantee the complete elimination of an enemy's ability to strike back. Some of them promised precisely that result, but Warren knew that had always been bullshit. There was no point in Li An tricking him in order to launch any of those types of attacks. She had to know the Alliance would survive and retaliate, and if the CAC strike had been successful enough to render a targeted response impossible, the response would be directed at the CAC's cities instead.

He stared at the screen, his eyes focused on a single heading. Level Four Operational Plans. He sighed and punched a key, bringing up a list of protocols. Level four was everything, a massive unrestrained assault intended to utterly destroy a Superpower and its population. Even the Unification Wars hadn't descended to all-out nuclear war, despite 80 years of almost non-stop fighting. But he couldn't think of anything else behind Li An's scheme. He'd been worried that the CEL-RIC situation would eventually lead to an all-out exchange, but now he was wondering if the CAC might beat those two Powers and start the final conflagration now.

The door slid open, and Anne Jackson stepped in. She had a troubled look on her face.

"What is it, Anne?" Warren's voice was coarse, grim. He could see something was wrong, and another problem was the last thing he needed.

"I just got a report from one of my deep cover agents in the CAC government."

He exhaled loudly. "What happened?"

"Apparently, Li An and several other senior Committee members left their secure facility in a submersible several hours ago." Jackson's face was somber, her voice heavy with worry.

Ryan felt his stomach tighten. "I can't believe this is happening." He stared up at his second-in-command. "She played me. They must be planning to attack immediately, hoping they've sowed enough confusion to prevent us from responding in time." He felt cold sweat dripping down his neck, and he struggled against the panic rising inside him.

He turned toward the workstation. "Activate AI Black-7."

"Activated, Mr. President. Awaiting your command." Black-7 was the Alliance's strategic strike AI, a computer that existed for a single purpose. To direct a comprehensive nuclear strike on the enemy.

Warren waved toward the guest chair as he stared at the screen. "Activate Plan Omega-12, target list to follow."

Jackson sat down and watched Warren.

"Plan Omega-12 now active, Mr. President. Awaiting target

list."

Warren swallowed, his throat tight with fear and tension. "Objective one, Central Asian Combine, maximum strike, all military and civilian targets."

He looked at Jackson for a second. She was staring back silently, her face pale. "Objective two, The Mohammedan Caliphate, maximum strike, all military and civilian targets."

He paused. The CAC and the Caliphate were the only two Superpowers that were inveterate enemies of the Alliance. It was possible he could persuade the others to stand down. He was trying to convince himself that was enough, to hold the line at the hundreds of millions in the two Powers he'd already targeted and not expand the cataclysm, but he knew that was wishful thinking. The other Powers would respond automatically to the attack on their allies, just as the PRC and CEL would in support of his own launch.

He sighed. "Objective three, Russian-Indian Confederacy, maximum strike, all military and civilian targets. Objective four, Europa Federalis, maximum strike, all military and civilian targets. Objective five, South American Empire, maximum strike, all military and civilian targets."

He took a deep breath, his chest tight and painful from the stress. "Review target profile."

The AI repeated the list of Powers back to him. Its voice was calm, almost cheerful. He wondered who had given an AI a pleasant voice when its sole purpose was to launch Armageddon.

"Lock in all parameters, and move Plan Omega-12 to stage two."

"Targets locked in. All weapons programmed with specific targets. All safety systems disabled." There was a short pause. "Plan Omega-12 at stage two. Awaiting final command criteria for stage three and launch."

"Final launch criteria under my voice command, Warren, Ryan, Alliance president."

"Warren, Ryan, president is now authorized to activate Plan Omega stage three and launch all ordnance. Do you wish to add anyone else to the authorized command list, Mr. President?"

"No…"

"Don't you think you need a backup, Mr. President?" Jackson spoke softly, calmly. "This is important. What if you are incapacitated? Or even if you can't get to a workstation? You know we'll have less than 12 minutes to react if the balloon goes up."

Warren turned from the screen and looked back at her. There was a hint of suspicion in his expression at first. "Who do you think I should add to the command list?"

"I don't know, sir." She paused, her voice carefully controlled. "One of the generals, maybe. Or one of the surviving cabinet heads?"

He sighed. The suspicion dropping away from his face. She was right, he realized. Li An could even have an assassin somewhere in the base. Hell, he thought, she didn't even need to kill him. Just locking him in a closet for 15 minutes would do the job.

"I don't trust any of Oliver's people, Anne. They were very convincing when they faced the choice between swearing allegiance to me and summary execution, but I don't think I want to put the fate of the world in their hands." He paused a few seconds. "The same with the generals. Besides, all our truly capable commanders are in the field fighting the war. We've got nothing here but inbreds from powerful political families. All they know how to do is wear fancy uniforms." He looked across the desk at his deputy. "Not exactly the people you want at the controls of apocalypse."

She nodded slowly, but she didn't say anything. She took a breath, looking back at him with a non-committal stare.

"You, Anne." Warren's voice was tentative. He wasn't comfortable giving anyone else the power to destroy the world, but she had been right. He needed a backup.

"Are you sure, Mr. President?" There was a look of surprise on her face. She was his direct subordinate at Alliance Intelligence, but there were a dozen others in the government who came before her in the line of succession.

"Yes, I'm sure. You're the only one I can think of with the

intelligence to handle this well." He stared right into her eyes. "Remember, Anne, I want to avoid this at all costs. We only launch the attack if the CAC or one of the other powers strikes first. Do you understand me?"

"Of course, sir." She sounded shocked that he would even question that. "A last resort. Only if our hand is forced." She returned his gaze. "Besides, you will be here to make the call. This is only a safeguard."

"Attention Black-7." Ryan's voice was ragged but firm.

"Yes, Mr. President. Awaiting decision on additional command personnel for program Omega-12."

"Jackson, Anne, Number Two, Alliance Intelligence. Full access, full authorization for Program Omega-12."

"Confirmed. Subject Jackson, Anne, Number Two, Alliance Intelligence is fully authorized for Program Omega-12."

Warren sighed. "No further authorizations."

"No further authorizations. Program Omega-12 is active, awaiting final order for launch."

Warren leaned back in his chair, rubbing his head with his hand. "I can't believe this, Anne. We're on the brink, staring straight down to hell itself." He was a wreck, struggling to sit still in his chair.

"Would you like a drink, Ryan?" Jackson was usually scrupulously formal, but she used Warren's first name this time.

"I don't know, Anne. I think I should stay clear-headed right now, don't you?"

She stood up slowly. "Yes, of course. I'm not saying you should go on a bender. I just thought one drink would relax you. It might help you focus better through the stress. You know, control your nerves a little. I know I could use one."

"Maybe you're right." He motioned to the bar along the war. Francis Oliver had the best collection of expensive liquor he'd ever seen. "I'll have a Cognac…a small one." He waved again. "I'm pretty sure I saw a bottle of Louis XIII over there." He wondered what Oliver had paid for that bottle. Warren was surprised any still existed. It had to be one of the last in the world, but now seemed an appropriate time to open it. "Join me. It should be an exceptional Cognac."

Jackson walked over to the bar and took out two snifters. She picked up the large bottle and opened it, filling each glass about 20% full. She set the bottle down and paused, holding her hand over one of the glasses and pressing a tiny button on her ring. A single clear drop fell into the glass, and she swirled the amber liquid, mixing it in.

"Here she said," handing one of the snifters to Warren. She held up her own glass. "To avoiding apocalypse."

Warren somehow managed a small smile. "I will drink to that." He clinked his glass against hers and brought it to his lips, taking a large sip.

"I was right." He took another drink. "It is magnificent. If we get through this, we'll finish it off as a celebr…" He reached up, putting his hands to his throat. His eyes were wide with panic, and he looked at her with a shocked expression.

"I'm sorry, Ryan, but I'm afraid Gavin Stark made me a better offer."

Warren stared at her, his face blank with shock. He was struggling to speak, but he couldn't get any words out. He tried vainly to get a breath, but a few seconds later, he fell to the floor, flipping backwards over his chair.

Jackson walked around, kicking him over with her foot and making sure he was dead. "She put her glass to her lips and drained it. "You were right, Ryan," she said. "It is outstanding Cognac."

She set the glass down and turned toward the workstation. "Attention Black-7."

"Black-7 active. Voice identification confirmed, Jackson, Anne, Number Two, Alliance Intelligence."

"Black-7, initiate Plan Omega-12, stage three immediately."

"Identity confirmed, Jackson, Anne. Authorization confirmed. Plan Omega-12 is now in stage three. Launches will begin in 60 seconds. Initial impacts projected, 16 minutes, 45 seconds."

"Black-7, the command center is compromised. Lock out all attempts to disengage Plan Omega-12, stage three."

"All changes locked out. Stage three proceeding. No cancellation orders will be accepted."

She smiled. It was done. She turned and walked to the door, opening it and stepping into the outer office. "The president does not wish to be disturbed. He is working on sensitive data."

"Very well, Number Two." Warren's assistant nodded.

She walked out into the hallway, heading toward the lift. She didn't have much time, and she was walking as quickly as she could without arousing suspicion.

She took the lift up to the surface, and moved swiftly across the scrubby grass to a series of outbuildings, glancing at her chronometer as she did. Seven minutes left.

She entered one of the buildings, a large storage shed. She pushed aside a pile of crates, revealing a small ground to orbit transport. She opened the hatch and slipped inside, closing it behind her.

She let out a deep breath. "Activate launch sequence."

"Launch sequence negative." The AI's voice was cold, robotic.

"I said activate launch sequence." She was beginning to get nervous.

The AI didn't respond, but a few seconds later an image appeared on the main screen. It was Gavin Stark.

"Hello, Anne. If you have activated this program, that means you have successfully initiated the Alliance nuclear offensive program. I would like to thank you for your service and your great competence. I'd like to say I never doubted you, but I knew the task I assigned you was a difficult one. Again, congratulations. I should have realized you would get the job done."

She was watching with a confused look on her face. This didn't make sense, why would Stark waste time on this now?

"Unfortunately, Anne, you are a victim of your own success, and you have become an extraneous asset, what I like to call a loose end."

He was smiling as he spoke, but his eyes were cold, like two black holes in the icy depths of space. "I have found that loose ends can be troublesome, and they are best dealt with decisively and permanently." He paused, his face still on the screen, the smile as broad as ever.

"But don't worry, Anne. You should have less than five minutes to wait, and then it will all be over. The CAC-Caliphate retaliatory strike projected for your target zone includes over 3 gigatons of burrowing warheads designed to penetrate and destroy Base Zeta. Since you are on the surface, I am sure you will be disintegrated by the first blast. It will be extremely fast, so I doubt there will be any pain."

She reached over, trying to open the hatch, but it was locked. She banged against it, trying to force it open, but it was too sturdy.

"Goodbye, Anne. And thank you again. Your service has been of great value."

Stark's face disappeared and the screen went blank, leaving her screaming and banging futilely against the hatch.

Chapter 26

Corridor Near Landing Bay
Shadow Legion Base Omicron
Asteroid Belt, Sol System

Cain raced down the hallway, with Breyer and Halligan right on his heels. The station had artificial gravity of a sort, but it was at best one-third Earth normal, and the three Marines had to take care not to launch themselves into the ceiling with each step. But they were veterans, and their armor was like a second skin to them. They had long ago mastered its use, and controlling the amplified strength in low gravity was almost second nature to them.

There was no time to lose. Stark's ship could take off at any second, and with Sand Devil away sending a communique to Mars, there would be no way to follow. The ship would get far enough from the station to engage its stealth systems, and Gavin Stark would slip away again. That was inconceivable to Cain, and he shook with unfocused rage at the very thought. He could feel the madness inside him taking charge, driving him forward, without doubt or hesitation. Stark had to die. That was all that mattered, and he was going to see it done no matter what it took.

He whipped around the corner, recklessly, without looking. He heard the shot first then he dove to the ground, bringing his assault rifle around under him as he fell. "Get back," he screamed to his comrades as he opened up, spraying the hallway with fire before he crashed to the floor.

He landed hard, rifle to the front, still firing. Then the pain hit. He could feel the heat on his shoulder, the blood pouring out of the wound. Then the flood of painkillers, driving the feeling away almost entirely, and a shot of uppers, clearing the fogginess from his head.

"Fuck," he growled to himself. "That was a damned rookie move, you stupid asshole." He felt rage, directed mostly at himself, and he struggled to maintain his composure, to deal with the combat situation. He looked down the hallway. There were two enemy soldiers, but both were down now. He stood up slowly, painfully and held his rifle out with his good arm. He stared down at his readout on the stock. The small red light along the side was flashing. Empty.

Halligan spun around the corner and ran down the corridor, his gun trained on the two enemy soldiers. He crouched down and looked at each of them, turning back toward Cain almost immediately. "Nice shooting, Erik. You got each of them in the head." He turned and took another glance. "Twice."

"I'm a damned fool, that's what I am. How many kids have I told to look before jumping out from cover?"

Breyer walked up from behind. "You ok, Erik?" He could see the hole in Cain's armor. "Maybe you should stay here and let us go on ahead."

Cain snorted. "Are you fucking crazy?" He tossed the empty assault rifle aside and extended his blade. "It's a scratch." He looked down toward Halligan and back to Breyer. He knew from the amount of blood pooling around in his armor it was a lot more than a scratch, but it didn't matter. If he was still breathing, the way was forward. He wasn't going to stop until either he or Stark was dead. Or both. "We don't have time for bullshit now. Let's move."

He turned and walked down the corridor. He could feel the trauma control system patching his shoulder. He still had some pain, despite the drugs, but Cain had been a Marine for almost 30 years, and he'd been to hell and back more than once. A sore shoulder wasn't going to keep him on the sidelines. It was time to kill Gavin Stark. Or die trying.

He stepped up to the next corner and peered around, far

more cautiously than before. He saw two men walking down the hall toward a set of double doors. They weren't wearing armor like the Shadow Legion soldiers. They looked a lot like… spaceship crew!

He took off at a run, banging into the sides of the hall as he raced to catch the men before they could get to the doors. He slapped one with the back of his armored hand, sending the man hard into the wall.

He turned to face the other, grabbing his arm. "Are you crew for Stark's ship?"

The man stared back, a terrified look on his face. He squirmed, trying to escape, but Cain's armored hand was like a vice.

"I'm not going to ask you again." He moved the blade next to the man's neck. "Have you seen one of these before? They cut through solid iridium. Your throat is like melted butter to a blade like this." Cain moved his arm a few centimeters closer. "Want me to show you?"

The man was whimpering, tears streaming down his face. "Yes, we are gunners for the laser turrets. We were ordered to report immediately for takeoff."

Cain stared down at the door then back to man held fast in his grip. He paused for an instant, thinking. Then he threw the terrified prisoner against the wall. The man slumped to the ground, unconscious.

Cain flipped a switch and a loud crack echoed through the hallway. His armor popped open, spreading like a clamshell, and he began to climb out. He winced when he pulled his stricken shoulder from its place. The med system had packed it with expandable, sterile foam, and some of it tore out, opening parts of the wound again, sending a fresh stream of blood pouring down his arm.

"Erik, what the hell are you doing?" Breyer was standing right behind him, watching the general squirm out of the various tubes and intravenous connections that tied a Marine to his armor.

"I'm going after Stark." Cain jumped free, standing in the

middle of the hallway, naked and dripping blood from his shoulder. "I'll never get on that ship in my armor." He looked down at the two motionless men on the ground. "But one of these uniforms should do the trick." He shot a glance over his shoulder. "You guys get back to the control room and see if Teller needs anything."

Breyer stood and stared for an instant, unable to believe what he was hearing. "Are you insane, Erik?" You want to sneak onto that ship unarmored and alone?"

"I came here to kill Gavin Stark, and that is exactly what I am going to do." He reached around the back of his armor, pulling a pressure bandage from the first aid kit. He twisted his body, trying to wrap it around his shoulder the best he could. He wasn't going to pass himself off as part of Stark's crew if his uniform was soaked in blood.

"Erik, you can't do this." Breyer's voice was strained. "You won't have a chance on that ship injured and alone."

Cain knelt down and flipped over one of the unconscious men, pulling off his uniform. "It's the best chance we're going get, Elliott." He slipped the pants on as he spoke. They were a little short, but not enough to draw attention. "If we let him get away now, we're back to square one." He slipped the shirt over his head, wincing as he twisted his wounded shoulder into the tight garment. "And he'll know we're after him. He's too damned smart. We'll never catch him again."

He turned and looked into his friend's eyes. "It's now or never." His gaze hardened, and he stared at Breyer like a block of solid marble. "And never doesn't cut it."

Breyer walked around, moving between Cain and the hatch to the landing bay. "Erik, this is crazy. I can't let you do it."

Cain stood up, fully clad in the dark blue uniform of Stark's naval crew. "Get out of my way, Captain." His voice was like ice.

Breyer stood his ground, his armored form dwarfing Cain.

Cain stepped forward, standing a few centimeters from Breyer. "I said get out of my way. Or I swear I will have you shot for mutiny." His tone was deadly serious.

"Mutiny?" Breyer didn't move. "But we're not Marines anymore, Erik. Are we? We're just a pack of hunters now. But that doesn't mean I'm going to let you commit suicide."

"Captain, I don't have time for this." Cain stared up at Breyer's imposing form, a good half meter taller than his own, unarmored body. "If you interfere with me catching Stark, I swear by the blood of Elias Holm, I will kill you."

Breyer could hear the inhuman determination in Cain's voice, the seething anger and hatred. There was something there that made his blood run cold, something raw and primal. Cain wasn't just a Marine chasing an enemy or a man seeking to avenge his friend. He'd become a personification of vengeance, an avatar of death.

Breyer was sure Cain had lost his sanity in his overwhelming drive to find and kill Stark. He didn't know if his friend would recover the part of him that made him who he was. Perhaps, if he managed to kill Stark, he might find his way back. If he survived, that is. Or he might be an empty husk, the man who had been Erik Cain burnt up by the fires of hatred. But Breyer knew he couldn't stop Cain, couldn't save him from his destiny.

Slowly, grudgingly, he stepped aside. Cain slipped by and moved quickly to the door. He turned back and looked at the two armored men standing in the hall, watching him helplessly. "Get back to the control room and hook up with the others. Then find a way to get out of here. This is my job now. I will see it done somehow."

Breyer and Halligan just stood and stared, neither of them able to force any words. Both men idolized Cain; they had followed him into battle after battle, and they'd held him up as the ideal for a Marine. He was commander, mentor, friend. And they both knew he wasn't planning on coming back.

Cain pressed the button and the hatch slid open. He took a step and stopped. He turned again, looking back one last time. "Elliott…" His tone had changed. The terrible voice of retribution was gone for an instant, replaced by halting words, choked with emotion and sadness. "If you make it out of here, do something for me."

"Anything, Erik." Breyer was barely able to croak out the words.

"Tell Sarah I love her." He paused and took a deep, rasping breath. "Tell her I loved her right up to the end. That wherever I am, I always will."

"I will, Erik." Breyer stood and stared at Cain, his body shaking with emotion. "I promise."

Cain nodded once. Then he turned and was gone.

"All ships, best possible acceleration." Campbell sat on John Carter's stricken flag bridge, staring at the scattered cluster of small icons that represented his fleet. He didn't have a single undamaged ship left, and he'd left half his fleet behind, pushing ahead with those vessels that still possessed significant thrust capacity.

He'd thought John Carter was one of the cripples, but Engineer Vandebaran and his people had worked miracles. The fires were all out, and the ship's vital systems were more or less stable. The damage control teams had even managed to get thrust up to 7g, though Vandebaran had urged Campbell to stay below 5.5 except in a desperate situation.

Campbell had been tempted to ask how much more desperate things could be, but he'd held his tongue. His engineer had given him more than he'd dared to expect, and he was grateful for the herculean effort.

He was enjoying a brief moment of relief from the crushing pressure of 5.5g acceleration. John Carter was about to begin decelerating as it approached the coordinates Vance had provided, and the ship would spend the next few minutes in freefall before engaging the engines again.

Campbell stared straight ahead, watching the disordered cluster of icons that designated his battered fleet. The main viewscreen was out, and it wasn't a top repair priority, so he'd been making do with the smaller screen on his workstation. He was trying to concentrate but all could think about was Gavin Stark.

He'd just watched thousands of his people die, good friends

and old comrades among them. Their blood was on Stark's hands, and Campbell knew millions of others were dead through the enemy's machinations. Gavin Stark had become the greatest mass murderer in human history, a significant feat, Campbell thought, considering some of those who had come before him.

Duncan Campbell wasn't easily excitable, tending to embrace a stoic outlook on life. But the mass death of war was all around, and Stark bore the guilt for all of it. The destruction of the Martian domes, the millions dead in the fighting on Earth, the deadly struggle between the Alliance Marines and Stark's Shadow Legions. It was all his doing. Stark had to die.

Campbell took a deep breath, watching the seconds pass slowly on the chronometer. Ben Jennings was out at Stark's base, with a damaged Torch transport and Erik Cain and a handful of Marines. It wasn't a very impressive force to confront the greatest evil humanity had ever faced, and Campbell was willing his ships onward, as if his thoughts could alter the physics of space travel and get him there faster.

He turned toward Commander Linken. "Bring the fleet to yellow alert. I want all ships ready for action as soon as we reach Stark's hideout." He turned his eyes back toward the screen in front of him. "Because we are going to blow that base and the entire asteroid it's built on to atoms."

"Yes, Admiral."

Campbell stared silently ahead. The blood of Mars was calling to him, and he intended to answer. Gavin Stark would pay.

"All weapons, prepare to fire on my command." Francisco Mondragon's voice echoed through every com unit in the fleet. His ships were completing their deceleration and taking position all around Stark's asteroid base. If it hadn't been for Cain and his Marines, he would have opened fire already.

"All weapons report ready, sir." Commander Wendell's tone was grim, feral. Everyone in the fleet knew their target. They carried the shades of thousands of dead with them into this fight, millions…Marines, naval crew, civilians. Against all odds, Erik Cain and his people had tracked down Gavin Stark, and now it was time for their hated enemy to die.

"Any energy readings from the base's weapons systems, Commander?"

"No, sir." Wendell's eyes flashed to his screen, confirming the readings he'd just checked. "All weapons systems inactive. No communication from the base. Nothing. They're just sitting there."

"Open a channel." Mondragon knew Cain and his tiny group of Marines were probably dead, but he had to be sure before he opened fire.

"It's ready, sir. On your com station."

He took a deep breath. "This is Admiral Francisco Mondragon, Alliance navy." His voice was dark, threatening. He didn't want to leave the slightest doubt he was completely willing to blow everyone on that station to hell. "You will surrender at once, or we will open fire. You have no chance. You are surrounded and hopelessly outgunned."

He had a sour look on his face. He wanted to kill these bastards, not capture them. He wanted it so badly he could taste it. But he couldn't give up on Cain and his people. Not until he knew for sure they were dead. He waited for a response, the seconds passing by with aching slowness.

Finally, the com burst to life. "Admiral Mondragon, this is General James Teller." The bridge erupted into loud cheers. "We are surprised to see you, Admiral. Damned happy, but surprised."

"We're here with Admiral Garret's complements, General. Do I understand you are in control of the station?" He was shocked to hear a friendly voice at the other end of the link, but he tried to hide it the best he could.

"Not exactly, Admiral." The stress in Teller's voice was more obvious than it had been at first. "We've taken the control room, but I'm afraid we're under siege and outnumbered."

Mondragon snapped his head toward Wendell. "Commander, order Major Winston's Marines to the launch bays at once."

"Yes, sir."

"Tell them Generals Cain and Teller need them." A little extra kick never hurt, he thought.

Mondragon turned back to his com. "General Teller, we've got three companies of Marines on their way to their assault shuttles now." He paused, a dark smile slipping onto his lips. "May I assume that might address your problem?"

"Indeed it would, Admiral." He could hear the relief in Teller's voice. "Indeed it would."

"Admiral, I've got a strange reading." It was Wendell, and he was turned around, staring over at Mondragon. "It's strange… intermittent energy readings. It might be a stealth ship taking off from the station."

"Detach 2nd Squadron at once. They are to pursue and destroy that vessel."

"Yes, sir." Wendell turned back toward his station.

"No!" It was Teller on the com. "Do not destroy that ship, Admiral. I repeat, do not destroy that ship. General Cain is aboard. He chased Gavin Stark onto the vessel."

Mondragon snapped his head around. "Belay that last order. Second Squadron is to pursue the ship and maintain contact, but they are NOT to engage without my specific command."

"Yes, Admiral."

"And launch the Marines as soon as they are ready."

He turned back to his com. "Help is on the way, General. And we've got ships chasing General Cain. Mondragon out."

He flipped off the com and stared at the screen. His 2nd Squadron ships were already altering course, angling to follow Stark.

My God, Mondragon thought, the meaning of what Teller had told him just sinking in. Erik Cain is on that ship, alone, facing Stark and his whole crew. God help him, the admiral thought grimly. He looked over at Wendell. "Tell Captain Janus I will skin him alive if he loses that ship.

Chapter 27

AS Pershing
Orbiting Columbia
Columbia, Eta Cassiopeiae II

Elizabeth Arlington sat on her flag bridge, trying to follow events on the ground, but her mind kept drifting down to sickbay. News of the attempted assassination had spread like wildfire through the fleet, and everyone was waiting to see if Augustus Garret would pull through, or if the navy would lose its beloved commander less than a year after the Corps mourned General Holm.

Garret's naval crews were veterans, an elite group of warriors almost unmatched in human history. But now they were distraught, and they walked through the corridors of the fleet's ships like zombies, unable to focus on anything but the fight going on to save the admiral.

Arlington was expecting to hear from General Gilson any minute, declaring the battle for Columbia won. The fleet and the Marines had blasted the disorganized remnants of the Shadow Legions forces with a massive nuclear barrage, and Gilson's people went in immediately, smashing into the wreckage of the enemy army and slaughtering Stark's soldiers wholesale.

As always, the enemy refused to surrender, and the last surrounded remnants were killed by their command teams, their own suits injecting fatal doses of barbiturates into their systems. But this time Stark's ruthless directive failed to implement completely, and almost a hundred prisoners had been taken, their suits too badly damaged by the severity of the nuclear exchanges to complete their deadly tasks.

The prisoners would be useful, she thought, at least for the research effort. But she found it difficult to give a shit if any of the Shadow Legion soldiers survived. She knew they were clones, created as slaves and conditioned to fight. She understood that their free will had been subverted. They'd been as wronged as anyone in the fleet or the Corps, worse in some ways, but Arlington was only human, and she'd seen too much death and destruction to overlook what they had done, voluntarily or not. She knew it wasn't fair, but that was how she felt.

"The perimeter ships are reporting a contact, sir, inbound from warp gate 2." The communications officer stared back at her screen. "It's a Martian Torch-class transport, Admiral. And it is initiating communications."

"To my station here, Commander." She flipped on the com unit. "Martian vessel, please identify."

"This is Captain Horatio Simpton from the MCS Mirage. I have an urgent communique for Admiral Augustus Garret from Roderick Vance."

Arlington felt a stab of pain at the mention of Garret. She sighed softly. "Captain Simpton, I'm afraid Admiral Garret has been wounded and is unavailable. I am Admiral Elizabeth Arlington. How can I assist you?"

There was a pause. No doubt, she thought, the news of Garret being wounded was a shock.

"Admiral, Mr. Vance wishes to advise that matters on Earth are entirely out of his hands, and he fears that Shadow Legion forces will assume full control of the planet unless your fleet can intervene in some way. Nuclear war is imminent, and Gavin Stark's Shadow Legion soldiers are set to launch their final conquest, under the command of Rafael Samuels."

Arlington felt a wave of anger. She was fleet, not a Marine, but a traitor was a traitor, and she felt the same rage at Samuels' mention as her friends in the Corps. She was sure at once; they couldn't let it happen. Not without trying to stop it. She knew with all her heart that Augustus Garret wouldn't sit idle while Earth fell under Stark's thumb.

"Captain Simpton, I am patching in Admiral Harmon, who is in acting command of the fleet." She turned toward the com station. "I need Admiral Harmon on this line. Now."

The officer acknowledged, and a few seconds later Harmon was connected.

"Elizabeth, what can I do for you?" Her voice was somber, perhaps even more than usual, Arlington thought.

I have Captain Simpton on the line. He brings a dispatch from Roderick Vance."

"Admiral Harmon, my compliments to you. I bring word from the Sol System, and I'm afraid it is not good. Mars has been devastated by an attack from Stark's forces, and Earth is on the brink of nuclear holocaust. The Martian fleet has engaged the Shadow Legion forces and won a Pyrrhic victory, one that has left it combat ineffective. And as soon as the Superpowers destroy themselves, Rafael Samuels will emerge with Stark's Shadow Legion forces and take total control. Once they are deployed throughout the globe it will be almost impossible to root them out."

Harmon was silent for a few seconds. "That's a lot to absorb, Captain." Her voice had changed, still grim, but now touched with sadness, sympathy. Camille Harmon was hard, some would say unfeeling, but that wasn't a fair assessment. She could feel her own pain, and she sympathized deeply with the suffering of others as well, perhaps even more so than most.

"Elizabeth, what is General Gilson's status?"

"I am expecting a formal declaration of the cessation of hostilities any moment, Admiral." Arlington glanced down at her readouts. "I don't have it yet, but I believe combat operations have ceased."

"Captain, you say the Martian fleet engaged Stark's ships?"

"Yes, Admiral Harmon. By all accounts, the battle was a holocaust, with both sides virtually destroyed. Unconfirmed reports suggest that Admiral Liang was killed.

There was another pause, longer than the last. Finally, Harmon spoke. "Elizabeth, I'm going to take my task force back to Earth immediately. You stay and collect the Marine forces as quickly as possible." There was a touch of concern in Harmon's voice. It was clear she wasn't comfortable splitting up the fleet, even with the reports that Stark's force had been badly mauled.

"Yes, Admiral." Arlington hesitated. Then she added, "It's what Admiral Garret would do, Camille."

Both officers knew Garret would have told them to use their own judgment and not to try and figure out what he would have done. But that was easy to say and far more difficult to do. Both officers had come up under Garret, served in various ranks in his famous campaigns. He was a living legend to both of them, just as he was to the lowest-ranking crew member hauling crates in the cargo hold. They were both gifted officers, well-respected in their own rights. But neither of them could escape the pull of Garret's brilliance.

"I want you to be careful. We still don't know what else Stark has out there." They'd all underestimated their deadly adversary, and Harmon was determined never to do it again. "I'm leaving Mike Jacobs and his people under your command. Put them on picket duty while you load up Gilson's people. Then follow me to Earth."

"Yes, Admiral Harmon." Arlington was already doing mental calculations, trying to figure out how quickly she could load Gilson's Marines.

"Captain Simpton, would you care to accompany my task force back to the Sol system? I'm afraid we'll slow you down, but it will be a lot safer."

"Thank you, Admiral Compton, but I'd better get back at my best possible speed and report to Mr. Vance. He will want to know you are coming." He paused for a second. "And also about Admiral Garret."

"Very well, Captain. Good luck to you and your crew. Give Mr. Vance my compliments, and tell him we will be there at our best speed."

Sarah was bent over Garret, her fingers deep in his chest cavity, her once-white gloves completely red with blood. It was the rusty orange color of substitute oxygenation fluid, not the bright scarlet of natural blood. Garret had lost all his own blood, and about 20 liters of the replacement too.

She'd been working on him for 18 straight hours, and she'd thought she lost him twice. But the Alliance's celebrated fleet admiral was tough as nails, and he simply refused to die. And Sarah Linden refused to let him.

"I'm ready to remove the heart. Initiate medpod maintenance of blood flow and respiration."

"All systems ready," the AI responded. "All circulatory function now transferred to remote system."

Sarah sighed, glancing across the pod at Alicia. She'd called for her assistant as soon as she saw Garret's condition. The two were a strong team, and Garret needed every edge he could get right now.

She reached her fingers around the tattered wreck of Garret's heart. She'd harvested cells earlier, and Garret's replacement was already growing in the lab. It was only a few hours old, still an invisible cluster of new cells. It would be two weeks before it was ready, and until then the medpod would have to keep the admiral alive, pumping his blood and forcing air into his tortured lungs.

Sarah had considered implanting a temporary mechanical heart, but she'd nixed the plan when she got a good look at the damage in Garret's chest. There was no way he could take an artificial unit, not until she was able to repair a lot of the injury. So she decided to keep him in a medically-induced coma in the medpod until his new heart was ready.

She looked up at the monitor, reading the vital signs as the machine took over for Garret's cardiovascular system. She was nervous, worried about how his savaged body would handle the mechanical pumps that would keep him alive until she implanted his new heart. The numbers looked good, she thought, feeling a tiny burst of exhilaration. Augustus Garret wasn't out of the woods, not by a long shot. But he wasn't dead yet, either, and considering the shape he'd been in when she first walked into the operating theater, that alone was cause for optimism.

"Alright, Alicia…let's see if we can rejuvenate some of this lung tissue." She took a deep breath. They'd been at it for hours, but she knew there was still a long road ahead. And she wasn't stepping away from the medpod until she was convinced Garret was stabilized. "OK, let's go. Left lung first…"

"General Tyler, I want to thank you for your support and for the bravery and skill of your soldiers." Cate Gilson was standing in the field, once a lush green meadow, but now a barren, dusty wasteland. She was watching her Marines boarding the transports as she said her goodbyes to Tyler. "We wouldn't leave so soon if it wasn't urgent." Elizabeth Arlington's communique had been a shock. Part of the fleet had already left for the Sol system to try and deal with the growing apocalypse there, and Arlington's task force was following, as soon as Gilson could get her Marines, what was left of them at least, loaded up and ready to go.

"No, General." Tyler stood facing Gilson. He was out of his armor, dressed in the light gray uniform of the Columbian army. His arm was bound tightly in a sling, a wound he took in the final hours of the fighting. He was wearing his last decent uniform for the occasion, the only one that wasn't torn to shreds or stained with the mud and blood of the battlefield. He was smiling…for the first time in a very long time.

"Your Marines lived up to their reputation yet again." He looked down at the ground for a few seconds. "I'm ashamed to say that I'd given up hope, and I apologize to you and your people for that. I will never lose faith again."

"Your people fought with courage I will never forget, General." Gilson's voice was sincere, her admiration genuine. "It was a privilege to fight alongside such brave men and women." She turned her head, looking around her. Everywhere her eyes went, there was destruction. Blackened grass, shattered buildings, the smoking ruins of war. And to the west, she knew, the heartland of Columbia was a radioactive hell, an apocalyptic battlefield, now silent, but still shattered and poisoned by the hell of total war.

"I can't imagine the task that awaits your people to rebuild their world, General. I have nothing to offer in the way of help besides my good wishes, but those are given with all my heart."

"You have done enough, General. The rest is our job." Tyler's voice betrayed his own exhaustion, but there was something else there too, a new energy, a hope for the future that had been absent from him for a long time. "I ask only one thing from you, General Gilson."

She looked back at him, an expectant expression on her face.

"Come back to Columbia one day. Come back and see what we have done, how we have rebuilt this planet that you liberated. That will be our tribute to your brave men and women who died here. To reclaim the world they freed for us, to ensure their sacrifices were not in vain."

She smiled again and extended her hand. "You have my word, General. I look forward to it, and I pray that visit comes in a time of peace and not in answer to another call of the bugle."

Tyler reached out his good arm, grasping her hand warmly. "A hope we both share, General. We have seen too much war, too much death." He held her hand for a long time before he let go slowly. "Fare thee well, Catherine Gilson. Until we meet again."

She nodded slowly. "Take care of yourself, General Tyler, and these people you have led so ably. You have saved them, saved your world. Now use your freedom well."

She turned and walked slowly back toward the transports, sighing sadly as she did. Tyler's war was over, at least unless Stark won everywhere else and got around to returning to Columbia. But her battle continued. Hers and the dwindling ranks of the Marine Corps. Earth, she thought, imagining the vastness of man's homeworld. What could her small band of exhausted survivors possibly accomplish there?

"You should have just let her die, Colonel." Flag Captain Josiah stared down at Tara Rourke's still form, lying peacefully in the medpod. "We're just going to space her ass anyway."

"You will do nothing of the sort, Captain." Camille Harmon walked through the door, her voice like iron. Harmon had always been a bit cold and mechanical in her bearing, but since her son had been lost beyond the Barrier with Terrence Compton, she'd become a virtual automaton, focused with razor-sharp precision on the job at hand. She stood just inside the room and stared at the chastised officer.

"I'm sorry, Admiral." The captain tried to backtrack, unsettled by the grim admiral's presence. "I…I just thought…"

"You thought that was the penalty for murdering a superior officer, or attempting to do so," she said without pause. "As well it is." She walked over and looked down at Rourke's unconscious form. She'd known Garret's tactical officer for several years. She had no idea what had happened, but she was sure there was more to the story than she knew.

She turned and nodded to Sarah. "Colonel Linden, I understand thanks and congratulations are in order. I am told you worked nothing less than a miracle in saving Admiral Garret's life." She paused, and a faint smile crossed her lips. "Thank you. From me, and from the entire fleet. The navy will be eternally in your debt."

Sarah returned the smile, though her exhaustion was obvious. "Thank you, Admiral, though I wouldn't characterize it as saving his life. Not yet, at least. I'm afraid he has a difficult recovery ahead, and many complications could arise."

"Still, thank you again. Augustus is a tough old bird, and he has the best doctor in the fleet." She smiled again. "Even if we had to borrow you from the Corps." She looked down at Rourke. "So what do you think? Did she just lose her mind? It doesn't make sense. She loved Garret. She was like a daughter to him. And her service record is spotless. She was an odds on bet to make the admiralty someday."

Sarah struggled to stay focused through the fatigue. "Well, I haven't had time to examine her. It was actually one of my staff who stabilized her and treated the gunshot wounds." Garret's Marine guard had shot Rourke four times, but none of the bullets had hit vital organs. A fully-equipped Marine's assault rifle would have torn her body to shreds, but Garret's guard had been unarmored, and he carried a small carbine for shipboard use.

Sarah took a weary breath. "But if I was pressed to take a wild guess, I would say Gavin Stark is behind this somehow. He is fond of using all sorts of experimental conditioning techniques, and I wouldn't be surprised if she'd been acting under some compulsion she couldn't control." She paused, glancing again at Rourke's still form. "I'd say there is a good chance this was an assassination attempt by Stark and that Tara Rourke was a pawn, as much a victim in this as Augustus himself."

Harmon nodded. The whole thing sounded insane…until you considered the players. Then it made perfect sense.

"I will examine her now, but I would also suggest you run a check on where she has been the last few years. Leaves, detached missions, hospitalizations…anything. Stark would have had to get his hands on her to implant conditioning this powerful, so see if there has been any time when you can't confirm her whereabouts."

"I'll take care of that right now, Sarah." She turned to leave but stopped and look back over her shoulder. "And, again, thank you. We've all lost so much, so many of us gone. If we'd lost Augustus too, I don't know if the fleet could have survived it. Everyone has a breaking point."

Sarah just smiled. She knew Harmon was talking about herself as much as anyone in the fleet.

Chapter 28

Stealth Ship Spectre
Asteroid Belt, Sol System

Cain leapt out from behind the crate, his good arm slipping around his victim's neck. He felt a wave of pain from his stricken shoulder despite his efforts to use only his right side. His muscular arm tightened like a vise, and he twisted, breaking the man's neck in a single quick motion.

He let the body drop slowly to the ground, looking around, making sure he was alone. He wondered for an instant if he could have incapacitated the man instead of killing him, but he quickly put it out of his mind. He wasn't going to take any chances. Unconscious men woke up. Bound men escaped their bonds. But dead men were reliable. They stayed dead.

Besides, he thought, Stark's crews were made up of scum and criminals, men and women who'd signed on to serve the psychopathic bastard. The Shadow Legion clones might be victims, slaves created to serve their evil master, but the spaceship crews had joined of their own free will. Cain had only one thought on that. Fuck them all.

He searched the man, finding a key card and shoving it in his pocket. The dead man had no weapons, and Cain hadn't been able to find any in the hold. He'd have to make do. At least any Shadow Legion guards he ran into on the ship would be unarmored.

He stepped up to the door, sliding his hand over the plate. It slid open, revealing a doublewide corridor. There was a lift at the far end, and a ladder next to it, leading both down and up.

Cain hurried down the hallway, stepping as softly as he could and listening for any sounds. There was a faint hum, the type of noise common on spaceships, but he didn't hear any footsteps. He reached out and grabbed the ladder, climbing down, quickly and quietly, to the lower level.

The humming was louder, and he walked toward its source. He knew the engineering spaces would be at the base of the ship, and he intended to disable the ship. He was determined to kill Stark, but if he failed...if he died in the attempt, he could give his comrades another chance to prevent their enemy from escaping.

He heard voices ahead, at least two different ones. They were having a discussion, but they didn't sound alarmed, so he figured no one knew he was there yet. He rubbed his hand along his waist, wishing he had a pistol or even a knife, but wishing didn't accomplish anything. He'd do this with what he had, even if that was only his bare hands.

He crept down the hallway, slowly, cautiously, remembering to keep guard behind him as he did. One Shadow Legions soldier coming down the ladder could end his quest for vengeance in an instant.

He ran his hand over the door plate, but nothing happened. "It's locked," he muttered to himself, his voice thick with frustration. Then he remembered the keycard he'd taken in the cargo hold. He pulled it out and put it into the slot. The door slid open, and he stepped inside, turning his head quickly, getting a comprehensive view of the room.

It was small, even by the tight standards of spaceship architecture. The reactor was to the side, behind a shield of reinforced polycarbonate. It was a compact design, and the core was no more than two meters in diameter. The engines were directly to the rear, two small units, with access panels for maintenance and repair. The room itself was no more than five meters square, and there were two crewman standing in the middle. They'd been speaking to each other, but they turned when Cain walked in.

"Who are you?" One of the engineers turned and walked

up to Cain. He had a suspicious look on his face, but he wasn't overtly hostile.

"I'm Simon. Alex Simon." Cain took a few slow steps, trying to get within striking distance without arousing suspicion.

"I don't know any Alex Simon." The engineer looked at his partner then shot his eyes back to Cain. "Stay where you are. I'm going to call the bridge."

Cain sprang like a tiger. He was on the first man in an instant, driving his fist under his adversary's ribcage with every bit of strength his muscular body could produce. The engineer doubled over and vomited up a spray of blood, falling to the ground, his eyes wide open, fixed, staring at the ceiling.

Cain knew his victim was dead, and he moved immediately toward the second man. His shoulder was wracked with pain, but he ignored it, swinging his leg around, taking the technician in the head with a powerful roundhouse kick. Marines fought most of their battles in powered armor, but their comprehensive training program taught them how to kill using whatever was available. Erik Cain was a deadly combatant, even with nothing more than his hands and feet.

The tech fell back, his head snapping around grotesquely on his broken neck. Cain rushed over, confirming he was dead and searching him for anything useful. Neither of the dead men had any weapons, but he grabbed their keycards and shoved them in his pocket with the first one.

He ran over to the control panel, sitting at one of the workstations. He looked at it for a few seconds, but he didn't touch it. Without any passwords it was too risky to mess around with the computer system. He looked around the room, trying to find something, anything he could use to scrag the reactor. He knew he was short on time. The crew might not monitor the surveillance system on a constant basis, but sooner or later someone would see the bodies in engineering or try and contact the two dead technicians.

Nothing. There was nothing useful. If he'd had his armor he might have accomplished something, but he couldn't think of a way to disable the ship, not with what he had.

"Fuck," he muttered under his breath as he moved back toward the door, tapping the plate and opening the hatch.

"You! Stay where you are." The voice came from the end of the hall, and Cain reacted instantly. He leapt back into the room just as the guard charged down the hallway, opening fire as he did.

Cain felt a sharp pain in his leg, and he looked down as he combat rolled back into a standing position. The burst of fire had caught him in the leg. It was just a flesh wound, but it hurt like hell.

He ran over to the side wall, moving around toward the door. The hatch had closed again, but he knew the guard would open it and come in firing any second. Worse, the whole ship would know there was an intruder aboard.

He pressed himself up against the wall, right next to the hatch as it slid open again. He was ready, focused, adrenalin coursing through his veins. It was time to kill again. Or be killed.

"Scan again. Look for energy leakage, a particle trail. Anything. But find that ship." Mondragon barked into the com, his voice angry, demanding. He had a whole squadron out looking for Stark's ship, but they hadn't found a thing. One minute it had been right there on their plots and the next it was gone. And that wasn't an answer he was about to accept. Not with Gavin Stark on the verge of escaping. Not with Erik Cain on that ship on his own.

His flagship was between his searching squadron and the rest of the fleet positioned around the enemy asteroid. The ships near the base were landing Marines, sending the help Teller and the other survivors of Cain's team needed. With any luck, they'd secure the facility and get Teller's people out of there before they were overrun. But Cain was a different story. By all accounts he was alone, trapped on Stark's ship, and his own fleet couldn't even find the damned thing. If they didn't manage to detect it soon, it would be gone. And as good as Erik Cain was, Mondragon didn't think he could take on Stark's whole ship by himself. Not and live to tell the tale.

"Admiral Mondragon, Captain Frieden reports that the Marines have landed, and they are moving into the facility." The communications officer was reading the incoming message aloud. "General Teller's people are still holding the control center, sir."

"Very well." Mondragon nodded perfunctorily. That was good news, but the prospect of losing Stark was weighing on his mind.

He turned back and stared toward the com station. "Any updates on the scanning sweeps?" It had been less than five minutes since he'd asked.

"No, sir." The com officer's voice was somber, all traces of his elation at the Marine landing gone. "There is no sign of it, sir. It's just gone."

Mondragon felt his fists clench in frustration. He stared at the screen, his thoughts a blur as he began to realize Stark was going to escape again. He wanted to scream, but he held onto his self-control. It wasn't over yet. There was still hope.

"Keep scanning, full power."

Teller heard the sound of combat outside the door. He and his companions had barricaded the entrance to the control room, ready to fight it out to the end if that's where things led. They had no idea how many of Stark's soldiers were still on the station, but they knew how many they'd killed, and they figured there couldn't be too many left. Enough to wipe them out certainly, but they'd resolved to hold the control room until the reinforcements arrived.

Now it sounded like relief was at hand. He ran back to the command chair – Stark's chair, he reminded himself – and tapped the com unit. "This is General James Teller, calling any Marine forces on this base. Please respond." He stared back at the unit, almost willing someone to answer.

"General Teller, this is Major Stanford Winston." Teller could hear the sounds of battle coming through the major's com. "We are almost to your location, sir."

A broad smile erupted on Teller's face. "Understood, Major." He turned toward the other three Marines trapped with him and nodded. "We are looking forward to your arrival.

"James, there's something wrong with this readout." Breyer was sitting at one of the workstations, eyeing the screen as he kept watch over the bound prisoners of Stark's staff.

Teller walked over. "What is it?" He leaned over Breyer's shoulder, taking a look for himself.

"I don't know, sir. Some kind of power spike." He stared back at Teller. "It doesn't make sense."

Teller turned toward the cluster of prisoners. "What is this?" He reached over and pulled up one of the captives with his armored hand, dragging him to the station.

The officer was defiant at first, but Teller squeezed his shoulder until he let out a yell and looked at the workstation. He stared for a few seconds and gasped. "The reactor is building an overload." His voice was shrill, surprised.

"What would cause that?" Teller turned the man around to face his armored form. His blade slid out of the sheath on his arm. "I want an answer. Now."

The quivering man could hardly speak, torn between fear of Stark and now the newer terror of this deadly Marine holding a molecular blade a centimeter from his neck. But most of all it was what he'd seen on the screen. "I don't know what is causing it, but this station's going to be blown apart if we don't stop it."

"How long?" Teller's voice was harsh, demanding. "I said how long?" He tightened his hand, squeezing the man's shoulder until he cried out.

"I don't know. Fifteen minutes. Maybe less."

"Can you stop it?" Teller loosened his grip slightly.

"I don't know." The man's voice was heavy with fear.

Teller motioned for Breyer to get up. "Well sit down there and try." Teller dropped the man in place. "And don't do anything stupid, or I'll pull your head off like a bug's."

The room shook with a sudden explosion, and the wreckage of the door fell to the sides. Half a dozen fully-armored Marines ran into the room, weapons ready.

"Major Winston reporting, General. The station is secured."

Teller turned toward the new arrivals. "Well done, General." He glanced back toward Stark's terrified officer, motioning for him to get to work. "I'm afraid we have another problem, however."

The hatch opened, but the enemy guard didn't enter. Cain stood still, holding his breath, not making a sound. The seconds passed by until his eye caught the shadow of his adversary, moving slowly forward. Cain watched and tensed his body, ready to strike.

He could hear his enemy's breath, see the shadow on the floor moving slowly, cautiously. He took a deep breath, feeling the tension in his legs, his arms. Then he sprung around, hitting the guard in the stomach with his foot.

The man doubled over, falling forward to the ground and dropping his pistol. Cain swung around behind his victim, driving his knee into the guard's back and reaching his arm around his opponent's neck. He pulled back hard, clamping on his enemy's throat, choking him.

Cain's shoulder was on fire, and he could feel the blood pouring down his arm as his dressings tore and his wound opened again. But he held firm, his grip like a deadly vice, draining the life from his adversary. He could feel the thrashing slow and then stop, and he gradually loosened his hands. He closed his elbow around his victim's neck and twisted hard, the sickening snap his insurance that his enemy was dead.

He scrambled around, reaching out and grabbing the gun laying on the ground a meter away. He shook his head, trying to push the pain out of his mind as he hauled the body over and searched for anything useful. He found two spare clips for the pistol, and he was about to search the man's utility pockets when he heard boots climbing down the ladder in the hall.

Time wasn't on his side. He was bleeding and losing strength, and the ship was alerted to his presence. He had to finish this now.

He took as deep a breath as he could and gripped the pistol

hard in his hand. It's time, he thought. It's finally time. He jumped up and ran through the door, firing at the descending guard as he did.

He saw the man lose his footing and fall to the deck, trailing blood behind him. Cain finished him with two shots to the head and threw himself against the wall next to the ladder, staring up cautiously.

He thought of Sarah, and he wondered if the image of her in his mind would be his last. He felt the ache, the terrible pain of realizing he would never see her again, never feel her soft hair in his hands. He only allowed himself an instant of remembrance, but no more before he pushed her back into his memories and focused on the matter at hand. After all these years of combat, of brutal fights all across occupied space…all the thousands dead, friends lost…he could feel it in his gut. He was about to enter his final battle.

Chapter 29

Outskirts of Paris
French Zone
Europa Federalis

Warren's command car raced down the blasted streets east of Paris, swerving around the gaping shellholes and piles of shattered rubble. He still couldn't believe the last message, and its meaning had only partially sunken in.

It had been a special top level communique, and the coded message it carried was one he'd never expected to hear. Black Zero. The CEL's code for an imminent full scale strategic nuclear attack. Armageddon.

He'd frozen in place when he first got the message. Then he'd resolved to stay where he was and die in his headquarters, surrounded by his men. All that had taken perhaps 30 seconds. Then his officers had grabbed him and forced him into the truck. He was the hero of the CEL, revered by the men he had led to victory, and they intended to save him anyway they could.

The truck screeched to a halt, and a cluster of soldiers pulled open the doors. "Please, sir, there isn't much time."

Werner stepped down from the truck, half under his own power and half dragged by his men. They pushed him forward to a waiting chopper. It was one of the few aircraft left on the western front - in the whole CEL, in fact – and they'd commandeered it to get their commander to safety. Or whatever would pass for safety in the post-apocalyptic world that was coming for them all.

Werner turned and stared back at his men, still arguing he

intended to stay with them, but they pushed him onboard and slammed the doors shut. He looked out, and his eyes caught Potsdorf, standing in the middle of the cluster of officers, staring up toward the chopper. He caught Werner's stare, and he stood firm and saluted the general one last time, just as the aircraft lifted off.

"No, go back." He stared up toward the cockpit, but the pilot didn't move.

"I'm sorry, General, but we have to get you to safety. There is no time."

"I don't want to be separated from my men." Werner's voice was hoarse, ragged. He stared down through the window to the cluster of soldiers gathered together, watching the chopper hurry away. They were all doomed, and they knew it. Paris would be targeted by multiple city-killers, warheads with yields of 20-100 megatons. Werner's officers were less than 8 kilometers from the city's center, still in the 95% kill zone.

"I'm ordering you to land this craft, Major."

The pilot just ignored the CEL general for a few seconds. Then he said, "I'm sorry, sir. Protocol requires you be evacuated to the safest location possible. Incoming telemetry reports we have less than eight minutes until initial impacts."

Werner turned and looked back toward the ground. He couldn't see his people anymore, but he knew they were there, standing where he'd left them. Where they would die.

Huang Wei sat in the Committee room, listening to the reports coming in one after another. He was terrified, shaking with fear as he sat before the assembled leadership of the CAC. He'd been hit hard by the news that Li An had been conspiring with the new Alliance president. He'd sparred with C1's wily master before, but he'd never imagined she would actually commit treason and make common cause with the enemy. Her actions had driven the CAC to the brink of launching a full scale strategic assault, even as the scanners picked up the massive Alliance launch that had beaten them to it.

There were almost 12,000 Alliance warheads now making

their way all across the globe. All five of the Powers in the CAC bloc had been targeted, and there was no question of the intent of strikes so large. Annihilation.

Wei had ordered the CAC's counterstrike, every bit as comprehensive and destructive as the Alliance's. Both sides would do everything possible to intercept the incoming warheads, but Wei knew that was pointless. The attacks were too massive, designed to penetrate the best defenses the Superpowers possessed. Enough warheads would get through. Every city on Earth would be destroyed, wiped off the face of the map as if by some biblical disaster. Factories, industry, military bases, power plants, infrastructure…in 20 minutes, virtually all of it would be gone. Destroyed, blasted to dust, and the twisted wreckage left behind would be poisoned with radiation for decades.

He couldn't believe it had come to this. A century of peace shattered, and in just over a year, mankind was falling into the abyss. It was worse than the world wars of the 20th century, deadlier than the Unification conflicts that wracked the globe for 80 years. Mankind was finally destroying himself. And this time there would be nothing left. Nothing but a few pathetic survivors, starving and sick with radiation, wandering through the wilderness.

Wei let out a deep breath. Thank heaven his predecessors on the Committee had built the undersea sanctuary for the CAC's elites. The Alliance bunker in Virginia would be destroyed, he knew, obliterated by the burrowing 50 megaton "diggers" that were even now heading its way. But the CAC facility was deep under the rocky bed of the South China Sea, safe from enemy ICBMs.

"Chairman Wei, we are receiving reports of enemy naval craft. They have broken through our cordon and are approaching the base."

Wei felt a cold chill run down his spine. He'd been scared to face the future, to deal with the almost total-destruction of the CAC. But he'd believed he and his fellow elites would survive. Now, he knew he was looking at his own death as well.

"All naval units are to intercept immediately." He'd lost all semblance of strength and dignity, and he was like a child begging for help.

"All vessels have been destroyed by Admiral Young's forces, Chairman." There was a short pause. "We are tracing multiple undersea warhead launches from the Alliance fleet."

Wei fell back into his seat, tears streaming down his face. It was over, and he knew it. In five minutes he would be dead.

The Virginia countryside was quiet, and the sun was bright in the late morning sky. Much of the Alliance outside of the cities was toxic and polluted, but the hills around the government's wartime base had been carefully cleaned up and preserved.

The grass was waist high, blowing gently in the wind. A man walking across the idyllic setting would never know he was standing above the largest underground facility in the world, a massive fortified base built to house the Alliance's government and its highest-placed politicians in time of war.

That base was now in an uproar, though the hysteria and panic were not apparent to an outside observer. The new president of the Alliance was dead, murdered…and the entire nuclear arsenal of the Superpower had been launched, an action that had triggered massive counterattack from all the other Powers.

Anti-missile batteries were firing from carefully-situated locations, filling the sky above the bunker with small, fast rockets, designed to intercept incoming warheads. There were similar systems around all the Alliance's cities, though none of them matched the massive array protecting the Virginia refuge.

The countermeasures shot down dozens of warheads, but the Alliance's enemies knew what it would take to penetrate the defensive systems, and missiles streaked toward the Virginia fields from a dozen trajectories, splitting into multiple warheads, each designed to burrow deeply into the ground before detonating. Only a tithe of them had to get through to do the job, but over half of them made it, redefining the term overkill as they did.

The first wave of warheads slammed to the Earth, exploding with unimaginable nuclear fury, sending huge clouds into the morning sky, black and heavy with the now radioactive dirt and shattered rock the bombs clawed out of the ground. The fallout clouds from the burrowers would be particularly radioactive, and they would spread death on the winds for hundreds of kilometers.

Wave after wave followed, each successive flight of missiles digging deeper into the savaged ground, tearing out the remnants of the Alliance's base, hollowing out the last refuge of the government that had ruled with brutality for over a century. The politicians and generals below were incinerated and crushed by cave-ins. They were blasted by lethal doses of radiation and burned beyond recognition.

When it was over the once beautiful stretch of rolling hills had become a ravaged and toxic wasteland, and in the crushed and melted remains of the Alliance government's last refuge, not a soul remained alive.

"Let's go. Get down behind that bank." The dropoff was about 5 meters, and Axe's people were climbing as quickly as they could, digging hands and feet into the cracks and holes in the concrete wall. The depression had been a roadway at one time, but now it was almost entirely grown over, with just a few chunks of old asphalt to give a clue what it had once been.

"Come on, Ellie." Axe reached his hand out to the girl. "I know you're scared, but we need to get down there now." Axe had seen the smoke trails in the sky, and he knew what they were immediately. He was hopeful his people were far enough away from the city to survive, but he knew they still needed cover.

The girl hesitated, afraid to climb down the steep embankment. She shied away from his hand.

"Ellie, please." He was hanging on the edge of the dropoff, his foot wedged into a large crack in the concrete. "You have to trust me."

She paused for a few seconds, staring back at Axe. She looked like she might run for an instant, but finally she reached out and took his hand.

He pulled her off the edge and grabbed her firmly in his

arms. She shrieked and squirmed, trying to escape, but he held her tightly and scrambled to the ground.

"Everybody, get down and cover your heads. And keep your eyes closed. Whatever you do, don't open your eyes until I tell you to."

He dove to the ground, holding Ellie tightly under him, just as the first warhead struck New York, and the blinding light flashed over them.

Axe stayed firm, his arms wrapped around the terrified girl, listening as the first blasts echoed over their position. He had no idea what was going to happen next, but he knew one thing for sure. The world would never be the same.

Chapter 30

Stealth Ship Spectre
Asteroid Belt, Sol System

Cain crouched on the ladder and thrust himself up hard, ignoring the pain in his wounded leg as he popped above the floor, staring down the corridor. His pistol was firing before his conscious mind even identified the targets, and two guards fell to the ground immediately. They had been heading toward the lift, and Cain had taken them both by surprise.

"That's six," Cain muttered to himself, scrambling across the deck, checking to make sure both men were dead. He grabbed their pistols, shoving one in the waistband of his pants, and he turned back toward the ladder, holding a gun in each hand. His shoulder hurt like fire, but he ignored it and gripped the gun tightly. He needed the firepower, and if that meant his shoulder was going to hurt more, so be it.

He was walking back toward the ladder when the alarm went off. That's it, he thought. Anybody who hadn't known he was there did now. He slid to the side of the ladder and peered up, ducking back immediately as a blast of gunfire erupted from above.

Fuck, he thought, leaning his arm out and returning the fire. He had to get to the upper deck. Stark was up there, and nothing was going to keep him from wasting that mad son of a bitch.

Six men, he thought…how many does that leave? He looked around the ship, trying to get a feel for the size of the crew. Ten more, he wondered…fifteen max? None of it really mattered. Not as long as they had him pinned down.

He looked around the corridor, searching for another way up. His eyes stopped on a ventilation grate, halfway down the corridor and about two meters off the ground.

He leaned out and fired half a dozen rounds up the ladder before ducking back. Maybe, he thought. Just maybe.

He made his decision in that instant. It was the only chance he had. He fired another burst of shots then he raced across the hall, shooting at the grate covering the ventilation shaft. It took five shots, but the thing fell off and crashed to the ground at his feet.

He didn't know if his body had enough left to do what he was planning, and he was sure either way it would hurt like hell. But there was no choice. He slipped the two pistols in his belt and took a deep breath, launching himself upwards and grabbing onto the bottom of the vent.

His shoulder erupted in pain, wave after wave of agony. Cain could feel every fiber of his being screaming for him to let go, but the grizzled Marine was still in charge. He gritted his teeth and exerted all the strength he had left, slowly pulling himself up to the meter-wide opening. He was almost in when he heard boots coming down the ladder.

"Fuck," he gasped, realizing he wasn't going to get up in time. He let go with one hand, reaching for one of the pistols. His other arm couldn't hold his body halfway up, and he fell back, barely hanging on.

He fired half a dozen shots, and the dark figure fell from the ladder and crashed into the deck with a sickening thud. "Seven," he whispered to himself.

He shoved the pistol back, but it slipped from his sweating hand and fell to the deck. He growled at himself, but there was no time to worry about it. He still had two guns.

He extended his arm again, pulling as hard as he could, shrieking at the pain when he could no longer stay silent. Blood was pouring out of his wounds now, and his uniform was covered with huge dark patches. But somewhere he found the strength he needed, and he pulled himself inside the large duct, just as he heard more steps coming down the ladder.

He wanted to lay back, to rest…even for a few seconds. But he knew he didn't have those seconds. He had to keep going. He had to see this through to the end. He pulled himself forward, slowly, agonizingly. He had to get to the upper deck. He had an appointment with Gavin Stark.

"Let's go." Teller's voice was loud, commanding. He'd led thousands of men into battle, but now he had just one thing to do…get his men the hell off the base before Stark's self-destruct sequence blew it – and them – to bits.

He turned and glanced at the prisoners. "Let's go. All of you." He had no doubt how Cain would have handled the situation, and he'd thought about doing the same thing. These men were not innocents; they were Stark's henchmen, and he didn't doubt each of them deserved death. But Teller didn't have the dark side Cain had always possessed. He couldn't sentence these men to die with a stare the way his friend could. Perhaps they would be executed for their crimes, but Teller wasn't going to shoot them in cold blood – or leave them to be vaporized.

The men stared back, and the fear in their eyes was plain. They didn't expect mercy from their enemies any more than they'd ever given it themselves.

"Now!" Teller roared. "Or I will leave you here to be blasted to atoms." Teller's mercy had a limit, and he was very close to it now.

The men leapt up and followed, moving out into the corridor, stumbling after the line of Marines heading to the airlock.

"Let's go. Move." Teller was urging the Marines forward. They had less than ten minutes, and he had to get everyone off the asteroid and blasted off before the reactor blew.

He'd already sent two groups out through the main airlock and back to the fleet. Admiral Mondragon had landed half a dozen retrieval boats, and there were two still on the surface, either of them big enough to handle Teller and the last of the Marines.

"You have 30 seconds to get into survival suits." Teller stared at the prisoners, waving toward the racks along the wall.

"Because in 31, we're depressurizing the airlock and moving out, and I'll be damned if I'm delaying that timetable for any of you." Mercy had its limits, and they weren't very far.

The terrified captives raced to the wall, climbing into the emergency gear as quickly as they could manage. Thirty seconds wasn't enough time, but fear motivated them, and they managed it somehow.

"Depressurize." Teller watched as the gauge on the wall showed the drop to vacuum conditions. Then he nodded. "Open the door. All personnel, onto the ships."

He waved for all the Marines to go, the last two leading the dazed prisoners in front of them. Teller took one final look behind him and scurried across the dusty gray surface and into the waiting ship.

"Take off," he yelled into the com, and he sat down on one of the benches and strapped himself in. "Let's get the hell out of here before this thing blows."

Cain winced again as he squeezed his shattered shoulder up through the small duct. The passageway had narrowed considerably, and Cain's large frame barely fit through the opening.

He'd lost one of his guns, but he still had the other two. He could see a shaft of fuzzy light ahead, and he knew it was another ventilation opening. If he'd kept his bearings, it had to be the bridge, or a compartment near there. He scrambled forward, pushing himself as quickly as he could. It wouldn't be much of a mystery to his enemies where he went, but if he could climb there quickly enough, he might get lucky and get out before they managed to pin him down again.

His stretched his hand as far as he could, his fingers gripping a small ridge around the inside of the vent. He pulled his face up and looked out into a small room. He let out a deep breath. There was no one there.

He knew he didn't have much time, seconds probably. He pushed against the grate, trying to knock it off, but he knew his strength was starting to fail him, and it didn't budge. He threw himself hard against it, with all the minimal momentum he could generate from his constrained position.

He kept it up, slamming into the grate, and each time his body shook with pain. Finally, it gave way, crashing loudly into the floor. Cain knew someone would have heard the sound, so he shoved himself out of the vent as quickly as he could, falling over and landing hard on the floor.

He felt the bone in his foot snap, a strange numbness for an instant, followed by more pain. His eyes were tearing and his mind was howling in his head, begging to surrender, to give up. The man had taken all he could, but the Marine was still holding, barely, clinging to the mission. And behind it all was the monster, the frigid creature of pure hate that now drove Erik Cain. This avatar of death didn't care about pain; it didn't care about survival. It only wanted one thing. And as long as it drew breath, it would keep going. Until Stark was dead.

Cain's instincts were true, even through the agony and fatigue, and somehow he found he had the guns in both hands, firing full as his enemies charged into the room. The firefight only lasted an instant, and when it was done, there were three more of Stark's men dead on the floor, and Erik Cain had taken another shot, this one in the thigh.

He'd slipped to his knees, but now he pushed himself back to his feet, somehow again shoving aside the pain and the weakness threatening to take him. He stared around the room, his eyes settling on a strange device along the wall. Cain was no engineer, but he'd been on dozens of spaceships, and he'd never seen anything like the glowing cylinder in front of him. Hmm, he wondered…what could that be?

The stealth device, he thought suddenly. It had been a guess at first, but then it all began to make sense. There wasn't a doubt in his mind, and a wicked grin slipped onto his face.

He stepped back and steadied himself against the wall, staring at it for an instant before he raised his arm and opened fire.

Chapter 31

MCS John Carter
Asteroid Belt
Columbia, Eta Cassiopeiae II

"We're detecting a large nuclear detonation, sir. Approximately 400,000 kilometers ahead, along our current course."

Stark's base, Campbell thought. Is it possible? He'd been on his way to attack the facility, but he had no idea who else might have beat him to it. Perhaps Stark had ordered the base destroyed after he'd realized it had been discovered.

"I want a full energy analysis on the explosion." Stark would never give up without a fight, Campbell thought...so if that was his base, it means he got away somehow. "And all ships are to scan full in all directions. I want any contact reported...energy, particle, whatever. Nothing is too small."

"Yes, sir." Christensen relayed Campbell's message through the fleet com. Then she activated the AI and instructed it to analyze the incoming data.

"Scanning data supports the sudden release of a previously-controlled fusion reaction of sufficient size to sustain itself for several seconds after loss of containment." The AI's tone was moderately androgynous, and Campbell had never been able to decide if it had modeled after a man's voice or a woman's. "Concentration of heavy materials in spectral analysis also supports the hypothesis of the sudden failure of a fusion power reactor encased in an asteroid. Probability 94%."

"Let's go a little closer in and have a look. Just to make sure." Campbell didn't trust Stark, and he was going to be damned sure he knew what had happened before he headed back to Mars.

"Any other contacts?" He asked almost as an afterthought.

Christensen was staring into the scope. "Just picking them up now, sir. Approximately 20-25 ships."

Campbell's head whipped around. He'd asked almost as a reflex. He hadn't expected to detect other ships out here. "Full report, Commander!"

"Definite spread pattern formation. The vessels seem to be searching for something. They are covering a wide dispersal pattern." She paused, staring into her scope. "Admiral!" Her voice spiked high with surprise and her head popped up. "They are transmitting Alliance protocols."

Campbell was surprised again. He hadn't expected to run into any ships out here at all besides Captain Jennings' Torch. But a whole Alliance fleet?

"Initiate contact, Commander."

"Contacts confirmed, sir. It looks like approximately 40 vessels, Admiral." The officer was reading the data as it came in. "Their original course suggests they were bound for the base, sir, but after the detonation, they altered course and they now appear to be searching for something."

"They're searching for the same thing we are, Lieutenant. We're on the same team, so let's join forces. Get me a channel." Mondragon sat in his command chair, staring at the plot of ships heading for him.

"Your line is open, sir."

"Attention incoming vessels, this is Admiral Francisco Mondragon of the Alliance navy. Please identify yourselves." There was a brief pause, about half a second each way for the signals to cross the space between the fleets.

"Admiral Mondragon, this is Admiral Duncan Campbell, Martian Confederation navy. Welcome back to the Sol system."

"Thank you, Admiral. May I assume that you are attempting to find the same vessel I am seeking?" Mondragon leaned back in his chair, waiting for the response.

"We were searching for a ship we believe carries Gavin Stark,

Admiral Mondragon. You may have more information than we do." Campbell paused. "We're simply going on the assumption that Stark escaped the destruction of his base and is out here somewhere in one of his stealth vessels."

Mondragon smiled. "Your assumption is excellent, Admiral Campbell. And yes, we are also searching for Stark's vessel. One of our people was able to sneak onboard, but we have been unable to locate the ship since leaving the vicinity of the base." He sighed softly. "I'm afraid we were caught rather close to the explosion, and by the time we were able to clear our scanners, the vessel had vanished from our scopes.

"Admiral Mondragon, the enemy vessel has reappeared on our scanning plots. It is 145,000 kilometers from our current position, moving at 3,850 kilometers per second."

Mondragon's head snapped around. "Lieutenant, advise General Teller. He has a strike team loaded up and ready for a boarding operation."

"Yes, sir."

Mondragon flipped his com back to Campbell's channel. "Admiral, we believe we have located Stark's vessel."

"We have too, Admiral." There was a grim tone to Campbell's voice. "We have too."

"All laser batteries, prepare to fire at my command." Campbell turned his head sharply. "Engine room, I want 3g thrust in 15 seconds."

Campbell turned and stared straight ahead. It was time. The butcher, the murderer who'd attacked Mars' cities…it was time for him to pay the price.

"Engineering reports ready, sir. Commander Vandebaran reports reactor up to 55% output."

Campbell nodded. "Very well." He allowed himself a feral smile as his eyes focused on the scanner. Vandebaran had exceeded all timetables. John Carter's reactor had been a pile of scrap, but somehow he'd managed to put it back together. The ship wasn't really combat-ready, not by any reasonable standard, but she was more than capable of blasting Stark's ship to atoms.

"I want targeting information updated every 15 seconds. Projected time to firing range, four minutes, ten seconds." Campbell took a deep breath. In less than five minutes, Stark would be dead. He didn't know how much comfort it would give to the displaced masses back home, but it would be a measure of justice at least.

"Admiral, I have an incoming message from Admiral Mondragon."

"Put it through, Commander."

"Admiral Campbell, my forces have a landing craft inbound toward the subject vessel. General Erik Cain is aboard, and Marines are en route to rescue him and terminate Gavin Stark. Please place your offensive operation on hold until further notice."

Campbell stared at the plot on the screen. He was looking at the small red dot that represented Stark's ship, but in his mind he was seeing the nuclear explosions on the surface of Mars, the magnificent domes cracking, shattering, falling to the ground in a sea of shards. Stark had to die. Nothing could be allowed to interfere with that.

"I'm afraid I can't do that, Admiral."

Mondragon was staring at his com unit, a stunned look on his face. "I repeat, Admiral Campbell. We have Alliance personnel both on that ship and inbound to it. Cease all offensive operations until further notice."

"I'm sorry, Admiral Mondragon. But there is simply too great a danger for the enemy to escape. If that ship is able to re-engage its stealth systems, we could both lose Stark."

Mondragon's faced hardened. He understood Campbell's motivations, but he wasn't about to let the Martian fleet blow that ship apart, not while there was a chance Cain was still alive.

"Admiral Campbell, I am going to ask you one final time. Stand down immediately and cease all offensive operations against that vessel." Mondragon's voice was like ice. "I am not going to repeat myself."

He stared down at the silent com for a few seconds then he

turned toward the tactical station. "Lieutenant, bring the fleet to battlestations. All vessels are to target the Martian fleet."

The officer stared back for an instant, his eyes glazed over with shock. "Yes, sir," he finally stammered.

An instant later the battlestations lamps came on, bathing the bridge in a red glow. Mondragon took a deep breath. He'd expected a lot of potential dangers when Garret had sent him back to Sol ahead of the rest of the fleet, but a battle with the Martians wasn't one of them.

"Give me an open channel, Lieutenant. I want the fleet and the Martians to hear this."

"Yes sir." A moment's pause. "You are live, Admiral."

"Attention all units, this is Admiral Mondragon. We are in pursuit of what we believe to be Gavin Stark's spacecraft. General Erik Cain is also on the ship, and we have detached a Marine boarding party that is currently en route." His voice was firm, even harsh. He wasn't going to let the Martians destroy that ship with Cain on it. Not while there was still a chance he was alive.

"I have requested the Martian fleet stand down and allow us to complete this operation, but my requests have been refused." He paused, staring at the com unit in his hand for a few seconds. "You are to stand by with all weapons ready. If the Martian fleet closes to within less than 100,000 kilometers of the subject craft, all units are to open fire. You are to attempt to disable rather than destroy the Martian vessels, however your priority is to prevent them from entering firing range of Stark's ship."

Mondragon made a chopping motion with his hand, and he leaned back. He could feel his heart pounding in his chest. His palms were soaked in sweat, and he was nauseous. The Martian fleet outweighed his, but they had massive battle damage too. He didn't know if his people could win the fight he was on the verge of starting, but he knew one thing. He wouldn't back down. Not while Cain and the rest of the Marines were out there.

"All Alliance vessels are fully-armed, and their targeting systems are activated, sir."

Campbell sat motionless on his chair, staring out at the screen and the two rough lines of dots facing each other. Would Mondragon really do it? Would he open fire on an allied fleet to save one man?

His mind was racing. He wanted Stark dead so badly he could hardly keep the thought from his head, even for an instant. If Cain was on that ship, Campbell thought, he was probably dead already. But he knew Mondragon would never relent. Not until he knew for sure. Erik Cain was one of the Alliance's greatest heroes, and his comrades would never leave him if there was the slightest chance he was alive.

"We're at 110,000 kilometers, Admiral." There was an uncomfortable pause. "If we're going to engage the Alliance fleet, we need to plot targeting solutions immediately."

Campbell didn't answer. He just sat, staring straight ahead.

"Down to 105,000, sir."

"Put me on a wide channel line."

"Ready, Admiral."

"Attention all fleet units, this is Admiral Campbell. The fleet will proceed on the current course, but no ship will fire except as I expressly authorize. All units are to assume positions surrounding the enemy vessel. You are not to interfere with the Marine operation underway, however, if the enemy ship engages its engines or activates its stealth system, all vessels are ordered to fire at once." He paused. "You are not to attack any Alliance ships unless our fleet is fired upon. In that event, you are to fully engage and seek to neutralize the attacking vessels."

There, Campbell thought, I blinked...but only with one eye. "Let's see if Admiral Mondragon meets me halfway," he muttered softly. He stared at the screen and waited. He knew he only had a middling hand, but he wasn't ready to fold. Not yet. He didn't thing Mondragon's cards were any better.

"Get that thing open. Now!" Teller was standing behind the docking collar as the technicians attached it to the hull of the stealthship. He was edgy, impatient. It had been just like Erik

Cain to sneak onto the enemy ship by himself, and damned the consequences. Teller knew Cain was ready to die to kill Stark, but taking on entire ship by himself was too much, even for the Marines' great stoic.

The two fleets had fallen into an uneasy standoff, Mondragon matching Campbell's compromise. But things were still tense, and Teller knew time was of the essence. He'd almost given up hope before, but when the stealth field went down he knew Cain was still alive and fighting. And his Marines were not about to abandon him.

"OK, you guys are all set." The technicians stood aside, allowing the Marines to crawl through the small tube connecting the ships.

Teller was first, dressed in fatigues, and carrying an assault rifle in his hand. He crawled through and jumped out into the enemy cargo hold, springing into combat position and scanning the room quickly. There was a body in the middle of the floor – probably Cain's work, he thought – but no live enemies.

He raced to the door, waving for the others to follow behind as he leapt out into the hall. There were bodies in the corridor as well, and one hanging down from a ladder leading to the upper deck.

He ran down to the end of the hall, looking up and down the shaftway. He couldn't see anything, but an instant later he froze. He could hear something, the sounds of fighting…from the upper deck. He felt his heart race. Unless Stark's people were fighting each other, it had to be Cain up there.

He reached out and grabbed one of the rungs of the ladder. "Let's go, Marines. It's time to finish this."

Chapter 32

Stealth Ship Spectre
Asteroid Belt, Sol System

Cain stood laughing as he stared at the shattered wreck of
Stark's stealth device. There were shards all around, and the
strange green light inside was extinguished. Cain had no idea
how the thing had worked, but he was damned sure it was a pile
of junk now.

He turned and moved toward the door. He was weak and
tired, and his body was wracked with pain, but he had a job to
do, and he'd be damned to hell if he was going to quit this close.

He opened the door and ran out onto the bridge, screaming a bloodthirsty war cry and firing with pistols in each hand.
His training and instincts took over and directed his shots with
deadly accuracy. There were half a dozen spacers on the bridge,
and he took down four of them in an instant.

He leapt forward, diving over a large console, firing behind
him as he did. He took the fifth of Stark's men in the shoulder then, an instant later, right through the eyes. He ducked
back just as the door opened, and two more guards raced in.
They took cover to either side of the door, crouched behind
two workstations.

Cain was gasping for air, every breath a searing agony. He
was covered in blood, and he was almost out of ammunition.
There were three men left in the room with him, perhaps the
only three on the whole ship. The last member of the bridge
crew had ducked behind a large structural support. Cain hadn't
gotten a good look at him, but he knew it had to be Stark.

"I am here for you, Gavin Stark. It is time for you to pay for your crimes." Cain was weak, his endurance fading. But somehow he managed to keep his voice loud and strong.

"Who is that?" Stark's voice boomed out from behind his cover. "What do you want?"

Cain felt a strange surge of energy, a power from somewhere deep within him, some recess in his mind where the darkest part of his soul dwelled. "I am Erik Cain, you son of a bitch." His voice rose to a booming crescendo. "And I am here to take your miserable life."

He threw himself over the console, rolling across the top, firing away toward the door. The two guards were taken by surprise by the bold move, and both fell to the ground, riddled with Cain's bullets.

He didn't even pause to watch them hit the ground. He spun around, diving forward to get a shot at Stark. He whipped up his gun and fired...and then he felt a hammer blow on his chest.

He stumbled back gasping for air, listening to the sucking sound from the hole in his chest. He saw Stark fall to his hands and knees, grasping at the abdomen. Cain's shot had found its mark as well. He struggled to stay on his feet, somehow, anyhow. He had to finish this.

Stark had dropped his pistol when Cain's bullet hit him, and he was crawling toward it, his eyes ablaze with terror and hatred. Cain still had one pistol in his hand and he aimed it at Stark's head and pulled the trigger. Nothing. It was empty.

Cain threw the gun at Stark and lunged forward, landing with agony on top of his adversary. He reached down and pulled Stark's arm out from under him, and they both fell, lying alongside each other gasping for breath.

It was a fight to the finish, a desperate, primal, feral struggle. Both men were critically wounded, and both were focused solely on the death of the other. This was a struggle that had begun years before, when Cain had almost shot his political officer. He and Stark had fought their battle for years, across the vastness of space, and uncounted millions had died. Now that contest was at an end. In seconds, a moment or two at most, one of them would stare down into the cold dead eyes of the other, and in that instant they would know victory.

They grabbed onto each other, grappling along the floor, pulling, gouging, driving determined fists into each other's battered bodies. It was as nasty as a fight can get, pure murderous combat, their tortured bodies rolling around the bloodsoaked deck of the bridge.

Stark shoved his hand deep into Cain's shoulder, clawing at the raw, uncovered muscle with all his strength. Erik screamed at the pain, and poured it all - the agony, the hatred, the memories of death and destruction – into one last effort. He whipped his body around as hard as he could, pulling himself behind his enemy. He doubled over in pain as he felt two ribs break, but he bit down and thrust himself up, on top of Stark, slipping his arm around his foe's neck.

Cain pulled back, straining with every fiber of strength, every ounce of love, hatred, even pain that was left to him. He tightened his arm, choking the life out of his enemy, driving his knee hard into Stark's back and holding him in place. He held on for Elias Holm, for the vengeance he had come to claim… but also for Sarah, so she might have a future unplagued by the likes of Gavin Stark.

Stark let out a muffled roar as he flopped around frantically. He reached up, pulled at Cain's arm, slammed his fists into his attacker's shattered ribs, but nothing could loosen the herculean grip. Cain had let the monster out completely, surrendering himself utterly to the vengeance-craving beast. He held on with more strength than he'd dared to imagine he possessed, and his grip was like iron, resolute through all of Gavin Stark's frantic efforts.

Slowly, steadily, he felt Stark's resistance weaken. He held on with all he could, feeling the last of his own strength drain from his body. The struggle had lasted no more than two minutes, though to Cain it had seemed an eternity. Finally, slowly, he loosened his arms, and let his enemy fall to the ground with a sickening thud.

He stared down at the cold eyes looking back at him, and he

smiled. Gavin Stark, the scourge of mankind, the greatest mass murderer in human history, was dead.

Cain looked up, but he couldn't see anything, at least not with his eyes. He'd fallen right next to Stark's body, a few seconds after his victory had been won. His vision was gone, and his hearing. Even the pain had faded. There was a vague sense of satisfaction, of having carried out his pledge to kill Stark, but even that dissipated quickly, and he found himself floating in space, strange images passing through his mind.

His mother. So long ago, yet now he could see her as if it had been yesterday. Not the emotional wreck that had remained after the family had been forced out of the Protected Zone, but the vibrant and happy woman she'd been before disaster had come for them all. Seeing her family driven from all they'd ever known and cast out into a vicious urban wasteland had been more than she'd been able to bear, and it had driven her mad. That was that image of her Erik had always remembered...the broken, silent, ghost of a woman.

Now he saw her as she had been before, when he was a young child...happy, smiling. His parents hadn't had much material wealth, but the family had been a happy one. Cain had forgotten all that, buried it under the frigid exterior he'd developed to survive. It had been a defense mechanism for most of his life, but now it broke down, and he wept inside for his lost family, for what might have been if they'd lived in different times, or if fortune had been less cruel. He felt the pain of loss, but he could only watch the images sliding slowly past him. He wanted to cry, to weep for all that was gone, but he couldn't. There were no tears. Only pain.

Other images floated by. Will Thompson, Elias Holm, Marines he'd comforted as they lay dying...and others he'd sent to their deaths. They'd visited him before, late at night, invading his dreams. Jax. He still thought of Jax every day. The big man had been closer than a friend, and the wound left by his loss had never healed. "Forgive me, brother." His lips moved, but he was weak, and the sound didn't come, just the aching thoughts deep in his mind.

He could feel the blackness deepening, closing in on him, and his thoughts grasped on one last image. Sarah. She had been there for so many years, always by his side, even when lightyears separated them. Even now.

His mind wandered, dancing across the years they'd been together, and the many times they'd been ripped apart by war. He knew he could never have survived so long, never have accomplished what he had without the strength she'd given to him.

He was grateful she'd come into his life, and he loved her without limit. But now he felt sorrow, a sadness so deep he could hardly fathom it. He knew he was dying, and he felt the pain his death would cause her, the loneliness she would feel when he was gone. He'd done what he had to do; he'd destroyed Gavin Stark. He'd known his quest might claim his life, but now Sarah would pay the price too. No, he thought, feeling the last of himself slipping away. "Live your life, Sarah," he whispered softly. "Find happiness. Don't spend your days mourning me."

He felt the darkness coming, and he struggled to hold on to her, to keep her image alive in his mind. But the blackness was too strong, and she faded away…then it swept over him and he saw nothing.

Chapter 33

AS Pershing
Earth Orbit
Sol III

"I just wanted to stop by and pay my respects, sir." Cain stood in front of Augustus Garret. He was wearing a spotless uniform, carrying his hat under his arm, in token of respect. "I just heard about Commander Rourke, sir."

Garret nodded, and Cain could see the sadness in his eyes. "Thank you, Erik. In the end, despite all we tried to do to help her, in the end she couldn't live with what had happened." His voice was soft, pensive.

Rourke had been cleared of any guilt in the attempt on Garret's life when Sarah identified the conditioning that had been implanted in her mind. She'd been kidnapped during her last leave, and Stark's people had done the deed, leaving her with perfect memories of an uneventful vacation. She'd carried the conditioning for almost four years, all through the First Imperium War, and it had finally been released by one of Stark's agents in the fleet sending her the trigger phrase.

Sarah's analysis had cleared Tara of any wrongdoing, but all her medical skills couldn't do anything about the animosity toward Rourke in the fleet. Augustus Garret was revered by the men and women he commanded, and they'd howled for Rourke's blood. Even after Sarah had removed the last of the conditioning, it was clear that, whatever future the navy had, Tara Rourke could be no part of it. Garret despised the injustice, but he knew the reality of the situation as well.

But Rourke's greatest challenge had been forgiving herself. She'd loved Garret as much as anyone in the fleet. More. She'd worked at his side, and she'd looked up to him like a father. In the end, despite all of Sarah's efforts, and Garret's too, she simply hadn't been able to deal with it, and she'd taken her own life. They had found her in her dress uniform, lying on her bed in a pool of blood. She'd shot herself and left behind a note for Garret, another apology that tore at his insides like a knife. He'd tried to help her, to assure her he didn't blame her, but to no avail. Some wounds were simply too deep to heal.

"Sit Erik. Stay for a while. I wanted to talk to you anyway."

Cain walked across the room and sat down alongside Garret. He knew his own survival had been the unlikeliest of all. He had been dead; he'd been sure of it, lying on the deck of Stark's ship. He'd felt his life slipping away, the last of his strength gone.

It had been Teller, and the Marines from Mondragon's fleet. They'd gotten there too late to intervene in the fight, and they'd found Cain on the deck, barely breathing. Teller had thought his friend was dead at first, but then he realized Cain was still clinging tenuously to life. They rushed in a portable medpod and got him into cryo-stasis before rushing him back to Mondragon's flagship.

He'd teetered on the edge of life and death for days, until Sarah arrived with the fleet and took over his care. She worked weeks on his shattered body, without sleep, almost without food, leaning over his medpod tirelessly, through all hours of the day and night. Finally, almost miraculously, he began to recover.

Eventually, he'd ended up next to Garret in sickbay, the two of them propped up side by side as their beautiful doctor supervised every moment of their convalescence. Garret's recovery took five months, and Cain's most of six. He'd only just been released a week before, and he'd just gotten word of Rourke's suicide.

"Erik, I have no idea what is going to happen…on Earth, in occupied space. The future is, at best, uncertain." Garret's voice was calm, soothing. Cain could perceive something else there too, sadness, regret. Cain had always known Garret had a lot of guilt and pain, but he was beginning to realize just how much self-recrimination the admiral carried with him. Cain had been privileged to have a number of remarkable friends and comrades, and he'd begun to understand how similar he and Garret were – and how different in some ways from the others.

"We still call ourselves the Alliance navy, the Alliance Marines…but the Alliance is gone. All the Superpowers are gone. Earth is in ruins."

Cain knew Garret was right. The nuclear exchanges between the Superpowers had been cataclysmic. Every city in the world had been obliterated. The world's industry was destroyed. Over 80% of the population had been killed in the conflagration, and the rest were staggering around in the wilderness between the hotspots, struggling to survive.

The colony worlds were truly on their own now. They would have to carry on without Earth's vast industry, learn to subsist for themselves. They would have to trade with other worlds for things their own planets lacked, and they would have to start immediately.

They would all be free as well, released from the control of the Superpowers and left to their own choices. Every world would have to form its own government, find its way forward. Cain didn't know how the Corps would fit into that new future, or the navy either, but he knew one thing for sure. Both institutions would be vastly smaller than they had been. Mankind no longer possessed the resources to support vast military formations.

"I guess old habits die slowly, Admiral." Cain didn't know what else to say. He'd always thought of himself as an Alliance Marine, and he had no idea what would come next. If there would even be a Marine Corps in the future.

"But they die sometimes, Erik. They get replaced by new things." Garret's eyes found Cain's. "Some of us will go on like before, leading the services into whatever future they have, even if that is only a slow and agonizing disbandment. That will be my role. There is nothing left for me but duty, Erik. Everything else important to me is gone."

Cain was staring directly at Garret, and he suddenly realized the true extent of the sadness the admiral carried. He opened his mouth to speak, but Garret raised his hand.

"Please, Erik, let me finish. I had my chances at happiness, long ago, but I passed them by. They are long gone, never to return." He paused, and for an instant Cain felt like Garret's thoughts were somewhere far away – or long ago. "You have suffered, Erik. You have fought with unimaginable bravery and fortitude. You have seen things no man should witness." He reached out and put his hand on Cain's arm. "But you are not used up like I am. You feel like you are, but you aren't. You have a chance at a future, at happiness."

Cain looked down at the sofa. "Sir…"

"My God, Erik, after all we've been through call me Augustus. I know it's a mouthful, but it's better than all the sir this and admiral that."

"S…Augustus, how can I abandon the Corps now?

"I didn't say abandon the Corps, Erik. Retire. Go on reserve status. Sam Thomas went back to Tranquility, but I'd doubt you'd say he ever stopped being a Marine." Elias Holm had recruited Thomas and a thousand old vets in the dark days at the beginning of the war. Back then, Garret thought, no one expected the 85-year old Thomas to come through as strong as ever…and for Holm to die on Armstrong, but that's what happened.

"Cate Gilson led the Corps through these final campaigns. Let her take the Commandant's stars. She won't do it without your OK. Give her your blessing, and then go live your life. A real life. One where you can get through your day without the stink of death all over you. You have love, Erik, someone to spend that life with you. Don't throw that away. I did. A long time ago. And for all my fame and glory, I still regret the choices I made." He paused. "Garret the hero has become my tormenter, Erik. Don't let Cain the hero become yours."

Cain sighed softly. The Corps had been his whole life. For all the sacrifice and struggle it had often demanded, it had been his home. Was it possible to live another way? To get up and smell the air, to walk through the woods? To live with Sarah, not just for short periods, but every day?

Garret had watched him quietly, but now he spoke again. "You are both young, though I've no doubt you don't feel that way. With the rejuv treatments, you are the physical equivalent of two people in your early thirties. You could still have children." He stared into Cain's eyes again, almost pleading with his friend to heed his words. "Do it for all of us, Erik. So that all the fighting, all the sacrifice, wasn't in vain. Be the reason we fought so hard and so long. One small island of sanity in the storm we've all traversed."

Cain sat quietly for a moment, considering Garret's words. Finally, he nodded slowly. "Maybe you're right, Augustus. I'll talk to Sarah about it." He managed a small smile. "I will think about everything you said. I really will."

Cain stood on the observation deck and gathered his thoughts. The collar on his dress uniform was tight, and he undid the top two buttons. He'd be a Marine until the day he died, but he knew he had changed too. He'd been thinking about everything Garret had said to him, and it had begun to make sense. He didn't know if it was the desperate final battle against Stark or something else, but Cain felt somehow…different. Perhaps he needed to take a different road forward.

He'd just come from the cargo hold, where he'd witnessed Rafael Samuels' execution. Cain had hated Samuels for years, ever since he'd become the greatest traitor in the history of the Corps, but now the whole thing felt somewhat anticlimactic. He'd only gone because he felt it had been his duty to go, but he'd felt no anger, no bloodlust. He'd watched Samuels die, but he felt no satisfaction. The shots that killed the great traitor didn't bring back a single dead Marine, nor rebuild a shattered city.

Stark was dead, the Superpowers destroyed. The long struggle was at an end. The cost had been high, more terrible than anyone could have imagined, but now it was time to move for-

ward. Samuels' actions had been unforgivable, and they were no
less horrific for the fact that Stark's crimes had been even worse.
But the time for war and hatred and vengeance was over.

The former Commandant had been captured on Earth,
during the last of the fighting. Camille Harmon had led the
fleet back to the Sol system too late to intervene in the orgy
of destruction unleashed by the Superpowers. Stark's plan had
worked exactly how he'd devised, and Samuels led the Shadow
Legion forces out of their bases and into the ravaged wastelands
to seize total control of the tattered remnants of mankind.

Harmon had reacted quickly and, without hesitation, she'd
launched a fresh round of nuclear death on Stark's bases and
heavy concentrations of Shadow Legion soldiers. Then Cate
Gilson had led the remnant of the Corps and the Janissaries
down to the surface to track down the survivors. The battle
had raged for three months, and when it was done, the Shadow
Legion armies were gone, and the Marines and the Janissaries
were shattered remnants, wispy apparitions of the massive fighting forces they had once been.

Earth was a radioactive ruin, and its people faced an ardu-
ous struggle for survival, but at least their future would be their
own. They would have no master, no creature like Gavin Stark
or Rafael Samuels to rule over them. Cain valued freedom like a
precious gift, but he wondered how the people of Earth would
feel, scavenging for food, fighting to stay warm, dying for lack
of basic medicines. Would they prize the freedom the destruction of the Superpowers left behind?

They would suffer unimaginably in their struggle to survive,
and it would be generations before there was any substantial
recovery or rebuilding. The Superpowers were gone, destroyed
by their own corruption and folly. The politicians who had
ruled the people were dead or scavenging in the same wasteland as those they had once ruled. Cain suspected the starving
refugees wouldn't take long to turn feral, and anyone who had
held power in the old system would be in grave danger if their
identity became known.

But for all of Earth's suffering, mankind had another future, one among the stars. Humanity had stretched its hand out into the galaxy, and on almost a thousand worlds, new civilizations grew. Some of these were tiny outposts on the fringes of explored space, others substantial colonies beginning to celebrate their first centennials. They faced enormous challenges ahead, but also great opportunities.

Would these worlds learn from Earth's mistakes? Would their people avoid the tragic errors their ancestors had made? Or would they tread down the same dark path, selling their freedom cheaply to politicians and power brokers who lie to them and tempt them with empty promises of security?

Cain didn't know the answer, but he tried to suppress the doubts he felt. He wasn't an optimist by nature, but for once, he wanted to be. He longed to believe humanity could learn, that they could truly appreciate freedom and embrace it above all things. But he just wasn't sure.

Erik Cain had unlimited confidence in a select few friends and allies who had proven their worth through years of fire and death. But he had no faith in most people, nor in mankind as a whole. He'd seen the consequences of humanity's choices, the cost good men and women had paid again and again.

In his heart he feared men would make the same mistakes again. These new colonies, now so optimistically embracing the future, would eventually begin to fight with each other instead of growing together. Democratic governments would give way once again to entrenched political classes, and the people would live their lives in willful ignorance. They would trade their freedoms willingly for empty promises of protection, and in so doing, they would ignore the deadly threat to liberty until it was too late once again.

Cain looked through the porthole one last time at the world of his birth. The holocaust wasn't apparent from space, but he knew what was happening down there, the billions dead, the millions more wandering through the nightmarish hell their world had become.

It wasn't just radiation Earth's survivors faced, but virulent plagues and huge areas contaminated with toxic chemicals.

Earth's Superpowers had unleashed every fearsome weapon they possessed during their flailing death struggles. Thousands more would die each day, succumbing to radiation sickness, disease, starvation. It would be years before the hell that had been unleashed receded, probably decades. The human suffering that would occur over those years was incalculable.

Cain stared at the deceptive beauty of the blue planet below, and he imagined what it was like to be down on its scarred surface, amid the suffering and desperation. For an instant he thought he should delay the departure, go down there himself to see what man's folly had wrought. But he shook his head and turned slowly away. Earth, whatever it had become, was his past, and he had time only for the future.

Chapter 34

Tangled Vine Inn
"The Cape"
Atlantia – Epsilon Indi II

The sea air was blowing across the rocky beach, carrying with it a heady mix of pine trees and the scents of the ocean. Erik walked slowly down the beach, enjoying the cool water washing over his bare feet. Sarah was next to him, brushing back her hair, wild and frizzy in the salty air.

They had come to Atlantia years ago, before revolution had swept the Alliance's colonies and launched them into more than a decade of almost non-stop warfare. Of all the places they had been, the rugged coastline of this idyllic world had called out to them both, and they had decided to make a home there.

Though they had both retired from active duty, they had other responsibilities, and they spent no more than half the year on Atlantia. Most of the rest of the time they were on Armstrong. Cain still had duties at the Academy, teaching to the vastly shrunken class of new cadets. Most of the old campus had been destroyed in the war against the Shadow Legions, but the few remaining buildings had been adequate to serve the needs of a vastly shrunken Corps.

Sarah was a director of the vast Marine hospital, now in the process of opening much of its unused space to serve the needs of the growing city of Astria. The damage from the fighting on Armstrong had mostly been repaired, and the planet and its capital city were growing, stepping up to take its place among the first tier of colony worlds, alongside planets like Arcadia and

Columbia.

Cain could hardly believe it had been two years since the last confrontation in the Sol system. The final moments of his battle with Stark had faded to a blur, and the terrible rage and vengeance that had driven him had begun to mellow into a sense of satisfaction over the accomplishment. He still had nightmares – he suspected he always would. But he'd also found some peace…and contentment. He'd always mourn for the friends and comrades he'd lost, but he'd come to realize they would want him to go on, to live his life.

"What time is the ceremony?" He turned and looked back at Sarah.

"In about 3 hours." She returned his gaze with a warm smile. "We should head back if you want time to shower and change."

Atlantia's inhabitants lived mostly along a winding, rocky coast that resembled Earth's New England, before it had been ravaged by war, pollution, and finally, nuclear holocaust. The planet was as close to a pristine paradise as any world man had found in the vastness of space, and its people tended to move at their own pace. Most of the former Alliance colonies had erected monuments of one kind or another – to the Corps, the fleet, or the individual heroes of the wars. But Atlantia was just getting around to dedicating its own, and General Erik Cain and Colonel Sarah Linden, as the colony's two most famous residents, were the guests of honor, despite their protestations.

Cain sighed. "Well, they're not going to let us out of this, so we might as well go get ready." He smiled and leaned in, kissing her gently. The morning sun was beating down on them, creating just enough warmth in the cool fall air. He wanted to stay where right where he was, but he understood duty, even if it had become something far less dangerous and burdensome that it once had been. "Let's go," he said, and took her hand as they walked back toward the house.

The statue wasn't a massive, hulking monument, like so many others he'd seen. It was simple, a little larger than life perhaps, but not inordinately so. It was a Marine, armored and standing at the ready, prepared to face whatever danger threatened.

Cain stared up at it, his eyes fixed on the bright new bronze. It wasn't a statue of General Holm or Admiral Garret - or even one of him - like so many worlds had erected. Indeed, it wasn't a general at all depicted up on the small marble pillar, nor even a junior officer. The Atlantians had built their tribute not to the commanders, not to the famous warriors covered in glory. They had chosen to salute the common Marine instead, the steadfast warrior who had done so much to buy mankind a chance at a future, paying with their blood more often than not.

Cain took Sarah's hand in his and he turned to leave, pausing for a last instant and smiling. He had served with that Marine, he thought, and thousands like him. Indeed, he had been that Marine long years before. They were all heroes, those who survived their service to see their own chance at a peaceful life, as he had…and those who'd fallen, the men and women who'd paid the price of freedom. Elias Holm, Darius Jax…and a legion of Marines just like them.

Cain had seen many monuments in the two years following the end of the war, some of them vast and overwhelming. But he decided this was his favorite. A simple honor to the Marines who had stood on the front lines, facing anything that threatened mankind. He stopped and turned back one last time, silently paying his respects to friends lost. Then he turned toward Sarah. He took her hands in his and he smiled. They had made it together, and the future was now.

The Crimson Worlds Saga Continues!
Introducing Two New Series
Available for Pre-Order Now!

MERCS

Crimson Worlds Successors I
Release Date: March 24, 2015
Available NOW for Pre-Order

Earth has been a scarred ruin for three decades, its scattered people struggling to survive amid the poisoned and radioactive wreckage of the final war between its despotic Superpowers. But out on the frontier, on a thousand worlds, mankind thrives and grows, building new civilizations and looking boldly to the future. But man has never been able to live in peace, and even Earth's sad fate has failed to slow the call to war.

Most of the colonies lack the industry and economic power to sustain their own armies and navies, and they look to the mercenaries of the Great Companies for aid in time of war. These futuristic condottiere contract themselves to the highest bidder, and the mightiest strike fear into the hearts of all who opposed them.

Darius Cain is the leader of the Black Eagles, the most renowned of all the Companies. A military genius, he has led his undefeated warriors from victory to victory. The Eagles command the highest rates of any of the Companies, and leaders bankrupt their worlds to pay their price.

But amid the ruins of Earth and on planets all across occupied space there are signs of a greater darkness, a force working in the shadows, waiting for the right moment to strike, to launch a final war to reduce all mankind to slavery.

As Cain slowly uncovers the truth, he must forge an alliance among old enemies, the other Companies his men have fought for years…and the twin brother he hasn't seen in a decade.

The Crimson Worlds are about to explode into a war that may be mankind's last.

Into The Darkness
Crimson Worlds Refugees I
Release Date: June 23, 2015
Available NOW for Pre-Order

Terrence Compton is one of Earth's greatest admirals, a warrior almost without equal. Alongside his oldest friend and brilliant colleague, Augustus Garret, he and his forces saved Earth from invasion by the robotic legions of the First Imperium's insane computer Regent.

There is just one problem. The First Imperium was cut off from Earth by the destruction of the sole warp gate connecting the two domains…and Compton and 300 of his ships are trapped on the wrong side, surrounded by the enemy and cut off from Earth.

Pursued by their deadly enemy, Compton and his fleet must flee into the darkness of unexplored space, seeking a new home. Their journey will take them deep into the heart of the First Imperium, to the silent, windswept worlds where the ancient raced that built the Regent once dwelled…and uncover the lost secrets of their disappearance 500,000 years ago.

Crimson Worlds Series

Marines (Crimson Worlds I)
The Cost of Victory (Crimson Worlds II)
A Little Rebellion (Crimson Worlds III)
The First Imperium (Crimson Worlds IV)
The Line Must Hold (Crimson Worlds V)
To Hell's Heart (Crimson Worlds VI)
The Shadow Legions(Crimson Worlds VII)
Even Legends Die (Crimson Worlds VIII)
The Fall (Crimson Worlds IX)

War Stories (Crimson World Prequels)

Also By Jay Allan

The Dragon's Banner

Gehenna Dawn (Portal Worlds I)
The Ten Thousand (Portal Worlds II)

www.crimsonworlds.com

Upcoming

MERCS
(Crimson Worlds: Successors I)
(March 24, 2015)
Available for Pre-Order Now!

Into the Darkness
(Crimson Worlds: Refugees I)
(June 23, 2015)
Available for Pre-Order Now!

Dragon Rising
(The Last War I)
(Summer 2015)

Made in the USA
Coppell, TX
14 October 2020

39759810R00185